THE
BOARDWALK
BOOKSHOP

SUSAN MALLERY

THE BOARDWALK BOOKSHOP

mira

ISBN-13: 978-0-7783-3329-6

The Boardwalk Bookshop

Copyright © 2022 by Susan Mallery, Inc.

For questions and comments about the quality of this book, please contact us at
CustomerService@Harlequin.com.

Mira
22 Adelaide St. West, 41st Floor
Toronto, Ontario M5H 4E3, Canada
BookClubbish.com

Printed in U.S.A.

To Dr. Angela I., who has a way more impressive résumé than me!
I hope you enjoy Mikki, Ashley and Bree as they deal with
the unexpected and discover just how strong they really are.
Sometimes love really is the answer...in all its forms.

THE
BOARDWALK
BOOKSHOP

ONE

"I thought there'd be more sex."

Bree Larton stared at her seventy-something-year-old customer, not sure how to respond. Bursting out laughing would be inappropriate and Ruth would take offense. "You need to tell me what you want so I can get you the right book," Bree said with a gentle smile. "You wanted a political thriller. Most of them aren't sexy."

Ruth, barely five feet tall but feisty as a badger, pursed her lips. "Not true. James Bond has sex all the time and he spends his day saving the world. I want a book like that. Ticking bombs, financial collapse, kidnappings and then everyone jumps into bed." She winked. "That would be a good book."

"I can do a sexy thriller. Maybe international?" Bree started walking toward that section of the bookstore. "A couple of options come to mind. Now, on the sexy part—do you want monogamy or can the partners play around?"

Ruth's eyes brightened. "I'd like them to play around, but nothing too kinky. And no groups. That's just too hard to keep track of."

Bree held in a chuckle. "All right. We'll limit the body parts, add a little European flair." She held out a book with a hunky guy on the cover. "If you like this one, the author has five more stories waiting for you."

Ruth, an unnaturally yellow blonde wearing cherry-red lipstick, clutched the book to her narrow chest. "I'll take it."

Bree suggested several additional authors. Ruth browsed for a few more minutes, then carried a stack of books to the register.

"I think I would have been a good sidekick for James Bond." Ruth passed over her credit card. "Back in the day, I was quite the looker."

"You still are," Bree told her.

Ruth waved away the comment. "I'm too old for espionage, but I wouldn't say no to dinner with a charming man." Her smile turned sly. "I'll just have to keep living vicariously through you."

"Sadly, I'm lacking a man these days."

Ruth leaned close. "What I admire about you, Bree, is that you're not holding out for love. You go after what you want. When I was your age, that wasn't an option. Not in polite society anyway. I was born in the wrong time."

Bree honest to God had no idea what to say. "I guess we have to work with what we have." She tucked a flyer into the shopping bag. "Harding Burton is signing here in a couple of weeks."

Ruth looked at the poster next to the counter. Her bright red lips curved into a smile. "He's a good-looking man."

Bree mentally shrugged. "I suppose."

"You don't think he's exceptionally handsome? Those eyes, that smile. Isn't he the one who was hit by a car and left for dead on the side of the road when he was just a teenager?" Ruth clucked her tongue. "So tragic. But he pulled through and walked again and now look at him." Her gaze darted to Bree. "You should have your way with him and then tell me all about it."

Bree held in a wince. "First, I'd never tell you about it and second, I don't date authors."

Between her late husband and her parents, she knew enough about the type to want to avoid them forever. At least on a personal basis. Work-wise, she was stuck. What with owning a bookstore and all.

"Harding seems exception-worthy," Ruth told her. "He might have some interesting scars you could trace and—"

Bree held up her hands in the shape of a T. "Stop right there. If you're interested in Harding's scars, go for him. How could he resist you?"

"I'm old enough to be his mother."

Grandmother, Bree mentally corrected, but kept silent. She had a soft spot for the ever-outspoken Ruth.

"Maybe he's into older women," she said instead.

"Wouldn't that be nice."

Ruth was still laughing when Bree walked her out of the store. Anson, Ruth's driver, was waiting in the no-parking fire lane. Anson helped Ruth into the Mercedes. Bree stayed outside until the car drove away.

Early evening on the beach in Los Angeles was nearly always magical but in June, if the skies cleared, it was the stuff of dreams. Warm air, palm trees, sand and surf. Honestly, she shouldn't admit to having any real problems in her life. Even Ruth's impossible book requests were insignificant when compared with the view outside the front door of her store.

Until six months ago, Driftaway Books had been located about two miles north and a good three blocks inland from the actual beach. Last fall, when the current space had come up on the market, Bree had stopped in to drool and dream. But beachfront came at a premium, and the square footage had been nearly double what she'd needed.

In one of those rare moments when fate stepped in and offered an unexpected opportunity, that very day two other women business owners had also been swooning over the same retail space. They'd agreed it was an unbelievable location, right there on the sand, but it had also been too big and expensive for each of them.

Impulsively, Bree had suggested they go get coffee together. Over the next hour they'd discussed the possibility of sharing the lease. Bree generally didn't trust people until she got to know them, but there had been something about Mikki and Ashley that had made her want to take a chance. By the end of the week Driftaway Books, The Gift Shop and Muffins to the Max had signed a ten-year lease and hired a contractor to remodel. Bree had changed the name of Driftaway Books to The Boardwalk Bookshop, the final step in fully claiming the business as her own. The first Monday after the holidays, they'd moved in together.

Bree looked at the long, low building. Huge display windows were shaded by blue-and-white-striped awnings. The large glass doors could slide completely open, blurring the line between retail and sand. She and Mikki, the gift-store owner, had their stores on either side, with Ashley's muffin selection taking up the middle space.

Big, bright displays showcased books, gifts and muffins, grouped together in seasonal themes. An array of beach books, sunscreen, flip-flops and wide-brimmed hats enticed tourists who had shown up to the beach unprepared.

Bree headed back inside, aware of the approaching sunset. She collected blankets and champagne glasses, then paused to straighten the poster announcing a book signing by Jairus Sterenberg, author of the popular *Brad the Dragon* children's books. Jairus lived in next-door Mischief Bay and was always a pleasure at signings. He was one of the few authors Bree liked. He arrived early, stayed late and asked only for a desk and a glass of water. The man even brought his own pens.

At the other end of the spectrum was a not-to-be-named famous mystery author who was a total nightmare. Demanding, slightly drunk and very handsy, he'd patted her butt one too many times at his last signing and had been banned from the store. Despite pleas from his publicist and a written apology from the author himself, Bree had stood firm. She owned The Boardwalk Bookshop and she made the rules. No literary books, no existential anything and no guys touching women without their permission. Not exactly earth-shattering, but she could only control her little corner of the world.

Mikki saw her and smiled.

"Once again, we're waiting for Ashley. Have you noticed that?"

"Young people today," Bree teased.

Mikki, a generally upbeat kind of person, with thick blond hair and more curves than Bree and Ashley combined, laughed. "I like that. I'm only ten years older than her, so if she's young, then I'm less old than I thought. Maybe I won't mind turning forty this fall."

"You're not seriously worried about it, are you?"

Mikki wrinkled her nose. "I don't know. Sometimes. Maybe. Forty sounds a lot worse than thirty-something."

"Forty is the new twenty-five."

Mikki's humor returned. "If I'm twenty-five, then Ashley's barely eleven. That could create some legal issues with our lease." She waved the bottle of champagne she held. "Come on. This needs our attention. When Ashley's done texting love notes to Seth, she knows where to find us."

They left the store and walked out onto the sand. With the approach of sunset, the temperature had cooled and the Friday crowd had cleared. The sky had started to darken, while the part that kissed the ocean still glowed bright blue with a hint of yellow.

To their left were a grove of palm trees, a handful of kiosks and a boardwalk that went all the way to Redondo Beach. To the right were more shops and restaurants, benches, parking and hotels. In front of them was the Pacific Ocean. Big, blue and tonight, unexpectedly calm.

They stopped about thirty feet from the shore and sat on the blankets. Mikki held up the champagne.

"Perrier-Jouët Blason Rosé," she said proudly. "Ladies Know Wine gave it 93 points and said it had 'delicious hints of sweet earthiness that complement fruit flavors including strawberry and peach with a hint of spice in this perfectly balanced rosé champagne.'"

Bree grinned. "I don't know which is more impressive. That you're branching out from traditional champagne or that you can quote a Ladies Know Wine review that well."

"I love Ladies Know Wine. I savor every issue. If Ladies Know Wine were a man, I would make him fall in love with me. Then we'd have sex."

"Earl would be crushed."

Mikki unwrapped the pink foil and tucked it into her khaki pants pocket. "Earl would need to get over it." She held up the bottle. "Look at the shape of that. It's beautiful. And the label. Kudos to the design team."

She held the cork in her left hand and used her right to grip the bottom of the bottle. Instead of pulling on the cork, as often happened in movies, she rotated the bottle several turns until the bottle and cork separated without a hint of a pop.

Last fall the three of them had signed the lease late on a Friday. They'd been so excited, they'd driven out to their new location. The sunny, warm day had promised a beautiful sunset. Bree happened to have a bottle of champagne in her car and had suggested they share it to celebrate their new venture. The following Friday they'd done the same and a tradition had been born.

The first time Bree had opened a bottle of champagne with her business associates, she'd popped the cork and the frothy liquid had spilled over. Mikki's expression of horror had been so clear as to be comical.

"You're letting out all the bubbles," she'd explained. "It changes the essence of the champagne and ruins the experience."

"*Ruins* is kind of strong," Ashley had pointed out. "It's still really good champagne. Better than what I usually have. Of course most of my champagne drinking is done at weddings where they're buying for two hundred, so price is a concern."

"Champagne needs to be treated with reverence," Mikki had told her. "Don't drink bad champagne."

From then on they'd alternated providing the Friday night sunset champagne. Ashley always ran her selection past Mikki, but Bree took her chances by picking it herself.

Mikki poured them each a glass, then put the bottle into the sand, pushing down a little to keep it upright.

"To us," she said, touching her glass to Bree's. "And to perfect sunsets."

Bree smiled and then took a sip. She closed her eyes as she let the bubbly liquid sit on her tongue for a second before swallowing. Mikki was going to ask her how she liked it, and saying it was fine was never an option.

"Delicious," she said, holding in her smile. "I taste a lot of berry with a hint of citrus. It's surprisingly creamy."

Mikki looked at her with approval. "That's what I get, too. It's really drinkable. I like it."

"Noooo! You started without me!"

The shriek came from behind them. Neither of them turned around. Instead, Bree held out the third glass and Mikki filled it. Ashley, a tall, slim redhead with big blue eyes and a full mouth, plopped down next to Mikki. Her lips formed a pout.

"You didn't wait," she accused. "You're supposed to wait."

"You're supposed to be on time," Mikki reminded her. "Every Friday you text with Seth and run late. You agreed either you show up on time or we're starting without you."

Ashley ducked her head. "I thought the pressure would help. Instead, I just feel guilty."

Mikki sipped her champagne. "I'm sure your chronic tardiness has to do with your mother."

Ashley laughed. "My mom can take your mom anytime."

Mikki grinned. "I don't know. Rita would bring her Eeyore self to the party and then talk about how everyone's good time depressed her."

"I can see that happening," Ashley admitted. "Then I'll toast to both our mothers. And Seth, who is amazing. I in no way feel guilty about texting with him. He loves me and I love him."

Bree held in a groan. "Yes, we know. It's all so wonderful."

Mikki bumped shoulders with Ashley. "She's jealous."

"No, no." Bree held up her glass. "You are welcome to your cooing and clucking relationship."

"We don't cluck. What does that even mean?"

"I have no idea," Mikki admitted. "Bree?"

"It's just an expression."

"*Clucking* is an expression?"

Bree chuckled, then glanced out at the sinking sun. Light reflected on the moving water. A family walked along, close to the waves. An older boy ran ahead, while the parents held hands with a younger child.

They looked happy, she thought, studying them the way she would an unfamiliar species. No doubt the mom and dad loved their children, took care of them. Mikki did that, too, with her two kids. And Ashley's parents were wonderful. But not all parents were good.

Mikki refilled their glasses. "Ashley, a lot of customers are talking about your brother's book signing. When are we going to meet him?"

"Monday," Ashley said. "He's moving into his new place."

Harding, Ashley's brother, after several months on the road for book signings and research, had returned to Los Angeles. He'd leased a house and was supposedly hard at work on book number three. In the meantime, he would be signing at The Boardwalk Bookshop where he would, no doubt, pull in a crowd.

Authors, Bree thought with a silent sigh. An annoying but

necessary species. Customers liked book signings, so she had authors come in.

"I can't wait to meet him," Mikki said. "Such an interesting story. Bree, are you excited about the signing?"

"More than words can say."

Mikki studied her. "That's sarcasm, right?"

Bree laughed. "Yes. That's sarcasm."

"How can you own a bookstore, love books and hate writers?"

"I don't hate them. I just don't want them in my life."

"You're so weird." Mikki turned to Ashley. "Help me out here. Tell her how weird she is."

Instead of joining in the teasing, Ashley dropped her gaze. "Yes, well, we should talk about Harding. Or more specifically, him and you."

Bree shifted back so she could angle toward Ashley. "I've never met the guy." Which meant there shouldn't be a problem. Unless...

"Does he need special treatment?" she asked with a sigh. "Only yellow M&Ms or French goat milk served in Waterford crystal?"

"Nothing like that," Ashley said, sounding worried. "He's great and I know you'll like him." She twisted her hands around her champagne glass. "I'm just, you know, afraid of what will happen."

Bree looked at Mikki, who shrugged.

"I have no idea what she's talking about," Mikki admitted.

"Me, either." Their normally perky, albeit tardy, partner wasn't making any sense.

Ashley exhaled sharply. "I'm afraid you'll hurt him."

"With my expertise in martial arts?"

Mikki raised her eyebrows. "You know Tae Kwon Do?"

Ashley scrambled to her feet and glared at them. "I'm being serious. Harding is my brother and I love him. He's been through

17

enough already. If you'd seen him the way I did after the accident, you'd be just as protective."

Bree stood as well. "Ashley, I'm sorry. We'll stop teasing. I can see you're upset but I honestly have no idea why."

"You're going to break his heart." Ashley blinked several times, as if holding back tears. "You're beautiful and funny and sexy and every man alive wants you."

"Except Seth," Mikki said, watching them. "Seth only has eyes for you, Ashley."

"Okay, sure, but every other guy wants you and Harding is going to fall hard. You'll sleep with him, then dump him and he'll be crushed. I know he seems strong, but his heart bruises easily." She swallowed. "You're my friend and I care about you, but he's my brother. Please don't crush him."

Bree stared at her, not sure what to say. Or think or feel, for that matter. She liked the beautiful and sexy part but was less happy about the assumption that she would sleep with Harding, then dump him, like she was some monster who preyed on vulnerable men. A slutty monster who left ruined lives in her wake.

She wanted to protest that her relationships were her business, that she was always bluntly clear on her expectations, or lack thereof, when she hooked up with a guy. If they chose not to believe her, then that was on them, not her. She never promised more than she could give. The expiration date was made clear and if they couldn't handle that, then she walked away before anything started.

But that wasn't the point. Ashley didn't want Bree to break Harding's heart. Funny how no one ever worried about Bree's feelings. Something she'd gotten used to a long time ago. She was always on her own—she had to protect herself, because no one else was going to do it.

"If you knew me better, you'd know I don't hurt anyone on purpose," she said quietly.

Ashley flinched. "I didn't want to upset you. It's just Harding's a regular person and you're you."

"Not every guy I sleep with falls for me," Bree pointed out.

"Most do." Ashley nodded toward the surf shop at the end of the block. "You slept with Sad Guy twice in January and he's still moping. It's pathetic."

"And sad," Mikki added in a low voice. "Poor Sad Guy."

Bree shot her a "stop helping" look, but Mikki only winked at her. Bree turned her attention to Ashley.

"I'm sorry you've been worried about me and your brother," Bree said. "I don't want to make things difficult for you and I certainly don't want to hurt your brother. I promise not to even get to know him. How's that?"

Ashley shook her head. "I don't want that promise. It's not right. And it's not realistic. He lives here. The only reason you haven't met him until now is his travel schedule. But you and I are business partners and now that he's back…" She sighed.

"Just don't break his heart."

"I won't."

Mikki stood. "Wouldn't it be funny if he broke hers?" She laughed. "I know it will never happen, but it's fun to think about."

"Less fun than you might think," Bree told her.

"I suppose that's true for you. All right, did we clear the air? Time for a group hug?"

Mikki held open her arms. Ashley rushed in, while Bree hesitated a second. She wasn't a hugger by nature—something she'd had to deal with since meeting Mikki, who hugged nearly as much as she breathed. She braced herself for impact and stepped close.

The three of them stood like that for a few seconds, then separated and dropped onto the blankets. Ashley held out her glass.

"This is really good champagne. Seth and I have another wedding tomorrow. His cousin, I think." Holding her glass steady, she flopped onto her back. "We have at least three weddings a month through Labor Day."

"You're in that time of life," Mikki told her. "Then you'll go years and not attend a single wedding. I'm only a few years away from having to deal with round two. My kids and their friends getting married."

"I never thought of weddings as having a season in our lives," Bree said. "But you're right."

She hadn't been to a wedding in forever. Not that she missed them. The promise to love each other forever wasn't one she believed in. Not anymore. She supposed she should—after all, her parents were as in love as they had been the day they'd eloped. But her own marriage had shattered any illusions she'd had about love being in the cards for her.

"I'll be in the store in the morning," Mikki said, checking how much was left in the bottle. "Then I'm busy with errands for the rest of the day. Sunday afternoon Perry and I are hosting the barbecue I invited you both to. The one for the kids and their friends. Sort of an end of school, start of summer party."

Ashley sat up. "How can you and Perry do things like that together? You're divorced."

"Yes, but we have children, so there's no escape. Besides, we didn't divorce because we hated each other. We just wanted different things."

Bree held out her glass so Mikki could pour in more. "Does Perry know about Earl?"

Mikki laughed. "No. Not anything I'd discuss with a man. Girlfriends won't judge."

Ashley smiled. "I'm used to hearing about him now, but the first time you mentioned you had a vibrator named Earl, I was shocked."

"I was fine with it," Bree murmured. To each their own. She'd rather have a man, but Mikki wasn't exactly the use-them-and-dump-them type. Bree could understand a woman needing an Earl in her life.

"You should try an Earl before you form an opinion," Mikki said primly. "Sexually, he's the best relationship I've ever had. He'd dependable, selfless and he never gets tired."

"I'd rather have Seth," Ashley muttered.

Bree nodded. "I'm in the actual-penis-over-a-mechanical-one category, but I say that without judgment."

"Thank you," Mikki said. "Earl and I are happy and that's what matters."

Ashley gave a strangled laugh. "You win." She held out her glass. "To Earl. May you never run out of batteries."

TWO

"Uh-oh. You made a face. Is it that bad?"

Ashley Burton did her best not to laugh. "I don't want to be critical," she whispered to Seth. "I know they're on a budget. But I'm afraid Mikki is having an unexpected influence over me." She sipped the champagne again and tried not to grimace at the overly sweet flavor. "It's that bad."

"We only have to drink it for the toast."

"Thank goodness."

A few months ago Ashley wouldn't have known good champagne from crap, but since partnering with Bree and Mikki, she'd had a crash course in the drink's finer points.

None of which would interest any of the other guests around them, she thought with a grin. They were just happy to watch their friends get married and enjoy a good meal and even better company. In her case, Seth. Some guys resented going to weddings, but Seth always enjoyed the party.

Today's event was in Redondo Beach at a big house off Pacific Coast Highway. No view, but beautiful grounds and plenty of space. The DJ was good, the buffet looked interesting and later, Ashley planned on dancing with Seth past midnight.

Their friends Krissy and Karl joined them. Karl looked around at the crowd and grimaced.

"I'm tired of weddings," he grumbled. "This is our third and it's only June. We've got one every two weeks all summer."

"I love a wedding," Krissy told her boyfriend. "And you love me."

"Which explains why I'm here." Karl rolled his eyes. "Why couldn't women enjoy baseball as much as weddings?"

Seth put his arm around Ashley's waist. "Think of this as the physical manifestation of the bride and groom's love for each other."

Karl chuckled. "There'll be plenty of manifesting tonight."

Krissy gave him a shove. "Karl, we're in public. Don't be gross."

"But you like it when I'm gross."

Seth shook his head. "Okay, I'm taking my beautiful girlfriend to our table and showing her off."

"Karl's in a mood," Ashley said when they were out of earshot. "I guess he really doesn't like weddings. What about you? Are you already tired of them?"

Seth shook his head. "Not if I'm with you."

She grinned. "The politically correct answer."

He brushed her mouth with his. "Hey, you're my girl. I want to make you happy."

"You do."

As she spoke, her gaze locked with his and she saw the love in his eyes. Someone bumped into them, breaking the contact, but her happy glow lingered even as they made their way across the reception area.

Seth was such a great guy and he had no trouble telling her how much she mattered to him. They'd been living together nearly three months and their relationship was just getting stronger. Soon, she told herself, Seth would propose and they would move into the next phase of their lives.

They found their seats and introduced themselves to their tablemates. Once the small talk died down, Seth turned to her.

"You remember I'm out of town Monday and Tuesday, right?" he asked, angling toward her and lacing his fingers with hers.

"Yes," she told him. "You texted me your flight and hotel information. Twice."

"I just want to be sure you know where I am."

She patted his arm. "Sweetie, I put a GPS tracker in your arm a few months ago. I know everything you do."

He laughed. "You did, huh? When did that happen?"

"You were sleeping."

"Track away. I have no secrets from you."

Which was pretty much true, she thought. Seth worked for Too Many Names Productions—a major movie producer. He was in the business side of things, managing the budgets of several productions. He liked to say he was the guy who explained to directors that no, they couldn't bring in three lions and a gorilla for a thirty-second shot, even if it "looked cool." Sometimes that job meant flying to a location shoot to audit the books. Normally, one of his staff would go, but on big-budget movies, he liked to do it himself.

"So you'll be okay?" he asked.

"Yes. Harding is getting his rental house on Monday and I'm going to help him settle in. I have my usual Tuesday volunteering at OAR. I'll be fine."

"But you'll miss me?"

She smiled at him. "With every breath." She leaned close. "When we get home, want to do some manifesting of our own?"

He laughed, then pulled her close. "I was hoping we would."

Mikki Bartholomew was willing to admit the haircut might have been a mistake. Her twice-yearly appointment for highlights and a trim had gotten out of hand yesterday with her saying the nearly always regrettable, "Let's do something different this time."

Ninety minutes later she was still a blonde but her hair was now barely brushing her shoulders. She tried to tell herself the shorter cut made her look younger and edgy, but she was pretty sure she was lying.

"I know better than to make a change when I'm restless," she murmured, poking at the potatoes boiling away on her six-burner stove. She always told her kids, "If you're feeling anything but levelheaded, don't do something that can't be undone." Technically, her hair would grow back, but meanwhile, she was stuck with a constant reminder that she'd broken her own very sensible rule.

She glanced at the clock on her microwave. She would give the potatoes another minute. She'd already cooked the bacon, reserving the fat. Her loaded potato salad wasn't healthy, but it was delicious and a family favorite. She'd prepped the burgers for the grill. The veggie burgers came ready to barbecue, so that was easy. Once the potatoes were cooling in the refrigerator, she would start on the corn salad. Closer to party time, she would make the green salad. She still had to get the chicken in the marinade, but that wouldn't take long. Perry would bring soda and beer, she had enough ice and dessert would be cupcakes Ashley would bring, and ice cream in the garage freezer.

"I think I'm ready," she murmured, grabbing two hot pads, then carrying the heavy pot to the sink.

She was expecting about thirty people for the afternoon get-together. Her in-laws, her mother, her two kids, a lot of their friends, Perry, of course, Bree, Ashley and Seth. An informal celebration of the start of summer.

Once she'd drained the potatoes, she dumped them into a massive bowl and poured the bacon fat over the top. She stirred them until they were coated, then carried the bowl to her garage refrigerator. When she returned to the kitchen, she found Sydney, her older child, sitting at the large island, a mug in her hand.

Mikki smiled. "It's barely nine. What are you doing up so early?"

Her daughter laughed. "Very funny. I meant to get up before this to help." She stifled a yawn. "Let me drink my coffee, then I'll be ready for you to assign me tasks."

Sydney, eighteen and possibly the smartest person Mikki knew, was back from her first year at Stanford. She'd graduated early from high school, ignoring Mikki's pleas that she stay for her senior year to enjoy all the rites of passage, like homecoming and senior prom. But Sydney wasn't a traditional kind of teen—she had a life plan and had wanted to get started on it as soon as possible.

Sydney held up a ceramic place card holder. "Really, Mom?" she asked, turning it so Mikki could read the front.

This has bacon in it. Not vegetarian.

"I want to be clear," Mikki told her. "At least two of your friends are vegetarian."

"They can eat lettuce. Plus, I know you bought them veggie burgers."

"I did and they need to eat more than lettuce. You should be supportive."

"You shouldn't enable them. We're living in a carnivore world."

"Technically, we're omnivores. I would have thought your fancy teachers up at Stanford would have taught you that. I want my money back."

"Too late," Sydney said with a laugh. "I blew it on textbooks and coffee."

Mikki pointed toward the stairs. "Go shower and get dressed. After breakfast you can help me, but there's no rush. I have everything under control."

"You always do," Sydney said, standing and stretching. "I'll be down in a few."

Mikki watched her walk away, envying her daughter's slim hips and narrow waist. She'd managed to escape the family curse of big boobs and easy weight gain. Will had inherited his father's lean build and broad shoulders, leaving Mikki alone to fight poundage creep. That reality meant she would only allow herself the tiniest portion of her potato salad later today, she thought as she walked into her small office.

She waited while her laptop whirred to life. She glanced at her email, then wished she hadn't. Third from the top, just below the notice of a sale at Zappos, was a reminder that her payment was due for her late September trip to Paris.

Mikki grimaced, then clicked on the email and read the cheerful note full of promises about the fabulousness of the itinerary and multiple opportunities for personal enrichment and sightseeing.

"Ugh. Why did I think this was a good idea?"

A question she should have asked before putting down a deposit to hold her spot. Not that she didn't want to see Paris. She did. But not by herself.

She'd been to London on her own, two years ago, and had discovered she didn't like to travel alone. While she wanted to be one of those brave, self-actualized women who could boldly walk into a restaurant in a foreign country and ask for a table for one, she'd been miserable and lonely and had counted the days until she could slink home and berate herself for not being more capable.

This time she had signed up with a group that put together tours for single women. She and nineteen other lonely souls would explore the sights of Paris.

Which hadn't been at all where she'd seen herself when she and Perry had divorced three years ago. She'd wanted more than the separate lives they'd been living, and he'd wanted her to stop bugging him to do things with her. She'd wanted to travel and take up new hobbies and grow as a person. He'd wanted to work on old cars with his friends and watch sports.

Oh, the divorce wasn't all him being stubborn and disinterested. She'd been too busy with her new business and the kids.

She'd been impatient and hadn't listened the way she should have. They were both to blame. But she had assumed—apparently wrongly—that three years later she would have her life together.

"I don't want to go to Paris by myself," she whispered. "Or on this tour." Yes, she would likely make friends with some of the women, but everything about the trip felt wrong. No, not wrong, just not what she wanted.

More of the restlessness that had led to the unfortunate haircut, she thought.

She clicked on the cancellation link and read the details. She could get back 90 percent of her deposit if she canceled within the next two days. So she would only lose fifty dollars.

After marking the email as Unread, she closed her laptop and returned to the kitchen. No more impulsive decisions, she reminded herself. She would think about why she'd wanted to go to Paris and whether those reasons were enough to take the trip. If not, she'd cancel. The fifty dollars wasn't the point. The bigger problem was something was going on with her and she really needed to figure out what it was before she did something a lot more impulsive than just cut her hair.

By eleven, Mikki was ready for the crowd to descend. Will, her younger child, had wandered into the kitchen close to ten, but he'd made up for his late arrival by putting out plates, glasses and flatware, then positioning big outdoor umbrellas around the folding tables.

"Anything else, Mom?" Will asked, leaning against the door frame, as if he were incapable of supporting his own weight.

At sixteen, he was tall and lanky—all arms and legs. He could put away enough food to feed the average family of four, and his idea of cleaning his room was to shove everything under the bed, but he was a good kid. He tried hard in school, he had a sweet, thoughtful nature he didn't want his friends to know about and he was always willing to help out.

Now Mikki smiled at the hopeful look in his eyes. "What's waiting for you this time?"

"Dad said we could look at new wheels for my car. You know, for my birthday. I wanted to get some ideas online before he got here."

"Your car already has wheels. Four of them. Why do you need more?" She did her best to keep the teasing tone out of her voice, but Will's slow grin told her she'd failed.

"Mo-om, you know what I'm talking about."

She did. Tires were mounted on wheels, but messing with him was fun. "Huh. Okay. If you say so. But the last time I talked to your dad, he said he was thinking of getting you a sweater for your birthday."

"No one's getting me a sweater." He crossed to her and pulled her into a bear hug. Still growing, he towered above her already. His dad was only five ten, so Will had gotten his height from some throwback relative.

"Go look at your wheels," she told him when he stepped back. "But when everyone starts arriving, come downstairs." She smiled. "Or I'll send your grandmothers to help you clean your room."

"You'd never do that."

"I might surprise you."

"You always have my back. It's just a mom thing."

With that, he walked down the hall. Mikki was still smiling as she turned toward the kitchen.

About twenty minutes later the front door opened.

"It's me," her ex-husband yelled as he walked into the kitchen, bags in each hand. "I have another load in the car," he said, leaving the bags on the counter then walking back the way he'd come.

"Hello to you, too," Mikki called after him, shaking her head as she poured ice into the big insulated tub they used for out-door parties. They'd bought it years ago and Perry had built a wooden platform on wheels to move it when it was full.

She layered ice and drinks as Perry returned with more bags.

"You said we were expecting around thirty people?" Perry asked.

"That's my best guess."

"Good. We should have enough. I'll take the leftover beers and the kids can keep the sodas."

Because he knew Mikki didn't waste calories on soda. If she was going to risk her ass getting bigger it was going to be over something thrilling like a glass of buttery chardonnay and a slice of brie.

Perry handed her drinks until the tub was full, then refrigerated the rest. He moved with an easy familiarity that came from once having lived here.

She and Perry had bought the house when she'd gotten pregnant with Sydney. When they'd divorced three years ago, she'd bought him out. His parents had decided to try condo life. He'd rented their house, a short three blocks away. She and Perry alternated weeks with the kids, so his parents' old house was perfect. Will had what had been his father's room and Mikki had helped convert her mother-in-law's sewing room into a bedroom for Sydney.

Mikki wasn't proud that her marriage had failed, but she appreciated how she and Perry had managed the divorce. They'd stayed friends, had taken care of their kids and managed to keep their relatives talking. His mother, Lorraine, was friends with her mother. Perry's father still referred to Mikki as his daughter. At the holidays and birthdays the seven of them had dinner together. On Christmas morning everyone showed up at Mikki's house to open presents. They were, happily, a modern, connected family.

"Need any help?" Perry asked.

Mikki laughed. "It's all good. Later, you'll man the grill."

"I can do more than grill."

True. Perry had been feeding himself for three years now. Lorraine had helped at first, but after a few months he'd told her he would be fine.

She studied her ex-husband. He was of average height and lanky, with thick blond hair and brown eyes. Not the most handsome of men, but solid and decent. Plus, he had a great smile. Back in the day, that smile had made her giddy.

She heard a car in the driveway. Perry headed for the front door and returned with Lorraine, his father, Chet, and Mikki's mother, Rita.

Mikki braced herself, then smiled broadly and called out a greeting. "Hi, everyone. Great day for a barbecue."

Her father-in-law gave her a big hug and a kiss on the cheek, but her mother stared at her openmouthed.

"Dear God, what did you do to your hair?"

Mikki held in a sigh. "I got it cut. I think it's perfect for summer."

"It's hideous. What were you thinking?"

Lorraine patted Rita's arm. "Don't say that. Change is good." She smiled warmly. "If you like it, I like it."

Slightly more diplomatic than her mother, but still not the response she'd been hoping for.

"I like it," Perry said, winking at her. "She looks like she did when we first met."

"You didn't even notice."

"I did."

Before she could point out he hadn't said anything, Will and Sydney raced down the stairs.

"Grammy, Grandma and Grandpa!" Sydney called.

Hugs and kisses were exchanged with all the enthusiasm of a family reunited after months apart. In truth, her kids had seen their grandparents several times in the past week, but Mikki wasn't going to complain. She liked that they were close.

Now that the whole crew was here, everyone got busy putting out the food and drinks. Will and his dad wheeled out the drinks tub while Lorraine and Rita fussed over the salads. Chet got the two big barbecues going and yelled out that he needed the giant spatula. Mikki supervised, although after all this time and practice, no one needed her hovering. The burgers had just been pulled from the refrigerator when the first of the guests arrived.

The next hour was a whirlwind of greetings and catching up. Will and Sydney's friends came in packs consisting mostly of couples. The newly minted boy-and girlfriends could barely untangle themselves enough for a hug, but they managed before wrapping their arms around each other again and heading for the backyard. Sydney had always been more interested in school and her friends than any guy, and Will hadn't had a serious girlfriend yet. Mikki knew it was just a matter of time until he, too, was caught up in the magic of first love.

Perry hadn't been her first love, but he'd been the one who had made her dream about a future together. Oh, to have those feelings back, she thought wistfully. The thrill of the first date, first kiss, first orgasm, first "I love you." Not that Earl wasn't getting the orgasm job done—he was. But he was short on verbal skills and post-sex cuddle time.

Ashley and Seth arrived, both carrying large bakery boxes filled with cupcakes frosted in a riot of summer colors.

"You cut your hair," Ashley said by way of greeting. "It's so short." She tilted her head. "I like it."

Mikki smiled at her as she took one of the cupcake boxes. "Thank you for lying, but I know it's a disaster. Just don't tell my mother I know. She'd revel in my regret."

"I like it a lot." Seth kissed her cheek. "Saucy."

"That's what I was going for," she said lightly.

She led the way to the backyard. Music was playing loud enough to annoy the neighbors, but Mikki knew there would be no complaints. The block had a party agreement—give warning and don't go past nine. She'd sent out a group email two days ago and had promised to wrap up by seven. While Seth and Ashley went off to mingle, she set out the six dozen cupcakes.

"We're going to have leftovers," Perry said, coming up to help move the treats from the boxes to large platters.

"Of Ashley's cupcakes? Unlikely. Will and his friends know they only get one each until the last hour of the party. Then they're allowed to descend. I doubt you'll find a crumb here at closing time. If you want to take a couple home, I suggest you hide them in the kitchen while you have the chance."

"I might do that." He collected the empty boxes. "No wine tasting today?"

Mikki often had blind tastings at her parties. She bought several different wines, put them in brown paper bags and had her friends guess which was from what country and which was the most expensive. No one ever picked correctly, not even her, but it was a fun way to learn about different wines and find new favorites.

"Too many teenagers," she said. "I didn't want them tempted."

"Just as well," her mother said, walking up to them. "You drink too much. All that wine tasting and drinking champagne on the beach every Friday." Rita's mouth twisted. "You take classes! About wine!"

Mikki laughed. "Yes, I do, Mom. I even took one about champagne. I enjoy learning and I meet nice people. You should come with me sometime."

An offer she made with her fingers metaphorically crossed, because the last thing she wanted was her mother tagging along, ruining one of her favorite hobbies.

"I'm not drinking with a bunch of strangers," her mother said, her tone thick with outrage.

Perry put his arm around his former mother-in-law. "Probably for the best. You're still a good-looking woman, Rita. You'd have all the men falling over you and that could get embarrassing."

Her mother clucked her tongue but didn't protest the compliment. Mikki agreed that Rita still looked good. She was full-figured, like her daughter, but had bright blue eyes and beautiful skin. She'd always been attractive—except for the constant scowl.

Mikki excused herself and walked across the yard, singing along with the Beach Boys' "Surfin' USA." She greeted a few of Will's friends, asked Bethany how nursing school was going, then joined Sydney and Bree at a table in the shade.

Bree looked up, her expression amused. "Did you know your daughter is leaving you to fly to the other side of the country?"

"I'd heard a rumor."

Sydney sipped her soda. "Come on, Bree. California's great and I love Stanford, but be real. All the action is on the east coast. Georgetown makes the most sense and they have the best program."

She set down the can and began ticking off items on her fingers. "First I graduate with honors, then I move and start at Georgetown. I want to get my JD and my MA in Eurasian, Russian and Eastern European studies."

Bree's eyes widened. "That's a serious commitment."

"I'm a serious woman."

"We used to be girls," Mikki said mildly. "Now we're women."

Bree grinned. "You can still be a girl if you want."

"Thank you."

Bree turned to Sydney. "And then what? A think tank? Working for the government?"

"I haven't decided. Planning out the next seven years is about as much as I can manage." She stood. "I'm going to help Dad and Grandpa with the burgers."

Bree watched her go. "Jesus H You-know-what. She's getting her law degree while getting a masters in Eastern European studies? Is that a thing?"

"Apparently. I was there when she was born, so I know she's mine, but how did she get so smart? Perry and I do okay, and Will's bright enough, but she's on a whole different level. I'm just grateful she's using her powers for good."

"At least in the near term. Twenty years from now she could be running the world." Bree paused. "You okay?"

"Why do you ask?"

"You're frowning. You don't usually frown."

Mikki instantly rubbed her forehead. "Don't say that. I refuse to turn into my mother."

"You're not."

"But Rita's a frowner."

"I'm sorry I said something."

Mikki picked up her can of diet soda, then put it back on the table. "Do you think I should go to Paris?"

"You said you wanted to."

"I'm having second thoughts. Everything sounds so grim. Twenty single women of—" she made air quotes "—'a certain age,' traveling together. There's a pathetic quality to it."

"Because of their age or because they're single?"

Mikki glanced toward the groups of teens sitting on the lawn. They were so happy, she thought. So full of promise. Jared kissed Mattie, then they smiled at each other, while Mikki looked on, fighting a sense of…she wasn't sure what. Loss? Envy? Confusion?

"I thought I'd have my act together by now," she admitted. "It's been three years since Perry and I divorced and I thought I'd be more…"

"More what?"

"Something. I don't know. I love the store. That makes me happy and the kids are doing well. I just don't want to travel to Paris with a bunch of women I don't know."

Bree sipped her beer. She was only a few years younger than Mikki yet Mikki frequently felt like the much, much older friend. Maybe it was because Mikki often seemed to be part of a different generation. She had kids and she worried too much, while Bree simply lived her life. Bree was so comfortable in her own skin. Nothing ever got to her, nothing ruffled her.

Being beautiful probably helped, Mikki thought, trying not to be bitter. Bree had huge brown eyes and curly hair that tumbled to the middle of her back. She was lean, athletic and had a confidence that Mikki couldn't imagine possessing. Bree could walk into any bar, look around and pick a guy. Ten minutes later they were talking like old friends, and an hour after that they were in his bed.

Mikki couldn't begin to understand how that even happened. She could never talk to a strange man—she wouldn't know what to say or how not to be embarrassed. Just the thought of it made her stomach clench.

"You're a traditionalist," Bree said. "I'm not judging, just stating the obvious. You don't want to go to Paris with a bunch of women because that was never how you saw the trip happening. You want to go to Paris with a man you're in a relationship with. You want to be a couple. You're lonely. I know you have Earl, but he only gets you so far." The corners of her mouth turned up. "So to speak."

Mikki stared at her friend. "Is that how you see me?"

"It's how you see yourself. You can try to ignore the truth, but it's still the truth. Most people are traditional. Look at Ashley and Seth. How long until they're engaged? Most people want to be in a relationship. It took you a while to figure out what it meant to be divorced, but now you have and you're ready for more. It's why you no longer want to go to Paris with a bunch of single women."

The insights made her uncomfortable. Was Bree right? Did she want to be involved with someone?

"I don't know," she murmured. "A man? Really?"

Bree leaned toward her and lowered her voice. "Don't worry. If you find the right guy, he'll still want you to have fun with Earl. You can make it a threesome."

THREE

Bree tightened her core, keeping her weight forward as Nicole, the Pilates instructor, counted down from eight. By three her stomach was shaking. By one she was breathing hard. But when Nicole said, "And slowly, slowly, lower yourself back down," Bree completed two more counts before lowering herself onto the floor.

Work on the Pilates chair was always challenging, but that was why Bree liked it. Physical activity should be difficult—at least at first. She enjoyed seeing improvement with every class, regardless of what she was doing.

"Thanks for your help," the older woman next to her said, wiping sweat off her face. "I've never gotten the reverse pull-up before." She chuckled. "My butt doesn't like to defy gravity."

"Mine, either," Mikki said from Bree's other side. She glared at Bree. "You make it look easy. I resent that."

"Come to class more often," Nicole told her. "Twice-weekly sessions make all the difference."

"I don't actually *like* exercise," Mikki said cheerfully. "I thought I made that clear."

They all walked toward the cubbies at the front of the studio. Nicole stepped close to Bree.

"Thanks for your help with the new client. You're one of the regulars I can count on to be there for the newbies."

Regulars? Was that how Nicole saw her? Bree was surprised. She didn't think of herself as being that predictable. "Happy to help."

"Jairus said the signing went well Saturday."

"It was great." Bree slipped into flip-flops. "Your husband is very popular with the younger crowd."

There had been over two hundred children at the signing. Jairus had read from his new *Brad the Dragon* book, then had signed well into the afternoon. She'd enjoyed the chaos and totaling the sales receipts at the end of the day.

Mikki joined them, groaning as she slid her feet into her sandals. "I'm already sore. That doesn't bode well for the rest of the day." She rubbed her butt. "I think I broke something."

"You'll be fine," Nicole told her. "Take a bath later."

"I'm not a bath person."

"Not into exercise or baths," Bree teased. "I'm hearing a lot of no from you."

"It's the fact that class is so early. What was I thinking, agreeing to a class that starts at six? I'm really an afternoon person."

They waved to Nicole and headed to their cars. Mikki yawned as they stepped into the still morning.

"The sun's barely up," she complained.

"It was daylight when you drove to class."

Mikki unlocked her SUV. "Was it? I was too sleepy to notice. See you at the store."

"Yes, you will."

Bree got into her Mini Cooper and started the engine. Unlike Mikki, she enjoyed early-morning exercise. She took a Pilates class twice a week and had a group surfing lesson every Thursday. A spin class membership allowed her to do drop-in sessions whenever she had the time.

She headed north to her quiet Santa Monica neighborhood. This time of the morning everyone was aiming for the freeway for their commute to work. She hit all the lights perfectly and was home in less than fifteen minutes.

Her house, an older bungalow with an added second story, had a small front yard and a single car garage. But the big patio and grass area out back more than made up for that.

She'd bought the place two years ago, using the money from the sale of the house Lewis had left her when he died. The kitchen had been remodeled, but the downstairs half bath and the master upstairs had desperately needed updating. She'd tackled the former a few months before, but was having a little trouble making decisions about her bathroom. Still, she was enjoying the project.

She parked and walked around to the back door. After letting herself inside, she went through the small mud-slash-laundry room to the kitchen and put a coffee pod into her Nespresso. Seconds later the machine gurgled to life.

Like many older homes in LA, her place had several craftsman touches, including built-in cabinets in the dining room and shelves in the living room. The front room fireplace was decorative rather than useable, but Bree was okay with that. This was her house. Just hers. There were no ghosts—at least not any that bothered her. She never brought anyone here. Certainly not the guys she slept with. Whatever past had existed, she didn't want to know.

An hour later she'd showered, dressed for work and had breakfast. After packing her lunch, she headed toward the beach. The morning was clear and beautiful, already in the low seventies. By noon it would be eighty. Good news for her and her friends. Hot weather meant crowds, which meant more business.

Before the store opened, Bree completed her orders for the week and opened the cash registers. Rita, one of her employees and Mikki's mother, showed up at exactly nine thirty. In the few months she'd been working for Bree, Rita had never been a minute late and always completed her shift. Bree respected the work ethic and found Rita's take on the world amusing.

"Have you seen my daughter?" Rita asked by way of greeting as she tucked her purse into her locker and put on the store apron. "She cut her hair. It looks terrible. What was she thinking?"

"I saw Mikki yesterday at the barbecue and this morning at Pilates. She looks great."

Mikki could carry off any haircut, Bree thought. Her appeal came from her lushness, her zest for life. Mikki drew people to her, regardless of her hair.

"It's horrible. I hope she grows it out. She needs the extra hair to balance her hips." Rita shook her head. "I warned her she'd inherited my body shape and she could get fat."

"Mikki's not fat."

"No, but she could be."

Bree couldn't help laughing. "Oh, Rita, my little ray of sunshine."

Rita glared at her. "You're mocking me."

"Only a little. Any other complaints?"

"I don't like the red, white and blueberry muffins."

"But they're our muffin of the month. With the Fourth of July coming up, they're very patriotic."

Ashley had come up with the idea of featuring a monthly muffin to celebrate the season, with red velvet in February and zucchini around St. Patrick's Day.

"They're not my favorite," Rita said with a sniff.

"Ashley will be crushed, but we'll get her through the pain."

"Now you sound like Mikki."

A nice compliment, Bree thought.

"I can't believe you're having another signing this weekend. Two in a row. That's a lot of work for me."

Bree nodded solemnly. "I agree. I know you usually work the signings because you're so good at keeping the line moving, but I didn't want to take advantage of you, so I gave you Saturday off."

"What?" Rita's eyes widened. "I'm not working the signing? I'm the glue that keeps them running smoothly. You can't have a signing without me. I'm indispensable. You'll have to put me back on the schedule. Doing a signing without me? What were you thinking?"

Still muttering to herself, Rita stalked out of the back room. Mikki stood in the doorway.

"I heard some of that," she said, her voice sympathetic. "My mother's in a mood."

"She's always in a mood," Bree said cheerfully. "Don't worry. I enjoy her quirks."

"I don't get it. Why did you hire her?"

"She's incredibly dependable, knows the inventory and really does help manage the signings."

"But her attitude."

Bree supposed some people would find Rita difficult, but not her. "Your mom has nothing on mine," Bree said. "Trust me, you have it easy."

"You've said that before. I'm not sure I believe you. Maybe I'll meet her someday."

Maybe hell will freeze over, Bree thought, but she only nodded. "Maybe."

They walked into the store. Rita and Lorraine, who worked for Mikki, opened the big glass doors. A dozen customers waited to get in.

Mikki put her arm around Bree's shoulders and squeezed. "I love it when they line up like that."

Before Bree could answer, a boy of maybe seven burst into the bookstore and headed directly for her. His face was red and his eyes filled with tears.

"I wasn't here," he said, his voice thick with emotion. "I

wasn't here for the signing and I didn't get a book. My mom promised."

Bree knelt. "I noticed, Griffin. I missed seeing you."

Griffin threw himself at her and hung on tight. "It's *her* fault."

Bree glanced at Griffin's harried mother, who grimaced. "His sister's dance recital ran late. Then there was traffic." Her expression turned pleading. "I don't suppose there are any extra signed books?"

"It won't be signed to me," Griffin said, wiping his face. "You promised, Mom. You said a book with my name in it was part of my birthday present. You *promised*."

His mother's face sagged. "How many times do I have to tell you I'm sorry?"

Bree stood. "I think I can fix this," she said, smiling at Griffin. "Just give me one second."

She went into the back. She'd had a few copies of Jairus's book personalized for regulars. She collected the one for Griffin, along with a goodie bag, and returned to the store.

"Would I let you down?" she asked him, handing him both.

Griffin stared at the book. "There was an extra?"

"Look inside."

He opened the book and saw his name in Jairus's big scrawl. The tears returned. "He signed the book to me! Look, Mom. He knows my name."

Griffin's mom shook her head. "That's incredible." She turned to Bree. "I don't know how to thank you. You've saved the day." She lowered her voice. "And my standing in the family."

"Not a problem. You know, with all the signings you can preorder the book so if you're not sure you'll get here, it will be waiting for you."

Griffin's mom sighed. "A great idea. Thank you." She held out her hand. "Come on, Griffin. Let's go pay for the book, then get you to baseball camp. You can read it tonight."

Griffin's smile was blinding. "I can't wait. Thanks, Bree. You're the best."

"You're welcome."

As she led them to the cash register, she passed Rita, who gave her a knowing smile.

"You should have had some kids. Not that you can depend on them." She shot her daughter a disappointed look.

Mikki only laughed and returned to the gift store. Bree rang up the purchase, thinking children had never been an option. Not when she'd been married to Lewis and certainly not now. She knew her limitations and understood the fears that she kept hidden from the world. No way she was putting a kid through that.

Ashley loaded the last of the cupcakes and muffins into the bakery boxes. Evan and Oscar, her main bakers, had started at two in the morning, as they did five days a week, finishing at nine thirty. Evan then went to his counseling job at OAR, her brother's nonprofit, while Oscar, a beefy, forty-something man with countless tattoos, delivered ten dozen muffins and cupcakes to the OAR coffee kiosk set up by UCLA before heading home.

The weekend baking was managed by a local culinary school. An instructor brought in students. The students got practical experience, she had product for Saturday and Sunday, while her guys had the days off.

Most mornings Ashley came early so she could check in with her team and verify inventory. Nothing was worse than running out of an ingredient at three in the morning.

Oscar wheeled the cart back into the industrial kitchen. "I'm ready to go, boss. Want me to put your muffins in your car for you?"

Ashley smiled. "I can handle it, but thanks for asking. I heard from our fruit guy. The first of the season's cherries have come in. I ordered two crates. I thought we'd make cherry muffins and those cherry almond cupcakes everybody loves. Could you make sure you have everything you need?"

Oscar's normally stoic face brightened in a smile. "Cherries, huh? Sounds good. We should have everything, except maybe almonds. I'll text you."

As he spoke, the overhead light illuminated his shaved head and the teardrop tattoo under his left eye. Ashley knew in his case, the tattoo was more than an affectation—the teardrop signaled that he'd killed someone and had served nearly twenty years.

He'd learned to bake in prison and had brought his skills to the outside world, only to discover that very few bakeries wanted to hire a former felon. Through his parole officer, he'd applied at OAR. Ashley had been about to expand Muffins to the Max and had taken a chance on Oscar. That had been three years ago. Evan, another former felon, had followed last year.

Sometimes she wondered how she'd gotten here. She was an ordinary woman, raised in the suburbs. She was supposed to have been a physical therapist. Instead, she owned her own business, rented kitchen space from her brother's nonprofit and employed two former felons who probably knew sixteen ways to kill her.

Not that she worried. Oscar was caring and loyal. She knew he would rip apart anyone who tried to hurt her. When she'd complained about her previous boyfriend being a jerk, Oscar had offered to have him "taken care of." She'd been pretty sure he wasn't kidding and had never mentioned the guy again.

"Dave said Harding is coming into town," Oscar said. "He's moving back?"

"He's rented a house nearby while he works on his next book. It's about grief, so expect him to bug you for stories. It's what he's doing these days. No one is safe. Well, except me. Ignoring Harding's accident, I'm mostly untouched by grief."

Oscar surprised her by lightly touching her arm. "That's what keeps me having faith in the world. I hope you get to stay that way for a long time."

She had no idea what to say to that. "Thank you" felt weird and "me, too" was too flip.

"Carrie's working the kiosk this morning," she said instead. "Maybe she'll make you a latte."

Oscar's expression tightened. "Not gonna happen."

"You drink coffee. I've seen you." She lowered her voice. "Is it the latte thing? Too mainstream?"

"You are pushing your luck."

"You'd never hurt me. So about Carrie. She's sweet on you."

"She's too young."

"You're the same age."

His dark gaze settled on her face. "I'm not talking about years."

A shiver rippled down her spine. Every now and then she was reminded that she and Oscar had almost no life experiences in common.

"You need someone to take care of you," she said firmly.

"I take care of myself."

"Then for sex. Come on. Flirt with her a little. You'll like it and I know she will."

"I can't hear you. Funny how that happens. Your lips are moving yet nothing's come out. Strange."

With that, he walked out of the kitchen.

"Text me about the almonds," she yelled at his back.

She didn't quite hear his reply, but was fairly confident it contained four-letter words in unique combinations. She was still laughing when she pushed the cart to her car.

She rented space at OAR. Their large building had come with an industrial kitchen neither Harding nor Dave, his best friend and business partner, had known what to do with. Ashley had seen the potential immediately. She'd come up with the coffee kiosk by UCLA. She sold the cupcakes and muffins to the foundation at cost and they poured the profits back into their programs. She'd also suggested they provide to-go meals for their clients.

She loaded her SUV with the boxes, then drove them to Muffins to the Max. She'd just finished loading her display case when the first of what she knew would be hundreds of customers arrived.

The morning "muffin with my coffee" crowd thinned out around eleven. At noon Elsie, her afternoon employee, arrived to take over. By twelve fifteen, Ashley was on her way to her brother's rental.

Under normal circumstances, she would be excited to have him back in Los Angeles. He was family and she liked life better when they lived in the same city. However, she couldn't shake her concern about Harding and Bree. Yes, she knew in her head that her brother was more than capable of taking care of himself. But in her gut and her heart, she worried. Probably because if she was to describe the perfect woman for her brother, that woman would have nearly all of Bree's characteristics.

She turned onto a quiet residential street and parked in front of an old-fashioned beach bungalow. There was a wide porch, big windows by the front door and a tiny front yard. An old Ford pickup was parked in the driveway.

The bungalows were common to the area—most had been built in the 1950s and few originals remained. Most had been either torn down and replaced, or had a second story added. You couldn't make the size of a lot bigger, but you could add square footage vertically.

The front door opened and Harding stepped outside, grinning at her.

"Hey, sis."

She dropped her purse and the baskets she was carrying and rushed into his open arms.

"You're finally back," she said, feeling the tightness of his hug. "Don't be gone so long next time. It was months."

"I know. Too long, for sure. Next time I'll break up my travel."

They stood like that for several seconds, needing to know that the other was okay. When he released her and moved back, she took a second to appreciate his easy stride and how healthy he looked.

His accident—when a car had hit him and the driver had left him for dead on the side of the road—had been nearly thirteen years before. She still remembered how he'd looked when they'd finally let her see him at the hospital. Bruised, battered and in traction, but what scared her the most was his stillness. He'd been in a coma for three days, machines helping him breathe.

The doctors had warned her and her parents that he was unlikely to make it and if he did, he would never walk again. Three months later Harding had been moved from the hospital to a rehab facility. Six months later he was walking. Three years after that he'd completed his first triathlon and had written about his experience. An instant bestseller, that book had launched his speaking career and led to the start of OAR. At thirty Harding had accomplished more than most people did in sixty years, and she was proud of him. But she would never forget how broken he'd been and how she had to protect him— even from himself.

He picked up the basket. "You dropped my muffins."

"And your cupcakes. I can't help it. I was happy to see you."

"Was?" he asked, his voice teasing.

"The joy is fading." She followed him into the house.

As she'd suspected, the rooms were small, but there was plenty of light, and the furnishings were nice. He led the way to the kitchen, passing the dining room where he'd already set up his computer. Across the narrow hallway were a bathroom and two bedrooms.

The kitchen had been expanded, allowing enough room for a table and chairs by a bay window. Harding had put out two place settings. As she sat down, he set out deli boxes she'd brought, and a pitcher of iced tea.

"You made tea," she murmured. "Mom would be so proud."

"I can cook. I choose not to. But come on, you have to admit the pitcher is impressive. I found it in one of the cupboards. There's also a silver tea service, but I'm saving that for important company."

"You are such a pain in my ass," she said, opening her sandwich box. She bit into the pickle. "Did you tell the folks you got here all right?"

"The second I pulled into the driveway. Mom worries."

They all worried, but Harding knew that. In some ways he'd recovered more fully than she and her parents had. He'd done the rehab, but they'd had to see his pain and suffering.

Ashley had been fifteen when he'd been struck. Overnight her world had changed. She'd been frantic about whether her only brother would survive, while dealing with both her parents practically living at the hospital for three months. They'd tried to split their time, so she wasn't alone too much, but she'd insisted they stay with Harding.

His accident had forced her to be self-sufficient. Whenever she'd gotten scared, she'd reminded herself that compared to what Harding was dealing with, she had it easy.

"How's the book going?" she asked.

"Slow. I'm just starting. Plus, I've been on tour for the new release." He picked up his sandwich. "I'm looking forward to the book signing. I finally get to meet the women you work with."

"They'll adore you."

He grinned. "Most women do."

Annoying but true. Harding was handsome in a boy-next-door kind of way. His brown hair had a slight red tinge and his large, expressive eyes were the perfect shade of hazel. He was fit, charming and articulate. Plus, the whole "left for dead" thing. Women loved that story.

"About the signing," she said slowly, not sure how to express her concerns. "We should talk about Bree."

Harding put down his sandwich. "What about her? My publicist says her store is one of the best." The smile returned. "Apparently, she's picky about who signs in her store, so thanks for making that happen."

If only it was that simple, Ashley thought. "You have to watch yourself around her."

He frowned. "What are you talking about?"

"Bree." She leaned toward him. "I adore her. She's a great friend and I would trust her with anything in my life. But I'm worried about you. She's just your type. She's gorgeous and well-read and athletic. You're going to want to go out with her and I'm afraid you'll fall for her. But Bree doesn't do relationships. She sleeps with guys a few times then dumps them. I don't want you to get hurt."

"Are you serious?"

"Very."

He relaxed back in her chair. "Ashley, I love you like a sister, but you're an idiot. Don't worry. I can take care of myself."

"I wish that were true. Bree's not like the other women you've dated. She's more the kind who would eat her young."

"I thought you liked her."

"I do, but I also have a healthy respect for her self-preservation skills. She absolutely won't get emotionally involved with a guy and you're just one big emotion. You practically cry at commercials."

He looked more amused than annoyed. "I don't cry."

"You do on the inside. Harding, just please be careful."

He studied her. "You warned her to stay away from me, didn't you?"

Ashley tried not to look guilty. "Maybe."

"Now I *have* to go out with her."

"Why? Don't be stubborn. Trust me. I know Bree."

"You can't protect me from the world, kid."

"I can try. Please don't ask her out just to teach me a lesson."

"Fine. I'll only ask her out if I want to go out with her. How's that?"

She held in a groan. "You make me insane." She stared at her lunch. "Now I feel awful about dissing my friend. I'm not sure I can eat."

He winked. "More for me."

FOUR

Mikki added another necklace to the display. The "sea creature" jewelry was selling well. Thin gold or silver chains were attached to a shark, a dolphin, a clown fish or an octopus. The price point was right and the necklaces were made by a local artist. She also carried wave bangles that could be stacked together or worn separately.

She loved her gift shop. There were seasonal offerings, stacks of colorful beach towels and lots of mugs with cute sayings. Tacky tourist gifts shared space with original paintings.

She liked how rearranging a display could increase sales and that flip-flops always sold well. She liked the smell of salt air, the quiet mornings, the busy afternoons. In high school she'd taken elective art classes, but she'd lacked the talent to be an artist. The gift shop gave her an outlet to play with color and texture and make money.

These days the store was a family affair. Lorraine worked for her, and Will was helping out this summer. Sydney was working for her dad. Next year they would switch, assuming Sydney came home next summer. Her daughter was already looking for internships. That child never rested.

Sales were up, Mikki thought, placing bottles of sunscreen on a shelf. The move last January had been great for her business. The first couple of years had been a struggle. The location hadn't helped, nor had her lack of retail experience. But she'd worked hard and the business had grown.

Still, for the first six months she'd been terrified she was going to go under. Perry hadn't wanted her to buy the store in the first place. They'd fought for weeks. She'd worn him down and he'd agreed reluctantly, insisting she was going to lose all the money they were investing. A threat that had kept her up at night.

Now, as she placed aloe vera next to the sunscreen, she wondered if that had been the first crack in her marriage. The fighting followed by her long hours at the store. They'd always had separate interests but when she'd bought the store, they'd lived separate lives. She'd practically been single before the divorce. Three years later she still was on her own.

That made her think about her conversation with Bree. Was she a traditionalist who wanted to be in a relationship? She'd certainly never expected to be alone this long. After the divorce she'd tried dating, but going out with men she didn't know had made her uncomfortable. She just didn't know how to date.

"Look!" Lorraine walked over with a small blown-glass turtle. "The delivery just arrived. Aren't they the cutest things? We have little sea lions, and I'm swooning over the otters. What about putting them in the front display case?"

Mikki grinned. "We won't be able to keep them in stock. Let's up the price by fifteen percent."

Lorraine laughed. "You're such a tycoon."

"I wish."

Mikki carried the turtle to the bookstore section. She found Bree and her mother stocking shelves.

"These just arrived," Mikki said, showing them the blown glass. "Plus sea lions and otters. This first shipment will go quickly, but maybe we could do a joint display when I get more in stock."

"We could put them with some children's books," Bree said. "The bright covers will complement the glass."

Rita pressed her lips together. "You can't put something that delicate with children's books. The kids will break them. Customers will get glass in their feet. Everyone will sue you and you'll lose the store."

Bree patted her shoulder. "I'm sure Mikki was thinking these would be in a case with the books. Because your point about the shards of glass is valid."

Rita looked pleased to be taken seriously. Mikki marveled at Bree's ability to deal with her mother. For her it was hard enough to have Rita on the other side of the building. No way she could work with her. Lorraine was different. Her mother-in-law avoided finding a black cloud inside every silver lining.

"I'll let you know when we get more in," Mikki said, returning to her gift shop. Her mother followed.

"The paper says the city is putting too many chemicals in the water," Rita said. "We're all being poisoned."

Mikki held in a sigh. "Why would the city want to poison its own residents?"

"I'm not saying they want to. I'm saying it's happening."

Mikki looked at the woman who had always worried about the unexpected. Rita had made her carry an umbrella to school, even though Southern California had maybe a dozen rainy days a year. Disaster was always right around the corner. Living like that must be exhausting.

Her parents had divorced twelve years ago. Her father, a quiet, unhappy man while married, had blossomed into an avid square dancer who had dated dozens of women. Sadly, he'd passed away unexpectedly eight years ago. Unlike her ex-husband, Rita hadn't changed at all after the divorce.

"Mom, why don't you date?"

Her mother stared at her in confusion. "A man?"

"Yes. I doubt you're secretly a lesbian. It's been years since the divorce, but I don't remember you ever dating."

"Why would I go out with some man who only wants to

steal my money or take advantage of me? No, thank you. I was married once. I'm not looking to do that again."

Lorraine walked over. "Rita, I just can't understand your attitude. You're a young, vital woman. You must want a little companionship."

Her mother shook her head. "You're plenty of companionship for me."

"But we're friends. Mikki's talking about a man."

"Not worth the trouble."

Mikki didn't like that she remembered saying exactly that herself recently, when Sydney had asked why she never went out. Was she turning into her mother?

"But you're barely sixty," Lorraine pointed out. "Do you want to spend the next thirty years alone?"

"Why are you two ganging up on me?" Rita glared at them.

With that, she walked off, obviously upset. Lorraine sighed.

"That woman. She's difficult. It hurts my heart to think how closed off she is."

Mikki nearly staggered as reality hit her up the side of her head. If her mother had thirty years left, didn't that mean Mikki had fifty? Fifty years! Holy crap—was she really going to rattle around in her big house with only Earl for company? The thought was simply too depressing to consider.

She didn't want to be like her mom—she wanted something more. Real companionship. Conversation, travel, laughter and yes, possibly sex with a man. No offense, Earl. She didn't want to get old and bitter. She wanted to be happy. She wanted more than she had. And if that was true, then she really needed to get off her butt and do something about it.

Bree studied the rows of chairs she'd set up in front of the podium. With the moveable racks out of the way, she could easily seat two hundred. She'd rented an extra hundred and fifty chairs. The side sliders could open, allowing the seating area to literally flow onto the beach, if necessary. She wasn't sure how many to expect. Harding Burton wasn't one of her regular authors.

Rita joined her. "Do we need that much seating? It's a book about rowing."

Bree held in a grin. "It isn't about rowing."

"It's called *Oar*."

"Objective, achievement, repeat. It's more of a life philosophy."

Rita's expression turned doubtful. "Then you put out way too many chairs."

"I'm not sure. He draws a crowd." *A mostly female crowd*, she thought.

The book was fine. Nicely written with interesting anecdotes. Not exactly earth-shattering since the idea of not giving up in the face of adversity had been around since primates started walking upright. Still, his story was compelling and his picture on the back of the book was pretty.

Three women in their twenties walked up to her with the slightly crazed look of überfans.

"Harding Burton's signing's here, right?" the tall brunette asked eagerly.

"This is the place." Bree glanced at her watch. "In a couple of hours."

The three women giggled. Rita made a strangled noise and stalked away.

"Can we pick our seats now?" another woman asked.

Bree waved toward the empty chairs. "Absolutely."

They raced to the front row and sat by the podium. More women followed until about thirty were claiming seats. Each held the book with a removable Paid In Full sticker. Bree had a firm rule—every attendee must buy a book. From her. None of that online buying and bringing it in. Her store was how she made a living and if you wanted to come to the book party, you had to pay the bookstore owner.

Twenty women waited patiently at checkout for their copy of Harding's book. As Bree wondered if she'd ordered enough, Mikki came over.

"Can you make an announcement about the signing? Lots of women are hovering on my side of the store, not shopping, just taking up space. It's annoying."

Ashley joined them. "They're buying muffins. I guess they want to keep up their strength."

"Because being around Harding is so taxing?" Bree asked, not sure what to make of the steady influx of customers. In the short time she'd been standing there, the line for the register had nearly doubled. She thought the *Brad the Dragon* signings were big, but she had a feeling this one was going to be record-breaking.

She pointed at Rita. "Go help at the register. Mikki, can you make the announcement that the seating is open? I'll get more chairs, then call my rep and see if I can get more books delivered."

"How many did you order?"

"Six hundred."

Mikki grinned. "Honey, you're going to need a bigger boat."

The signing was from three to five. By two thirty, Bree had run out of even emergency chairs and she was down to two cartons of books. Dozens of customers had settled on the sand outside. Bree set out the portable speakers. People might not be able to see Harding, but they could hear him.

Once the books ran out, she'd started a list of those who still wanted an autographed copy. With luck, she could convince Harding to come back and sign them for her. She really hated to lose the sales.

She'd just finished checking the speakers when she turned to find Ashley hovering.

"Don't tell me he's running late," Bree said.

"He'll be here any second." Ashley shifted uneasily. "I'm sorry about before."

Bree stared at her. "I have nearly six hundred women waiting to hear from your brother, who isn't here yet. I have no idea if he's a decent speaker, so there's that. Plus, I ran out of books. What on earth are you sorry about and why are we discussing it now?"

Ashley held her ground. "About you not getting involved with him. I was wrong and I hurt your feelings. I'm sorry. It's not my business what you do with my brother."

Bree's brain took a second to process that. "Don't tell me you've been worried about that all this time. Ashley, honey, I have no interest in your brother. He's a way to bring in customers. As for dating him, there are plenty of guys out there. I don't need to get involved with your brother."

"But I—"

Bree cut her off with a quick shake of her head. "Stop talking and go find him. Drag his sorry ass into the store so I can stop worrying he won't show up. Authors. What was God thinking?"

Before Ashley could move, Bree heard a verbal wave crash across the store. It started at the entrance and worked its way to where they were standing. The sound was part sigh, part moan and all happy. She turned and saw a guy walking toward them.

Bree recognized him from his picture and was curious to see how the real thing matched up to the hype.

He was about six feet, lean but strong. There was a faint hesitancy to his gait, no doubt lingering damage from his injuries. His hair was more brown than red, and a little wavier than his sister's, but there were similarities. The big eyes—his hazel rather than blue—and the full mouth. His jaw was stronger, his shoulders broader.

And then he smiled.

An audible gasp came from behind her. Bree had to admit it was a killer smile, good enough to make a woman want to do about anything just to see it again. Thankfully, she was done being a fool over any man.

She walked toward him, her hand outstretched. "You must be Harding. Nice to meet you. I'm Bree. Welcome to my store. Let's go back to my office. Otherwise, I fear your fans will attack and leave nothing behind but a few bones and teeth."

"There's an image," he said easily, his large hand engulfing hers. "Good to finally meet you. Ashley's told me so much about you."

"I can imagine. It's all true."

She ignored the heat she felt from his touch and the way her girl bits offered a quick "yes, please." As they walked toward the back of the store, she heard murmurs of protest from the crowd.

"Five minutes," she yelled. "Then he's all yours."

"I wish," one of them called.

They stepped into her office. Harding closed the door behind him and gave her that smile again.

"So you're Bree."

"Most days, yes."

"I like the hair."

The non sequitur had her blinking at him. "Excuse me?"

"The curls. I've always had a thing for curly hair."

"Lucky me. Can we focus on the book signing?"

"Sure."

"How do you want to handle things? Your publicist says you do a brief talk. Do you want to read from your book?" Something she'd never understood. An author reading his own words was the definition of boring. Except for children's books. But writers were inherently weird and she'd learned to go along with the quirks. Especially when those quirks meant several hundred book sales.

"I'll speak for twenty minutes, then sign," he said.

"Great. So I only ordered six hundred books. I didn't think

you'd pull in so many people and a lot of them are buying multiple copies."

"They're nice for gift giving."

"I'm taking names for those who can't get a copy today. Are you open to coming back to sign them?"

"Of course. Just tell me when and I'll be here." He put his hand on her upper arm. "Whatever will make this go smoothly for you, Bree, I'll do."

She couldn't tell if he was being flirty or funny or nice. Under other circumstances, she would want to find out, but not right now. Unless he was being nice, in which case, he should stop because she sure didn't trust that.

"I have pens for the signing," she said. "Plus the bookmarks your publicist sent. I mocked her for sending a thousand. I should have paid more attention. Do you want anything to drink? Water? A latte? Tequila?"

His hazel eyes brightened with amusement. "You have tequila?"

"Sure. This is LA, so it's the good stuff."

"Maybe after the signing. For now just water."

From behind the closed door came a faint chant of "Harding. Harding. Harding."

"Is it always like this?" she asked, thinking she really should have said no when Ashley suggested the signing with her brother. If only she wasn't such a sucker for cash flow.

"Mostly." He started for the door. "Shall we?"

She followed him out into the store, then quickly walked around to the side where she could observe without getting in the way. The second they saw him, the crowd came to their feet. The cheering, whistling and stomping shook the building.

Mikki joined her. "You're hating this," her friend said cheerfully.

"Why do you say that?"

"You're not a fan of celebrity."

Something Bree never discussed but Mikki wasn't wrong. Bree had grown up with famous parents—at least in literary circles. She'd seen grown men weep at the privilege of being in the same room as her parents.

Mikki put her arm around her. "Hang in there. Three hours from now this will be over. If nothing else, he's good-looking."

"Interested?" Bree asked, her voice teasing.

"Too young, plus, you know. Earl."

"He might be better than Earl."

Instead of laughing, Mikki shook her head. "Don't get me started on that. I'm dealing with some stuff. But you go for Harding if you want. You'd make a cute couple."

"I don't couple."

"Yes, one day we'll discuss that."

Mikki returned to her side of the store. The crowd had quieted and was listening intently as Harding spoke.

"I met Dave in rehab," Harding was saying. "He broke his neck in a diving accident. One centimeter. It's the difference between walking and being in a chair. The difference between having the use of your hands and not." He gave a self-deprecating smile.

"It all comes down to independence. The first time I realized not being able to move meant I couldn't piss on my own was a moment I'll never forget. A nurse had to put in a catheter and I couldn't change that. I couldn't move. I could barely breathe. I had more broken bones than not, but all I could think about was that pretty nurse sticking a tube up my dick and how it was going to hurt like hell. I nearly gave up a thousand times."

He shrugged. "My family would tell you I was brave, but I wasn't. I was scared and I hurt and I felt my life was lost to me. Then I met Dave at rehab. We were roommates. He'd been there a couple weeks longer than me. He had it all figured out. He knew a way a guy in a wheelchair could off himself and that was his plan. Did I want in?"

The crowd gasped. Bree was surprised as well—she hadn't read this in either of Harding's books.

He gave everyone a moment to take in his words, then leaned forward.

"In that second, as I realized what he was saying, I knew I wanted to live. No matter what it took, I would heal from what had happened to me. I was stronger than the jerk who'd left me on the side of the road. I told him if he wanted to do that, I wouldn't stop him, but it wasn't for me."

Harding's smile returned. "Dave told me I'd passed the test and that I could stay in the room with him. He didn't want to be with some victim. He wanted a friend who was willing to do the work. We stayed up all night talking and OAR was born. Objective, achievement, repeat."

The crowd burst into applause. Harding waited for quiet before continuing.

"Six months later I limped out of that rehab facility. I went from walking to running. I fought my way to my new normal. There were plenty of setbacks. But I refused to give up and Dave was right there with me. I competed in a marathon, then a triathlon. I finished second from last, but I finished. Dave and I started our foundation."

Bree sensed he was wrapping up his talk and moved to the table she'd set up near the register. She and Rita had already put out stanchions. She connected them with retractable rope, then hoped Harding wasn't too much of a talker when he signed. With this many people wanting a piece of him, they could be here for hours.

When he'd finished speaking and moved to the table, she handed out sticky notes to those wanting the book personalized. She had Rita help him by opening the book and putting the sticky note with the recipient's name next to it. Should anyone talk too much, Rita gave her a little stink eye and the line kept moving.

Harding was friendly but not gross. No matter how low cut the T-shirt, he didn't leer. Several women passed him phone numbers, but he always pushed them back.

And so it went for an hour, then two. By the time the third hour had started, Bree was ready to surrender. Thank goodness the line was dwindling. She followed the last woman in to start taking down the rope and stanchions.

"I thought we could get some dinner," the third from the last woman in line said. She was a gorgeous twenty-something with big boobs and long blond hair.

Mikki eighteen years ago, Bree thought with a grin, wondering how many invitations Harding had fielded today.

"Thanks," he said easily. "I already have plans."

"How about tomorrow?"

His smile turned regretful. "Thank you but no."

Her expression tightened and she snatched up her book. "Whatever."

The last two readers finished up with him and walked away. Harding stood and stretched. "Good crowd."

"Too many people, if you ask me," Rita said with a sniff. "Just buy the book. Why do you need it signed?"

Harding chuckled. "I like you, Rita. You say what you think. Not enough people do."

Rita glared at him, as if not sure he was messing with her or telling the truth.

"Thanks for not giving up on the line," Bree told him. "I'm used to a couple hundred avid fans, but nothing like this. You're an attraction."

"Or an oddity. You'll let me know when the rest of the books come in for me to sign?"

"I'll get in touch with your publicist when I receive the shipment."

"Or you could just text me." He pulled out his phone. "Give me your number."

Saying no seemed churlish, although it was her first instinct. Reluctantly, she offered the information, then immediately received a text from him.

"I'll let you get on with your evening," she said, picking up two of the stanchions.

He grabbed two more and followed her to the rear of the store. "Have dinner with me."

She opened the closet door. "You have plans."

"Yes. With you."

She tucked the stanchions into place. He did the same and they faced each other.

He really was nice to look at, she thought. He was a couple of years younger, but she would guess experience wise, they were equally matched. Obviously, he appealed to her physically, but attraction was easy.

"No," she said simply.

"Why not?"

"I don't go out with writers, and I promised your sister I wouldn't break your heart."

He grinned. "You *are* a heartbreaker. Of that, I'm certain. I'll be right back."

He walked across the store. Bree put away the rest of the stanchions and started on the chairs. She was on her third armful when Harding returned, Ashley at his side.

"I'll take care of these," he said, collecting the chairs she held. "Ashley wants to talk to you."

"Go out with Harding," Ashley said, her expression guilty. "I shouldn't have said anything."

"It's fine. I don't want to."

"Liar," Harding said, walking past them for more chairs. "Of course you want to hang out. I'm charming."

He was, but she was more concerned about Ashley. They were business partners, in a way, and she didn't want any awkwardness. This, she reminded herself, was why she avoided relation-ships. They were always complicated.

"I'll feel better if you have dinner with my brother," Ashley told her earnestly.

"You've lost your mind."

"Possibly."

"You're begging me to go out with him?"

"Yes."

"Whatever." Bree waited until Harding walked by with yet more chairs. "Fine. Dinner. Tomorrow. But just so we're clear, it's only dinner. You're not my type."

He paused to wink at her. "Too bad, because you're defi-nitely mine."

FIVE

Mikki resisted the urge to offer Bree more coffee. Or make waffles. She always went into "Mom mode" when she was nervous, which was usually fine, but Bree didn't enjoy anyone hovering. Still, it was difficult not to stare over her shoulder.

Bree looked up from Mikki's laptop. "You know I have no experience with online dating sites."

"Yes, but you're a guy magnet. I refuse to turn into my mother, so I have to put myself out there. My clients are mostly women. My days revolve around work and my kids, and my kids won't need me much longer. Nothing about my lifestyle brings me into contact with single men, so meeting someone online makes the most sense."

She'd been practicing that little speech for nearly three days, ever since she'd realized she was merely a passenger in the journey of her life, rather than driving the car. Or whatever vehicle one had for one's life journey. She needed to *do* something. Soon.

She forced herself to sit at the kitchen table, across from her friend. At her request Bree had come by this morning to help Mikki pick which online dating site seemed best for her. Nothing too flashy or young or complicated.

"You sure you want to do this?" Bree asked. "Single guys are everywhere."

"For you, maybe. I couldn't do what you do."

"Which is?"

"I don't know. Talk to them. You just start a conversation. I don't have that skill."

"We're talking right now."

"You're not a guy I might want to date. I started dating Perry in high school. He's the only man I've ever loved."

Bree's expression turned pained. "Please tell me he's not the only guy you've had sex with."

"There was someone before him. Briefly."

Her first high school boyfriend. The sex had been fast and uninspiring, but yes, they'd done it. There was also a guy she'd slept with after the divorce, but she didn't like to think about that awful experience.

"I could live into my nineties," Mikki told her. "I don't want to be alone for the next fifty years. I want to care about someone. I want to be cared about. You're right—I'm a traditionalist." She pointed at the laptop. "So let's find me a man."

One corner of Bree's mouth turned up. "You're very brave from the safety of your kitchen."

"We should take advantage of that."

Bree turned the laptop toward Mikki. "I think this is the best one for you. The singles are a little older and it's easy to navigate. You get a month's free trial, so you really have nothing to lose. You just have to build your profile."

All the air seemed to flow out of Mikki's lungs. Her stomach flipped and she had the strongest urge to start a pot roast.

"Now?"

"You're back to being a coward. Yes, now." Bree started typing. "Are you comfortable using your real first name?"

"What other name would I use?"

"I don't know. We'll go with Mikki." She typed. "You're a businesswoman."

"What? I work in a gift shop."

"You *own* a gift shop. Embrace your success. How about entrepreneur?"

"That makes me sound more successful than I am."

Bree looked at her. "How?"

"I don't know. It just does."

"Now you sound like your mother."

Mikki glared at her. "Don't be mean. Fine. Entrepreneur."

"You want to lie about your age?"

"Why would I do that? At some point the guy's going to see me in person. I'm thirty-nine."

She tried not to wince. She was going to be forty. She practically had adult children. How had time gone by so quickly?

They went through likes and dislikes.

"Don't you dare say you like walks on the beach," Bree told her.

"But I do."

"It's a cliché. Be more creative. You enjoy wine tasting and intelligent conversation. You want a man who's funny without being mean. You know how to change a tire, but you'd rather not. You want to travel and learn things, but aren't really into anything like mountain climbing or backpacking."

Mikki stared at her. "How do you know all that?"

Bree's expression turned self-satisfied. "I observe."

Mikki waved at the computer. "All that. Say that. It's really good."

They spent fifteen minutes picking out pictures for the profile.

"You're not applying for a receptionist job at the local church," Bree grumbled, scrolling through the picture file. "Don't you have something sexy? Maybe you in a bathing suit?"

"I don't take pictures of myself in a bathing suit. Who does that?" She pointed at a picture of herself at the Santa Monica pier. "What about that one? At least I'm out of the house."

They finally settled on three pictures, including one from a wine-tasting class. As Bree uploaded them, Mikki wondered if she was making a mistake, bothering with an online dating site. Was she really going to meet anyone that way? It seemed so random.

"Maybe I should think about this," she murmured. "I'm not sure online dating is for me."

Bree hit a couple of keys, then smiled. "Too late. Your profile is up. Brace yourself for the onslaught."

Mikki felt nauseous. "There won't be an onslaught. I'll hear crickets. I'll be humiliated."

Bree stood. "You underestimate yourself. Guys are going to want to go out with you."

"I'm not sure I can date."

"You'll learn. It's not hard. When you find a couple of guys who interest you, set up something casual like coffee. Meals last too long. You need an escape."

"Now you're scaring me. Why would I want to escape?"

"They might be boring. You might not have chemistry."

"They might be serial killers?"

"Unlikely, but yes." Bree grabbed her bag. "I'll see you tomorrow at the store."

Mikki walked her to the front door. "Thanks for helping me this morning. I appreciate it. Sort of."

Bree laughed. "You're going to like being part of a couple."

"I agree. It's getting there that's going to be difficult."

She closed the door behind her friend and faced an empty house. The kids were with their dad for the week. Despite being legally an adult, Sydney had slipped right back into the every other week routine when she'd gotten home from college.

Mikki had her usual Sunday chores: changing sheets, laundry, menu planning. Although for the next few days she only had to feed herself. That was hardly worth the effort of planning out a menu.

She worked her way through her list, circling through the kitchen every hour or so as she eyed her computer. After her trip to the grocery store, she went on a walk through the neighborhood, then spent an hour in the garden. Around four she returned to the kitchen and sat down in front of her laptop.

"It's too soon," she told herself, even as she logged in to the dating site. "No one will have—"

Her inbox notification was blinking. She carefully clicked on it, then sucked in a breath as a hundred and twenty-seven messages loaded.

"That can't be right," she murmured.

But it was. There were over a hundred messages from men who, apparently, wanted to meet her.

"Or not," she said as she scanned the first dozen.

Three were offers to have sex and one was some woman looking for a date for her brother in prison. Delete. She read a few more. Several replies were from guys in their twenties, looking for an older woman. Delete, delete.

A professional dog walker offered to take care of her puppy. She wasn't sure if that was a guy looking for work or making a very weird sexual advance. Just to be safe, she got rid of him, and deleted anything that looked remotely weird, including three in which the men talked about how big their penises were. Yuck. Once she'd cleaned up the replies, she was left with about forty.

A lot of them were variations on a theme. "You seem nice. Let's meet for drinks."

"Love your picture. I'm a single dad with three girls. How about coffee?" And so on.

Mikki kept reading, not sure what she was looking for. How was she supposed to know who was nice and who would freak her out? And jumping from an online posting to coffee seemed really sudden.

"Hi, Mikki," she read. "I think we know each other. I'm Duane Merrell and our daughters were friends in elementary school."

The message went on to explain he'd been divorced for three

years and that if she was who he thought, he would like to talk on the phone or get together for a drink. He left his phone number.

She didn't remember him at all, but she thought she remembered Sydney having a friend with his daughter's name. That would be easy enough to check.

She read a few more messages, then logged out. The volume of replies should make her happy, but instead she felt confused and restless. There were too many options and she wasn't sure she was ready to take the step of getting in touch with one or twenty of them.

She went online and searched *how to be successful at online dating*, then read a few articles. The information wasn't exactly comforting. One suggested she meet guys at a coffee shop not too close to home, and when she left, she should take a longer route past a police station, so she wasn't followed.

"Yup, not doing that," she said, snapping her laptop closed. "No guys, no police station, no long route home."

But if she didn't want to find someone online, she needed a different plan. That or spend the rest of her life alone, slowly turning into her mother.

Bree drove to the restaurant Harding had suggested. It was on the pier in Redondo Beach, so not somewhere she usually ate, but she knew the area. He'd offered to pick her up, but that was a no-go. She didn't invite people to her place—not friends and certainly not some guy. They'd have dinner and that would be the end of it. Yes, he was attractive and she'd enjoyed his talk yesterday, but dating him would be too complicated.

She handed her keys to the valet, then walked inside. Harding was already there, talking to the hostess. For a second she allowed herself to admire the view. He was as good-looking as she remembered. Attractive without being threatening. His stance was casual, his clothes appropriate. When he saw her, he gave her a smile that had her regretting sex wasn't on the menu.

"This is our first date," he told the hostess. "I'm super excited."

"Super excited?" Bree repeated. "Did you just say that?"

"I did."

They were shown to a table overlooking the ocean. The big, open windows allowed them to hear the waves and the people on the beach. Soft music played on hidden speakers.

"Nice restaurant," she said. "How did you find it?"

"Dave said it was epic."

Bree laughed. "Epic works."

He leaned toward her, his gaze intense. "Why did you say yes to dinner?"

"Because your sister begged me to."

His mouth twitched. "She didn't."

"I'm sorry to say she absolutely did. I was shocked. I mean, how sad that you need a relative shilling to get you a date? I would have thought being so famous and all, you'd have your choice of women, but apparently not."

"You're saying this is a pity date."

She held in a smile. "Uh-huh. I'm a giver."

"You're beautiful."

The unexpected compliment flustered her—something that never happened.

"Don't change the subject," she said, telling herself she didn't care what he thought of her looks. "We were discussing how pathetic you are."

"My least favorite topic."

Their server walked over and told them about the specials, then took their drink orders. When he'd left, Bree glanced out the window.

"Great view. Ashley said you're moving back to LA. So you've lived here before?"

He nodded. "It's my home base. I've been gone, doing some writing and touring. I stayed away longer than I should have."

"Did you have a secondary home base for the travels?"

"I stayed in Aspen a couple months to get into my book."

"Nice. I've skied there."

His expression brightened. "You like to ski?"

"I like most physical activities." She held up her hand. "No sex jokes, please."

"But they're the most fun."

"Maybe, but no." She locked her gaze with his. "I mean that, Harding. We're not sleeping together."

"You say that with a lot of intensity. Do you expect me to leave?"

"I don't know. I just want to be clear."

"But you're attracted to me. I can tell. Just like you know I'm attracted to you."

"Interesting but irrelevant."

"You have rules." The smile returned. "I like it."

He was way too easy to be with, she thought. Too easy to like. The server brought their cocktails. As Bree picked up hers, she reminded herself to be careful. Liking someone, being vulnerable, was dangerous.

"Tell me about your next book," she said, knowing writers loved nothing more than talking about their work for hours. "Is it another memoir?"

He shook his head. "No. It's nonfiction. I'm not creative enough to write anything else. I'm exploring grief. What it's like to experience it, the forms it takes and most importantly, how people who have lived through grief find the strength to not just move on but thrive."

"The OAR philosophy meets emotional rather than physical challenges?" she asked lightly.

"Something like that. So if you know anyone who's gotten through grief, have them get in touch with me."

She thought about what she'd lived through, first with her parents and then with Lewis. Was it grief? Probably more like rage, she thought, knowing she would never discuss that with Harding, or anyone.

"What's your writing process?" she asked.

He studied her. "You can't possibly be interested in that. Why would you ask?"

"You're a writer."

His expression turned knowing. "So I want to talk about myself? Not all writers are like that."

"Most are." She sipped her drink. "I was married to a writer. Unpublished, but he had all the characteristics."

Harding chuckled. "You're a bookstore owner who loves books but hates writers?"

"*Hates* is strong. Let's just say I'm clear on their limitations. But I do love the end product. Fiction, nonfiction, inspirational, travel, poetry. I love it all. Oh, nothing literary, but otherwise, I'm a fan."

"He wrote literary?"

"He tried," she said lightly. He'd wanted to be famous, like her parents. For him, it had never happened.

"Your second book is doing well," she said, mostly to stop talking about Lewis. "You and your publisher must be happy. It's different than your first book."

"You read it?"

"I read both of them. You have a compelling style. Clean, but with an eye for detail. That story you told, where Dave tested you by offering you a way to kill yourself. Did that really happen?"

"Every word is true." Harding looked at her. "I'm the face of OAR, but Dave does the hard work. He's the one with the courage and drive."

He picked up his drink, then put it down. "My story is tragic. Teenager hit by car and left to die. It makes a good headline.

But I had so much support. Not just my family, but friends and the community. Then the media got ahold of it and I became a national phenomenon. Strangers sent me letters and prayed for me. Specialists flew in. Dave was a star athlete who dove into a pool and broke his neck. No one wrote about him. No one offered to modify his house for free or followed his progress in the local paper. He sucked it up and learned to deal. I had it easy. I was never in it alone. A lot of people are. I get that."

She thought about all the work that Harding glossed over. The pain, the fear, the endless days and weeks of sweating to exhaustion, never knowing if he was making progress. Yet, to him, Dave was the hero. Not just Dave, but countless others who had to figure it out on their own.

She knew about being alone, though not in the context he meant. She supposed there were different kinds of suffering. Life with her parents. Her marriage to Lewis. Looking back, she wondered why he'd married her. For a while she'd thought maybe he'd been in love with her, but now she doubted he ever had. Maybe he'd seen her as a way to be close to greatness—at least as he saw it.

"I lost you," Harding said quietly. "Where did you go?"

Nowhere she was going to talk about. "I was just thinking about what you went through."

"Not just me. My whole family. My accident changed us all."

"It made Ashley strong," Bree said. "She's doing so well with her business. What she did takes courage."

Ashley had gone to college for physical therapy, but after completing her four-year degree, she'd realized that wasn't her passion but was instead a reaction to Harding's accident. She'd changed directions, going to culinary school and opening Muffins to the Max.

"I'm glad you like her."

"I wouldn't have leased space with her if I didn't."

"You're not willing to work with someone you don't like?"

"No way. I own a small business. I work too hard to play those kinds of games with employees and business partners."

"You're a good role model."

She dismissed that comment with a flick of her wrist. "You don't know me well enough to say that. Besides, your sister thinks I'm heartless and cruel to men."

"Are you?"

"No." She smiled. "I'm clear on what I do and don't want. No commitments, nothing long-term. Maybe we'll last just the night or maybe a week. But don't expect more from me."

"Want to tell me why?"

"Nope."

"Do you know why?"

She remembered being six and telling her mother she was hungry. Her nanny had been gone for some reason. Her mother had snapped at her.

"Your father and I are working. We're writing. Can you understand that? We can't be interrupted every few hours because you have a grumbly stomach. When your nanny gets back, she'll take care of you. Can you possibly wait until then and leave us alone?"

Bree remembered how rejected she'd felt. How small and unimportant. "But I haven't eaten since yesterday," she'd whispered.

Her mother had glared at her without speaking, then had stomped down to the kitchen where she'd made a couple of sandwiches and had poured a glass of milk. That done, she'd turned back to her daughter.

"She'll be back later today. Until then, try to manage things yourself. Understand?"

Bree looked at Harding. "I'm very clear on why I don't get involved with anyone."

"But you were married."

"Yes."

"I'm guessing whatever happened there reaffirmed your belief system."

"It did."

He smiled. "Want to talk about it?"

"No."

"Want to admit you're attracted to me and regretting your no-sex rule?"

She liked his confidence and the way he used humor to make a point. "I don't believe in regrets."

"Want to order dinner?"

"I think that's the best plan."

SIX

"This is the village." Seth pointed to the map on his tablet. "There are dozens of hotels and restaurants. Plenty of shopping."

The pictures were pretty, Ashley thought, snuggled next to him on the sofa. "Whistler is north of Vancouver, right?"

"Yes. About seventy-five miles, most of it on a wide highway, so it's easy driving. I was thinking we'd go before the big snow."

She laughed. "I'm not a fan of the little snow, either."

"How about mid-October?" Seth asked. "There are biking trails, and the leaves will be changing color."

She liked the sound of that. "You mentioned a canoe tour. I'd like to learn how to paddle a canoe."

He flipped to another picture. "Then we'll do that as well."

She pointed. "You want to rent an ATV, don't you?"

"Kind of."

"I don't get the thrill of being bounced around. How about you do that while I visit the spa?"

He kissed her. "Deal." He put the tablet on the coffee table and pulled her close. "If you email me some dates you can get away, I'll check availability. We'll fly to Vancouver, rent a car and drive to the Whistler Four Seasons."

"While that sounds amazing, I don't think we need to spend that much money."

"Maybe just this one time. To make it really special."

Her breath caught in her throat. Special as in...*special*? Her heart rate doubled. "What do you mean?" she asked as casually as she could.

"The anniversary of our first date is in August," he said. "The first time we said *I love you* was in October." He touched her cheek. "Let's celebrate that. We'll spend a few days in Whistler, at a fancy hotel. We'll explore the area, do the things we talked about, have nice dinners. I want it to be a trip we'll always remember."

"I'd like that," she whispered. If he proposed, she would remember that trip for the rest of her life.

"Me, too."

Her heart rate returned to normal while she consciously slowed her breathing. She wasn't interested in a big wedding—that had never been her thing. She wasn't the kind of person who dreamed about six bridesmaids and centerpieces in her colors. She wanted to be married to start on the next phase of her life.

Should Seth propose, she hoped he would be open to a simple wedding. She'd rather put the money toward a house or a college fund for their future children.

She reminded herself not to assume. Maybe the trip was just a trip. But the thought that it might be something more, something amazing, nearly made her giddy with happiness. Because Seth was the one. Of that she was sure.

Mikki didn't like being indecisive. She prided herself on making a decision and living with the consequences either way. Like her haircut. She hadn't dithered—she'd done it, and had regretted it, but that was a separate issue. More than two days after joining the dating site, she had yet to answer anyone. Nor had she read the additional messages. She was scared, uncomfortable and she really, really wished she could suck it up and go on a date already.

If only she had a little more experience. There were those

three disastrous dates a few months after she and Perry had separated. But the guys hadn't really interested her, and she refused to think about the mistake of sleeping with one of them. It had all been so off-putting.

She glanced at her ex-husband, walking next to her on the beach. They were at their biweekly beach cleanup volunteering session. Something they'd been doing for two years. They signed up online for two hours of walking the beach and picking up trash. It gave them a chance to talk about their kids while doing a good deed.

Perry had started dating within a couple of months of their separating. According to Sydney, there had been a steady stream of women for the first year, then things had calmed down. He'd had a few longer-term girlfriends. She wasn't sure of Perry's social status now, nor did she want to ask. Going to her ex-husband for dating advice seemed weird, even for their friendly relationship.

She dropped several empty beer cans into the trash bag Perry held. It was nine and the beach was still relatively quiet. By eleven the sand would be covered with towels and chairs. Summer was always busy.

"My folks want to get Will those driving lessons for his birthday," Perry said, returning to a topic he'd first broached a couple of weeks ago.

Mikki had balked, then had agreed to research the specialized driving school. She wasn't sure about giving a seventeen-year-old race car driver skills.

"He still wants to be a NASCAR driver," Perry continued. "As soon as he turns eighteen, you know he'll start racing locally. Better to equip him with the tools and experience to keep him safe."

"I don't like it," Mikki admitted. "Why can't he want to be a doctor or a zoologist?"

"Why a zoologist?"

"I don't know. It seems less risky."

"Cars are his passion. You can delay the inevitable but can't stop him."

Things she knew to be true. She also knew Will was a good kid. Mostly sensible and responsible.

"Fine," she said, stopping by a pile of paper plates and napkins. "Tell them to sign him up. I'm not happy they'll be giving him the cool birthday present, but I'll live with it."

Conversation shifted from Will to Sydney and her ambitious plans for her life.

"She gets her smarts from you," Perry said.

"I wish." Mikki chuckled. "She's a throwback or the next step in evolution. Maybe both. At least when she's the ambassador to some European country, we'll have an excuse to visit her."

"We will."

And speaking of travel, Mikki thought. "I've canceled my trip to Paris so I won't need you to take Will."

Her ex-husband frowned. "I thought you were excited about Paris."

"I was, but I don't want to travel with a bunch of people I don't know." She groaned. "I sound like my mom."

"You're nothing like Rita." They headed toward a pile of trash close to the waves. "I should have taken you to Paris like you asked. You always wanted to go. I was wrong to say no."

Nice words, she thought, knowing it would never have happened.

"I fought just to get you to take a family driving trip every few years," she said lightly. "You would never have flown to Paris."

He'd always said their home life was so great—why bother going anywhere else.

"I regret that," he told her. "And I'm sorry. I was young and immature. I should have listened more, done more of what you wanted. I really am sorry."

She stopped to face him. Perry looked as he always did—like

a decent guy who you could depend on. She'd loved him once. They shared children, and a past.

"I know my stubbornness is one of the reasons we got divorced."

"It wasn't just you," she told him. "I'm just as much to blame. I had the kids to distract me and once I bought the business, I threw myself into that."

"You wanted me to take classes with you and travel. I could have done that."

She shrugged. "It was a long time ago. We've both moved on."

Something flickered in his eyes. "You're right. We have. And speaking of that, I bought a house."

She took a step back and stared at him. "What?"

He smiled. "I bought a house. A bungalow near the beach."

Her mind couldn't grasp the information. "What about your folks' place?"

"They want to sell," Perry told her, starting along the beach again. "They want the cash for their retirement."

She fell into step with him. "Lorraine never said anything. What about the kids? Is there room at the new place?"

"Yes. There are enough bedrooms, even if they're small. The lot is big, so I'm thinking of adding a master downstairs."

"So this is a done deal?"

"I close in a couple of weeks."

"Congratulations," she murmured, hoping she sounded sincere. She didn't begrudge Perry getting a house of his own—she was just surprised.

"I want you to come see the place when I close," he told her. "I'd like your advice on updating. You've always had a good eye for design and color."

"Of course. I'm happy to help. And good for you," she added. "With the kids getting older and starting on their own lives, you would have been lost in your parents' house. Good move."

"Thanks. I think so, too."

They continued to walk along the beach. The morning was warm and sunny, the salty air fresh as she inhaled. Mikki told herself to enjoy the moment and think about how great her life was. There was absolutely no reason to feel that everyone was moving on. Everyone but her.

Bree scanned in the box of books, then set them on the cart to be shelved. A few years ago new releases were always the last Tuesday of the month. These days new releases happened every week—a schedule she liked. It gave people more reasons to come into the store.

She enjoyed checking in the deliveries. Opening the boxes, seeing the actual book for the first time outside the online catalog. There was something about seeing it in person. Feeling the weight of it, breathing in the new-book smell.

Funny how much she loved her bookstore. This was where she belonged. As a teenager she'd vowed to never even enter a bookstore, let alone own one. But the summer after junior year of college, she'd needed a job and the one at Driftaway Books had paid more than any other.

The reason for the higher pay was simple. Lewis Larton was demanding, self-important and a stickler that anyone who worked for him knew everything about American literature. He preferred but didn't insist on a master's degree. Few applicants could answer his rapid-fire questions, and those who could rarely lasted a week.

She still remembered being shocked at how handsome Lewis had been. About a decade older, he had that intense, "I'm smarter than everyone" air about him—something that usually annoyed her. But for some reason she had been immediately attracted to him.

She remembered his long-suffering sigh as he'd scanned her application.

"You're a business major." His tone had been accusing. "I have no interest in you."

She'd smiled at him. "Ask me anything. I might surprise you."

"I doubt that." He glanced back at her application. "Bree Days. Name two authors who share your last name."

She'd been careful not to smile. "Naomi and Gearard Days."

"How do you know that?"

"They're my parents."

Lewis's surprise had been comical, and she'd instantly gotten the job. At the time, she'd mistaken his attention for interest, rather than a sycophant's desire to be close to someone who knew such famous literary writers.

She'd been so young, she thought. She'd never had a chance. Falling for him had been as inevitable as the fact that one day he would shatter her heart.

Time heals, she reminded herself, scanning in more books. In her case, the wounds were scarred over and she'd never risk believing in love again. A lesson she should have learned from her parents.

Still, despite the pain Lewis had caused her, she'd ended up here—with a life exactly how she wanted it. She had dozens of casual friends, a great house, the store and male companionship on her terms. Always on her terms.

Which was why she hadn't gotten in touch with Harding. She'd been tempted—their dinner had been better than she'd expected. He was interesting, funny, attentive. Under other circumstances, she would have gone home with him and enjoyed the night. Perhaps even two. But he was a complication she didn't need. Not only was there the Ashley issue, but Harding struck her as the kind of man who led with his emotions. He was kind and sincere. While she didn't mind the former, she was wary of the latter. Sincere people had expectations she had no plans to meet.

She rolled the cart into the store. Shelving books was almost meditative. She concentrated just enough to quiet her mind, allowing her to relax into the moment.

A Beach Boys song came on the overhead speakers. She kept their music in regular rotation because she enjoyed their mostly upbeat lyrics and the steady rhythm. Around her, customers browsed. A half dozen teenagers crowded around Ashley's display. Ashley put the cupcakes they wanted in a bright yellow bakery box.

Mikki's gifts often pulled in an older clientele with more money. To Bree's delight, those customers frequently wandered over and bought books. She did love a customer who carried out a heavy bag.

"I've been thinking about you."

The familiar voice came from behind her and caused an instant, take-me-now reaction pretty much everywhere in her body. The jolt of wanting told her it was definitely time for her to get laid, although not by the man causing the reaction.

Harding smiled at her. Before she could stop herself, she smiled in return, knowing she looked as pleased as she felt, which was bad and stupid.

"I've given you a couple of days, because you seemed as if you'd prefer that. Calling right away would make me seem needy and that's not sexy. But it's been enough time, so we should have lunch."

He held up a bag from a local sandwich place.

"What if I'm not hungry?" she asked, instinctively wanting to put the cart between them. Not for physical protection—she wasn't afraid of Harding. At least not in that way. But for other reasons she wasn't going to define.

"It's lunchtime. You should eat."

"Maybe I have plans."

"Change them."

"You're assuming a lot."

His hazel eyes held her gaze. "I assume nothing. I'm hopeful and I brought sandwiches. Come eat with me."

She told herself it was just a sandwich. There were picnic tables on the beach. A half hour out of her day didn't mean anything. She'd walked away from dinner with Harding without so much as a kiss. Surely, she could eat lunch with him and not do anything self-destructive.

"Fine. Give me a second and I'll meet you out front."

She pushed the cart into the back room, told Rita she would be back in less than an hour, then walked out of the store.

Harding had already claimed a table and was setting out their meal. He'd dressed in jeans and a T-shirt. The light breeze mussed his hair in a way that was very appealing. As she approached, she saw a faint scar by his elbow that went up the side of his arm and disappeared under his sleeve.

Remnants of the accident or something else? Not that she would ask. She'd already shown too much interest in him.

"Caprese sandwiches," he said, sliding one toward her. "It seemed like a day to go vegetarian."

She opened the can of organic soda. "You have vegetarian days?"

"Sure." He flashed her a grin. "Then I eat a burger. Life is all about balance. How are you?"

"Fine. How's the writing going?"

He shook his head. "Nope. I'm not going to fall for you trying to make every conversation about me. We have more interesting things to talk about. Like your parents."

Disappointment had her putting down her sandwich. She wouldn't have pegged him for a literary snob.

"You're a fan?" she asked lightly, telling herself at least now she wouldn't want to sleep with him.

"Not my thing," he said. "But it's interesting that you're their daughter."

"Why?"

"You don't have any literary books in your store. You don't feature your parents or use their celebrity to bring in business."

"Not my thing," she said, repeating his words.

"You don't get along?"

"Stop interviewing me."

He leaned toward her, as unrepentant as a puppy. "I can't help it. I want to know everything about you. You're fascinating. You could totally work the daughter of famous writers thing into the store, but you don't. In fact, you do the opposite, yet you own a bookstore."

"Owning the store is more about circumstances than any plan on my part."

"Tell me about your parents. Just one thing. Then we can change the subject."

She eyed him for second, then exhaled. "Fine. My father is distant. Not cold, just unaware. The existence of any world beyond what he's writing and my mother is a constant surprise to him. When I was little, I always thought he had no idea who I was until someone told him."

"And your mother?"

Bree remembered the Christmas she'd turned eleven. She'd asked how they would celebrate.

"Oh, dear God, again? When are you going to let go of the ridiculous Christmas charade?" Her mother had stared at her in obvious disappointment. "Fine. What are your expectations? Give me a list and be precise, please."

Bree had learned to hide her hurt. She'd stood straight and said, "I want a Christmas tree and a stocking. Don't put out the stocking until Christmas morning, and none of the presents should be from Santa. Just you and Dad."

Her mother had nodded stiffly. "Write it all down. We'll be dining with friends Christmas Eve, but I'll arrange a dinner for the three of us on the day. Is that sufficient?"

It wasn't, of course. Bree had wanted a real family holiday, with people who hugged and gave her presents because they wanted to, not because she insisted. Fortunately, that had been her last Christmas at home. The following year she'd gone away to boarding school. A solution that suited both her and her parents.

"My mother isn't a fan of the holidays," she told Harding. "Not because they wasted money, but because they took effort and energy away from her work." She gave him a wry smile. "After all, they are two of the greatest literary voices of their generation."

"That can't have been easy."

"There were complications."

"But you married a writer."

"Yes, I did." She picked up her sandwich. "One would assume I'd learned my lesson, but one would be wrong. Besides, Lewis was more bookstore owner than writer, even though he wouldn't agree with me on that."

Harding stared at her. "The bookstore was his."

"Yes."

"You must have had a hell of a divorce lawyer."

He assumed that she and Lewis had split up. She didn't correct him. If he knew she was a widow, he would probe. The man was writing a book on grief, after all.

"What have you been doing for fun?" she asked to change the subject.

"Exploring the area. Jogging on the beach." His humor returned. "It's a very LA thing."

"It is. Have you tried surfing? Also very LA."

"I've taken a couple of lessons. It's a lot harder than it looks. Some of my fine motor skills aren't what they should be. It's hard for me to balance on a board. Do you surf?"

"I take a class every Thursday morning. I enjoy getting out on the water. I'm not very good, but I have fun."

She studied his features, his relaxed posture, and thought

about how he was a successful writer, had started a foundation and recovered from a life-threatening accident.

"Why aren't you married?" she asked. "You're what? Thirty? Isn't it time?"

He laughed. "You sound like my mother."

"That doesn't answer the question. Do you have issues?"

"We all have issues." The smile faded. "I want to get married. Like most people, I want to be part of something. I've been in love, but I've never felt strongly enough to want to commit to spending the rest of my life with her."

"Maybe you like the limelight too much. Getting married might make you less shiny to your fans."

"Harsh," he said gently. "And no. I don't actually like being a celebrity. I do it for the foundation. Every dollar we raise is one more dollar we can use to help people."

"That sounds altruistic."

"Why do you have so much trouble believing the best of people?"

"Because when I assume the best, I'm always wrong."

He leaned toward her. "What are the odds of you kissing me when we get up from this table?"

And just like that, the awareness was back. All she had to do was bend toward him a few inches and their mouths would touch. She wondered how he kissed, what he tasted like, if he wanted her on top. Would he take things slow or did he like it fast and hard?

She felt the tingles of arousal between her legs and a need to have his hands on her breasts. As she registered the sensations, she deliberately leaned back.

"Thanks for lunch," she said. "I appreciate you stopping by but this isn't going to happen. Go find someone else to play with."

"What if I'm not playing?"

She stood and collected her trash. "We're all playing, Harding. The fact that you haven't figured that out is the reason you and I are never going to happen."

She walked back to the store. Once inside, she tossed her wrappers and recycled her can, carefully pushing thoughts of Harding from her mind. She was good at letting go—in some respects, it was her superpower. And now was the time to use it.

SEVEN

Mikki took a couple of days to deal with Perry's news about the house. She wasn't sure why the thought of him buying his own place rattled her. Maybe it was the physical manifestation of him getting on with his life, while she felt stuck. She didn't think it was anything about their divorce. That had happened three years ago—she hardly wished they would get back together. But it sure was something.

She waited until the store was relatively quiet, then approached her mother-in-law. "Do you have a second?"

Lorraine looked up from the empty box she was wrapping in seashell paper for a display.

"Of course. What's up?"

"You didn't tell me you and Chet were selling your house."

Lorraine blinked. "I didn't? We've been talking about it for a while. I'm sorry. I wasn't keeping information from you. I thought we'd discussed it." She put down the box. "Real estate prices are high right now and with all the improvements Perry made, it's a good time to sell and invest the money for our retirement. He said he was ready to look for a place of his own, so we moved forward. Are you upset?"

"No, just surprised. No one said anything." Mikki smiled at her mother-in-law. "It's fine. He told me about the house he bought. It sounds perfect. You and Chet are keeping the condo?"

"Yes, but we're thinking of buying an RV."

"You've been talking about that for ages. Are you really going to do it?"

"We'll want to visit Sydney back east. And if Will starts racing cars, we can follow him on the circuit." Lorraine grinned. "Keep an eye on him for you."

Mikki wasn't sure her son would enjoy being followed around the country by his grandparents, but she was kind of happy with the idea.

"Perry mentioned he'll need to do some remodeling," Lorraine added. "He's probably going to ask you for help."

"He talked about wanting to add on a master bedroom. He'll need a contractor."

Bree and Rita walked up.

"Who needs a contractor?" her mother asked. "Are you remodeling again? There's nothing wrong with your house, Mikki." Rita turned to Bree. "My daughter loves to decorate and paint and change things. New tile, different flooring, bigger windows. Always something."

Bree looked at Mikki. "You do that yourself?"

"I do some work, but mostly I come up with a design, pick out the materials and have professionals do the hard stuff. I can paint, but I'd never try to put in a window." Mikki looked at her mother. "The contractor isn't for me. Perry's bought a house that needs work."

Lorraine nodded. "You know how good Mikki is at pulling a room together. Perry wants her help."

"Why doesn't he ask his girlfriend?"

"What girlfriend?" Mikki and Lorraine asked together.

Rita grimaced. "Perry's buying a house. Men need to be motivated to do that sort of thing. A new woman in his life would do that."

Which made sense, Mikki thought. If Perry was buying a house with a woman, or for a woman, things had to be serious.

"I hope she's nice to my kids," she murmured.

Bree raised her eyebrows. "You don't know there *is* a girl-friend."

"There is," Rita said flatly. "She's probably twenty-five."

"That's depressing." Lorraine shook her head. "Perry would never do that."

"All men do that."

Lorraine smiled at Rita. "I'm going to ask him and if you're wrong, you're buying me a muffin."

They walked away.

"You okay?" Bree asked.

"Not if the girlfriend is twenty-five. I don't care if Perry's involved with someone, it's just a big change. The house. The woman."

Bree laughed. "I say again, you don't know if there *is* a woman."

"Maybe not now, but there will be eventually. Perry won't spend his life alone."

"Maybe he'll sign up for a dating site and answer some of the messages sent to him." Bree's tone was pointed. "Unlike other people I could mention."

"You're judgy."

"You're scared."

Mikki knew that was true. She *was* scared. "I don't want to be humiliated," she admitted. "What if some guy takes one look at me, then leaves?"

Bree laughed. "No way. Have you seen yourself?"

"I'm overweight and nearly forty."

"You're a walking invitation to fuck."

Mikki felt her mouth drop open. She consciously closed it. "I think that's the nicest thing you've ever said to me."

"It's true. Sure, you're not skinny, but come on. The curves, the big blue eyes, your smile. You're nice, you bake and your kids are nearly grown. What's not to like?"

"Is that how you see me?"

"It's how everyone sees you."

"So I should go answer a couple of the messages?"

"That or stop talking about it."

"How do I know who to respond to?"

"Didn't you say there was some guy you used to know? Unless you remember him being a jerk, answer him."

Mikki hesitated.

Bree narrowed her gaze. "Do. It. Now."

"Fine. Whatever. But I won't like it."

Mikki retreated to her office where she opened her laptop and typed Duane's name into a search engine.

Seconds later she clicked on links and discovered he was a professor of economics at UCLA and affiliated with several international economic nonprofits. He was also nice-looking, with massively broad shoulders and what looked like serious muscles under his suit jacket. More significant, he looked familiar.

She did a search under his daughter's name and discovered that yes, she was an old friend of Sydney's, and Duane really was her father.

"I'm doing this," Mikki said firmly as she logged in to the dating site.

She searched for Duane's message. When she found it, she stared at his number for several seconds, then picked up her phone to text.

Hi. It's Mikki. I saw your message on my page.

She paused, not sure what else to say. Did she mention coffee? Suggest a phone call? Ack! Why was she so bad at this?

She added a wimpy It was nice to hear from you, before hitting Send, figuring she would let him take things from there. She was surprised when three dots instantly appeared.

You texted! Hi. I was surprised to see your profile

on the site. Surprised in a good way. Let's have dinner and catch up.

Dinner? Just like that?

Aren't we supposed to start with coffee and work our way up to dinner?

I remember you being charming and fun. Let's risk dinner.

Charming and fun? Her? How was she supposed to resist that?

Sure. Dinner it is. When and where?

He suggested Friday at a restaurant in Hermosa Beach. Mikki agreed, then wrote down the details.
See you then, she texted.

Looking forward to it.

Me, too.

Which she was. Mostly. Just as soon as the urge to throw up passed, she would mean every word.

Ashley clicked to the next slide on her PowerPoint presentation.
"Your shift hours aren't a suggestion," she said. "People depend on you to show up on time. Your tardiness means someone else has to stay late. When you have a job, you're part of a team. If you mess up, other people suffer."
Five foster kids, aged fourteen and fifteen, watched intently. Each of them had brought their new work permit to the session. Minors in California had to have a permit to hold a job. Until age sixteen, their hours were limited, especially on school days.
Ashley moved to the next slide. "You want to be neat and

tidy when you get to the job. If you're wearing a uniform, keep it clean and in good condition. That's on you."

She explained how some jobs would give them a uniform, but they had to pay back that cost over time. Last week she'd explained about how taxes were withheld and how to open a bank account. In future weeks she would offer classes on managing money and budgeting. These kids had different priorities than most. For many of them, turning eighteen meant aging out of the foster-care system. They could find themselves with nowhere to live and no support system. One of OAR's missions was to help teens when they aged out of foster care with training, access to resources and even financial assistance.

Working while they were young—gaining experience, a work ethic and contacts—helped them beat those odds. OAR had created a certificate program for teens. Upon completion, they could attach that certificate to their application. Local employers understood that OAR teens were ready to do the job. They knew what was expected and if there was a problem, the employer could contact OAR directly.

Ashley finished up her PowerPoint and answered all the questions, then told her group she would see them next week. She'd just closed her laptop when Dave, her brother's business partner and the president of OAR, wheeled into the room.

"One day you need to tell them who you are," he told her, his voice teasing.

"Harding's sister? They already know that."

"I was talking about the whole entrepreneur thing. That you employ people yourself and are responsible for their livelihoods. That kind of information gives you street cred."

She laughed. "I prefer to be the nice lady who gives them information. Besides, they all know about Muffins to the Max. There aren't many secrets here."

Dave was a good-looking guy. A year or so older than her brother, with broad shoulders and a muscled chest. He'd been a skilled athlete before his accident and continued to be active. He played basketball a few nights a week and belonged to a group that sailed—all while in wheelchairs. He was a tireless advocate, constantly seeking accessibility for people in wheelchairs as the norm rather than an exception.

Back when she'd still been in high school, she'd had a mad crush on him, but he'd only ever treated her like a cross between a cute puppy and his friend's much, much younger sister. She'd gotten the message. She'd been devastated, but she'd moved on. Now she and Dave were friends and she enjoyed her volunteer work at OAR.

Dave took her laptop case and put it on his lap, then led the way out of the room. "You like having your brother back home?"

"You know I do. He was gone way too long. Oh, our parents are visiting soon. You'll want to see them."

"I will."

Dave got along well with her parents. They appreciated how he'd been supportive when Harding had first gone into rehab. They were also generous donors for the foundation.

They went to the back of the building and paused by the exit. "I can't believe you're messing with your brother's love life."

Ashley groaned. "He told you about that?"

"He tells me everything. You should know better than to warn him about a woman. Harding loves a challenge."

"Bree is going to be that," she muttered, then shook her head. "I was momentarily struck stupid. It happens."

"And you're still worried."

She looked at Dave. "I can't help it. Bree's great. You've met her. Every guy wants her. She's just that kind of woman. Only despite being famous and successful and all that, Harding's a regular guy at heart. If he likes her, he'll be totally into her and she's not going to appreciate that. I don't think Bree sets out to be cruel but at the end of the day, she's emotionally fine and a lot of the guys are shattered." She sighed. "The irony of that statement is if I were in trouble, I'd turn to Bree and I know she'd be there. It's specifically a guy thing."

"Maybe I should go out with her," he teased.

"She would chew you up before breakfast."

He handed her the laptop case. "Then I leave her for your brother."

"A wise decision." Ashley leaned down for a quick hug.

"Leave Harding alone," Dave said when she straightened. "He's got to figure this out on his own. He's a big boy."

"I know you're right. I know I shouldn't have said anything. It's just, I'll always remember how he looked the night after the accident."

"All the places he shattered have healed stronger than before. Harding can take care of himself. Trust him." Dave smiled at her. "Besides, maybe the one who gets hurt in all this will be your friend."

Ashley laughed. "Unlikely."

Bree massaged coconut oil into her hair. When her long curls were saturated, she pulled them back into a loose braid. She wiped her hands on a towel, then gathered up her wet suit and made her way from the parking lot to the sand.

A little before six on a Thursday morning, the beach was mostly deserted. There were a few die-hard joggers on the sand, a dozen folks on the boardwalk and a handful of her classmates waiting to start the day's lesson.

Surf class was one of her favorites. Riding the waves required perfect coordination between her head and her body. She wasn't very good, but she was able to get up on her board and that was what mattered.

She called out a greeting. Everyone smiled and waved. Dalton was already there, talking about the rainstorm a hundred miles west that would increase the size of today's waves.

"The new guy's here," Dalton said, glancing over Bree's shoulder. "Let's suit up."

Like the other women in the class, Bree had opted for a simple one-piece bathing suit. A bikini looked cute in the movies but in real life wasn't practical when getting in and out of a wet suit. She preferred not to risk flashing a tit at some unsuspecting family.

She'd just pulled the wet suit to her waist when Dalton said, "Everyone, this is Harding."

Bree spun and saw Harding exchanging greetings with the group. She stared at him, not sure how she felt about his being here. She'd mentioned her surf class, but she never thought he would join.

"Is this okay?" he asked quietly.

No. The correct answer was absolutely not. Only she was happy to see him in a way she shouldn't have been, and she liked how he looked in board shorts and a T-shirt.

"Are you stalking me?" she asked.

"I'm interested. I like to think there's a difference. If you're bothered, I'll take a different class."

Dalton walked over. "You know each other?" He carefully put himself between Bree and Harding, as if prepared to protect her.

Not prepared, she told herself. Dalton would absolutely protect her. It was in his nature.

"We're fine," she said easily. "Harding is my business partner's brother. He did a signing at the store. I didn't know he was taking the class. It's okay."

Dalton's gray eyes met hers. "You sure?"

"Yes."

He smiled. "Then let's get in the water, people. Some of us have real jobs to get to."

Bree finished putting on her wet suit, then picked up her board and headed for the water. Harding walked with her.

"I've taken a couple of private lessons with Dalton," he said.

"How did it go?"

He grinned. "Not well."

She laughed. "Then you'll fit right in."

While the rest of them went into the surf, Dalton took a few minutes with Harding. They worked on the sand, perfecting Harding's ability to slide from lying on the board to the classic surfer's crouch.

Bree paddled out past the waves and sat with the group until Dalton and Harding joined them.

The morning was cloudy and cool. Seals swam between the boards, bumping into their legs. Seagulls circled.

"Ready?" Dalton called.

The group yelled they were. Bree lay on her board and felt the water taking her toward shore. She positioned her hands, resting more on the palms than the fingers, and checked that her feet and legs were pressed together. As the board skimmed along the crest, she clenched her core, drew her knees to her chest and rose, in one almost-smooth movement.

She'd just found her balance when a seal zipped by, nudging her board and sending her tumbling into the ocean. She inhaled when she shouldn't and came up coughing and choking on the salt water.

"Why did you do that?" she yelled loudly, then choked a little more, before grabbing her board and hanging on while she caught her breath.

Dalton paddled over. "You okay?"

"Stupid seals."

"Probably a boy seal hitting on you," he teased.

"He needs to work on his opening line." She scrambled onto her board. "I'm fine."

"You took in a lot of water. Do you need to throw up?"

"You're so romantic."

He grinned. "Just being practical."

She turned back toward the ocean and made her way past the

breakers. While she caught her breath, she watched her class-mates surf. Okay, not really. She watched Harding.

He paddled out, got into position and totally couldn't find his balance. His timing was good, but he didn't have the ability to make the smooth transition from lying to standing. She was pretty sure he had the muscle strength. The little she'd seen of him told her he was impressively buff, so it was something else.

She caught a couple more waves before riding the last one into shore. Harding was already on the sand, his board stand-ing next to him as he unzipped his wet suit.

"You okay?" he asked as she approached. "I saw you fall when we first went out."

"A seal plowed into my board. Dalton thinks he was flirting with me but I think it was all about revenge."

Harding smiled, but it was less broad than it had been before. She noticed his lips were blue and he was shivering.

"You're freezing," she said, looking around for his stuff. "Where's your towel?"

"I'm fine. The water's colder than I thought."

She watched him closely.

"Stop," he told her. "Sometimes I don't regulate my body temperature normally. No big deal." One corner of his mouth turned up. "At least I wasn't bossed around by a seal."

"He didn't boss me. He knocked me down, which isn't much better. Which towel is yours?"

He pointed and she shoved it at him, then helped him peel off his wet suit. Once it was on the sand, she took the towel and vigorously rubbed his back and arms. She ignored his muscles and how good it felt to touch him.

"This is nice," he told her.

"Yeah, yeah, it's medicinal." She tossed the towel at him, then shrugged out of her own wet suit and picked up her towel.

She dried off quickly before slipping on the cotton sundress she'd worn. From here she would head home to shower and then go to work.

"How long were you and Dalton together?" Harding asked as he pulled on a T-shirt.

She glanced at him, trying to guess what he was thinking. "A week, maybe two. When things ended, he suggested I might like surfing. He was right."

"He's a good guy," Harding said. "He's been patient with me."

An interesting response. "You're not jealous?"

"Not my style. We all have pasts. Yours is just more interesting than mine."

"I doubt that."

"It's true." His hazel gaze locked with hers. "Why did you let me think you were divorced? You're not. Ashley said you were a widow."

"Ashley talks too much." But she said the words without a lot of energy. Harding was bound to find out the truth eventually. "I didn't want to be a subject for your grief book. Writers tend not to respect boundaries."

"You're sexy when you generalize."

"And here I thought I was sexy all the time."

"You are."

"Thank you."

He looked at her. "What happened?"

"With Lewis?" Nothing that she was going to tell him. "He had cancer. Lung cancer, which was unexpected because he never smoked and he was in his early forties. He went into remission, then it came back."

Which was all true, she thought. Not anywhere near complete, but not dishonest, either. Harding didn't need to know how Lewis had told her he'd fallen out of love with her. He didn't need to know how those words had nearly broken her, nor that when Lewis had wanted a second chance, she'd been weak with gratitude. And a fool. Such a fool.

She wanted to tell herself she should never have loved him, that she should have seen through him. But how was she supposed to know?

"I'm sorry you went through that," Harding said.

It took her a second to realize he was talking about Lewis's dying—not the rest of it.

"Thank you. Now, let's get you to your car, so you can go home and rest."

"I don't need to rest."

"You're still shaking."

"You do that to me."

She laughed. "Right. It's all me."

They collected their surfboards and started for the parking lot. She slowed as she realized he was limping.

"You're hurt," she said.

"I'm okay."

Because of the accident, some things must be more difficult for him. He'd pushed himself too hard. Not that she would say that—she had a feeling Harding wouldn't listen.

On pavement, he walked more easily. He leaned his surfboard against his truck then escorted her to her Mini and helped her secure hers on top of her car.

"Very California," he said. "You wouldn't see a surfboard on a Mini in New York City."

"Probably not." She tossed her tote bag in the back, then faced him. "You did good today."

She had more to say, but before she could continue, he stepped close, brushed a strand of hair off her face then leaned in and kissed her.

The unexpected feel of his mouth on hers should have annoyed her, but instead of getting pissed and pushing him away, she found herself leaning in. She wanted this. Wanted him. His lips were cool and salty. He placed his hands on her waist, not tugging her toward him, just resting them there. A comfortable weight, she thought, raising her arms so her fingertips settled on his shoulders.

He kept the kiss light, which she appreciated. Guys who just went for tongue were usually bad lovers. At least give it a second, first. Rushing the kissing usually meant a man was going to rush everything else.

She struggled against the need to press her body against his, to learn how they fit. She wanted to follow him home to his place, share a shower, then share everything she had in his bed. She wanted the touching, the gasps as he explored her, the mind-clearing pleasure of an orgasm.

Which wasn't going to happen, she reminded herself as she deliberately broke the kiss and stepped back. Not with Harding. He wasn't the casual type, and even if he was, she knew better than to risk getting too close to him. There was something about him that screamed danger, and listening to those warning signs was how she kept safe.

"Nice," he said softly. "Very nice."

For a second they just looked at each other, then she got in her car and drove away. As far as she was concerned, the kiss had never happened. Better for both of them that way.

EIGHT

"Don't be nervous," Sydney said. "Just relax and be yourself."

"I'd really rather be someone else," Mikki admitted, pressing a hand to her stomach. "This was a bad idea."

"Come on, Mom. You should be dating. It's past time. Duane's a great choice. Even if it doesn't work out, you'll have some practice. Plus, you don't have to worry about him spiking your drink."

Mikki turned her attention from her reflection and the worries that her dress wasn't flattering to what her daughter had just said.

"You worry about guys putting drugs in your drink?"

Sydney groaned. "Don't focus on that. Yes, it's a concern, but not for tonight. We know Duane. He's a good guy and a good dad. I was sad when Shalee had to go to another school. We lost touch. But if you and Duane fall madly in love, we can be stepsisters."

"I'm not marrying Duane."

"You don't know that."

"At this point I just want to get through the evening without projectile vomiting."

"Good goal," Sydney teased. "Mom, you look great. Don't think of this as a date so much as meeting an old friend."

"We were never friends. I met him what, three times when we did drop-offs for sleepovers?"

Sydney waved that comment away. "Pretend you're old friends. Or that this is a practice session for someone else you're going to meet." She pushed Mikki out of the bedroom. "Go."

Mikki wanted to protest, but she knew if she backed out, she would never go on another date and she would eventually turn into her mother. Not a future she wanted.

"Text me if you need me to come get you," Sydney said.

Mikki hugged her. "You're very sweet. I'll be fine. It's just Duane, right?"

"You know it."

Mikki gathered her courage and her handbag and walked to her SUV. On the drive to the restaurant, she tried to distract herself with thoughts of inventory and how it was already July, so she needed to be planning the holiday season. She'd already ordered her themed inventory, but what about displays and special mailings?

The work thing lasted until she pulled up in front of the restaurant and realized there was a valet. She scrambled forever for her key fob, then handed it over and took a ticket. It was only then she realized she didn't know how much valet parking cost and wasn't she supposed to tip the guy and what if she didn't have change and had she ever really valet parked on her own?

That uneasy string of thoughts was followed by a sense of dread. Maybe she wasn't up to the challenge of dating. Maybe—

No! She squared her shoulders and marched toward the restaurant. She'd been divorced for three years. She was smart, successful and according to Bree, a walking invitation to, well, the f-word. She could deal with a valet and have dinner with Duane. This was a good first step and she was going to dazzle herself. Later, she would be proud. So there!

She walked inside and immediately saw Duane. He was taller than she remembered, and better-looking. His sandy-blond hair was a little long and his shoulders were huge. So manly, she thought as he saw her and smiled. His eyes crinkled and his whole posture turned welcoming. He looked like a kid who'd gotten his first bike for Christmas.

"You made it," he said, walking toward her. "It's good to see you, Mikki."

"Good to see you. It's been a while."

"Too long."

He nodded at the hostess who seated them. The restaurant was small and trendy, with a pretty outdoor garden. They were shown to a corner table by a trellis.

Duane held out her chair for her, then took his seat. "You found the place okay?"

"Yes. I used my nav system. I don't get to Hermosa Beach much, but it's nice."

"I like it. Lots of good restaurants." He hesitated. "I was surprised to see your profile online. I didn't know you and Perry had divorced."

"About three years ago."

"It's about the same for Anne and me." He chuckled. "I confess, I'm nervous."

He was? "Why? Don't you date?"

"Sure, but this is different. When our daughters were friends, I had a little crush on you. Just, you know, in my head. You were funny and sexy."

She nearly fell off her chair. "You're mixing me up with someone else. You barely knew me and you probably saw me without makeup or even a shower."

"I'm not taking it back."

What was she supposed to say to that? Fortunately, their server appeared. Mikki ordered a glass of red wine that she would nurse all evening. She wouldn't risk more than that when she had to drive.

"So you're in the economics department at UCLA. That's impressive."

He waved away her comment. "I like what I do. Tell me about you."

"I own a gift store on the beach. I moved to my current location six months ago and share the space with Bree, who owns The Boardwalk Bookshop, and Ashley, who owns Muffins to the Max."

"You really are an entrepreneur."

"A small business owner."

"There's no difference. Small businesses employ nearly half the workforce and account for over 60 percent of new jobs every year."

"I'm more impressive than I thought," she joked.

"You are."

Their drinks arrived. Conversation turned to their children. Duane's kids were slightly older than hers. Shalee was his youngest.

"What went wrong in your marriage?" she asked. "Or is that too personal?"

"No question is too personal," he told her. "We had the usual ups and downs. About six years ago Anne was diagnosed with lupus. We were all devastated and worked as a family to help her deal with the illness. I took on more responsibilities at home and she started going to retreats to learn meditation and have alternative treatments."

He shook his head. "I felt her slipping away, but everything I did only made things worse. One day she told me she didn't like me very much anymore and wanted a divorce. Two months later she moved to Santa Fe where she lives with three other women. She seems happy."

Mikki didn't know what to say to that revelation. "Are the three women roommates or, um, something more?"

"I haven't asked. What about you and Perry?"

"Nothing that dramatic. We'd been drifting apart for years, mostly because we wanted different things. I thought we should travel and have new experiences and he didn't. One day divorce seemed inevitable."

She smiled. "We're actually better divorced than we were married. We're friends, and we co-parent. Every two weeks we participate in a beach cleanup effort where we pick up trash for a couple of hours. I'm a little bit proud of how we've managed."

"You should be." He cupped his glass in his large hands. "Have you traveled much since the divorce?"

"No. It's been difficult for me to figure out how to make that work. I haven't dated much and going on my own hasn't been much fun."

She wasn't going to talk about her disastrous trip to London. That would make her sound pathetic and she wanted him to think well of her.

"Do you travel?" she asked.

His smile returned. "A fair amount. I work with an international nonprofit that helps developing countries establish economic policy. I also travel for fun."

An international nonprofit that established economic policies? Sure. And she'd just ordered several sets of dancing penguin mugs for the store.

He looked at her. "What are you thinking?"

"That I need more hobbies. Or to study medicine. I feel so ordinary, while you're helping countries figure out economic policy."

"It sounds more interesting than it is."

"I doubt that."

He leaned toward her. "Tell me about the hobbies you have now."

"Mostly learning about wine through Ladies Know Wine. They sponsor tastings and virtual classes. A few times a year they host a wine conference." She tried to keep her tone from turning wistful. "I want to go, but it hasn't worked out yet."

The timing was relatively easy. The problem was more that she didn't have anyone to go with. Most of her friends were married and didn't want to take a weekend away from their families. Bree was single, but Mikki wasn't sure she was a "girls' weekend" kind of person.

Which was why Mikki was out with Duane. She wanted to meet someone so they could do things together.

Their server took their dinner order. Duane told her funny stories about some of his students while she made him laugh by explaining her mother's ability to find rain in every sunny day. While enjoying their meal, they argued over who played the best James Bond and agreed the Dodgers were going to have a bad late summer.

"Are you seeing anyone?" Duane asked after their plates had been cleared.

The unexpected question had Mikki laughing. "As in dating? No. If I was, I wouldn't be out with you. I mean, there's Earl, of course, but he hardly counts…"

Horror swept through her. Heat burned on her cheeks and she honestly wanted to die. She'd been having such a good time. Duane was easy to talk to and nice to look at and everything had been going so well. Why had she said that? Why?

Duane raised his eyebrows. "If you could see your face," he teased. "Now I'm intrigued. If you're not seeing anyone, then who is Earl?"

"I can't," she whispered, her voice strangled. "Please don't ask. I'm not seeing anyone. I swear. It's too humiliating to discuss. Just, please, can we talk about something else?"

She saw him weighing her request, which made her feel even worse about mentioning Earl. He was so nice and friendly and open. The evening had been going so well and she'd ruined it. Even if he didn't pressure her, he would wonder and it would become a thing. He might even not want to see her again—all because she couldn't keep her mouth shut.

She swallowed hard, stared at the table, so as not to see the judgment in his eyes and murmured, "Earl is my vibrator."

There were two beats of silence. She looked up in time to see Duane throw his head back and laugh. The delighted sound drew glances. The women's gazes lingered on Duane. Mikki agreed he was attractive, but more interesting to her was the whisper of hope that he wasn't disgusted.

He laughed for several seconds, then reached out across the table to capture one of her hands in his.

"You're amazing," he said with a chuckle. "You named your vibrator Earl?"

"He's been a part of my life since the divorce. Giving him a name seemed the right thing to do."

"Okay. I get that."

He rubbed his thumb across the back of her hand. The movement sent little tingles up her arm. They settled in her breasts in a way she hadn't felt in a very long time.

Duane's eyes crinkled with amusement. "I'll admit I'm slightly intimidated, but I think I'll take on the challenge." He grinned. "I'd say pistols at dawn, but given the subject matter, that takes on a connotation not entirely appropriate at dinner."

She laughed. "Thank you for understanding. I didn't mean to blurt it out like that."

"I'm glad you did. When a woman like you is at stake, a man needs to be clear on the competition."

Oh, my. He was good. Better than good. He was a fantasy.

They ordered coffee and talked until the manager came over.

"We'll be closing in a few minutes," she said. "If you'll give me your valet receipt, I'll have your car pulled around."

"Closing?" Mikki said. "But it's only—"

"Ten thirty," the manager said firmly.

"It can't be," Duane said, then glanced at his watch. His eyes widened as he returned his gaze to Mikki. "We've been here over four hours."

He sounded as surprised as she felt. The time had flown by. They handed over their valet tickets, then he stood and helped her out of her chair. They walked through the empty restaurant. Outside, the evening was cool. Duane tipped the valet, then handed her her key fob.

"I had a great time tonight," he said, staring into her eyes. "I'd like to see you again."

The tingles returned, this time racing through her body as if they were too excited to settle. A feeling she totally understood.

"I'd like that, too."

"Good."

He leaned close and brushed his mouth against hers, then whispered in her ear, "Think of me when you play with Earl."

She felt her cheeks flame. "You didn't just say that."

He chuckled. "I absolutely did. I'll call you tomorrow."

Before she could figure out what to say, he opened her car door. She ducked inside and waved, then drove out of the parking lot. On her way home she couldn't stop smiling. Okay, the Earl part had been unfortunate, but the rest of the night had been so much nicer than she could have imagined. Duane was even better than she'd hoped and for some reason he seemed interested in her. It had been, she admitted to herself, the best first date ever.

"You're glowing," Ashley said when Mikki walked into the store the next morning.

Mikki had been smiling since leaving the restaurant. She was fairly sure she'd smiled in her sleep.

"I had such a good time," she admitted. "Duane was great. Funny and nice and smart. He thinks Daniel Craig is the best James Bond, but that's a flaw I can live with."

Bree walked over, a mug of coffee in her hand. "Did you sleep with him?"

Ashley rolled her eyes. "She didn't sleep with him. It was a first date."

"I didn't sleep with him," Mikki agreed.

Bree's expression turned knowing. "But you were tempted."

"A little."

"To do what?" Rita asked, joining them.

"Sleep with a guy on the first date," Bree said cheerfully.

Mikki groaned, knowing that now her mother would get involved in the conversation. "Why did you say that?"

Her mother turned on her. "I raised you better than that. Now that you're nearly forty, turning into a slut is not a good look."

"I'm not turning into a slut. Besides, a woman wanting sex with a man doesn't make her a slut. Don't say that." She glared at Bree. "Why do you make trouble?"

"I can't help it." She smiled at Rita. "I'm just teasing. Don't be mad at her. At least she's dating. Maybe he'll be interested and they'll get married."

Rita pressed her lips together. "Unlikely. Who is he? Does he have a job?"

"He's a professor," Mikki told her. "At UCLA. And he works with an international nonprofit that helps developing countries grow their economies. He has his doctorate."

"Dr. Duane," Ashley teased. "I like it."

Even Rita looked impressed. "That sounds good," she said grudgingly. "But I doubt he'll ask you out again."

Now it was Mikki's turn to look smug. "He already has."

Duane had called that morning, delighting her with his enthusiasm.

"We have a date set up."

Bree held up her coffee. "I'm so proud. Congratulations."

"Thank you. I'm happy."

Her mother eyed her, as if dying to point out that somehow

Mikki would blow it. Fortunately, all she did was grumble under her breath and wander away. Ashley and Bree moved closer.

"Tell us everything," Ashley said. "Start at the beginning and go slow."

"Highlights only," Bree told her. "We have to open the store in twenty minutes."

Mikki laughed. "It was a great evening." She told them how he'd looked and the way they'd talked and actually shut down the restaurant. "Oh, and I accidentally mentioned Earl."

Ashley blanched. "You didn't. Really? Was he upset?"

"He laughed. He said he's looking forward to the competition."

Ashley grinned. "I like him, Mikki. A lot."

Mikki sighed happily. "Me, too."

Love was in the air and Bree didn't like it one bit. She kept her crabbiness to herself, but the feeling remained. Ashley was always all romantic because of Seth and how good things were and now Mikki had gone on a great date. They'd spent the past two days giggling together. Bree was torn between wanting to join in and needing to avoid them completely. She wasn't in love—she would never be in love. She wasn't even seeing anyone, which was fine.

Only Harding had kissed her.

She'd tried to forget that, but every now and then she remembered how his mouth had felt on hers. Worse, she kept flashing back to how he'd been cold and shaking on the beach, but she would bet her ass he would be back in class next Thursday, determined to get up on his board. Harding didn't give up. At least not on physical challenges. She wasn't as sure about his staying power with people.

She rang up several customers, helped a mother of twin seven-year-old girls find a new series, then stared longingly toward the beach. The need to do something physical was powerful. Take a spin class or go for a run. Anything to exhaust herself to the point where she couldn't think.

But Rita had the day off and Bree couldn't leave her other employees by themselves, so she told herself she would go running later.

She funneled energy into shelving books. When she was done, she would move around a few displays.

Ashley walked over with a muffin on a small plate. "Cherry almond," she said. "They're delicious."

Bree wasn't sure if a sugar rush was a good idea or not, but still, she took the muffin. "Thanks."

"Mikki seems happy," Ashley said.

"Yes."

"I hope it works out for her and Duane. She hasn't dated much."

"Duane sounds like a smart guy. I predict he'll fall hard." She glanced at Ashley. "He might even rise to Seth level adoration."

"You're sweet." Ashley paused. "Are you seeing much of my brother?"

"There's a jump in subjects."

"I know. I'm too curious to be subtle." Ashley shrugged.

"And worried?"

"A little."

"Don't be," Bree said flatly. "Your brother and I are never having sex."

Ashley held up both hands. "Whoa, too much information."

"Why? You want to know if we're involved. We're not and we won't be. I'm not sleeping with Harding."

"Why not? He's not good enough for you?"

Despite her mood, Bree smiled. "Ashley, pick a side. Do you want me seeing him or not?"

Ashley laughed. "Sorry. Knee-jerk reaction. I thought you liked Harding. I know he likes you."

"I don't like men. You know that. I have brief, relatively meaningless relationships with them, then I move on."

"Oh, which you can't do with Harding. Interesting."

"It's not interesting. You are a complicating factor."

Harding was the bigger problem, but Bree wasn't going to admit that. A feeling in her gut warned her he wouldn't be as easy to walk away from, and she didn't need to get laid badly enough to take the risk.

"Can we change the subject?" she said.

Ashley studied her for a second, then nodded slowly. "Of course. They say it's going to rain on Thursday."

"It doesn't rain here in the summer."

Ashley grinned. "Would you rather talk about my brother?"

Bree held in a groan. "Nope. So rain. Who would have thought?"

NINE

Mikki parked in front of the two-story house. Like many in the area, it had a big wraparound porch and a detached garage. The yard was overgrown. Still, there was a good feeling to the place, she thought as she walked to the front door.

Perry opened it before she could knock. "You made it."

"You know I can't resist a remodel," she said, walking into the living room. "So far I like it."

The front room was big, with plenty of windows. There were built-ins on either side of the fireplace. She crossed to them and opened the glass doors.

"Original," she said, rubbing the ornate hinges. "Keep these. They're charming." She touched one of the shelves. "You probably have several coats of paint. I'm guessing the wood underneath is beautiful. Stripping the paint off will be worth the hassle."

She looked at the baseboards. "They're probably the same wood. The floors are decent."

He showed her the dining room that had been painted a hideous purple with lavender trim.

"What were they thinking?" she asked with a laugh.

"It's awful," Perry said. "But come on. Give me credit. I saw past the paint. You taught me that."

She smiled at her ex. "After all these years, you're finally listening. I'm so proud."

The half bath was as awful as the dining room. Ugly paint and worse tiles. But good bones.

"You'll have to gut this," she told him. "It's a big job. You'll need to hire someone."

The kitchen was spacious and recently remodeled. The previous owners had done a nice job with the cabinets and quartz countertops. Even the paint color was a neutral light gray.

"You got lucky in here," she said. "It doesn't need anything."

"Come see the backyard. It's huge."

They walked outside. The landscaping was just as overgrown as in the front. A big pool was off to the left, with murky water and cracked tiles.

"This is a mess," she said. "Did you get an estimate on repairing it?"

"I did, then I fainted," Perry joked. "I got a good deal on the house so I can afford to make the repairs. Come look at the other side of the yard. I want to show you where I'm thinking of adding the downstairs master."

He explained where he would put the addition, including an en-suite bath and walk-in closet. They went inside and she saw how the entrance to the addition would be off the sunroom.

"That would work," she told him. "But doesn't the house already have three bedrooms?"

"Sure, but they're not huge."

"Still, the kids won't live with either of us much longer. Will's going to be a senior, and next summer Sydney will probably have an internship at NATO."

Perry put his arm around her. "Don't miss them before they're gone."

"I can't help it. My babies aren't babies anymore."

Time went by so quickly. It seemed like only a few weeks ago she'd told Perry that she was pregnant with their firstborn. Now, all these years later, they were divorced and he'd bought his own place.

She leaned against him. "You did good. The house is really nice. If you want my help with the changes, I'm happy to give you ideas."

"Of course I do."

She thought about what her mother had said and stepped away. "I'm assuming you're seeing someone. Won't she want a say in how you remodel the place?"

Perry frowned. "I'm not seeing anyone. Why would you think that?"

"You bought a house. Is it really just for you?"

He glanced away. "For now."

"So there is someone."

She thought about her date with Duane and almost mentioned she understood the thrill of a new relationship, then stopped herself. She and Perry had stayed friends, but discussing their respective love lives seemed a little weird.

"Regardless," she said. "I'll offer suggestions and mock you when you don't take them."

"Thank you. Are you sure you like the house?"

She looked around and nodded. "I have envy in my heart." She laughed. "Don't get me wrong—I love where I live. It's home. But this place has so much potential."

"I'll take any help you want to give me," he said. "Let's set up a time to talk seriously. I'll even provide dinner."

Bree glanced at her laptop. "The Mother's Day promotion brought in a lot of business for me," she said.

"Me, too." Mikki wrinkled her nose. "Although we can't compare year-over-year numbers because this was our first Mother's Day in the new location. I think we'll do well for Father's Day, too."

Bree glanced at Ashley, who threw up her hands and laughed. "I'm just in this meeting to say yes to whatever you two decide.

My muffins and cupcakes have a very short shelf life. As long as we have customers, I'll sell whatever I have."

"Must be nice," Bree said, knowing Ashley's business model and hers were completely different, yet still complemented each other. "The Mother's Day baskets worked really well. Do we want to create more of them for Christmas and Hanukkah?"

"I think we should." Mikki passed around sheets of paper. "I've come up with a few ideas. For Dad, for teens, for the grandparents."

Bree studied the options. "What about a checklist? Customers could read the options, choose three or five or ten items, then show up later and get exactly what they want. There could be lists of books and different gifts. They could pick the basket, how many and what types of muffins or cupcakes."

"It's more work," Mikki said, sounding doubtful. "Will we be able to find enough seasonal labor?"

A good question, Bree thought. In the past she'd always been able to find holiday help, but custom baskets would require even more.

"Plus a workspace to assemble and store," Bree added.

Ashley tapped her tablet. "Custom baskets are a great idea. We should also have a selection of premade baskets for customers who are last-minute shopping or who can't be bothered to pick and choose. But either way, Bree's right. We don't have the space. But we could rent it at OAR."

Bree had to consciously keep herself from leaning back. The instinct to withdraw had nothing to do with baskets and everything to do with her interest in and wariness about Harding.

"OAR?" Mikki looked confused. "They rent out space?"

"Not usually, but hey, it's us." Ashley smiled. "They have a huge building they bought for cheap. The top floor isn't used at all. We could rent a couple of big rooms—one for assembling and the other for storage. Some of the kids who come there might be interested in a holiday job."

Mikki looked doubtful. "Would they be reliable?"

"There are programs at OAR to help these teens learn how to be successful in the workforce."

Bree had no interest in going to OAR for any reason, but wasn't about to say that to her friends. Renting space there would probably be their cheapest option.

"Let's get more information," Bree said. "Pricing, availability of extra help. If the numbers make sense, we'll move forward with a bigger selection of baskets."

"I'll get with Dave today," Ashley said, typing on her tablet.

They chatted for a few more minutes, before returning to their respective stores. Bree felt her phone buzz, pulled it out and glanced at the screen.

Hey.

She waited, but that was all Harding said. She stared at the single word, stupidly happy to hear from him. She'd been thinking about him too much lately. Reliving the kiss, telling herself he wasn't worth the energy she seemed to be spending on him, wishing he would get in touch with her and fighting the voices in her head that warned her not to get involved. He was exhausting her, all without doing anything beyond being on her mind, which was her problem, not his.

Hey, she texted back. Seconds later her phone rang.

"I thought we were texting," she said when she picked up, hoping her voice didn't sound too happy.

"I really wanted to talk to you, but didn't know if you were busy with work."

"I'm between meetings." She sank onto her office chair. "Why aren't you writing?"

He chuckled. "I've done my five pages and I have an interview with a widower in the morning. I'm working."

"That's what they all say, while they're secretly playing Solitaire and eating Oreos."

"I love Oreos. Who doesn't like Oreos?"

She held in a laugh. "Why are you calling me?"

"I needed to hear your voice."

The simple sentence was a punch to her gut. She wanted to scream at him not to talk like that, not to flirt and tease and say nice things. Whatever he wanted from her wasn't going to happen.

"I don't date," she said flatly. "I'm not kidding, Harding. I don't do relationships."

"So you've said. How about coming to the OAR headquarters so I can show you around and impress you with how much everyone likes me? Plus, Ashley just texted me about you three maybe renting space. You can see it and make your decision."

"I can't. I'm busy."

"I haven't said when."

Yeah, she knew that. "Harding, don't make this more than it is."

He sighed. "You won't go out with me and you won't sleep with me. Where does that leave me?"

"Alone with your Oreos."

"Come to OAR. I want you to see it. We're doing good work there. You'll like it, I promise."

No. She meant to say no, but somehow what came out was, "Fine. I'll go see OAR, but that's it."

"You said yes!" He sounded delighted. "I can't believe you said yes. I could squeal."

She burst out laughing. "Squeal? Seriously?"

"You're not easy, Bree. I'm celebrating every victory."

"What's the end game?"

"Getting you to trust me."

"You need another goal."

"Thursday," he said, ignoring her comment. "After surfing. You said yes."

She shook her head. "You're too weird for words. I have to go back to work now, because I have a real job."

"Nothing you say can bring me down. See you Thursday."

"Yeah. See you then."

She hung up before she could say something dumb like "let's get lunch." Or "I was wrong. I will sleep with you."

Both would be a mistake—possibly unrecoverable. She shoved her phone back into her jeans and returned to the store. She'd barely made it halfway to the registers when she heard a familiar, "Hello, Bree."

She tensed as she turned toward the tall, lean man standing in the aisle. On the surface he was attractive, in that LA beach kind of way. Sun-bleached hair, permanently tan. He wore a Hawaiian shirt over cargo shorts.

He'd been a mistake, she thought grimly. Although she'd been clear on the short-term nature of their relationship, he hadn't believed her.

Sad Guy, as Mikki and Ashley called him, showed up every few weeks to try to get back together. He didn't stalk her, exactly. He was just always there. Having his business a couple of blocks away didn't help.

She looked at him without speaking.

He took a step closer, which made her want to back up, but she held her ground.

"Sleep with me," he said bluntly. "One more time. I need to know it's not as great as I remember. Then I can get over you."

She ignored the outrageousness of his request and thought how the name Sad Guy suited him. Everything—his posture, his eyes, the set of his mouth, screamed sadness. Even though she'd been clear on the ground rules, she supposed she had some responsibility in what had happened. She normally vetted her partners more thoroughly, but she'd been on edge because of the move. Change was hard for her and that had been a big one.

So when he'd come on to her at a local bar, she'd said yes. And now they were both paying the price.

"No," she said, meeting his gaze. "It was exactly what I told you. A couple of nights and nothing more."

His expression tightened. "You're a bitch."

"Yes, so not anyone you should want to be with."

"You think I *want* to feel like this? I hate it. And you."

He walked out of the store. Bree watched him go, wondering how long before he showed up again. Chemistry was funny. Sometimes people wanted what they wanted, regardless of how bad it was for them.

Rita joined her. "Isn't that the young man who owns that surf shop? I don't like surfers, but his business does well. You could do worse. You're not getting younger. Flirt with him and see what happens."

Bree looked out at the sand and the ocean beyond. "You're sweet to worry about me, but I'm one of those women meant to take care of herself."

"You have a sec?"

Ashley looked up from her book. Seth stood by the chair across from the sofa, a folder in his hand. He looked concerned. *No*, she thought, putting down the book and uncurling her legs so her feet rested on the floor. Serious, but not worried.

"Sure." She patted the cushion next to her. "What's up?"

He dropped the folder on the coffee table and settled next to her. His warm thigh brushed hers in a way that made her insides tingle.

Even after nearly a year, she still got butterflies around him. Still anticipated their evenings together. She thought of things to say to him during the day, couldn't wait to see him again. They were good together. In love. Being with him made her happy.

He smiled at her. "Things are really great between us."

"I agree."

The smile turned into a grin. "I would be sad if you didn't."

"You're saying it would be awkward if I wasn't crazy in love with you?"

"More than that. You'd break my heart."

He held her gaze in a way that made her chest tighten. His expression was intense and she had the unexpected feeling their conversation was about to surprise her.

Was he proposing? But he couldn't be. They were casually dressed and they'd had dinner and what about the trip to Whistler? She'd been so sure he was going to do it there.

"We're both in a good place," he continued. "My work, your business. You have your volunteer commitment with OAR and I'm pretty sure I'm going to get a promotion."

Oh, God, oh, God, he *was* going to propose. Her hands started to shake. She knew what she was going to say, but she'd really been hoping for something a little more romantic and memorable. Still, this was Seth and she loved him. She was ready.

"With the hot real estate market, I thought this was a good time for us to buy a house."

She stared at him, unable to fully take in his words. "A house?"

He took her hands in his. "I know you've sunk every penny into the business and I'm fine with that. I have the down payment. Your business will grow so that investment will be part of our future. We'll co-own the house as joint tenants with rights of survivorship." His expression turned hopeful. "What do you think?"

"You want us to buy a house?"

"It's time. We're ready."

She pulled her hands free and slid back on the sofa to see him more clearly. Sure, they'd casually talked about getting a house at some point, but his bringing it up seemed...something.

He passed her several sheets of paper. "I've run the numbers and we can get a decent three-bedroom, two-bath place in this area. Our lease is up in four months, so that gives us time to find something and get settled. We want the right place. I'm hoping we'll be there about five years before we trade up."

The math made sense, she thought as she scanned the papers. If he was providing the down payment, then they could certainly afford to do it.

"It's an odd way to organize our future," she said. "I mean, buying a house before we're even…"

She pressed her lips together, not sure how to say *engaged* or *married* without him thinking she was pushing things. Only wasn't buying a house together a big deal? Shouldn't they have an actual life plan first?

"What?" he asked. "Is it too soon? Don't you want a house?"

She told herself she was smart, successful and perfectly capable of speaking the words. That saying what she thought and felt and wanted was her right, even though she was terrified.

Really? Terrified? Wasn't that a little old-fashioned? She and Seth were equal partners in their relationship. Both their feelings mattered.

Determined to be mature and self-actualized, she calmly said, "I'm surprised we're talking about buying a house when we've never discussed getting married. One doesn't necessarily need to come before the other, but I think we should have an overall plan."

There! She'd done it. She said the M word without bursting into flames. Only looking at Seth, she didn't feel especially good about it—not when his shoulders slumped and he turned away.

"You thought we'd get married."

The disappointment in his voice had her desperate to call back the words. Shame and embarrassment made her want to scramble farther away, but she stayed where she was, telling herself thinking about marriage was the natural next step, considering the fact they were in love, living together and talking about buying a house.

He looked at her, his eyes deep with pain. "You want to get married."

She had no idea why this was so uncomfortable or why she felt defensive, but both were true. She cleared her throat and did her best to keep her tone level. "I take it you don't."

"No. I don't."

"To me or anyone?"

The pain on his face deepened to anguish. "This isn't about you, Ashley. I love you. You know that. I just don't want to get married. You never said anything so I was hoping you felt the same way."

There was too much coming at her too fast. Confusion and disappointment joined the sense of shame she still couldn't shake, along with a big dose of WTF.

"You love me but you don't want to marry me," she clarified. "I don't get it. People who love each other get married. We talked about having kids."

"I still want that." He leaned toward her. "I love you. I want to spend the rest of my life with you." He tapped the papers that had fallen to her lap. "I want to buy a house and get a dog and love you forever."

"You're not making any sense. Why one without the other? What's the big deal about getting married?"

His mouth twisted. "I could ask you the same question. Why do we have to get married?"

Because they did. Because it was normal and stable and while she'd never been one to dream about a big wedding, she'd always seen herself with a husband and a family. She wanted that normal, regular life.

"What's your objection?" she asked, rather than try to answer his question. "You're not very radical, socially. You support other institutions."

He drew in a breath. "When people get married, they stop trying. They get lazy and take each other for granted. I want to spend my life with you because that's what we both want. Not because it's expected. I want you with me because being with me makes you happy. Not because you're stuck and don't see a way out. I want us to always try to make the other person happy, to live out our dreams together. Marriage is an excuse not to put in the effort."

Which all sounded okay, but felt wrong. She crossed the room as she gathered her thoughts.

He watched her cautiously. "Ashley, you've seen it. Couples get married and suddenly she's bored and he's spending all his time with his friends. They're not happy anymore. While they were dating, even living together, everything was great. They were in love. But once they're married, they both give up. I'm not giving up on us or you. I want us to always have the very best from each other."

"So life is one long audition? There's no time to relax? What if I get the flu? What if I throw up for three days? Am I not trying hard enough?"

He crossed to her. As he approached, she folded her arms across her chest.

"I don't mean it like that," he said, looking into her eyes. "I'm talking about taking each other for granted. I'm talking about waking up every morning and consciously deciding we want to be together. I want an awareness of how great we have it and how good our lives are. I want us happy."

His vision of their relationship sounded exhausting, she thought. There were about a dozen flaws in his argument, but she couldn't articulate any of them right now. Not when she was sad and tired and crushed to find out the man she loved more than anyone in the world didn't want to marry her.

"I can't talk about this anymore," she said, stepping back. "I need to think."

"You're mad."

"I'm not." *Mad* didn't describe what she was feeling. Maybe there weren't words. "I'm in shock, I guess. I thought we were in the same place. I thought we were heading toward something. We've been together almost a year and I never knew you didn't want to marry me."

"Ashley, please. I love you. I need you to be okay with this."

"I don't even know what this is."

She turned away only to realize she couldn't escape in a one-bedroom apartment. She grabbed her bag and her car keys.

"I'm driving to the beach to go for a walk." She glanced at the clock. "I'll be home by nine."

Seth hovered behind her. "Can I come with you?"

"No. I need to think."

He looked stricken. "I love you. Believe that. The rest will work out."

She left without responding. Her stomach roiled, her heart was heavy and she had no idea what to believe or feel. All she knew for sure was that Seth didn't want to marry her, and understanding that changed everything.

TEN

Bree didn't know what to expect when she arrived at the OAR headquarters. Ashley's description of the building hadn't given her much of an idea beyond the fact that it was big. She arrived at the industrial complex and found a warehouse-type structure—three stories with parking front and back. There was no fancy sign and the landscaping was minimal. The only characteristic slightly out of the ordinary was the large ramp leading to the front door.

She walked into a large, open foyer with a three-story ceiling. The space was huge and bright with turquoise-and-yellow walls. There were clusters of seating areas and an unoccupied reception desk. She waited a couple of minutes but when no one appeared, she texted Harding.

I'm here.

Be right there.

Seconds later Harding walked toward her. Even though she told herself he was just some guy and she wasn't all that interested in him or them or sex, her insides got all fluttery, which was annoying as shit.

"You made it." He smiled as he approached.

Her happy reaction still on her mind, she stepped back to avoid physical contact.

"Interesting wall colors."

He stopped a couple of feet from her and shoved his hands into his front jeans pockets. "The secret to joy is bright colors. There have been scientific studies. We avoid institutional gray. And sharp edges, whenever possible. Curves are less threatening."

"I have no idea what you're talking about." She tried not to notice his big hazel eyes and slow, appreciative grin. The man got to her. She didn't want him to, but he did. She thought about him at odd times, wishing they could… She could…

But she couldn't take the chance, she reminded herself. She wasn't strong enough to survive yet one more person she trusted ripping out her heart and tossing it in the trash.

"Bright walls help people to feel comfortable when they come here," Harding said. "We focus on foster kids about to age out of the system. We help them find housing, get them into college, teach them life skills. Less than four percent of foster kids graduate with a college degree, compared to 46 percent in the general population. And don't get me started on the number of young women who end up pregnant by age twenty-one."

"I thought you'd focus more on people with physical disabilities."

"We started with that, but it seemed too on the nose."

The comment came from behind her. A man in a wheelchair moved toward them. He was more classically handsome than Harding, with dark hair and a chiseled jaw. His shoulders and chest were huge. Bree had the feeling he could snap her like a twig.

He held out his hand. "I'm Dave, Harding's partner in crime."

"Bree. Nice to meet you."

"Glad you could come by. We're doing good work." He flashed her a smile. "Technically, I'm doing the work, while Harding is just the pretty face that dazzles the donors."

"I don't know," she murmured. "Your face is very nice, too. I would guess you have your share of fans."

Dave chuckled. "She's discerning. I like that. Come on. Let's take a tour. Want to ride on my lap?"

Bree laughed. "Are you flirting with me?"

Harding stepped between them. "He is and he's going to stop right now."

Dave winked. "Just playing with you." He waved at the big, open space. "This was why we wanted the building. We can host a fundraiser for five hundred in here." The smile returned. "Plus, the guy who owned it got in trouble with some loan sharks and needed to sell fast."

He waved to the left. "Kitchen, admin offices. Small staff, to keep costs down. We depend on volunteers. You should think about doing that. We're always looking for mentors and businesspeople in the community."

Harding put his arm around her. "This is a no-pressure visit."

Dave sighed. "Can I hit her up for money?"

"Sure, but only three figure donations."

"You're killing me, man."

Dave pointed to the other side of the building. "Classrooms, lecture halls. We're thinking of turning the second floor into a halfway house, but we're mired in government paperwork. Might need to do that somewhere else."

They started toward the back of the building.

"Currently, we have a network of places for our kids to stay when they age out of foster care," Harding told her.

"They turn eighteen and they're just thrown out?" Bree asked.

"Pretty much." Dave stopped in front of an elevator. "A couple state programs keep the teens in the system while they finish high school or college, but there's not enough money for the need."

"There's never enough money." Harding waved her into the elevator. He and Dave followed.

"So if a foster kid turns eighteen in March, that's it?" she asked. "Even if they haven't graduated?"

"Yep," Dave said, rolling out onto the third floor. "We try to fill the void."

He motioned to a long hallway. "The space Ashley mentioned is down here."

"Tell her about the former felons," Harding said.

"That's kind of a sideline. We try to employ former felons who can't get a break. Most of them can't find work or housing."

Harding opened a door. "Like Ashley's guys."

Bree felt her eyes widen. "Your sister employs felons?"

"As bakers. You didn't know?"

Bree shook her head. Ashley hadn't said anything, although she wasn't sure how one would drop that piece of information into a conversation.

Still, it made her think differently about Ashley. It made her seem more... Well, Bree couldn't say what, but something.

She looked around the huge, sunlit room.

"The room across the hall is the same as this one," Dave said. "If you want it, it's yours. The rent will be fair. Ashley said it was just for the holidays, but think about a year lease. You'd have long-term storage and we'd have cash flow. Win-win."

"Let me take some pictures." She pulled out her phone. "Then I'll get with Mikki and Ashley and we'll make a decision."

She could see why Ashley had thought the space would work. Here they could easily put together baskets. They could store the finished items in the room across the hall. This would be a great solution.

They returned to the first floor. Dave excused himself to make some calls. Harding showed her around the various meeting rooms and they walked through the huge kitchen.

"During the day we have boxed lunches available for the teens and staff," he said, pointing to the stacks of boxes in the refrigerated cases. "Prices are in dollars or volunteer credits. The teens earn credits by helping out around here."

"So no one goes hungry," she murmured.

"Yeah, that's one of our goals. At night Ashley and her team take over, baking for the store. The smell is incredible at four in the morning."

She was usually asleep at four, but saying that might send them down a path she didn't want to go. All right, she *wanted* to go, but knew she shouldn't.

"You've done a lot," she said, glancing at him. "You and Dave are impressive."

He leaned against a stainless-steel counter. "Yeah? You're impressed?"

She ignored the teasing in his voice. "Does he resent that you can walk and he can't?"

"Probably. Not all the time, but I'm sure he thinks about it." His tone turned serious. "Dave makes it look easy, but it isn't. Our world isn't built for those lacking in mobility. There are laws, but the real world doesn't always pay attention. We have a fundraiser in a few weeks. Come with me. I want to show you off and have you see what I do."

She ignored the *show you off* comment and said, "I'm not looking to find you even more impressive."

He grinned. "I do look good in a suit. Come on. It'll be fun. Ashley and Seth will be there, along with some famous faces. You can stargaze."

"Not my style."

"Then hang out with me. Please, Bree."

She could ignore the teasing, but the honest request was more difficult.

"I'll think about it."

"Good. So are you up for kissing and maybe some light petting in my office?"

She held in laughter. "I'm not making out with you in your office."

"You name the place and I'll be there."

"Not happening."

"Then lunch?"

"I could do lunch."

"I have a date." Mikki held in a wince as she realized she could have been a little less blunt.

Will looked up from his tablet. "Okay."

"With a man," she clarified, then wished she hadn't. "I mean it's just a date. We're not serious. But I wanted you to know because…"

She groaned. Why had she started down this rabbit hole? "I'm going to be gone this evening and that's all."

Will leaned back in his chair. "Mom, it's fine. You have a date, but he's not going to be my stepdad." He gave her a lazy smile. "I'm not a kid. I get it."

How nice that one of them did. "Good. I ordered you tacos. They'll be here at six thirty." She smiled. "No parties, no hard liquor."

He chuckled. "Yeah, I already knew that part. I'll be studying racing technique videos." He looked toward the front of the house. "That's a sound."

She didn't hear anything, but before she could ask, Will was heading toward the front door. He flung it open, then looked back at her.

"No *way*! Why didn't you tell me? Mom, seriously, how could you not say something?"

"I have no idea what you're talking about."

As she spoke, she heard the low rumble of a car engine. Was he talking about Duane's car?

Her teenage son shot out the door, leaving her to hurry after him. She found him staring openmouthed at a sleek convertible.

Duane got out and smiled at her, then turned to Will, who had practically thrown himself across the hood.

"Is this your ride? Man, she's beautiful. I've seen them online, but no one around here has one. It's a twin turbo V8, right? Zero to sixty in what?"

Duane grinned. "Three-point-seven seconds."

Will nearly swooned. "You ever do that? Man, I'd like to get her on a track. Although she's kind of sweet for that. Still, the lines. What a beauty. I could hear you driving down the street. She can sing, you know?"

Duane looked at her. "So he's into cars."

"Yes, he is. Will, say hello to Duane."

"Oh, right. Hi." He held out his hand, then looked back at her. "You never said."

"I didn't know." She still didn't.

Will groaned. "Mom, this is an Aston freakin' Martin Vantage Roadster."

"I like the color."

Will closed his eyes. "I don't know who she is or why she's pretending to be my mother."

Duane laughed, then opened the driver's door. "Want to go for a quick drive?"

Mikki thought she was going to pass out. "No way. He's only seventeen and—"

Duane winked. "It's okay. I have insurance." He looked at the teen. "You'll stay at the speed limit."

He wasn't asking a question, but Will nodded and said, "Yes, sir. I will," right before sliding behind the wheel.

"We'll be right back," Duane told her. He got in the passenger side.

They talked for about a minute before the car roared to life. Mikki honestly didn't get the appeal but she knew Will would be talking about the Aston Martin something-something for days.

She went inside to worry about her outfit. Duane had said

to dress casually, which had left her unsure about her options. She finally settled on taupe cropped pants, a lightweight, scoop-neck twin set and flats. She'd used a lotion with a subtle sheen on her arms and shoulders. Until the sun went down, she would be carrying the sweater rather than wearing it.

She fluffed her hair, reapplied lip gloss and paced until she heard the rumble of the fancy car. She stepped outside in time to see Will spinning with his arms wide open.

"Best day ever!" he announced before stopping and grinning at her. "That is a car, Mom. I know you love your SUV but you should so get one of those."

"I'll put it on my to-do list."

Will laughed. "I wish." He bounced up the stairs to the porch, kissed her cheek and opened the front door. "Have fun. I'll be good. Tacos at six thirty."

She watched him walk inside. "I'll be home by eleven."

"Okay." He waved as he walked back to the family room. "I'm texting Anderson to tell him what just happened. He's not going to believe it."

She got her bag and sunglasses. It was only a little after four—early for a date, she supposed. Which meant Duane had something planned before dinner.

As the thought formed, she felt a quiver of worry and anticipation in the pit of her stomach, then told herself not to be silly. They weren't going somewhere to have sex. Who did that? Plus, he wouldn't have told her to dress casually for that, would he? And speaking of sex—if they did go in that direction, should she start waxing? She never had, but she'd been reading a lot of articles on dating, and a few of them had mentioned it. Jeez—it was tough enough to get her brows waxed. How was she supposed to let them rip off hair down there?

One more point in Earl's favor, she thought. He was never that judgy.

She turned and nearly ran into Duane, who was standing right outside the front door. She awkwardly took a step back.

"I'm ready," she said.

"You look amazing." He leaned in and kissed her lightly on the mouth. "You smell good, too."

"Oh." She felt herself blush and wasn't sure what to say in return. "You do, too," seemed weird. "Thank you."

He escorted her to the car.

"Did you want to drive?" he asked, his tone teasing.

"Thanks, but no." She sank onto the leather seat. "It's nice."

He got in next to her and grinned. "Will enjoyed it."

"He did. Thanks for that. So you're willing to use my kid to win my heart?"

"I'll take every advantage I can get." His dark gaze met hers.

He couldn't possibly think he needed help, but she didn't say that. "You said to dress casually. So where are we going?"

"To the La Brea Tar Pits."

She stared at him blankly. "For real? The tar pits?" That was their date?

"When was the last time you were there?" he asked, his voice filled with amusement.

"I'm not sure. With the kids on a school trip."

"Exactly. You haven't been just for fun without worrying that someone is going to get lost. There's a lot to see."

The tar pits? Unexpected, but okay. "I do love a woolly mammoth," she admitted, only to slap her hand over her mouth. "That came out way more dirty than I thought it would."

He smiled at her. "I'm more a dire wolf guy, but we can see both."

Distance-wise, they didn't have far to go, but in LA traffic was always a consideration. They got stuck for a bit on the freeway, and then on Wilshire Boulevard before Duane pulled into a parking garage. He'd already purchased their tickets, so they walked right in and headed for the outdoor exhibitions.

The La Brea Tar Pits were a working archeological site, with a museum and educational programs. Their first stop was the observation pit where visitors could experience what it was like to be part of a real excavation. Most of the fossils were casts, but a few were real.

They went by the Lake Pit, an iconic location where a woolly mammoth was caught in the tar lake as other mammoths looked on.

"This always reminds me how life is hard for wild animals," she said. "The unexpected isn't always easy."

"You're softhearted."

"Isn't everyone?"

"No."

"You say that with such certainty."

They paused by the display. He glanced from the woolly mammoth to her.

"You don't believe there's cruelty in the world?" he asked.

"Sure, but it's the exception."

"I'm glad you think that."

She angled toward him. "Why don't you?"

"The economic reality in developing countries is as heartbreaking as this," he said, motioning to the tableau. "It just plays out differently. The world has never been fair. The work I do, internationally, tries to change that."

"A worthy goal."

He gave her a wry smile. "I fail more than I succeed."

"But you don't give up."

"No. I'm softhearted, too."

They moved through the museum. He tried to sell her on the qualities of the Dire Wolf, but she stayed firmly in the woolly mammoth camp. As they walked around, he took her hand in his, an act that nearly made her hyperventilate. Silly, but there it was—tingles and awareness.

When they returned to his car, he asked, "Do you like Italian food?"

"I do."

"Good. I know a little place in West Hollywood I think you'll enjoy."

They headed east and a little north, crossing into West Hollywood, and parked by a restaurant called Cecconi's.

"Have you been here?" he asked as he escorted her inside.

"No. It looks nice."

There were checkered tablecloths and lots of plants. The tables were well spaced and she could smell garlic and basil with a hint of truffle oil. Her stomach growled.

He'd made a reservation. She liked that he'd planned out their date—it made her feel he'd put some thought into their time together. So far, she had to admit, this dating thing was kind of fun.

"Yes or no on the tar pits?" he asked when they were seated.

"I had a good time and I learned a lot. A definite yes."

"Good."

They scanned the menus, then ordered drinks. After their server left, Duane leaned toward her. "Tell me how you came to own a gift shop? Did you start it yourself?"

"No, I bought it a few years ago." She paused. "Perry's parents own a couple of construction equipment rental franchises. Backhoes, Bobcats, that sort of thing. When Perry and I got married, I went into the family business."

"Running a backhoe?" he asked, his voice teasing.

"I wish, but no. In the front office. Lorraine handled the books. It was fine, but not especially interesting. A few years later we bought out the busier franchise. Perry loved it, but eventually he hired someone to take my place so I could spend more time with the kids. Once they got older I needed something of my own. There was a gift store that had always been a favorite of mine. I got to know the owner and one day she asked if I was interested in buying the business."

"You were."

"I was, but Perry refused to even consider it."

She thought about how he'd told her they couldn't afford it and even if they could, she didn't know the first thing about retail. They'd fought for weeks.

"Why didn't he trust you?"

"I only went to high school. I'd never owned a business before."

"You'd worked in one for years. Retail is different, but you strike me as the kind of person who does the work."

"Thanks. That's how I see myself, but he didn't agree. It wasn't a happy time. It was the closest we'd come to divorcing until we actually did."

The server returned with their drinks. They ordered appetizers and agreed to split a pizza. When they were alone again, she said, "He never forgave me for pushing him. When I bought the business, he refused to help. He wouldn't even go look at it for a year."

There had been more. Perry had resented the time she spent at work, even though she was supposed to understand the nights he stayed late.

"Maybe it was the beginning of the end," she admitted. "I was too independent." She held up her hand before he could say anything. "What I mean by that is every relationship has unspoken rules."

"You broke them by wanting something of your own," Duane said, staring into her eyes with such intensity that she felt herself swooning. "You were supposed to stay in the family business."

"Something like that." She had to struggle to steady her breathing. "About the time we separated, he came around. Now he's very supportive." She smiled. "We really are great together, now that we're not together at all." She laughed. "Ironic, I know."

"But a happy outcome."

She thought about what she'd told him. "Does it bother you that I didn't go to college?"

"No, why?"

"Some people care about that."

"I care about who you are." He kept his gaze on her face as he grinned. "And how you look."

"Oh."

"You sound surprised."

"I'm not that, you know, special. You should see my business partner, Bree. She's incredible. Beautiful and athletic and confident."

"Not my type."

"You haven't met her."

He shrugged.

"You don't like beautiful, confident women?" she asked, not sure why she felt the need to defend her friend.

"I very much like beautiful, confident women." He touched her hand. "Like you."

"But I'm not."

"Oh, you are. Obviously, you have no idea how I see you, which is probably for the best. If you knew the power you had over me, I'd be at a serious disadvantage."

Was he joking? Was this supposed to be funny? Only he didn't look as if he was teasing her.

"So," he said slowly, "about Earl. What color is he? I assumed pink, but after doing a little research, I've discovered there are a rainbow of possibilities."

She groaned. "We're not discussing Earl over dinner."

"When would you like to discuss him?"

Despite her embarrassment, she laughed. "Fine. He's light purple."

"I hope to meet him one day."

"That is never going to happen. Now, let's talk about something else."

He leaned across the table and lightly kissed her. "You pick the topic. I'm happy to sit here and listen to you all night long."

ELEVEN

Ashley carefully piped glaze onto the muffin. She normally did that back at the OAR kitchen, but had been concerned the glaze would get smudged in transit. Better to do it quickly in the store. If nothing else, the familiar movements would give her something to focus on that wasn't the sick feeling in her stomach and the sense of dread she'd been unable to shake for two days.

Seth doesn't want to marry me.

Those six words had haunted her since their conversation. They'd surrounded her, mocked her, echoed, screamed and embedded themselves into her now-shattered psyche. He claimed to love her and wanted to spend the rest of his life with her but wouldn't, for reasons she couldn't comprehend, marry her.

She knew she was still in shock, still trying to take it all in and make sense of what he'd told her. Her emotions ebbed and flowed like the tide—none of them positive, most of them accusatory. She must have done something wrong. She must not be pretty enough or smart enough or something not enough. Did he mean he really didn't want to get married or was he simply not interested in marrying *her*? And why oh why did the fact that she wanted to get married and he didn't make her feel ashamed and small? As if she had to justify herself. Because somewhere deep inside she couldn't help wondering—if she was as together and independent as she claimed, she wouldn't care about getting married. Only she did. A lot.

She was confused and embarrassed. She wanted perspective. She wanted to talk with someone who would explain it or at least make her feel less like a loser, only she didn't know who. Not her parents. The second she told them what Seth had said, they would hate him forever. Her friends would be on her side, but she couldn't help thinking they would secretly pity her for falling for him. Which left her alone and upset and more than a little nauseous.

"Hey, so I've been thinking about the basket project."

Ashley spun and found Bree standing by the counter, a tablet in her hand.

"What?"

Bree glanced up at her. "The baskets. I saw—" She paused and frowned. "Are you okay?"

Ashley closed her eyes. No, she thought weakly. She refused to believe her emotions showed on her face. She was stronger than that.

Mikki breezed up, looking all glowy and happy.

"What are you girls up to?" she asked, her eyes sparkling with humor.

Bree kept her gaze on Ashley. "Ask *her*. Something's wrong."

"I'm fine," Ashley lied.

Mikki studied her. "You're not. You've been crying and your hands are shaking. That's the wobbliest glaze line I've ever seen you draw."

Ashley set down the pastry bag and wiped her hands on a towel. Great. She was so bad off, even Bree had noticed.

"It's Seth," Mikki said flatly. "It's always the man. Am I right? What did he do?"

Ashley tried to think of something flip that would distract them or make them laugh. If only a meteor would fly into the ocean, but there was only blue sky and a light breeze outside the store.

"He wants us to buy a house together," she said.

Bree and Mikki exchanged a glance. "Why is that bad?" Mikki asked. "It makes sense. You get engaged, you buy a house, you get married. I'm confused."

Bree's gaze tightened. "You flinched."

"Seth doesn't want to get married."

Mikki's expression was completely blank while Bree looked confused. Ashley sucked in a breath.

"He said he's in love with me and committed to us. He even talked about having kids. But he doesn't want to get married."

"Why not?" Mikki asked. "Why have kids and not get married? That's just confusing."

Ashley fought tears. "He said when people get married, they stop trying. It's like they have what they want, so there's no effort anymore. He wants us to choose to be together."

"Uh-huh." Mikki's gaze narrowed. "That's a pile of crap. Dump his ass."

"What? No. I love him. I'm hurt and scared, but I'm not going to break up with him."

At least she didn't think she was. Right now she didn't know anything.

"Do you believe he loves you?" Bree asked.

"Yes. He's kind and considerate and affectionate. He does all the good boyfriend stuff." She blinked away more tears. "I don't understand."

"Do you believe he means what he says about marriage?"

Mikki turned on Bree. "You're taking his side?"

"I'm asking questions. He's not wrong about people taking advantage of their partners in a marriage. It happens."

"She said he said people stop trying." Mikki pointed at Ashley. "That's totally different than taking advantage of someone."

"It sounds the same."

"Look, I'll admit after a few years of marriage, it's easy to forget to show up every minute. Perry and I drifted apart, but I don't think being married had anything to do with it. We were living separate lives. So we split up. But at least we were willing to commit to each other. Fully commit. Not being willing to stand up in front of God and your friends means something."

Bree raised her eyebrows. "You have a lot of energy on the topic."

"Marriage matters, especially if there are children. Didn't you want to marry Lewis?"

Bree took a step back. "Yes, but that was different."

"It was exactly the same. Ashley is in love with Seth and wants to spend her life with him. Of course she wants to get married. I can't believe I liked him." Mikki sounded frustrated. "I believed in him. Stupid jerk. Now I have to hate him."

"Don't," Ashley said quickly. "Don't hate him. I don't want that. I just…" She wasn't sure how to finish the sentence. "I wish I could understand what was happening with him."

She'd heard all the words, but didn't know what they meant—not in the context of their relationship.

"Not everyone has to be married," Bree said. "Some couples stay together for years and never get married. They're fine with it. Could you be?"

"I don't know. I was never that girl who planned a big wedding, but I always saw myself as being married. It's what you're supposed to do."

"I'm surrounded by traditionalists," Bree said lightly. "You should talk to Seth and tell him what you're thinking."

"I know. And I will just as soon as I can figure that out for myself."

Because right now she was one giant wound. He'd been her everything and having that change, having her be so uncertain, left her feeling lost and more alone than she ever had.

Bree pulled a bottle of champagne from the refrigerator in the break room and collected three glasses. She'd chosen a bottle of Veuve Clicquot for their Friday night ritual. Ashley was already waiting by the door, a couple of blankets draped over one arm.

"You're early," Bree said, noting Ashley still looked pale. Obviously, things weren't better with Seth.

"I've been looking forward to this all day," her friend admitted. She offered a wan smile. "It's going to be the highlight of my week."

Mikki joined them and glanced at the bottle. "An excellent choice," she said. "It always makes the top five champagnes from Ladies Know Wine."

"As long as we have their seal of approval," Bree teased. "Shall we?"

They walked out of the store and onto the sand. The sun was low against the horizon, appearing larger than normal, sending ribbons of yellow and orange across the water. The sky was a thousand shades of blue from the palest right by the ocean to nearly violet on the eastern horizon. Ashley and Mikki spread out the blankets while Bree opened the bottle. Once they were seated, she poured them each a glass.

"Before we start, I don't want to talk about Seth," Ashley said. "I'm exhausted and depressed and I just want an hour to think about something else."

"Done," Mikki said, touching her glass to Ashley's. "We won't mention him."

"I agree," Bree said, clinking glasses with her friends. She took a sip of the crisp, bubbly champagne and stared out at the ocean. The early evening was still warm and the beach was crowded. The scent of sunscreen lingered.

"We got the contract from Dave at OAR," Mikki said. "I'll have my lawyer look it over and let you know if there are any concerns."

"We'll have plenty of room," Bree said. After her visit to

OAR, she'd reported back that if they went ahead with the holiday baskets, they should definitely lease the space. "And a large service elevator in back."

"Plus, we'll have twenty-four hour access to the building," Ashley added.

"For a 3 a.m. basket pickup?" Mikki asked with a laugh.

"I'm just saying we can get in and out when we want." Ashley glanced at Bree. "What did you think of what they're doing at OAR?"

"I was impressed. I didn't know about foster kids aging out of the system. There should be a better plan than simply tossing a foster child out when they turn eighteen, even if they're not done with high school."

Ashley nodded. "It's a problem."

"Dave was impressive," Bree added. "He's pulled the whole organization together."

"I always tell Harding that Dave is the brains of the operation," Ashley said with a grin. "He keeps my brother in line and I like that."

"Is he married?"

Mikki looked at Bree. "Interested?"

Bree laughed. "No. Just curious. He's very good-looking."

"He's not married," Ashley said. "He's more of a serial dater."

"He's in a wheelchair, isn't he?" Mikki asked.

Both Ashley and Bree nodded.

"So how serious is his injury?" Mikki asked. "Can he, ah, you know?"

"Have sex?" Bree asked. "Surprisingly, we didn't discuss that."

Mikki turned to Ashley. "Well?"

"We never dated."

"You had to have discussed it at some point. You've known him for years."

Ashley held up her glass. "Sure. 'Hi, Dave. Can you get an erection?' We talked about it all the time." She sipped her champagne. "From what his various girlfriends have said, it's definitely not an issue. Why are you so interested?"

"It's the obvious question. Why didn't you two ever go out?"

Bree was surprised when Ashley flushed.

"I'm Harding's little sister. I'm practically family."

There was something in her tone, Bree thought. "You had a crush on him."

Ashley groaned. "When I was seventeen. He wasn't interested, the crush went away. We're friends. Can we please stop talking about Dave, his penis and my crush?"

"Whose penis do you want to talk about?" Mikki asked, then started laughing. "I'm in a mood tonight."

"You should call Duane," Bree told her. "Let him take advantage of you."

"I'm not ready for that. I like him and he makes me tingle, but it's going to be a while until I'm ready to let him see my naked butt."

Bree chuckled. "He won't be looking at your butt."

They touched glasses as Ashley pulled her legs to her chest and rested her forehead on her knees.

"You two are the worst," she grumbled.

"We are," Mikki said happily. "And that is why you love us."

"*Love* is really strong," Ashley told her. "*Tolerate* is a better word."

"Don't cheapen the moment by lying."

This, Bree thought. This moment, this laughter, this friendship. It was unexpected, but she liked it. These women had, in a short period of time, become important to her. Their weekly ritual grounded her and made her feel she belonged. After so many years of being alone—even while married to Lewis—she was surprised and happy to feel a sense of being part of something.

"But you hate fire pits," Mikki said, unwrapping her sandwich.

She and Perry sat at an old picnic table he'd brought over to his new house. He'd wanted her to help him choose the best paint color for the downstairs, offering the bribe of lunch from her favorite deli. They'd agreed on a pale taupe color that would blend nicely with the woodwork, once it was stripped and stained.

"You said they're messy and everyone wants one but no one uses them."

She should know—she and the kids had begged him for a fire pit, but he'd refused. She'd had one installed a year after the divorce, settling on one fueled by propane rather than wood. Not as fun, but easier for her to handle on her own.

"I've grown and changed," he told her with a grin. "You use yours all the time. The kids love it. I'm going to put in the same kind when I redo the backyard."

She pressed her hand to her chest in mock surprise. "Next you'll be telling me you like Brussels sprouts."

"No one grows that much."

She laughed. "Okay, a fire pit it is. I think you'll really like it. You were right about the wood ones. They're a lot of work. Where are you going to put it?"

He pointed to the far end of the patio. "I'm extending that. There's still plenty of room in the backyard."

"That's a good place for it." She paused to figure out which direction they were facing. "It's the north side of the yard, so there should be plenty of shade in the summer. Nice."

She bit into her corned beef on rye. Perry had good ideas about the house. He'd shown her the preliminary design for the master suite addition. The closet was huge and she loved the layout of the bathroom.

"You'll be happy here," she told him.

He glanced at her. "That's my plan. I should have bought my own place a while ago. My folks made it too easy on me, renting me their house."

"Why would you say that? It worked out for everyone. The kids were close to both of us and you did a lot of work, fixing up your parents' house. It was a win–win."

"I was lazy."

His blunt statement surprised her. "In what way?"

"A lot of ways. I was lazy in our marriage. I liked how things were and never wanted anything to change. Mostly because you took such good care of me. I should have tried harder to be what you wanted."

"You said that before. Why is it on your mind now?"

"I've been doing some thinking lately."

A casual sentence, she thought. But there was something about the way he said it. Warning bells went off, causing her to drop her sandwich and stare at him as awful thoughts popped into her brain.

"Oh, God, you're sick!"

"What?"

"You have some disease or something. What is it? Tell me!"

He surprised her by laughing. "I'm not sick. Can't a man give a little thought to his behavior without being close to death?"

"I don't know. Can he?"

Perry smiled at her. "I'm not sick," he repeated. "Look, the kids are getting older and we're moving into another phase of our lives. Don't you ever take stock of things?"

She thought about how the realization that she could live another fifty years had prompted her to sign up for that dating site. Because of that, she was going out with Duane.

"You're right," she said, picking up her sandwich. "It's good to reflect and make positive changes."

"Sometimes I think about what could have been. If things had been different for us."

Did he? She'd given that up a while ago. There were regrets, of course. She'd wanted a third baby but Perry hadn't been interested. She'd wanted them to have date nights and take trips together. But none of that had happened and in so many ways, things were easier between them since the divorce.

"I'm glad we're where we are now," she told him. "We get along. That's nice for us and for the kids."

He studied her for a second before biting into his sandwich. "Sydney and Will are going to come over and help me paint. Want to join us?"

"Sure. Let me know when and I'll make sure things are covered at the store."

He stood. "Let me go get the tile samples."

As he walked back into the house, she wondered if she should mention Duane. If she kept seeing him, he would need to meet Perry. And she really should tell Perry she was dating before he heard it from one of their children. Only she wasn't sure what to say or how to say it, so she decided to put it off for a few more weeks. It wasn't as if her dating life would make any difference to her ex. What they'd had was long over and well in the past.

"You can't be here."

The voice came from behind her. Ashley jumped and spun, only to see Oscar walking into the OAR kitchen.

Her normally stoic baker scowled. "It's two in the morning. This is the third time this week I've found you here when you should be home sleeping."

He moved close and glared at her. "What's going on?"

He was a big guy—not just tall, but incredibly strong. Plus, the whole air-of-menace thing he had going on. Ashley drew herself up to her less impressive five foot seven and glared right back.

"You're not the boss of me."

A muscle twitched at the corner of his mouth. She'd hoped for a little more—a slight smile, maybe—but all she got was the twitch.

"You can't be here," he repeated, his tone slightly more gentle this time. "It's not good for you. You're at the store all day long." His gaze sharpened. "Why are you avoiding Seth?"

"I'm not."

The lie was involuntary. She inhaled sharply. "Not exactly. I mean, I don't want to talk to him right now, but that's not the same as avoiding him. One is more conscious. I'm just, um, catching up on work."

"You trying to convince yourself or me?"

"Mostly myself. You already know I'm lying."

Oscar's dark gaze settled on her face. "He hurt you?"

"No. Not in the way you mean. I thought…" She pressed her lips together, not sure how much to share. "I just found out we want different things." She held up her hand. "He loves me and wants to spend the rest of his life with me. That's what he keeps telling me."

Oscar studied her with an intensity that made her think he could read her mind. Finally, he said, "Hiding doesn't help. Hiding gives the problem more power. Every time you hide, it grows until you're overwhelmed. If you believe in Seth, give him a chance to make it right. If you don't believe in him, walk away and find someone you can trust and respect."

He was right, she thought. "How come you give such good advice about my love life but you won't ask Carrie out for coffee?"

"One does not equate to the other."

"She's sweet on you."

His expression hardened. "Don't go there, little girl. It's not your business."

"I think you should consider asking her out. It would be nice for both of you." She paused as a thought occurred to her. "Is it because you're gay? You never said, so I'm assuming you're not, but if you are, I'll stop pushing women on you."

While Oscar didn't physically move even an inch, somehow his posture turned menacing. "Did you just ask me if I'm gay?"

"It's a reasonable question."

"No, it's not."

"There's nothing wrong with being gay. A lot of people are. I get that. Even bisexual makes sense to me. I mean, a lot of things in nature exist on a spectrum."

Oscar muttered something and walked over to the pot of coffee she'd started an hour before.

"Go home," he told her, pouring coffee into a mug.

"So no on the gay thing?"

"No."

"I'm just going to say, one last time, that Carrie knows about your past and she's okay with it. And she's pretty and funny and—"

"Go home!"

His voice was a roar. Ashley jumped slightly, then pulled her bag out of a drawer.

"You are Mr. Grumpy Pants tonight, aren't you? Fine. I'm going home. But don't think we're done talking about Carrie."

"You should be afraid of me."

She looked at him. "Really?"

His set mouth relaxed slightly. "No. I'd never hurt you."

"I know that, Oscar. Have a good night."

"You, too."

Her good mood lasted all the way to the apartment building. As she pulled into her parking spot, she found herself spiraling back into sadness and bewilderment. She'd been avoiding Seth for nearly a week and at some point they had to talk. The problem was she wasn't any closer to knowing what to say than she had been when he'd first said he didn't want to marry her.

She let herself into their apartment, expecting to find the living room empty and dark except for the single lamp Seth always left on for her. Instead, the room was bright and he was sitting on the sofa—obviously waiting for her.

"You're still up," she said in surprise. "It's late. You have work tomorrow."

"You do, too." He stood. "You've been creeping in after midnight nearly every night this week, yet you're up early to deal with the store."

"I haven't been sleeping well."

He crossed to her and took her bag. After setting it on the table by the door, he pulled her into his arms.

"I'm sorry," he whispered, holding her close. "Ashley, I've hurt you and I never wanted to do that. I love you. Please believe me. I apologize for bungling our conversation about the house. I should have been more prepared and handled things better."

His familiar embrace, the warmth of his body and the sincerity of his words eased some of her tension. She hugged him back, wanting to erase the past few days and go back to where they'd been before.

After a few minutes he tugged her over to the sofa. They sat angled toward each other. He held one of her hands in his.

"We have to talk," he said, his voice gentle, "to straighten this out. I screwed up and I'm sorry."

Cautious optimism flared. "What does that mean?"

"We hadn't discussed marriage. We'd talked about our future, but never the M word." He smiled briefly. "That made me think, or rather hope, that you weren't interested in the trappings of marriage. That you wanted what I did."

"A committed relationship without getting married," she said flatly, as her optimism crashed and burst into flames.

"Exactly." He squeezed her fingers. "We can do it. The house will be set up so if one of us dies, it automatically goes to the other person. We sign medical directives allowing us to make decisions. We will be one hundred percent committed for the rest of our lives."

She pulled back her hands. "Until one of us gets lazy. What

happens if I agree to this and I get pregnant? You still won't marry me."

"We don't have to be married to have children."

"Not biologically, but what about them? How are we supposed to explain Mommy and Daddy aren't married? How are they supposed to tell their friends?"

His eyebrows drew together. "It's not that big a deal anymore. Lots of parents aren't married."

"Because they're not in love with each other." She slid back on the sofa. "Your argument against marriage is that people get lazy. They stop putting effort into the relationship."

"Yes," he said carefully.

"What happens if I have a bad pregnancy? What if I'm sick for three months and can't do all the things around here you expect me to do? What if I gain thirty pounds and it takes me a year to lose the weight? What if I never do? Does that fall under your categorization of—" she made air quotes "— 'getting lazy'? Am I not giving enough? Am I not trying hard enough?"

"You're taking my words too literally."

"Your words are all I have. I get what you're saying about some people taking advantage of the institution of marriage. I agree we've seen couples who phone it in. But the way you talk about the relationship makes me feel like one slip, one bad afternoon, and we're done. No one can live like that. The person you love is supposed to be the one place where you can relax. Where you can completely be yourself without being judged or pressured. Loving someone, committing to someone, means giving them a break, taking care of them more than they take care of you because if both people are doing that, then it's marriage at its best."

His shoulders slumped. "You're looking at this emotionally, not logically."

"We're talking about love, Seth. There is only emotion."

She thought he would snap back. Instead, he rose and pulled her to her feet.

"You're exhausted," he said, pushing her toward the bedroom. "You've been staying out late, avoiding me and thinking about this. Get some sleep. I'll take the sofa. We'll talk again in a few days when we're both rested."

She wanted to point out there was still so much to say. Only he was right—she was exhausted.

"Thank you." She walked into the bedroom and shut the door behind her. Even in the middle of this pile of shit, he was being nice, which she would never understand. If he was so willing to be the good guy, to be caring and supportive, why couldn't he see that marriage was important to her?

She wouldn't get any answers tonight. For the next few hours she was going to let it go.

TWELVE

Bree scanned the sales report, pulling up the May numbers from the previous year to do a direct comparison. Six-plus months in, she had to admit the move had been good for business. Sales were up every single month since January—by nearly 38 percent in May. She wasn't sure how much came from the new location and how much from walk-in traffic drawn by Ashley and Mikki's businesses, and she wasn't sure it mattered. The Boardwalk Bookshop was doing even better than she'd hoped.

She'd had to increase her orders, which made her account reps happy. The children's section was up the most, and the other departments weren't far behind.

The store phone rang.

"Boardwalk Bookshop," she said, smiling at the happy numbers. "This is Bree."

"Hello, Bree. It's Idalina Gray. How are you?"

The warm tone and the friendly question implied that Bree should know her caller. She had a strong sense the name should be familiar. But how? Was she a fitness instructor? Spin? Not Pilates—she mostly worked out with Nicole. Was she one of the ridiculously perky CrossFit women who—

"Your mother's publicist," Idalina said into the silence.

"Oh, right." Her mother's publicist? Why? "Nice to hear from you."

Not really, she silently added, wondering why on earth Idalina would be calling her. Bree couldn't remember the last time they'd spoken. Five years ago? Six? She hadn't talked to either of her parents in at least a year or seen them since Lewis's funeral.

"Your mother would like to have a signing in your store," Idalina said.

"Why?"

Her mother hadn't set foot in the store since before Lewis had died, and then only briefly. Neither of her parents had ever signed in the store—not even when he'd owned it.

"What do you mean, why? It's a *New York Times* reporting store, with a lovely reputation. You have very successful signings with great attendance. What dates would work for you?"

"None," Bree said flatly. "I'm not setting up a signing with you. If my mother is so eager to show up here, she can get her ass on the phone and call me herself."

There were several beats of silence before Idalina murmured, "I'll pass on your message," and then hung up.

Bree slammed the phone in place. "You have ruined my day," she shouted at the phone. "I was having a really good day before you called."

"Knock, knock."

Mikki stood in the doorway.

"What?" Bree snapped, then sagged back in her chair. "Sorry. My anger is spilling over. You're the innocent bystander."

Mikki took the visitor's chair. "What's wrong? And don't tell me you're fine. We both know you're not. If you resist, I'll be forced to use my mom voice and neither of us want that."

The combination of concern and irreverence nearly made Bree smile. She motioned to the phone. "My mom's publicist called to set up a signing. As if."

Mikki's eyes widened. "Your mother is a writer? Why didn't I know that? Oh, wait. You never talk about your family. Your mother is a writer? For real?"

"My father, too. You ever hear of Naomi and Gearard Days?"

"Probably," Mikki said cautiously. "Oh, wait, I know them. They're iconic literary writers. They're a big deal." She stared at Bree. "Holy crap, those are your parents? But they're famous and important and you don't carry literary fiction. Oh, I get it. The ultimate rejection of who they are and what they do. Good one. You know, you probably need therapy."

"I tried. Didn't take."

"Still, you might reconsider a second round. Your parents. Are they both alive?"

"Yes and living in Manhattan. They also have a summer place in the Hamptons and that cottage in Switzerland. My father goes there to write. It's the only time my parents are ever apart. They're still very much in love with each other. Their only child was more of an interruption and annoyance than a family member, which is why we don't have a lot of contact."

"I'm still in shock," Mikki admitted. "And processing. Can you see the hourglass over my head?" She paused. "So you were never close to either of them?"

"No. I've always felt my dad's neglect was more organic, if that makes sense. He constantly seemed surprised that I existed. I'd walk in the room and I could see him trying to remember who I was. Mom, on the other hand, simply couldn't be bothered."

"We always blame the mother," Mikki murmured.

"Shut up."

Her friend smiled. "So we hate Mom. I get that. When was the last time she did a signing in the store?"

"She hasn't. It was never important enough for her. When Lewis owned it, there weren't a lot of customers and no prestige. My parents are all about how things look when it comes to their books. Every event has to be perfect. I just don't know why she's bothering me now."

"Does she have a new book out?"

Bree realized she had no idea. She typed on her computer,

then shook her head. "Her last release was six months ago. No way she's still on tour." She scrolled down the screen, scanning as she went. "The reviews were fantastic. They're saying this is her best novel yet."

"I still hate her."

Not the most mature response, but one that made Bree feel taken care of. "Thank you."

"What happens now? Are you hosting a signing?"

"I told her publicist if she wanted to sign here, she could call me and ask herself." Bree stood. "Trust me, that will never happen."

Mikki rose. "If it does, let us know. We'll protect you from her."

"I don't need protection."

Mikki hugged her, an act Bree found surprisingly comforting.

"Of course you do," Mikki murmured. "She's your mother. Of all the people on the planet, she's the one most able to cut your heart into tiny pieces and then serve them to you in a tart."

"That's a disgusting visual."

"Yeah, and I wasn't going for cannibalism. It came out wrong, but you know what I mean."

"I do."

"I appreciate you getting up so early," Ashley told her brother as she poured them each a mug of coffee.

She'd asked to come over, but now that she was here, she was wishing she hadn't decided to talk to him. She trusted his advice and his willingness to keep her secrets, but she didn't know how to explain her situation without sounding like a fool. She was the woman who had fallen for the guy who didn't want to marry her. That wasn't something to be proud of.

He still looked rumpled—as if he'd gotten out of bed minutes before her arrival. He was barefoot and wearing loose sweats and a T-shirt. He stretched before taking the coffee and smiling at her.

"This isn't early. Thursdays I'm up before dawn for my surfing lesson."

Ashley sat at the small kitchen table and laughed. "Thursday you're up early so you can spend time with Bree at *her* surfing lesson. You're practically stalking her. It's kind of pathetic."

"I'm willing to be pathetic for her."

Ashley raised her eyebrows. "Are you sure that's a good idea? First, and no offense, but women aren't attracted to men they find pathetic. Second, Bree's made it clear she's not looking for a relationship. When someone tells you the truth, you should listen."

As she said the words, she had a bad feeling she was also speaking to herself. A thought that wasn't comforting.

"I'll take my chances," he told her. "Bree's worth the risk."

"What's your end game?"

"Two kids and a mortgage."

She knew he was half kidding, but still, the comment hit her hard. Unexpected tears filled her eyes. She turned her head, but not before he saw she was upset.

"Hey, sis," he said softly. "You can't be that worried about me and Bree. What's up with the tears?"

"It's not you," she said, then tried to laugh. "It's me."

He ignored her sad attempt at humor and let his "I've got all the time in the world" expression slide into place.

They sipped their coffee while she tried to figure out what to say.

"You can't tell Mom and Dad," she began. "I mean it. They won't understand and everything will change and—"

"Did he hit you?"

"What?" She stared at her brother, who seemed to show only casual interest in the question. *A facade*, she thought. Calm on the outside and ready to rip Seth apart on the inside.

"No, he didn't hit me. Nor did he get angry with me. It's not like that."

She clutched her mug. "Things are good between us. Really good. We're going to Whistler in the fall, and based on how he talked about the hotel and that it's the first anniversary of us saying we loved each other—" she looked at Harding "—I thought he was planning to propose."

"But he's not?"

"No."

She told him about the house and how he wanted to have kids with her, but he didn't want to marry her. That he believed people got married and then stopped trying. That they got lazy and took each other for granted.

When she stopped talking, Harding drained his coffee cup.

"What do you think?" he asked.

The tears returned. "That I've fallen in love with a man who isn't going to marry me."

"Do you believe he loves you?"

"I don't know. I used to."

His dark gaze met hers. "Do you believe he loves you?"

Ashley let the question sit in her heart. In every other area of their lives, Seth was everything she'd ever wanted. He was hardworking, thoughtful, kind, smart, funny. He treated her well and wanted the world to know he adored her.

"He loves me."

"And you love him."

"Less now."

Harding ignored that. "You can't get past your feelings enough to look at what he's saying logically. Is it possible to have committed partnership without getting married?"

"Of course. The legal stuff can be worked out. That's not the point."

"Isn't it? He's offering you everything you want."

"Not marriage. I want to be married."

"Why? You're not a wedding planning kind of person. I've never heard you daydream about a dress or a honeymoon."

"That doesn't mean I don't want a ring on my finger. Marriage is what people do. They fall in love and decide to spend their lives together, then they get married. If you're going to pair bond in this society, then you damn well better cough up a marriage proposal."

"Seth doesn't want to get married."

She groaned. "That is why I came to see you. Something I'm starting to regret."

"That's because you're still in your emotions. You say you want to be married because that's what people do. But why? You've never been a rule follower. You quit a great job to start over making muffins. You have two ex-felons working for you. When the opportunity to work with Bree and Mikki came up, you didn't hesitate. You've always been strong and willing to take risks."

He grabbed her free hand and squeezed her fingers. "Why is marriage so important? What about the ring makes things different for you?"

She pulled free of his touch. "That's hard to explain."

"That's my point. Until you can articulate something beyond it's what you want and it's what's expected, you can't have a real conversation with Seth. He's coming at the situation from a different perspective. You need to understand his point of view and he needs to understand yours. Then you can decide what matters the most to each of you."

Which all sounded fine, but she wasn't hopeful. "If Bree came to you, said she loved you and was willing to be with you and have kids, but wouldn't marry you, would you do it?"

"Yes."

"Just like that?"

"I want Bree. If those are her terms, I'm fine with them." He raised one shoulder. "Would I rather marry her? Sure. I want to stand before God and everyone I care about and say this is the one I've chosen. This woman forever. I am hers and she is mine. But it's not a deal breaker. As long as I have her in my life, I'm getting everything I could possibly want."

She eyed him suspiciously. "You're saying that metaphorically, right? You're not in love with her."

Harding smiled. "Not yet."

"You're so annoying." She sighed. "Why do I care so much about being married?"

"I don't know, but you do."

"I think it's because his unwillingness to be married feels personal. I think I don't believe it's all women, it's just me. He would marry someone else but he won't marry me."

"Do you really believe that?"

"Not in my head. I know he loves me. But it feels that way when we talk about it." She gave him a faint smile. "You're right. I have to figure this out. I need to get past the emotions to what's important to me."

Which sounded logical, but she had no idea how to do it.

Harding rose and pulled her to her feet. "Have a little faith in the man and have more faith in yourself. You'll get there. And if it turns out he's a jerk, I'll whack him with my surfboard."

She laughed, then started to cry. Through it all, Harding held her tight, because her big brother had always been there for her. And she knew that would never change.

"A handsome man is looking for you," Lorraine said, her voice slightly strained.

Mikki ignored the flash of guilt as she glanced over her mother-in-law's shoulder and saw Duane standing by the check-out counter. His broad shoulders and easy smile had her heart fluttering and her girl bits tingling. Not anything she wanted to experience under Lorraine's watchful eye.

"That's Duane," she said, trying to sound casual.

Lorraine glanced between the two of them. "I didn't know you were seeing anyone."

The guilt level tripled. "I, um, am. Excuse me."

She walked up to him. "Hi. You're in my store."

"Yes." His gaze met hers and the smile returned. "That okay?"

She laughed. "Yes. It's a store. You're allowed to be here. Although I am a little surprised."

"I wanted to see where you work. So I can picture it when I'm fantasizing about you."

When he what? "You fantasize about me?" she asked before she could stop herself.

He leaned close and whispered, "All the time. You're a terrible distraction."

Oh. She opened her mouth, then closed it, not sure what to say to that, but liking how his words made her feel.

"Well, this is my store," she said, hoping she didn't sound as flustered as she felt. "Where I, um, sell things."

"It's nice. It feels like you." He glanced around. "Warm and welcoming and a little unexpected." He returned his attention to her. "Could we step outside? I want to ask you something."

"Of course."

She paused, not sure if she should say something to Lorraine. Until this exact second, having her mother-in-law work for her had never been a problem. Yet suddenly, there were pitfalls she didn't know how to deal with.

Telling herself Lorraine would figure it out, she led the way outside.

The afternoon was hot and sunny, the beach crowded. Duane motioned to a bench in the shade of the building. They sat next to each other.

"How's your day going?" she asked.

"Good. I've been on a conference call since three." His expression turned rueful. "The time differences can be a killer."

"Three in the morning?"

"That's the one. I get more involved with my volunteer work when school is out," he told her.

"Developing economies wait for no man."

"Exactly. So I wanted to ask you about a Ladies Know Wine event."

"A tasting? I'm on their email list for local events. I didn't get anything from them."

"Not local." His gaze met hers. "They're having a big wine celebration up in Monterey. It's over a long weekend. I thought we could go."

To Monterey? For a long weekend? With him? Her and him, together? As in…

Could she do that? Did she want to?

She thought about how much she liked Duane and how great his body was and knew that yes, of course she wanted to do that, but wanting to and being ready were two very different things.

Sex was complicated. Not just the doing or not doing, but the preparation. She needed to lose twenty pounds and get some new lingerie and possibly wax. Plus, it had been forever since she'd had sex with a man and while she was sure she would remember how, she was nervous and scared and—

"Stop," he said gently. "Let me finish before you freak out."

"I'm not freaking out. I'm calm. I'm a rock."

"Yeah, if you could see your face." He took her hand in his. "Two hotel rooms. As much as I want us to make love, it's too soon. I don't want to scare you off. So we'll take sex off the table and just spend the weekend together. What do you say?"

Disappointment wrestled with relief. The latter won, allowing her to relax enough to say, "I'd like that a lot."

"The two hotel rooms? Going away with me? The wine event?"

She smiled. "All of it."

He gave her the dates. "It's only a couple of weeks away. Is that too soon?"

Maybe if she stopped eating completely, she thought. "It's perfect. The kids are with Perry, so I'm free."

"Excellent." He leaned in and lightly kissed her. "I'll get the tickets and make reservations. We'll have a good time." He whispered in her ear, "You might want to bring Earl. In case things get heated."

She laughed as she pushed him away. "Earl's a stay-at-home kind of guy."

"I still look forward to meeting him."

"That is never going to happen."

He rose and drew her to her feet. "I don't know. I can be persuasive."

He walked her back to the store, then kissed her again. "I'll text you the details."

"I look forward to it."

He left and she practically floated into the store. But once she was inside, her former mother-in-law hurried over.

"You two seemed friendly."

Mikki thudded back to earth. "We are."

She wasn't sure what to say after that. Pointing out that she and Perry had been divorced for three years seemed unnecessary, and she wasn't sure mentioning Perry's previous girlfriends would be helpful.

"I've been alone a long time," she said. "I'm ready to find someone. Please don't repeat this, but the last thing I want is to end up like my mother. I could live another fifty years. I want to do that with a partner."

Her mother-in-law's mouth tightened. "Of course you have every right to date whomever you want. I just always thought... hoped, really...that you and Perry would find your way back to each other. You have children together and most of the time, your marriage worked."

Mikki hugged her. "I'm sorry. I don't want to hurt you, but

neither of us wants that. Perry and I are good just the way we are."

"I know. I'm being silly." Lorraine patted her arm. "I'm glad you're happy."

"Thank you."

Lorraine nodded and walked away. Mikki told herself she wasn't doing anything wrong. But Lorraine's talk about Perry had caused a leak in her happiness bubble. Hopefully, a weekend away with Duane would help her get it back to floating.

THIRTEEN

The restaurant was one of those small neighborhood places with a patio and an eclectic menu. It was crowded enough that Bree was sure the food was good, but not so busy that it had moved on to trendy and self-important. She stepped out of her Uber and saw Harding standing by the entrance.

He looked good, she thought, both pleased to see him and annoyed with herself for accepting his invitation to dinner. They weren't dating—there was no reason to spend time with him. But somehow she'd been unable to refuse. She hadn't even been snippy when she'd said yes.

She knew the exact moment he spotted her. His whole face lit up and he started toward her. She forced herself to let him come to her. But that power play totally failed when she practically threw herself at him. She wrapped her arms around him and melted into him, oddly needing the feel of his body.

He was lean and strong, and everything about him appealed to her. She thought of him after their surfing lesson—how he was always shivering and she had to help him out of his wet suit so she could dry and warm him. He was exhausted but still made jokes. She thought of the scars and his limp and the way he pursued her and how she knew in her gut that his very goodness and his idealism were as lethal as his warm, sexy kisses.

"You're so beautiful," he said as they walked toward the restaurant. "Way out of my league."

"You're handsome enough."

That earned her a head-thrown-back kind of laugh.

"Handsome enough?" he asked, escorting her inside. "So not so good-looking as to take your breath away, but not so ugly that you're ashamed."

"Exactly."

"I can live with that."

He gave his name to the hostess, who led them to a corner table on the patio. The sky still had tinges of pink from the sunset, and heaters stood on guard, should the temperature dip below seventy-five. LA was a city that didn't do cold.

They sat across from each other. Harding leaned toward her. "Tell me about your day."

"I sold books."

"Did you think about me?"

She had—which she wouldn't admit. Getting close to people wasn't especially safe for her. Every now and then she made exceptions—like Mikki and Ashley. She worked with them and being standoffish would complicate things. But even as they got to know each other, she kept up walls to protect herself. What Harding wanted—at least what she sensed he wanted—was something else entirely. He would want to burrow deep inside her soul, learn all her secrets, then tell her his. He wanted them to be a part of each other's lives, entwined. He wanted a relationship. He was that kind of guy.

"I'll never be what you want," she told him.

"Maybe I'm superficial and I'm only interested in you because you're hot and I'm pretty sure you're great in bed."

She smiled. "I wish you were that shallow, but you're not." She leaned back. "Tell me about *your* day."

"I heard from a guy I knew in high school. He has a web design company and wanted to talk about me doing an update on the OAR website."

"He was looking for work?"

"Yup."

"What did you tell him?"

"That I had a web person, but I'd let him know if that changed. Then I gave him the names of a few businesses I know that might be looking."

"Have you talked to him since high school?"

"Once or twice. We weren't friends, if that's what you're asking."

"He wasn't at your side after the accident?"

Harding's warm expression never changed. "No. He was an avoider."

"People who avoid things that scare them. Like you maybe never walking."

"Not everyone can handle the bad stuff. I get that."

Their server took their drink orders, then left.

"But now he wants something from you," she pointed out. "That seems selfish."

"I don't judge."

"Everyone judges. Do you still have friends from high school?"

"A few."

"What about old girlfriends?"

She expected him to laugh, but instead he exhaled. "I had a steady girlfriend when I got hurt."

Bree wished she hadn't asked. Based on the slight tension in his body, the story didn't have a happy ending.

Stupid cow bitch, she thought grimly. *Dumping him after he was hit by a car? Who did that? What kind of selfish, mean-spirited—*

"She was there every day," he added with a shrug. "Faithful, supportive. She took shifts with my folks and Ashley so I was never alone. She read to me, made me eat, told me I'd get better. Told me I was strong enough to beat the odds."

"Oh." Bree rearranged her mental thoughts about the unknown teen. "She sounds great."

"She was. I knew she was falling more and more in love with me. I knew she was preparing herself to commit to me for the rest of our lives, no matter the outcome. She was that strong."

"What happened?"

He looked at her. "I ended it." He held up a hand. "Not for some altruistic reason. I wasn't saving her or being brave. I just didn't care about her as much as she cared about me, and having her visit every day really started to bug me. Just give me five seconds to myself. Don't get involved in every physical therapy treatment. She was obsessed and she really got on my nerves."

The words were so at odds with what she'd been expecting that she burst out laughing. And once she was laughing, she couldn't stop.

"Shame on you," she said as she tried to control her outburst. "That poor girl was willing to give up everything to stand by you. Why aren't you appreciative?"

"She had a grating laugh. It's not my fault."

"See," she pointed out. "Judgy. I knew it. By the way, I will never take care of you. You're not grateful enough."

"If you took care of me, I'd be extra grateful."

Their server returned with their drinks. As Bree wasn't driving, she'd gone simple and hard core. A vodka martini with a twist.

"Ask me about Lewis," she said, surprising herself and no doubt stunning him. "You want to."

"What do you want me to know? Beyond the fact that he was a writer, which is the one thing you don't like in a man, so that's confusing."

"He was older," she said. "Worldly, or so it seemed to me. Not in a well-traveled way, but with a smug, well-read snobbishness I should have hated and yet somehow found delightful."

"Better-looking than me?"

She looked at Harding. "Yes," she lied.

"Damn. At least I thought I was cuter."

She smiled. "You have other qualities."

"Such as?"

"You don't remind me of my parents."

"Did he?"

"In a way." More than in a way, she thought, then amended her answer. "Very much, actually, so his ignoring and thinking less of me was no big deal. I had a huge crush on him. I think with him I thought maybe I would finally get what I'd always lacked from my parents. Attention and love. Only I never expected it to work out, so the pain of not having that was familiar. Am I making sense?"

"Yes. We humans always seek out patterns."

"One day he looked at me over a carton of books and said he was in love with me."

She still remembered how shocked she'd been. How happy. He'd kissed her and she'd been lost.

"With Lewis, I had it all," she continued. "The intellectual, literary bullshit I was raised to expect and a man who adored me. I'd finally found someone who cared."

"He was irresistible."

"At the time."

She talked about how she'd been months from graduating with her business degree and had thought she would take a job in New York or London. But Lewis loving her had changed her plans. She'd stayed and worked in the bookstore.

"You gave up your future for him."

"That wasn't how I saw it. I was happy. My parents met him and were impressed." She finished her drink. "My mother pulled him aside to ask if he was sure he wanted to marry me. I didn't seem like his type."

What Naomi had really said was she didn't think Bree was

good enough, but there were some secrets she wasn't willing to share.

"We were married and I'd never been happier. I ran the store while he wrote."

"What about kids?"

"Lewis wasn't the type."

"Are you?"

She had been at one time, but now? "Not really my thing."

"Why not? You'd be a good mom."

"You can't know that about me." What she knew for sure was she never wanted her child to feel about her the way she felt about her mother.

"Then Lewis got sick?" he asked, obviously letting the kid thing go.

"No, then he divorced me."

Harding stared at her in surprise. Their server showed up and explained about the specials. They quickly made their selection. Harding chose a bottle of wine. When their server left, he waited for her to continue.

"He told me he wasn't in love with me anymore," she said flatly, skipping over how those words had made her feel. She'd been knocked to the ground and left for dead by his rejection of her. She'd been lost and confused and willing to do anything to change his mind. Not that he'd offered that option.

"He said he hadn't loved me for a while. That I was no longer interesting to him." She wished she'd ordered another drink. "I had no idea he was unhappy. I was as in love with him as ever."

"What did you do?"

"I moved out. The house was his, the store. Without him, I had nothing that mattered. A small savings account, a trust fund from my parents. I rented an apartment and hid out for nearly a year. My mother said she wasn't surprised, of course. She told me I'd been lucky to have Lewis for as long as I did." She faked a smile. "I wasn't good enough for him."

"I try not to dislike people I've never met, but I'm not a fan of your mother."

"She would charm you."

"I don't think so."

She sipped her water. "I got a job in a bank. I was a teller. It was a start back to regular life."

She'd learned, over time, that it wasn't the death of her marriage that had destroyed her. It was the loss of Lewis loving her. She'd been so sure she'd finally found the love that had been absent her whole life, only to have it ripped away. In the months after her divorce, she'd come to see that she was the problem. There was something unlovable about her.

Their server appeared with a bottle of wine. He opened it and had Harding taste it, then poured them each a glass.

Bree clutched hers tightly in her hand. "Two years later he came back. He said he'd made a horrible mistake and he missed me. He begged me to give him another chance." She offered Harding an empty smile. "It never occurred to me to say no or even question him. I didn't care that I was finally getting myself back together, that I'd healed. Instead of thinking of protecting myself, I jumped back into my former life and found that I could breathe again."

She remembered waking up in their bed that first morning. How she'd lain in the sunlight, breathing in familiar smells. Lewis had slept next to her, the heat of his body, the feel of the sheets—all of it so perfect. The open wound that was her heart had healed.

"Only something wasn't right," she said. "I tried to make our relationship what it had been before, but I couldn't. I don't know if my heart was too broken or what, but we never found our way back to our past and we couldn't seem to go forward."

She looked at Harding. "Three months later Lewis was diagnosed with lung cancer. He went through chemo and all kinds of drug treatments. There were a couple of years of remission. By the time it returned, I'd figured out the truth."

Harding's gaze locked with hers. The sadness in his eyes told her he'd guessed her darkest secret.

"He knew about the cancer before he asked to reconcile."

She nodded. "He knew the disease was terminal and if nothing else, I was good at taking care of him. Which I did. Until the end."

"Why did you stay?"

"I don't know. By the time I understood what was happening, he was close to the end. He didn't have anyone else. Maybe I figured I deserved it because I'd been so stupid. Giving up everything for a man who never loved me."

"Do you mean that?"

"Sometimes I think he loved me as much as he could—at least for a while. Maybe that's just wishful thinking on my part. Regardless, he died and he left me his house and the store. I sold the house as soon as I could and moved to where I am now. I made changes in the store."

"No literary books?"

She smiled. "None at all. It's my store now. Lewis wouldn't recognize it."

Nor would he be happy with her changes, but she was fine with that. Whatever she'd once felt for him had long since faded—destroyed by how he'd used her feelings against her. She'd given him all she'd had, all she was, and he'd taken advantage of that. In a way, her parents' indifference was kinder. At least they'd never pretended to be more than they were.

"You said before he never published?"

The question surprised her. "No. He wasn't good enough. After he died I sent a few of his manuscripts to my mother, who informed me they were awful. As she'd always had a soft spot for Lewis, I knew she was telling the truth."

"Did you keep them?"

"No. I shredded the copies and deleted the files. I moved on." Some days she liked to pretend she'd never known Lewis at all. A silly game but one that made her happy. "And that is my Lewis story." She tilted her head. "You probably want to ask me about my grief now."

Harding seemed startled by the statement. "You mean for my book? No. I don't. You're not ready to talk about it."

He was wrong, she thought. So very wrong. The mistake he made was to assume she had feelings bottled up inside her. The truth was she felt nothing. She worked hard to feel nothing. She kept herself apart, didn't let anyone into her life.

Their salads came. Conversation turned to OAR and the holiday basket plan. Bree mentioned how Duane had shown up at the store, freaking out both Mikki and Lorraine.

"Mikki's mom works for you, right?" he asked.

"Yes, Rita is my best employee. She's not the most cheerful person on the planet, but she works hard and her attitude doesn't bother me."

"It's an interesting dynamic," he pointed out. "You work with Mikki's mother, she works with her mother-in-law, you're dating your business partner's brother."

She put down her fork. "We're not dating."

"Oh, but we are."

"Harding. Don't make this more than it is."

His beautiful hazel eyes filled with determination. "Don't make it less than it is." His tone turned conversational. "Why won't you sleep with me?"

The blunt question surprised her. Before she could form an answer, he said, "You know it would be good between us. We get along, we're both relatively physical people. I know you've thought about how my hands and mouth would feel on you. God knows I've thought about coming inside you."

His words made her shiver as liquid desire poured through her. Of course she'd thought about how they would be together.

Him inside her, pushing her closer with every stroke. She'd masturbated to thoughts of him over the past few weeks, her fingers a poor substitute for what he could do to her.

"No," she said, even as her breasts tightened and she felt dampness between her thighs. "I'm not doing that with you."

"Then do it to yourself and let me watch."

Despite her wanting and her wariness, she laughed. "Not that, either. Harding, we're not going there."

"Because you're afraid."

"Because it's not a good idea." And yes, because she was afraid. Of him, of them, of caring. Of getting so lost, she never found herself again. Of a thousand things she couldn't articulate and instinctively feared the way animals feared fire. She didn't have to know what it was to know it was bad for her.

He surprised her by smiling. "Your loss." His humor faded. "I'll wait. When you're ready, I'll be here."

"Don't be. I'm not worth it."

"Is that what you think?" he asked.

She looked at him steadily. "Harding, that's what I know and it's something you need to figure out sooner rather than later."

Mikki had been looking forward to the painting party at Perry's house, but as she pulled into the driveway, behind his truck, she felt more than a little anxiety and some niggling sensation that under other circumstances she would label as guilt.

Telling herself she wasn't doing anything wrong didn't seem to make her feel better. She was divorced—she was allowed to date. In fact, getting on with her life was a sign of mental health. She supposed her uncomfortable feelings came from her mother-in-law's comments and the fact that Perry had always been the one to have a significant other.

She told herself it was fine as she walked to the front door, knocked once and let herself in. "It's me."

"In the dining room," Sydney called.

Mikki dumped her bag by the door, paused to admire the bare wood of the built-ins, then walked into the dining room where she found her daughter taping the windows. The woodwork had already been sanded. Cans of stain stood on an old table.

"Dad and Will are in the family room."

Mikki went through the house. Sure enough, Will was cutting in primer while Perry was on a ladder, painting the ceiling. He worked the roller expertly, covering the flat surface with bright pink paint that would turn white when it dried. The specialty paint allowed you to see where you'd missed when putting a coat of white on top of another coat of white.

"Hi," Mikki called. "Everyone's working hard."

"We are," Perry said cheerfully. "Glad you could make it."

Will sprang to his feet. "Hey, Mom. Want to take over? I'll help Syd tape, then we'll stain the dining room woodwork."

"Sure."

She'd worn old clothes and a scarf to protect her hair. She took the brush from her son and knelt on the floor to continue cutting in primer just above the baseboard.

"Most of the sanding is done," Perry told her, dipping his roller into a paint tray. "I thought it would take too long to do it myself so I hired professionals. The wood's in great shape."

"I saw the built-ins by the fireplace in the front room. They're beautiful. I guess all those layers protected the wood."

"Now we'll stain them and they'll last another fifty years."

His tone was friendly, his body language easy. Mikki relaxed, figuring either Lorraine hadn't said anything about Duane or if she had, Perry didn't care. Which made sense. She had no idea why she'd been worried.

"I'm using the same stain we picked at the house," he continued.

The medium tone had blended well with the hardwood floors and cabinets, she thought. "It's one of my favorites and it wears well."

"I have the master bedroom drawings back from the architect," he said. "When we're done here, I'll show you the design."

"I'd like that."

Perry finished the ceiling, then helped her prime. Once that was done, they each took a side of the room and began painting the walls. At noon Mikki ordered sandwiches from their favorite place and Will went to get them. She and Sydney set up paper plates and sodas at the picnic table on the deck.

"I want to finish my room before I go back to college," Sydney said. "So everything feels settled when I come home for Thanksgiving."

Perry joined them. "I'm going to put in double-paned windows upstairs."

"You don't have to be here for that," Mikki told her. "So once we get your room painted, you'll be good to go." She glanced at Perry. "When's your move date?"

"Right around the time she goes back to college. I don't need the addition done for me to live here. My parents' house closes the Tuesday after Labor Day."

Mikki smiled at her daughter. "And you'll be heading out just before then. So we'll get a few of your friends to carry the heavy pieces and the rest of us can join in to cart the little things. It should take less than a morning."

"Thanks, Mom. You're a good organizer."

"I try."

Sydney grinned. "Remember when we drove to Washington, DC, and you'd planned our whole route? We had to drive a certain number of miles every day to make it to the next hotel reservation."

She did. Organizing a cross-country car trip for the family hadn't been easy—especially with Perry resisting in every way he could.

Sydney pointed at her dad. "Remember how you wanted to

turn back the first three nights? You kept grumbling the trip was a waste of time and money and we wouldn't learn anything."

Perry shifted uncomfortably. "I should have been more cooperative."

"It was still a good vacation," Mikki said quickly. "We had a great time."

"I loved the Smithsonian," Sydney said, passing a diet soda to Mikki. "The exhibit on the first ladies was the best."

Will walked in with two big bags of food. "What first ladies?"

"That time we went to DC," Sydney said.

"I liked the Air and Space Museum," Will told her, passing out sandwiches. "Plus, Dad and I went to a Nationals' game and it got rained out and we couldn't find the car." He grinned as he sat across from his sister. "That was the best."

"Getting wet and losing the car?" Perry asked, sitting next to him.

"We were hanging out. It was good."

There had been plenty of disasters, Mikki thought, but lots of fun, too.

"Not like when we went on that cruise with the grandparents," Sydney grumbled. "That was so awful."

"The vacation never to be mentioned," Perry murmured, grinning at Mikki, who winced.

Both sets of grandparents had planned a family cruise to Alaska. They'd given it to Perry, Mikki and the kids for Christmas. Perry had been his usual uncooperative self about the whole thing, but Mikki had been dealing with her own dread. Her parents had been fighting and the thought of being trapped on a cruise ship with an older couple on the verge of divorce had made her uneasy.

Sure enough, her mother and father had started in on each other at the airport and had never let up.

"At least they left at the first port," Sydney said, then patted Mikki's arm. "No offense, Mom."

"I wasn't the one screaming, so no offense taken," she said. "It did get peaceful when they were gone."

Her parents had flown home and had filed for divorce the following week.

"I don't remember any of this," Will complained.

"You were too little," Perry told him. "Be grateful it's all a blur. I still remember your grandmother sleeping on our little sofa the first night."

Mikki did, too. Rita had refused to share a bed with her husband after one of their fights, but there weren't many places to go on a ship.

"I'm glad you and Dad were never like that," Sydney said. "You two got your divorce right."

"It's an odd thing to be proud of, but I am." She smiled at Perry.

"It was all because of you," he told her. "You kept telling me we had to think of the kids."

"I like when you think of me," Will joked. "You should do it more."

They finished lunch and returned to work. By late afternoon the woodwork in the front and dining room had a coat of stain, the dining room had a first coat of neutral color and all the downstairs ceilings were painted. Mikki helped Perry clean brushes and rollers in the garage.

"This was fun," he said, tapping the tops back on the cans.

"It was and we were efficient."

He stood and looked at her. "You've been really great with the house. I appreciate your help. I'd like to say thank you by making you dinner."

"You keep promising to make me a meal, but I've yet to see any actual food."

"Prepare to be amazed. I'll text you some dates and times."

Surprising, but okay. "I look forward to it."

FOURTEEN

Ashley thought maybe she'd gone to a dark place, but apparently, kale and rhubarb paired better than she would have expected. The mini muffins, medium green in color on the outside and paler green on the inside, had a slightly sweet flavor—from the rhubarb. She placed several on a plate and walked through the bookstore until she spotted Bree rearranging a display. When she reached her friend, she motioned to the muffins.

"Something new."

Bree stared at them doubtfully. "Why are they green?"

"I used kale."

Bree visibly shuddered. "In a muffin? Are things that bad?"

"Things are great. Sometimes I experiment."

Bree reluctantly took a muffin and nibbled on the edge. "Okay, less hideous than I thought."

"I'll design an advertising campaign around you."

Bree laughed. "They're not bad. Weird, but not bad. How much experimenting are you doing?"

"I also have pesto, pine nut and parmesan muffins. They're really good."

"And also green? Is the color a thing?"

Ashley tried to think of a funny comeback but she was too tired. The sleepless nights, the constant questioning herself, the wondering if she was wrong or if Seth was unreasonable, had left her feeling as if some energy vampire had left her drained on the side of the road.

"I don't know what to do," she admitted.

"He loves you. Are you clear on that? Because he does."

Ashley set the plate on a stack of books. "So we're not talking about the muffins anymore."

"You never were."

"Well, I was when I mentioned kale." She drew in a breath. "My mind is going round and round like a hamster on a wheel. I can't settle. My head says he's entitled to his opinion. My heart is broken."

"Because what he's saying feels like a personal rejection."

Ashley nodded. "I can't get past the question of is it really marriage to anyone or is it marriage to me? And then I ask myself why I have to be married. Why is that such a thing for me? Other people don't get married—not a lot but some. It's not like he's asking me to dress up like an elephant."

"You'd be a cute elephant."

"Thanks." Ashley looked at Bree. "I just want him to want to marry me."

"I know."

"You were married. Someone wanted to marry you. Mikki's been married. Most women I know have received a proposal."

"It's not just the proposal."

"No, it's not. It's everything. The rite of passage, the piece of paper, the ring, the commitment. The knowing that we're going to try to make it work for the rest of our lives. People stay in love. You were in love with Lewis when he died, right?"

Bree hesitated just long enough for Ashley to take a step back. "No," she said with a whine. "Don't say it was awful at the end."

"I loved him less."

"So marriages fail. You're proving Seth's point."

"I'm not," Bree told her. "You want what you want. That's fair. The question is, can you see yourself being happy with Seth and not marrying him? You love each other, you're commit-ted. Is there any part of you that could consider a permanent arrangement that didn't involve marriage?"

No! Ashley only thought the word, but it was very loud in her head. Not get married? What did that even mean? She wanted the sureness of marriage. She didn't want to spend the rest of her life explaining why she and Seth were different.

But if she went down that path, wasn't she saying what other people thought was more important than what she and Seth thought?

"I don't know," she admitted. "I don't know if I could do that."

"Maybe that's the question you need to answer. Maybe live with the idea for a few weeks and see if your feelings change."

"Why do I have to be the one to change? Why can't Seth change?"

The words came out sharper than Ashley had intended. Rather than snapping back, Bree lightly touched her arm.

"Seth isn't here right now, or I'd be telling him the same thing. Or you could."

"What?"

"Ask him to live with the idea of being married while you live with the idea of not being married. Then you meet and talk about it."

Ashley stared at her muffins. "That's so reasonable. I never thought of him having to look at things from my point of view. I just assumed..." She shrugged. "I don't know what I assumed. I guess that he'd already considered all the options. But what if he hasn't? Maybe he has outdated views of marriage. Maybe he—" She paused when she saw Bree shaking her head. "What?"

"Don't take the next step. You're already hoping he'll come around. Living with the idea of not getting married means just that. You accept the concept and see how it makes you feel.

Talking about Seth changing his mind violates the whole point of the exercise."

"But I don't want to change. I want him to change."

"Which is why you're at an impasse."

Ashley knew Bree was right but she didn't like it. "Why couldn't he have a different flaw?"

"Is there a good flaw?"

"He could hate cats. I could live with a man who hated cats."

"Sorry, kid. You're stuck with the one you already have."

"Hello, Bree."

Bree stiffened, her cell phone against her ear. She'd been so excited about a new shipment of books that she hadn't bothered looking at her screen before answering. Normally, she wasn't worried about who might call, but every now and then she found herself on with someone she would rather not speak with. Someone like…

"Hello, Mother," she murmured. How wrong would it be to simply hang up?

"I'll skip the pleasantries that neither of us care about," her mother said briskly. "Obviously, you felt it was important to speak to me, so here I am. Calling."

"I didn't need you to phone me. I simply pointed out that if you wanted something from me, you should ask directly and not go through your publicist. Very passive-aggressive and a bit of a surprise."

There was a pause, then a deep sigh. "I thought you'd prefer the request come from an unrelated third party."

"No, I wouldn't. But while I have you on the line, what do you care about signing in my store? You never have. I don't even sell literary books."

"Yes, you've made that very clear. Which is not the point. I would very much like to sign in your store, if that can be arranged."

Bree pulled the phone from her ear, stared at it a second, then replaced it. "Why?"

"My not signing there is becoming a problem. You're my daughter, you own a bookstore. There are obvious expectations."

Bree was pleased when she didn't flinch emotionally or physically. She was surprised, but not disappointed.

"Since when have you cared what other people think?" Bree asked.

"Again, not the point. May I have a signing in your store or not?"

Her instinct was to say no—self-preservation dictated that she avoid her parents as much as possible. Yet, to refuse would make her look petty.

"Of course," she murmured. "Have your publicist get in touch with me and we'll set up a time."

"Thank you. I'll avoid stating the obvious and pointing out you could have done that in the first place."

"But then you and I wouldn't have had this wonderful conversation. How long will you be in town?"

"Just overnight. Your father is in Switzerland. Writing. He won't be joining me."

"Thanks for the update."

"Is that sarcasm?"

"Does it matter?"

"Not really. All right, Bree. I'll wait to hear the date and time. I really will be flying in and out."

Translation: *I won't have any time to see you.*

"I understand."

Her mother hesitated, as if not sure if she should say something else. Seconds later she offered a quick, "Thank you and goodbye," then hung up.

Bree put her cell back into her jeans pocket, then returned her attention to the box of books she'd been unpacking. But the joy in the task had faded and she felt an odd restlessness she couldn't explain.

She grabbed her handbag and hurried out of the back room into the store where she found Rita by the cash register.

"I'm going out for an hour."

Rita nodded as she waved the next customer over. "I don't need supervision. I'm not some moody teenager."

Bree resisted the urge to hug her crabby employee and walked to her car. She had no idea where to go. Usually, she'd look for a spin class or go for a run, but neither option appealed. She started her car, thinking maybe she would take PCH for a few miles to clear her head.

But instead of fighting summer traffic on Pacific Coast Highway, she found herself easing into a quiet, older neighborhood, then parking in front of a small house.

Ridiculous, she told herself. She didn't even know why she'd come here. She didn't need anyone—she never needed anyone. She was self-sufficient and capable. Skills she'd learned early and well. What did her mother's indifference matter? It was hardly news. Nothing her parents did affected her—not anymore.

The driver's-side door opened and Harding smiled at her.

"Unexpected, but very nice. While I'd like to think you're here for a booty call, I know I'm not that lucky. So what's up?"

She stared into his familiar hazel eyes and saw affection and a hint of concern. His hair was mussed, as if he hadn't bothered to comb it after his shower. His T-shirt was worn, his jeans faded. All of which was just window dressing, she thought. What mattered was that Harding was the strongest person she knew. He was tough, he was compassionate and he didn't play emotional games.

She released her seat belt and threw herself against him. He caught her, his arms pulling her close and holding her tight. There weren't any questions, just the warmth of his body and the steady beating of his heart.

"Nothing happened," she told him, still hanging on. "Nothing at all."

"Sometimes that's when it hurts the most."

She drew back enough to meet his gaze. "Don't give me your emotional bullshit. Save that for the followers."

One corner of his mouth turned up. "You think you're tough."

"I am tough."

She waited for him to point out that if she was all that, she wouldn't be clinging to him right this very second. But Harding being Harding, he didn't.

He shifted so his arm was around her, then kissed the top of her head. "So no on the sex?"

She couldn't go there—not on her best day and certainly not now when she felt laid bare by a conversation that didn't matter at all.

"Not happening."

He glanced at his watch. "It's nearly noon. Why don't I buy you a sandwich and we can talk about all sorts of things that are unrelated to the nothing that happened before?"

"What if I want extra tomato on mine?"

"Bree, when it comes to me, you can have everything you want."

Mikki spent the drive from LA to Monterey doing her best not to throw up. She wasn't carsick so much as nervous. Very. Sitting next to Duane in his fancy car, talking about kids and weather and international exchange rates—a conversation during which she had very little to add—she tried to distract herself with thoughts of the weekend wine classes, but it wasn't enough. Not when she was going away with a man who wasn't Perry for the very first ever time in her life.

She kept stealing glances at Duane, noticing how close they were sitting together. Every few minutes she pressed her lips together to keep from making a squeaky noise. Reminding herself that they were simply two friends heading off to learn about wine didn't work at all. Duane was a man, not a friend. A man she found attractive and had kissed and thought about having sex with. Even though he'd said that wasn't going to happen, she couldn't help wondering if it would and if it did, was she okay with that?

They arrived at the hotel minutes before she thought she might mentally implode. Duane pulled up at the valet. He smiled at her.

"We're going to have a great time," he told her, squeezing her hand. "Thank you for agreeing to this."

She nodded because her heart was in her throat, which made it impossible to speak. Oh, God, oh, God! Why had she agreed to go away with a man? She wasn't ready. She wasn't sophisticated enough. She was nearly forty, overweight and she didn't know enough about how international currencies worked to survive the weekend.

Duane came around and opened her door while the bellman took care of their luggage. She grabbed her handbag and stepped out.

The four-story hotel overlooked the water. They were steps from Cannery Row, with shops and restaurants and crowds of tourists. The sky was blue, the temperature a perfect seventy-eight degrees. Seagulls called, and the air smelled of salt, coffee and sunscreen.

Duane settled her hand into the crook of his arm and led the way into the hotel. Mikki did her best to look as if she belonged. Did everyone know she was away for the first time with a man she wasn't married to? Not that it mattered. She was being ridiculously old-fashioned. But the sense of being stared at, and judged, added to the tightness in her chest.

Duane checked them in. The bellman led the way to their adjoining but not connecting rooms.

They went into hers first. There was a king-size bed, a sitting area with a fireplace and an incredible view of the water. The bathroom was huge, with a tub for two and a walk-in shower large enough to host a cocktail party. She spied beautiful toiletries with a label she'd only seen in magazines.

Duane's room was similar. The bellman left the suitcases and took the tip Duane offered. When he'd closed the door, leaving them alone, Duane pulled her close and settled his hands on her waist.

"You doing all right?" he asked, his voice concerned.

"I'm fine."

Her voice came out a little higher pitched than she'd planned. He smiled.

"Have you been away with anyone since the divorce?"

She shook her head.

He stared into her eyes. "Nothing will happen. I'm not here to seduce you, Mikki." He smiled. "I want to. Let me be clear. I have trouble being in the same room as you without getting a hard-on, but I can live with that. I want to spend time with you, and have us get to know each other. I want to go to the Ladies Know Wine events and sit across from you at dinner, wondering how I lucked into a date with an incredibly beautiful, sexy woman who makes me laugh and count the seconds until I can see her again."

She absolutely had no idea what to say to that. It was the most amazing speech anyone had ever given her and while she reveled in the *beautiful* and *sexy* part, she was really focused on the hard-on. Really? From being around her?

"Thank you," she whispered. "For all of this."

"You're welcome."

She put her hands on his shoulders. "We're going to have a great time."

"We are." His gaze locked with hers. "Sex is absolutely out of the question. That's why we don't have connecting rooms. I wasn't sure I could withstand the temptation."

"And if I decide I'm okay with it?"

Passion darkened his eyes. "I'd be naked in a heartbeat." His expression turned rueful. "I think we both know you're not ready."

"I want to be," she admitted. "But I'm not."

He lightly kissed her. "I suggest we unpack, then explore. We can go pick up our tickets. If I remember correctly, class starts at four. I made dinner reservations for seven."

"You're dazzling me."

"Good. That's the goal."

"Did you fill out your application already?" Ashley asked a boy who was maybe seven.

He smiled at her and handed over a sheet of paper. "We want a grown-up dog," he said happily. "Everyone wants a puppy, but older dogs have trouble getting adopted, so we're going to take one of those. He's going to be my new best friend."

"I'm sure he is." Ashley smiled at the boy.

The Saturday adoption event had been a big success with area shelters bringing dogs and cats to the huge parking lot by the beach. Seth's company asked employees to volunteer and Ashley had come along. They were manning the registration table.

As always, Seth was funny and charming. He patiently explained the process, joked with the kids and reminded everyone that a local pet store had a tent where new pet owners could find everything they needed.

She pointed the boy and his parents in the direction of dogs, trying not to notice the pregnant woman's wedding ring set. Obviously, they were a family. He'd proposed, she'd said yes and now they had a child with a second on the way. Nothing out of the ordinary—nothing that required an explanation.

She'd been doing her best to take Bree's advice and live with the idea of not getting married. The problem was, the more she thought about *not* being Seth's wife, the more she wanted him to change his mind. It was that old adage to not think about a pink elephant. Soon, there was nothing else on your mind.

Once their shift ended, Ashley and Seth started back for his car.

"That was fun," he said. "Makes me want a pet. We both work a lot, so a cat would probably be better than a dog." He smiled at her. "Although I really did like a few of those dogs. What do you think?"

"About you getting a dog?"

He stopped and looked her. "About *us* getting a pet."

"Who would own it?" she asked. "Would it be yours or mine?"

His mouth turned down. "Ashley, do you have to go there?"

"Why not? I think I'm asking a reasonable question. Who would own this mythical pet? We can't both be responsible for it. Who does the vet call with a health update? Who is the emergency contact?"

She crossed her arms. "How is all this supposed to work? Like if we want new dining room furniture. Do I buy the table and you buy the chairs? I guess we could go room by room. I'll be responsible for the bedroom set, but you furnish the living room."

They faced each other by his car.

"You're upset," he said. "I'm sorry. I didn't want this to be complicated."

"Well, it *is* complicated. I don't get it. I don't understand the process. What part of it is transactional? Do we keep an inventory of who owns what? How would we handle joint expenses? Do we each have a bank account and then put money into one we share?"

"That could work."

"So we make lists and check enough boxes and then it's fine?" She walked around to her side of the car, needing a barrier between them. "You know what I like about the idea of being married? I like that you don't have to answer any of those questions because you own it all together. The dog, the dining room set. It's easy and I understand it and it's nice. I like that marriage is basically about hope. Hope for the future, for a life together. For always. Do marriages fail? Sure, but couples who aren't married break up as well. I'm not looking for a guarantee, but I am looking for commitment and shared goals. I want someone who will take care of me and who I will take care of, no matter what."

"I want that, too."

"Yeah, right. Until I don't make you breakfast some morning and you decide I'm not trying enough."

He stared at her. "Is that what you think I mean? Ashley, I love you. I want to spend the rest of my life with you because you are the most amazing woman I've ever known. I want to make you happy. I want us to grow together and have a family." He gave her a faint smile. "And maybe a dog."

Which sounded great, but somehow still left her feeling rejected and unsafe.

"I want to get married," she told him, then held up her hand. "Let me finish. I was talking to Bree and she suggested I try to live with the idea of not getting married. That I mentally embrace everything you said. That we would be committed forever, buy a house, start a family, be faithful. We'd figure out the logistics, but we would agree we were going into our next phase with the assumption that it was for the rest of our lives."

Hope brightened his eyes. "Do you think you could do that?"

"I don't know, but here's the thing. If you want me to try to wrap my mind around your way, then you have to try just as hard to embrace what I want. You have to imagine us getting married. Not the wedding—I don't care about that. We can elope, go to City Hall. Whatever. But you and me, married. We have rings and we share a last name. Everything else is the same. The house, the kids, the dog. But we do it married."

He nodded slowly. "That's fair. I'm in. But how do we do

that? See the other side and seriously consider it? Do you want us to talk about it more?"

"God, no," she said, then gave him a smile. "Believe it or not, I don't like fighting with you."

"I don't like us fighting, either." He put his hands on the roof on the car. "What if we send each other five articles on the subject. You send me information on why it's better to be married and I send you five on why a committed relationship is as good or better."

"I like that."

"Me, too. I'll even go you one better." He flashed her a grin. "I'll read a bride magazine."

"How would that help?"

"How would it hurt?" The grin widened. "On the way home we'll stop and buy one of those magazines. I promise to read it cover to cover." His humor faded. "I mean it, Ashley. I want us to figure this out."

She knew he did, just like she knew he loved her. The problem was, she wasn't sure it mattered. They still wanted different things. But at least they were trying.

"One bride magazine for you," she said lightly. "To keep things fair, when we get home, I'll read about Joint Tenants with Rights of Survivorship."

"Then we'll meet in the middle." He circled around the car and put his hands on her shoulders. "When it comes to you, I always want to meet in the middle."

She raised herself onto tiptoes and kissed him. "Me, too."

FIFTEEN

"I'm not usually buzzed during the day," Duane said, lacing his fingers with Mikki's as they strolled back to the hotel after their Everything You Wanted to Know about Merlot class.

"I agree. I'm glad we don't have anything scheduled this afternoon. I want to sober up and drink a lot of water." She laughed. "And my mother will be delighted to hear you're not a day drinker."

"Was she worried?"

"Probably. My mom enjoys looking for things to go wrong. It's just how her brain works."

"You have a positive outlook," he said. "It's nice."

"I'm cheerful. According to my mother, I was a happy kid." She grinned at him. "Of course when she says it, it's an accusation."

"You're an only child?"

"Yes, that's why I wanted two kids. I always wanted a sister or brother." She wrinkled her nose. "My parents fought a lot and because I was the only one around, I was their excuse for arguing. A sibling would've been a nice distraction."

"I'm one of four," Duane confessed. "I'm the youngest and I couldn't wait for my sisters to leave home so I could have Mom and Dad to myself."

"Four kids and three of them girls?" She shook her head. "You were spoiled."

"Constantly."

"Now I know why you're so good with women."

He chuckled. "I do know my way around the gender." He pulled her to a stop on the sidewalk. "Just to be clear, none of this is a line. I mean everything I say to you, Mikki. I'm crazy about you."

They'd been to nearly a half dozen wine classes, had shared a wonderful dinner the night before and slept in separate bedrooms. She was getting to know Duane and the more she knew, the more she liked. Now, as he looked at her with two parts sincerity and one part concern, she knew he was telling the truth.

He pulled her close and lightly kissed her, then took her hand again as they started walking.

Duane was a toucher—much more so than Perry had ever been. Oh, sex had always been good for both of them, but the rest of the time, he hadn't wanted much physical contact.

Duane was different. He was always reaching for her hand or hugging her or stroking her arm. She liked the closeness, the connection. Even when they stopped to chat with someone, he rested his fingers on the small of her back. Like they belonged together.

They paused in front of a gift store window display. He leaned close.

"Yours is better," he whispered.

"You were in my place five seconds. You can't possibly know if my displays are better or not."

"No one has better displays."

She laughed. "You didn't just say that."

"I did."

She met his gaze and tried not to sigh over how good-looking he was and how great she felt in his company.

"What would you be doing now if you weren't with me?" he asked.

She glanced at her watch. "Working. Saturdays are busy. How about you?"

"Thinking about you."

"Oh, come on. Be serious."

"I am serious, but I can give you an alternative answer. I'd work on a monetary policy, then go for a bike ride. Then I'd think about you."

"Our lives are so different."

"I can teach you to ride a bike."

"I know how to ride a bike."

He chuckled. "Just checking. You said before you'd moved your store about seven months ago. Were you in business with Bree and Ashley then, too?"

"No. We just met in December when we all showed up to drool over the store for rent. It was bigger than any of us needed and way too expensive. Bree suggested we lease it together and here we are."

"That was bold."

"It could've been a disaster," she said. "What if we hated each other? But we didn't. We're friends. Every Friday night at sunset we take a bottle of champagne out onto the beach and hang out."

"I made you miss that."

"You were worth it."

He drew her hand to his mouth and lightly kissed her knuckles. "I'm glad you think so. Tell me about Bree and Ashley."

They'd reached the hotel. Rather than go up to their rooms, they found chairs on the patio overlooking the water.

"Bree's amazing," Mikki said. "Independent, beautiful, strong." She paused, thinking about her friend. "She's wise in ways that constantly surprise me, but terrified to let anyone in emotionally. But I trust her, which probably sounds weird."

"Not at all. You know where you stand."

"On the outside, but worming my way in. Ashley's a sweetie. Determined, smart. She's living with a great guy. Well, less great now."

Duane's expression turned questioning.

"Seth isn't interested in getting married. He wants to be committed, buy a house together and have kids, but he's anti-marriage. Ashley's trying to figure out which is more important to her. Getting married or being with the man she loves."

"Tough decision."

"Maybe. Seth is a sure thing. If she leaves him, knowing they love each other, she chances never loving anyone as much. Or being loved as well."

"Is that what you told her?" he asked.

Mikki shook her head. "I told her to dump his ass."

Duane laughed. "I haven't met either of them, but I agree. Marriage is more than a tradition. It's an economic necessity. In societies where there are more married couples, there are fewer children in poverty, and less violence." He smiled at her. "Women bring out men's better angels."

"I didn't know."

"It's true. Children do better with two loving parents, and women have more options when they have a steady partner. Men are happier when they're married. Women are frequently less happy when they're married, statistically speaking, but hopefully, men are working on that one. I can recite actual numbers, but the bottom line is unless Seth can articulate a reasonable argument, he needs to put a ring on it. Otherwise, he's just a jerk."

She smiled at him. "You have a very strong opinion."

"I do. Where do you stand on the marriage front?"

She didn't know how to answer. "Are you asking if I see myself getting married again?"

His gaze was steady. "Yes."

Was it just her or had things gotten awkward?

"I, ah, don't want to spend the rest of my life alone," she said cautiously, wanting to be honest, but not wanting to be seen as needy. Which was an interesting concern considering he'd been the one to bring up the subject.

"What are you thinking?" he asked.

"That I'm suddenly nervous I'll say the wrong thing. No wonder Ashley is having trouble talking to Seth about her feelings. There's some societal assumption that women want to get married and men, what? Have to be caught or tricked? Isn't that incredibly old-fashioned? But women get a symbol of the engagement while men don't. There's no engagement ring for a man."

He grabbed her hand. "Mikki, I'm not trying to set you up. I like you and I wanted to know if you're open to this going somewhere."

Wow. Just wow. Her heart pounded in her chest and she wondered if she was blushing. "I admire your ability to just say it like that."

He looked at her without speaking. She sucked in a breath. "I'm open to this going somewhere, too."

"Good." He leaned close and kissed her. "Now, we're going to change the subject before this gets too awkward."

"An excellent idea."

"You're being ridiculous," Bree said as she began shucking the fresh corn she'd brought.

Harding poured charcoal onto the grill. "You wouldn't have dinner with me at my house. We're not at my house."

They weren't. They were in a park, shaded by trees and flanked by families out for a barbecue on a beautiful summer evening.

"My point is I wasn't going to have dinner with you," she told him.

His smile was knowing. "Obviously, that wasn't your point at all."

"You think you know everything," she grumbled, telling herself she should be annoyed and yet oddly wasn't.

She liked Harding. There, she'd said it. Or at least admitted it to herself. She liked being around him. He was steady and blunt. Characteristics she'd never thought to look for in a man but now found she wanted. Not that they were in a relationship—they weren't. But they were friends and she could deal with that.

"Why were you gone so long?" she asked. "And why are you here now?"

He pulled a bag of marinating chicken pieces from his cooler. "You said you'd make grilled corn salad. It's my favorite."

"Ha ha. Why did you leave LA for so long? You weren't really on tour and doing research the whole time, were you?"

Rather than answer, he lit the charcoal. "The coals will take a while to heat up."

She stared at him. "You're being evasive. You're never evasive. It was a woman. You left because of a woman!" She was both pleased with herself for figuring it out and intrigued. "What went wrong?"

He handed her a bottle of beer. "Nothing. That was the problem. We couldn't get things off the ground."

Her gaze involuntarily dropped to his groin. He groaned.

"Not that. Emotionally. We dated for six months and decided to move in together. It was nice, but not spectacular. I wasn't in love with her."

"Was she in love with you?"

"I don't know. She said the words, but I never believed her."

She sipped her beer. "So you ended things with the high school girlfriend, and this one. Commitment issues?"

"Standards. I want to be seriously in love with everything that goes with it. When that happens, I'll pursue the woman until she gives in or runs me over."

"But not in an illegal, stalkerish way."

He smiled. "Metaphorically. Not literally."

"So you were running away."

The smile disappeared. "I don't run away."

"You left your home to avoid a woman. What would you call it?"

"A strategic change of circumstances."

"So much crap," she told him with a laugh. "What happens this time? Are you going to run away again?"

His gaze locked with hers. "No. I'm home permanently."

She waved her drink. "Don't look at me significantly. I'm nothing to you."

"That's not true."

"Fine, we're friends."

Humor brightened his hazel eyes. "Great. Then go with me to the OAR fundraiser, *friend*."

"You're very determined." She took another drink, then started to tell him "absolutely not" only to find herself inadvertently saying, "All right. But only as friends."

"Who kiss."

"I don't kiss my friends. Your sister and I have never kissed."

"We're boy-girl friends. It's different."

She didn't want to admit he was right, but he was. Their relationship was unlike any other in her life. There was something about him—something that made her wish...

No, she thought firmly. *No wishing, no dreaming, no what-if-ing.*

She set the shucked corn on the plate. Once the coals were hot, she'd quickly grill the ears then cut off the kernels and add them to the salad. With nothing else to do but wait for the barbecue, she sat across from Harding.

"Now that you know I have emotional issues, tell me why you were so upset the other day," he said, watching her carefully.

Not unexpected, she thought. After she'd shown up at his house and had clung to him like a lost toddler, he hadn't asked any questions. But he had to be curious and, knowing him, possibly concerned.

She could lie. She could invent a friend with a sick puppy or a—

"My mother called. She wants to have a signing at the store." Bree waved her beer. "Apparently, people are wondering why she hasn't made an appearance in her daughter's bookstore."

"And she doesn't want to explain she's a heartless bitch?"

He spoke calmly, without a lot of energy, but the words still had impact.

"I wish it was that simple," she admitted. "Her just being mean would be easier for me."

She glanced down at the picnic table. There were several sets of initials carved into the worn surface. She wondered if M.J. + R.Z. were still together.

"When I was twelve I asked her if she regretted having me."

Harding reached across the table and cupped her chin, forcing her to look into his hazel eyes.

"What did she say?"

"That *regret* wasn't the correct word. Having a child wasn't what they'd expected and far more time-consuming." She forced a faint smile. "I took them away from what was important."

"I'm sorry."

"It wasn't news," she told him, not wanting to remember how, at the time, she'd told herself to stay strong. That flinching or crying would distract both of them from the point of the conversation.

"I'd researched boarding schools and had picked two that most appealed to me. I explained that both of them had holiday and summer programs that would keep me busy."

"Translation," he murmured. "You wouldn't be coming home."

"Exactly. My mother was impressed with my thoroughness and used her connections to get me admitted the following September. That was the last time I lived with them."

His brows rose. "What about after high school?"

"They'd moved to the east coast, so I came back here to go to college. I lived in the dorms, went on holidays with friends, or took trips through different programs." She picked up her beer. "I had a wonderful education, saw much of the world and made lots of friends. I was happy."

"Happier than you would have been with them." He studied her. "But always moving. Never going home with the same friend twice in a row. Never duplicating the experience. Not because you get bored, but to keep anyone from getting close."

His words made her stiffen. She consciously relaxed her body. "Stop trying to get in my head. You'll never succeed."

"I can make good guesses. Were they surprised you ended up with Lewis?"

"Yes, but not for the reason you think. My parents thought he was too good for me. I overheard my mother telling him he could do better."

"Did he punch her?"

Bree laughed. "No, but he did say I was the love of his life, which made me feel good. Back then I still believed we had what my parents had—a true love that would consume us. I was wrong."

"You wouldn't be happy with a consuming love. You're too independent and strong."

She was surprised to find she agreed with him. "With the hindsight of a few years, I know you're right. No romantic relationship is going to make up for what happened with my parents. I needed to find my own way and have a relationship separate from them."

"Which didn't happen with Lewis."

"No."

"Has it since?"

She shook her head rather than blurt out the truth. Risk love again? That was never happening. Why would she want to open herself up? Love was for other people—but not for her. She wouldn't let anyone close enough. Fool me once and all that. Not loving was the only thing that kept her safe.

"Love should be a partnership," he said.

"You speak from experience?"

He smiled. "If by experience you mean love gone wrong, then yes. But I see it with other people. My parents have a good partnership. Some of my friends. I want that. Each person strong when the other is weak. Shared goals. Shared values."

"You're an idealist."

"Sometimes. You're a pessimist."

She laughed. "And proud of it." She paused. "Harding, thinking this way doesn't make me sad. I don't have unrealistic expectations and that's better for me. Safer. I see the world as it is, not how it should be."

"I shouldn't have walked again and yet here I am."

"Sitting," she joked, then sighed. "Sorry. Okay, yes, you beat the odds. But that's different. You worked hard, you had great doctors. What does that have to do with not believing in love?"

"But you do believe in love. If you didn't, you wouldn't be running from it so hard."

"You're obsessed with the topic."

"Maybe because I'm falling in love with you."

Bree hadn't seen that coming. She stared at Harding, aware of the sounds of the families playing in the distance, the smell of the charcoal briquettes heating. A plane flew overhead and birds chirped in a nearby tree. Yet, the world reduced itself to this moment and this man.

"Don't," she said, scrambling to her feet. "Don't."

"Fall or admit it?"

"Both."

She folded her arms across her chest as if trying to hold something in, or maybe just to protect herself. Love? *Love?*

"Why would you say something like that to me? We were doing fine and then you had to go and—"

"Ruin things?" he asked, standing. "Bree, you can't be surprised. I've told you I'm crazy about you."

"Not like that. Not with words."

"If you don't believe in love, why do my feelings matter?"

A reasonable question, she thought. And one she couldn't answer.

"They just do."

She grabbed her bag and ran to her car. As she pulled out of the parking lot, she caught sight of Harding standing by the picnic table. Alone and watching her go.

SIXTEEN

More than a week after her weekend away with Duane, Mikki still couldn't stop smiling. They'd had a great time—conversation had been easy, they'd laughed a lot and seemed to agree on most things. Just as thrilling, the sexual chemistry had been a mini-miracle. The more she was around him, the more she liked him—a reality that both thrilled and terrified her. The last guy she'd fallen for had been her ex-husband over twenty years ago. She wasn't sure she remembered how and what to do. But she wouldn't let fear get in the way. She would channel her inner Bree and keep showing up.

She pulled into Perry's driveway. He'd asked if they could talk about Will's upcoming birthday and she'd offered to stop by on her way home from work. He was waiting at the door.

"How was the move?" she asked as she approached the front steps. Perry had moved the weekend she'd been in Monterey.

"More work than the kids expected," he said with a grin, letting her inside.

In the living room, Perry's basic, beige furniture sat uneasily in the charming space.

"I know," he said with an easy grin. "Not the right style."

"Maybe an area rug would help."

"I need to get some new pieces. These were fine at my folks'. Maybe you can give me some ideas."

"Sure. We can go to a few stores, if you'd like. I'll offer suggestions but you'll have to make the final choices. You'll be living here, not me."

His gaze slid to her, then away. "Let's go look at the addition. It's framed and the roof is on."

She followed him into what would be the new master. "This is bigger than I realized. I love the windows."

He showed her the closet and bathroom layout.

"It's perfect," she said, thinking it was a little large for just him. Not that he would stay single forever. Perry was a good man. To be honest, she was a little surprised he'd gone so long without a steady girlfriend.

He led the way into the kitchen. She was surprised to see two place settings at the island. The kids were with her this week, so she knew he wasn't eating with one of them.

"You're having someone over for dinner?" she asked, thinking it was strange he would invite her over when he had a date later.

"No. I made some appetizers for while we talk about Will." He grinned. "I'm going to tempt you with a nice rosé so you'll go along with my plan."

Appetizers? Perry? Weird, but okay. "I'm always up for wine, but you don't like rosé."

"I said that before I'd tried it. I've had a couple and they're nice." He pulled a bottle from the refrigerator. "It's the pink. That's tough to overcome."

"I can see how that would be an issue for a lot of guys."

She took a seat while Perry poured the wine. Then she nearly fell off her chair when he put a tray of very fancy-looking appetizers in front of her.

"Mini crab cakes with crème fraîche," he said. "Mini tarts with seasoned cream cheese and topped with poached shrimp. Last but not least, cucumber-and-dill-stuffed cherry tomatoes."

She looked from the food to him and back. "Did you, ah, make these?"

"I bought the crab cakes and the crème fraîche, but I made the other two."

"But you can't cook like this."

"I've been watching some cooking shows and teaching myself. Sometimes I ask my mom for tips."

All the words were in English, but they didn't make sense. The Perry she'd known had barely been able to scramble eggs and never spent any time in the kitchen.

He sat across from her and smiled. "Help yourself."

She took a couple of each appetizer and bit into the mini tart with shrimp.

"Delicious," she said, hoping she didn't sound too surprised. Perry cooking. Who knew?

"About Will," he said, picking up a stuffed cherry tomato. "I know we talked about me getting him new wheels, but I've changed my mind. I want to take him to a couple of NASCAR races. We'd make a weekend of it."

"Will would love that," she said with a sigh.

"You don't want me to do it?"

"I don't want him to race cars. I know he's a great driver, but when I think about him crashing, it scares me."

Perry watched her without speaking.

"I know," she continued. "I have to let him follow his dreams. Oh, wow. His grandparents are giving him racing lessons. You're taking him to NASCAR. Everyone's gift will be nicer than mine."

"We could share the NASCAR costs if you want. It's a big present, after all."

A nice solution and a generous compromise. "Thank you. I'd like it to be from both of us." She laughed. "As long as I don't have to go."

"You'd be welcome."

"Nothing about it appeals to me." She nibbled on a crab cake.

"We're going to have to be creative for Sydney's birthday. Get her something as fun. Maybe an eco-vacation."

He sipped his wine. "Okay, you can take her on one if you want."

"Really? You don't want to study a rain forest in your downtime?"

"Not this week."

"At least we've solved the issue of Will's big birthday gift. I can cross that off my to-do list. And I'll start thinking about what to get Sydney. It's only three months away. I joke about eco-vacations, but I'm not sure that would make her happy. I'll dwell on it."

She looked around the kitchen. "The previous owners did a nice job on the remodel. I wouldn't change anything in here."

"So you like the house."

"I do. The location is perfect and the original features are so charming. You'll be happy here."

"You could be, too."

She stared at him, not sure what he meant. Was he thinking of asking her if she wanted to buy the house from him? No, that didn't make sense. Why would he—

His smile turned rueful. "I said that wrong."

He shocked the crap out of her by taking her hand in his.

"Mikki, I miss you. I miss *us*. We divorced too hastily and I take the blame for that. I should have realized what I had."

His gaze was steady and direct. "I'd like you to think about us getting back together. I'm still in love with you and I'm hoping you still have feelings for me."

She opened her mouth, then closed it. Honest to God, she didn't have any words beyond the voice in her head screaming "What?"

"You're the reason I bought this house," he continued, his gaze still locked with hers. "I saw it and immediately thought of you. We could be happy here. Start over, a little older and wiser."

She pulled her hand from his. "I'm seeing someone."

She hadn't intended to blurt that out, but was glad she had.

Perry nodded slowly. "Yeah, my mom mentioned there was a guy. The one with the Aston Martin?"

The wave of guilt surprised her. She found herself immediately wanting to backpedal or apologize, which was ridiculous. She and Perry had been divorced for three years. She was allowed to date if she wanted. She could have gotten married fifteen times over.

"Yes, he's the one I've been going out with," she said quietly.

"Is it serious?"

"I don't know. We haven't been dating all that long."

She wasn't sure what *serious* even meant when it came to her dating life. Or maybe she simply couldn't think. The shock was too great. Feelings for her? What did that mean? No, wait. She didn't want clarification. Just thinking about those words made her uncomfortable.

She waved her hand. "You're not still in love with me."

"How would you know?"

She ignored the question. "We're friends. Good friends. We get along, we co-parent. This works for us, certainly better than our marriage ever did."

He exhaled slowly. "I wasn't supportive enough. I think about that a lot. I should have gone to London with you. We could have had a great time together. I've been working on changing, to be a better husband."

"You were a good husband. I don't want you to think otherwise. We just didn't grow in the same direction. We wanted different things."

"What if we could want the same thing?"

What was she supposed to say to that?

"We had our chance. We had it and we screwed it up." She wished he'd never said anything about feelings. "Don't do this.

We can't change the past and I don't want to change where we are right now. We're in a good place. That's enough."

"We can influence the future. I'm not giving up on us."

"There is no us. Not anymore."

He surprised her by smiling. "We'll see. You and I are good together. I think there's still a connection. Maybe I'm wrong, but I want one more shot."

Once again, the man left her speechless. "I don't even know what to say."

"You didn't say no. That's a start."

"The wedding colors are lavender and sage," Seth said as he pulled into the church parking lot to attend yet another wedding.

Ashley glanced at him. "How would you know that?"

"The invitation. It was lavender and sage."

"How can you remember that?"

He flashed her a grin. "Hey, I've been doing my reading and now I'm a wedding expert. Ask me anything."

"Who chooses lavender and sage as their colors? I don't think they look very good together."

He leaned close and kissed her. "I guess we're about to test your theory."

She sighed. "Seth, you know considering marriage is a lot more than knowing wedding colors, right?"

His humor faded. "Yes. It's about whether or not I see us having everything we want, while married, rather than not married. The wedding is just window dressing." His smile returned. "But it's still fun to talk about lavender and sage as their colors."

He got out of the car. She hesitated before following, telling herself this was his way of showing he was trying. He'd already read a half dozen bride magazines and all the articles she'd sent him. In return, she'd started on a book that explained why marriage was a bad idea and read the articles he'd sent her. Earlier today they'd gone to a couple of open houses to start learning about the local real estate market.

Except for disagreeing on whether or not to marry, they were in a good place, she thought, slipping her hand into his.

They walked into the back of the church and saw the bridesmaids lined up for a picture. Sure enough, all their dresses were pale lavender. As she and Seth found seats, she saw the best man—in a black tux with a sage vest and bow tie.

"Told you so," Seth whispered in her ear. "I, for one, can't wait to see how they've decorated for the reception. I wonder if they'll use chargers. I'd go with silver rather than gold. Better with the wedding colors."

She held in a laugh. "Now you're just scaring me."

Two hours later the guests were in a banquet room, waiting on the bride and groom. Servers circulated with white and red wine, along with the wedding's signature drink: a lavender-sage sling.

"You were right," Ashley said, taking one.

Seth nodded toward the round tables, where silver chargers sat under white dishes topped with sage-colored favor boxes, each decorated with a sprig of lavender.

"They went with chair covers. They're like three fifty each and they have at least two hundred guests. It's a dumb way to spend seven hundred dollars."

Ashley looked at the chair covers. "I didn't even notice."

"This is my thing now. Want to talk about the centerpieces?"

Before she could answer, Krissy and Karl joined them. Krissy hugged them both before holding out her left hand.

"Look! We got engaged."

Ashley was unprepared for the stab of envy that shot through her. Krissy and Karl? She didn't know things were that serious.

"Did you? That's wonderful. Congratulations." She admired

the ring, a princess-cut diamond surrounded by smaller stones. "It's so beautiful."

Karl shifted from foot to foot. "It reminded me of her when I saw it."

Seth patted the other man on the back. "Good for you. Always go with your gut when it comes to jewelry."

"How did it happen?" Ashley asked, knowing that was the next question.

"He took me to dinner at our favorite place," Krissy said happily. "I had no idea what he was going to do."

As she detailed the surprise proposal and how the entire restaurant staff had been in on it, Ashley told herself she was fine. The knotting sensation in her stomach was no big deal and she was a nice enough person to be genuinely happy for her friend. Their engagement had nothing to do with her.

The problem was, she didn't quite believe herself.

She nodded in all the right places and after congratulating her friend again said, "I was just heading to the restroom. If you'll excuse me."

"Oh, I'll come with you," Krissy said, linking arms with her. "Be right back, boys."

So much for a second by herself.

Ashley handed Seth her drink and went off with Krissy. They made it halfway across the room before Krissy turned to her.

"How about you two? Any idea when Seth's going to pop the question?"

Ashley told herself that this was the perfect opportunity to practice her half of her deal with him. "We're not getting married. It's not our thing."

Krissy came to a stop and stared at her, openmouthed. "You're breaking up?"

Her voice was loud enough to carry to the far reaches of the room. Several couples turned to look at them.

"We're not breaking up," Ashley said quietly. "We're in love and we're happy."

"So why aren't you engaged?"

"We're not interested in getting married."

Krissy stared at her blankly. "Why not?"

"We don't need to be married to know that we want to spend the rest of our lives together. We're committed to each other in every way possible. We're starting to look at houses."

Ashley was proud of herself for getting through the speech. She wasn't a hundred percent on board with the idea but she could possibly see herself getting there. One day. Maybe.

"But you want to get married," Krissy told her. "How can you not? It's what happens next. You get married and have kids."

"We don't need to be married to have children."

"No, but I don't understand. What's really happening here?"

She was spared from answering when Seth and Karl showed up.

"I thought you two were going to the bathroom," Karl said.

Krissy stared at Ashley for a minute, then offered a fake smile.

"It's okay. I won't say anything." Her gaze slid to Seth, as if she suspected he was the problem. "We'll see you two around."

She took Karl's arm and led him away. Seth frowned.

"That was weird. What happened?"

Ashley looked away from her friend. "Nothing. We're fine. Everything is perfectly fine."

"You're in a mood," Rita grumbled before turning away and pushing a cart of books toward the center of the store. "Keep this up and I'll ask for a raise."

Bree watched the older woman stalk away and knew this time Rita's snippiness was her own fault. She *had* been in a mood for days. She also hadn't been sleeping, couldn't eat and no matter how many miles she ran or biked, she couldn't stop thinking about Harding. Or rather what he'd said.

I'm falling in love with you.

Love. She didn't believe in love or trust people who said they loved her. Why couldn't he just want to fuck her? She'd still say no, but at least desire made sense to her. She could trust wanting, but love?

"Asshole," she muttered before doing her best to focus on work.

She helped customers, rang up purchases, rearranged displays and, after the store closed, dusted every single shelf. It was nearly ten by the time she admitted that she was avoiding going home because at least at work, she could stay busy enough to pretend she wasn't thinking about Harding. Plus the whole lack of sleep thing.

I'm falling in love with you.

The words echoed in her brain, making her feel raw and exposed. Or worse, vulnerable. She didn't do vulnerable—not ever. No one got inside. She never shared her heart or put herself at emotional risk. She'd spent the first twelve years of her life begging for her parents' attention and the last two of her marriage knowing she'd been played. Love was for suckers and she was never going to be a sucker again.

She checked all the doors, set the alarm, then let herself out the back. On her way to her car she saw the lights on above the surf shop, where Sad Guy had an apartment.

Before she knew what she was doing, she found herself walking purposefully toward his building. While she had no interest in the man, he had said he wanted to have sex with her one more time, so he could get over her. Fine. If he wanted to have sex, she'd have sex with him. She would give herself to another man.

The coldhearted act of betrayal would destroy whatever was going on between her and Harding. He would be horrified and realize she was an awful person and then he would go away. Problem solved.

She reached the side door and rang the bell. After a few seconds his voice came over the small speaker by the bell.

"Yes?"

"It's Bree. You said you wanted one last time. I'm here."

Seconds later he buzzed her in.

Sad Guy was waiting at the top of the stairs. She did her best not to look at him as she walked into his large, airy apartment. She'd been here a couple of times last January. The furniture was the same—a beachy combination of palm prints and hardwoods. She dropped her purse onto a side table and toed out of her shoes.

"I don't understand," he said.

She forced herself to look at him. "I'm here for sex. That's what you said you wanted. One last time."

Hope blossomed in his eyes. Hope that kicked her like a son of a bitch.

"This doesn't mean anything," she told him.

He surprised her by smiling. "With you, it never does."

He moved toward her. Bree braced herself for his kiss and his touch. She had to do this—if she slept with Sad Guy, then she won. She wasn't sure what, exactly, but she knew the victory was there, just out of reach.

He pulled her close, pressing his body against hers. He was already hard and pushed his erection against her belly. Hot breath scalded her cheek. He brushed his mouth against hers.

"You smell good," he whispered, continuing to grind his dick against her. "I've been thinking about this for so long."

Bile rose in her throat. She ignored the sensation and deliberately wrapped her arms around him before parting her lips. Only the second his tongue touched her, she knew she couldn't do it. Worse, she was going to throw up.

She pushed him away and darted for the half bath. She barely had time to jerk up the toilet seat before she vomited a bunch of fluid and the remains of the half sandwich that had passed for dinner.

She dropped to her knees as she waited to see if there was more. Her stomach heaved a couple of times, then quieted. She tried to slow her breathing and fought against the burning in her eyes. Her life was already shit—no way she was going to cry. She'd given up on tears long ago.

After standing, she rinsed out her mouth, then faced Sad Guy. He stood in the doorway, watching her warily.

"Let's do this," she said, reaching for the hem of her shirt.

"Jesus, Bree, what the hell?" He took a step back, his expression sad and confused. "We're not doing it. You were so disgusted, you threw up."

"That's not why. My stomach has nothing to do with you. I'm ready."

He stared at her for a long time, then shook his head. "You should go."

She didn't want to be here, certainly didn't want to have sex with him, yet his words hit her like a slap. Her flinch was involuntary and she would have given anything to stand there strong and defiant, but she had nothing left inside and crumbling in front of him wasn't an option.

She hurried to the living room, grabbed her shoes and her purse and ran down the stairs. When she was out in the quiet night, she breathed in the salt air and told herself she would be fine. She was always fine. This was a little bump in the road—nothing more.

Once in her car she found herself heading in the opposite direction of home. As she got closer to Harding's house, she told herself it was too late for her to show up, that he might be asleep. Only she knew he was a night owl who rarely was in bed before midnight.

Maybe he was with someone. Maybe some fan had come by, and right this second he was screwing her brains out. They were both naked and so much for falling in love with her. She couldn't depend on him—she'd always known that. He was—

"Stop!"

She screamed the word into the car, then gripped the steering wheel tighter. She was slipping over the edge—she could feel it. The broken places she'd thought were healed had all come apart. Lewis had played her and maybe Harding was doing the same.

Only she knew he wasn't and if he wasn't, then what if he was telling the truth and he did care about her? How was she supposed to survive that?

She pulled up in front of his house and turned off the engine. Sure enough, lights were on, spilling into the darkness. She sat in her car for several minutes before surrendering to the inevitable. She walked up to the front door and knocked.

Harding answered, wearing jeans and a T-shirt. His feet were bare, his hair mussed and his smile—her heart lurched—his smile was a little crooked and all welcoming.

"Hey, you," he said, then stepped back to invite her in. "I haven't seen you in a long time. I've missed you."

She walked inside and glared at him. "That's it? I haven't spoken to you in days. I won't take your calls or answer your texts. I've totally ghosted you and all you can say is you missed me?"

He shoved his hands in his front pockets and shrugged. "I did miss you."

"I slept with Sad Guy."

She spoke defiantly, glaring at him, braced for the accusations and hurt. He was going to explode, then toss her out.

Harding didn't speak. She watched the smile fade, but otherwise, she had no idea what he was thinking.

"Just now," she clarified. "I drove over here from there."

He started for the kitchen. "You want water? Or something stronger?"

She followed him, waiting for the onslaught. But instead

of screaming, he pulled a square-ish bottle from a cabinet and poured liquid into two glasses. He handed her one.

"One of my favorites," he told her. "Casa Noble. This is their Anejo tequila. They age it for two years in French white oak barrels."

She took the glass, watching him warily. "You sound like Mikki's lectures on champagne."

He smiled. "I like Mikki."

He motioned to the family room, as if they were going to sit down.

"What's wrong with you?" she asked, her voice more shrill than she would like. "Why aren't you angry? Why aren't you yelling at me or throwing me out?"

"Because?"

"Because I fucking slept with another man. You're supposed to be in love with me. My doing it with someone else should matter."

"It does." He stared into his glass. "I'm surprised and hurt. Obviously, me telling you how I felt set you off. I'm not saying it's my fault. Your actions are your responsibility. But I knew you'd have a reaction. I wasn't expecting this one." His smile returned, but this time it was sad. "My bad."

"That's it?"

"What more do you want? I'm not happy, Bree. Is that what you need to hear? I'm not. But we're not dating, let alone exclusive. You've made it clear you're not interested in a relationship with me and while I don't believe you, I can't say you haven't been honest. Can we go sit down?"

Stunned by his words, she followed him to the family room. She huddled in a corner of the sofa, while he sat in a club chair, facing her.

"Why did you tell me?" he asked, his voice still surprisingly calm. "I don't believe you're cruel, so it wasn't to hurt me."

"I wanted you to be disappointed," she admitted, putting

her glass on the end table next to her. "I wanted you to send me away."

"So I'd be the one to end things," he said, more to himself than her. "Interesting. And by doing that, I'd reinforce your belief that you can't trust anyone and it's not safe to give your heart."

"I really don't want to talk about that." She sipped the tequila. It was smoky with a hint of spice. "This is nice."

They looked at each other. She didn't see any anger, only hurt in his beautiful eyes. He wasn't going to scream and he wasn't going to accuse, but she'd cut him.

She told herself to leave, that this was better. Eventually, he would see that she wasn't worth it, that being with her would be a disaster. He would understand that she could never love him back and—

"I couldn't do it," she blurted, then returned the glass to the table and wrapped her arms around her midsection. "I tried. I went there to do it. He'd come by a few weeks ago, asking for one last time so he could get over me, so I knew he was a sure thing."

Harding's mouth turned up at one corner. "How many guys aren't sure things?"

"Not many. But this was different. This wasn't about getting laid. I didn't want him touching me or kissing me and then…" She swallowed hard. "I threw up. It was awful. I tried to have sex with Sad Guy and I puked out my guts, then he told me to leave."

Her eyes burned and her chest ached, but she refused to deal with any of it.

"I guess he was less of a sure thing than I thought."

Harding's lips twitched. She glared at him. "Are you laughing at me?"

He put down his drink and stood, then walked to her and drew her to her feet.

"I'm happy," he said, pulling her close. "Really, really happy."

She shoved at his chest, trying to push him away. As he stepped back, she lunged forward and hung on to him.

"That's incredibly stupid," she muttered into his chest. "How can you be happy?"

"You care about me."

"What?" The word came out as a yelp. This time she did step back so she could glare at him. "I don't."

He grinned. "You so do. Otherwise, why bother with Sad Guy? You care enough to work really hard to mess it all up. Which, by the way, you did with incredible style. Points to you."

The realization that he was telling the truth nearly sent her to her knees. No and just no. Care? She didn't care. She wouldn't let herself.

"I don't like you at all," she insisted. "You're not my type."

"Bree, I'm your fantasy. Admit it. Charming, good-looking, strong, sensitive. I'm pretty much everything you've ever wanted."

She took a step back. "This is you trying to make me feel better?"

His smile faded. "Sorry. You're right. So let's deal with the situation at hand. You like me and we both know I'm crazy about you. Stop doing dumb shit and I won't tell you I love you again. Not until you're ready to hear it."

"I'll never be ready."

She thought he'd take offense, but he only smiled. "I can live with that."

"No! Go find someone less broken."

"We're all broken and your breaks fit mine."

"You don't have any." She glared at him. "Why can't you get mad at me?"

"I can, just not over this."

"What if I'd slept with him?"

"You didn't."

"Answer the question!"

He smiled. "What if I had?"

She looked around for something heavy to throw at his head. "You make me insane."

"I know it's hard when I'm reasonable. You're going to have to learn to live with that."

She wanted to tell him she didn't have to learn to live with anything. That he was nothing to her and whatever he thought they had, he was wrong. Only instead of screaming or finding a lamp to toss, she walked up to him and wrapped her arms around him again.

"Hold me," she whispered.

"Always. For as long as you need."

"I wish that were true."

He pulled her tightly against him and rested his head against hers. "I keep showing up, Bree. At some point I'm hoping you'll start to notice that."

"We're not having sex."

He chuckled. "I agree. But soon. And until then, I'm just going to hang on."

She wouldn't trust him—that was too big of a risk. But just for tonight she was willing to pretend that in the end, it was all going to be fine.

SEVENTEEN

"Your mood is worse than Bree's," Mikki's mother announced. "What is wrong with you two girls?"

Mikki wanted to point out that as she was closer to forty than thirty-nine, perhaps the word *girl* didn't apply. She wasn't sure what was up with Bree—her friend had been avoiding both her and Ashley—but she knew what was wrong with herself.

She was pissed. The more she thought about what Perry had said, the more pissed she got. How dare he interrupt her suddenly going in the right direction life with a harebrained idea of them getting back together? They were divorced. Done. D.O.N.E.

Sure, they were friends and she liked his company. They did well together as parents and he made her laugh. She could trust him with things like car problems. He had grown and changed, which was nice, but no reason to get back together.

Mikki needed to talk to someone and wasn't sure who to trust. Certainly not her mother-in-law who hadn't told her about Perry's new house and had told him about Duane. Her nonwork friends had all known her while she'd been married and had gone through the divorce with her, so she wasn't sure she wanted to tell them what he'd said. As for Ashley and Bree, sometimes she wasn't sure where they stood on the friendship scale. They worked together and hung out a little. They'd only known her as a single woman and—

"Fine," her mother said, her lips pursed. "If you don't want to talk, fine. I'm only the person who gave birth to you."

Mikki brushed off the teapot she'd just unpacked and set it on the counter. "I'm sorry, Mom. I have a lot on my mind."

Rita waited expectantly. Mikki glanced around to make sure no one was nearby. But the store wasn't open and the staff hadn't arrived.

"It's Perry," she began.

"He's getting married!" Her mother tsked. "Is she still in her twenties? Dear Lord, tell me she's older than Sydney."

"What? No, he's not getting married. Not exactly."

"Is he gay? After all this time? I never thought he was, but these days people surprise you."

Mikki gave a strangled laugh. "He's not gay. He wants to…" She tried to find the right words. "Perry says he's still in love with me. I'm the reason he bought the house and he wants us to get back together."

It was rare to see her mother speechless and under other circumstances, she would enjoy the moment. But right now she found herself anxiously waiting for the other woman's comments, which was so strange. Her mother telling her what to do rarely went well.

"That's ridiculous," her mother told her. "Get back together? It's too late. You two had your chance and now it's over and you've both moved on. I would never have gotten back together with your father. We had a terrible marriage and I was well rid of him."

Mikki tried not to wince. "Mom, we've talked about this. He's my father and it makes me uncomfortable when you say bad stuff about him."

"So I'm supposed to suffer in silence? All those fights, all those times he was distant? He would go weeks without talking."

Um, not exactly, Mikki thought, what with the daily fights. But she didn't say that. There was no point.

"You can't go back. Everything is different now." Her mother shook her head. "Still in love with you. Idiot. He's lazy. He doesn't want to bother finding someone new. Getting back with you is easy. You take good care of him and he gets the life of Riley. Well, I say not happening."

Mikki told herself that her mother meant well. In a way, Rita was defending her, if one ignored the whole "He's only interested in you because he's lazy and you bake a good pot roast."

"Did you tell him about Duane?" her mother asked.

"I did and he said he already knew."

"Lorraine told him."

"She is his mother."

"Still, she works for you. What happened to loyalty? I'm disappointed in Perry. He should stand up and be his own man. He snaps his fingers and expects you to come running?"

"He didn't snap his fingers."

"He was always entitled. He always wanted to do what he wanted to do, with no thought about you or the children."

Mikki wished she hadn't said anything. As usual, her mother's advice made her want to do the exact opposite. Not flattering, but true.

"Remember the fights you had about the Dodgers tickets?" Rita asked.

"Mom, that was a long time ago."

"He insisted on expensive season tickets, even though you had babies to raise. Then he got upset when you didn't drop everything to go to the games with him, week after week, even though you'd told him you didn't like baseball. Remember how he would go with his friends? Every home game he would leave you with the house and children."

"I remember," Mikki said dutifully. "But he stopped getting the tickets a few years before the divorce so we could spend more time together."

"But you didn't."

No, they hadn't. She tried to remember why not. Had that been right when she'd bought the business? Had she been the one gone all the time? Looking back, she wondered why he'd sold the tickets. He'd always loved going to the games. He'd been a Dodgers fan since he was a kid. Had he been reaching out to her and had she not noticed?

Ack! That didn't matter, she reminded herself. As her mother had said, however much she hated to agree with her, the past was the past.

"Mom, it's okay. We're not getting back together. It was just a strange thing for him to say."

Rita looked doubtful. "You never could deny that boy anything. Remember how you quit community college to work in the family business? Remember how Perry said no to another baby? You have a good head for business, Mikki, but when it comes to Perry, you go where the wind blows. If Perry wants to get back together, be careful. There's something about that man that makes it hard for you to say no."

An unexpectedly perceptive comment, Mikki thought, stunned and more than a little unsettled by her mother's words.

"I'll be careful," she promised.

Rita didn't look convinced.

Ten hours later Mikki was still mulling. She walked to her storeroom and opened the refrigerator. It was her turn to provide champagne. Originally, she'd decided on a Billecart-Salmon Brut Rosé Champagne, but the beautiful color reminded her a little too much of her evening with Perry. She would save that for another Friday night.

Instead, she reached for a lovely bottle of Tattinger Brut La Francaise Champagne. Ladies Know Wine said the emphasis on the chardonnay gave it wonderful structure and a ten-plus on drinkability. Mikki intended to have her full share this evening.

Forty minutes before sunset she took glasses and her blanket to the front of the store. Ashley was waiting there, a blanket over her shoulder and a large, square tote bag in her hand.

"I brought food," she said sheepishly. "I know we don't normally eat while we enjoy the sunset, but tonight just seemed like we should… I don't know. Indulge."

Mikki took in the shadows under her eyes. "You okay?"

"Mostly."

Bree joined them, holding a bottle of Veuve Clicquot. She waved it.

"You told me to always have extra on hand. I listened."

"But it's my turn," Mikki said, displaying her bottle.

"She thinks we're going to need more than one," Ashley pointed out.

Mikki thought about Ashley's silence and Bree's snapping and her own hellish few days.

"You're probably right. I should have thought of that myself."

They walked out onto the sand and found an empty area where they could spread out their blankets. Mikki sat in the middle and opened the Tattinger while Ashley unpacked a cheese plate, two kinds of crackers, sliced melon, a tray of cured meats and a box of cannolis.

"I'm suddenly starving," Bree murmured.

Mikki filled each of their glasses. "Happy Friday, everyone."

"Happy Friday."

Mikki stared at her glass. "So who wants to go first?"

"What do you mean?" Bree asked, putting a piece of brie on a cracker.

"We're all obviously dealing with a bunch o' crap," Mikki said lightly. "Extra liquor, food. This is not our normal sunset watching."

Bree looked out at the water. "I'm fine."

"You're such a liar."

One corner of Bree's mouth turned up.

Mikki reached for one of the plates Ashley had thoughtfully

provided and added melon, a couple of slices of salami, along with cheese.

"I'll go," Ashley said, then chugged about half her champagne. "I took your advice, Bree."

"That might not be a good idea," Bree murmured, looking at her. "I'm deeply flawed."

"Maybe, but you were right about Seth. We're trying to see the marriage thing from each other's point of view. Seth has been reading bridal magazines and articles on why the institution is so important to society. We went to a wedding last weekend and he knew about chair cover rentals and even guessed the colors based on the invitation."

Mikki heard the sadness in her voice. "But?" she asked gently.

Ashley blinked several times as if holding back tears. "I don't care about the wedding—I care about being married. A friend of mine got engaged unexpectedly, and it hit me really hard. She was happy and she had a ring and Karl loves her and wants to marry her."

"Seth loves you, too," Mikki said, thinking Ashley's boyfriend was an idiot. They were together and in love—he needed to cough up a proposal.

"She asked when we were going to take the next step," Ashley continued. "I told her it wasn't for us. I got all the words out and I really tried, but I felt uncomfortable and she freaked out and I was just so sad after."

She turned to them. "I just want Seth to marry me. I don't know how to be any other way."

"So you're breaking up?" Bree asked bluntly.

"What? No. I love him. He's a really good guy. He's trying and we looked at houses and I can see us together for the rest of our lives. He'll be a great dad. He's funny and patient and he pays attention to details."

"Maybe he'll change his mind," Mikki offered hopefully.

"Maybe. I just don't know how to get over this marriage thing."

"Give yourself more time," Bree told her.

Ashley nodded. "You're right. The articles he's sent me are interesting and I do get his point. If half of marriages end in divorce, why am I so determined to start something that will probably fail?"

"Now you sound like my mother," Mikki said. "Do you really want to go there?"

Ashley managed a faint smile before finishing her champagne and refilling her glass. "Anyway, that's me. Both in love with Seth and sad." She reached for a piece of cheese. "Let's talk about someone else."

Mikki looked at Bree. "You go. What's the problem?"

Bree looked out at the ocean again. "I might be considering the possibility of dating Harding."

Mikki looked at Ashley, who appeared as confused as Mikki felt.

"You're already dating him."

Bree glared at her. "I'm not. We haven't been out. I don't date and I certainly haven't been dating him. I don't do relationships."

"But you go to lunch and you surf together and you had dinner at the park the other night." Ashley frowned. "Isn't that dating?"

"No. It's something else."

In many ways Mikki admired Bree, but she had to admit her friend was a little twisted. "So you've been hanging out, not dating, but now you might start dating?"

"Maybe. I haven't decided."

Mikki nibbled on a piece of gouda. "And that decision is noteworthy enough to require an extra bottle of champagne?"

"Yes."

"But you like Harding," Mikki said. "And he obviously adores you."

"I don't want to talk about that."

Ashley exchanged another confused look with Mikki.

"But you're now going to start dating him?" she asked, sounding doubtful. "Does my brother know you're this weird?"

"I've told him I have issues."

"Is that what we're calling it?" Mikki asked under her breath.

Bree shot her a glare. "Hey, I can hear you."

"You're sitting right next to me. Of course you can hear me."

Bree finished her champagne and filled her glass. "This is why I hate relationships. They're so... So..."

"Relationship like?" Mikki asked.

"You think you're funny but you're not."

Mikki put her arm around Bree. "Oh, but I am. Every single day. It's a thing. Admire it or not, but it exists."

Bree sighed. "I'm not good at being with someone. I don't like it."

"You don't trust it," Ashley said.

Bree scooted back and stared at her. "I didn't say that."

"You don't have to. You hold back, emotionally. In some ways you're the most open person I know. It's all just out there. But you don't let anyone in because you were hurt so much. It's safe to trust Harding, though. He's a good guy."

"I'm changing the subject," Bree said, looking at Mikki. "So what's your problem?" She paused. "That came out more harshly than I expected."

Mikki drank more champagne. "I know what you meant. You just want us to stop talking about you." She thought about her week. "I can get both of you to stop thinking about your own problems in one sentence."

Ashley and Bree leaned forward to look at each other. They both shook their heads.

"Not happening," Ashley said.

Mikki eyed the cannoli, which she knew would go right to

her thighs. She would wait, she told herself. Then just eat one. Or maybe two.

"Perry's still in love with me and wants to get back together."

"What?"

"He said that?"

Mikki drank more champagne. "Told you so."

Bree shifted so she could face Mikki. "He wants to get back together?"

Mikki's smugness faded as emotions flooded her. "I couldn't believe it," she admitted. "I was at his place to see the addition and he told me he bought the house because he knew I'd like it. He talked about how much he's changed and how great we were and how he was still in love with me."

"But you're dating Duane," Bree said. "You like Duane."

"That's what I told him." Her chest tightened. "We're done. It's been three years and I don't think about us getting back together. But now he's said it and I can't forget it and I made the hideous mistake of talking to my mother, who reminded me that when it comes to Perry I always give in and I don't want to."

"So don't."

"I won't," Mikki said firmly. "I mean, why would I want to go back to what we had?"

"It would be different." Bree reached for a cannoli. "You said he'd changed. He knows about wine now. And you do get along really well with the kids and all."

"You're not helping. I don't want to get back together with him."

Bree didn't look convinced. "If that were true, why is this a problem? You tell him no and move on." She looked at Ashley. "You're quiet."

Ashley sighed. "It's nice. He wants to marry you twice. I can't get Seth to do it even once."

Mikki hugged her. "I'm sorry. I shouldn't have said anything."

"No, it's fine. I mean, you can't not talk about your life because of me." Tears pooled in her eyes. "I'm okay."

"Yeah, we all see that," Bree said drily.

"I will be okay," Ashley amended. "Eventually. For what it's worth, I say Perry deserves another chance. You didn't break up because you hated each other. You have a lot in common. You gave him close to twenty years of your life. Shouldn't you take a little time to be sure you're doing the right thing?"

A sentiment Mikki hadn't been expecting. "But we're divorced."

"People get remarried all the time."

"But I like Duane and I'm not in love with Perry."

"Maybe you could be again. I'm just saying, isn't your history worth something?"

Mikki rubbed her forehead. "You shock me."

"I know. I try to mix things up."

Bree shrugged. "I don't have any advice. I can argue either side. Why didn't you date for nearly three years after the divorce? Maybe you were waiting for Perry to come to his senses."

"No. That's not it at all. Duane. Why do I have to keep saying his name? I like him. I want to have sex with him. Those are not the feelings of a woman still in love with her ex-husband."

What was wrong with everyone? First, her mother telling her she couldn't stand up to Perry, now Bree and Ashley taking his side.

"We're changing the subject," she announced. "Right this second. Talk about something else."

Bree busied herself opening the second bottle of champagne while Ashley ate a cannoli.

When their glasses were refilled, Mikki stared out at the sunset. "I hear the Dodgers are having a good year."

Her friends laughed.

"I hear that, too," Bree said. "And let's toast to that."

★ ★ ★

"You okay?" Seth asked Saturday at breakfast.

Ashley smiled wanly. "Too much champagne."

She and her friends had finished the two bottles and had gone back to the store for a third. Seth had to pick her up, which meant he would also have to take her to work to get her car.

His gaze lingered on her face. "Is that all? Or has something been bothering you all week?"

She did her best not to look guilty or defensive. The encounter with Krissy haunted her and even as she told herself not to be ridiculous, she couldn't shake her sense of unease.

"My parents are coming into town," she said.

One eyebrow rose. "Yes, I know. Honey, I get along great with your parents. Don't worry."

"I know. It's not that." She picked up her coffee, then set it down. "I just don't want to tell them what we're doing."

"Living together? They know that."

"No, the whole *I'll consider not getting married and you'll think about getting married.* I don't want to talk about that with them. If they know how you feel, they'll probably get mad at you and…"

She paused, not sure what her parents would think. Would they tell her to cut and run or would they encourage her to hang in there? She honestly didn't know.

"It's not anything I want to deal with right now."

Seth leaned toward her. "Are you upset that Krissy's engaged?"

"What? No." She gave what she hoped was a genuine laugh. "I'm happy for her. I'm not sure about getting engaged to Karl because hey, Karl, but if that makes her happy, then good for them."

His gaze was steady. "You sure?"

"Absolutely. I'm still finding my way with the whole *let's not get married* thing and I don't want to drag my parents into the conversation." She wished she'd never said anything, but she was stuck now. "Can we please not discuss it?"

"Sure. I hadn't planned to bring it up." He reached across the table and touched her hand. "You're sure you're okay otherwise?"

"Yes. Positive."

A lie, but hey, it was early and she had a hangover. At this moment truth was way too much to expect.

"You know I love you," he said. "Right?"

This time her smile was genuine. "I do know that, Seth. You love me a lot. And later you're going to drive me to work because of the champagne thing."

Some of his worry faded. "Happy to do it. You're my best girl and I'm the very accommodating significant other."

Not the fiancé, she thought sadly. Not the husband. The significant other. The life partner. The man who didn't want to marry her.

EIGHTEEN

Mikki opened her front door to find her mother-in-law on her porch. Odd, considering they would see each other in a couple of hours at work.

"Lorraine," she said, stepping back to let the older woman inside. "What's up?"

"I wanted to talk to you privately."

Mikki didn't like the sound of that. She stopped in the middle of the living room but didn't ask her mother-in-law to sit down.

Lorraine gave her a tentative smile. "About Perry. He mentioned he'd had a talk with you and I thought—"

"He what?" Mikki's voice was a shriek. Perry had told his mother he was still in love with her?

"I know, I know. It's awkward. That's why I wanted to stop by. So we could come to an understanding." Lorraine patted her arm. "It would be wonderful if you two could find your way back together. You were always so happy."

Holy crap, this was *not* happening. "You mean up until we got a divorce." Mikki told herself to stay calm. "We're not having this conversation. You've always been good to me and wonderful with the children and I love you, but no. This isn't your business and you don't get to have an opinion. At least not one you share with me. Perry and I have made our divorce work. That should be celebrated. But that's all it is. A successful divorce."

Lorraine sighed. "But if you could just give him a chance. He's changed so much and it's all for you. He loves you, Mikki."

"Stop! Just stop. I'm not kidding. You need to stay out of this. You don't have the right to push me on anything when it comes to Perry. Can you understand that?" The last thing she needed was her mother-in-law messing in her personal life.

"I know you're right. I just can't help thinking you were too hasty—"

Mikki stepped back. "What are you doing? Do you hear anything I'm saying?"

Her mother-in-law grimaced. "You're right. I'm sorry. I just wanted you to know that I know. I won't say anything to Rita, and we don't need to talk about this again." She paused. "Unless you need someone to listen. I could do that."

"Thank you, but again, no."

"You're angry."

"I'm not happy."

"I've made a mess of things."

"Actually, that was Perry, but you didn't help."

Lorraine nodded. "I'll see you at work." She paused.

Mikki couldn't tell if she was going to make another run at saying she and Perry should get back together or if she would leave it alone. Fury boiled inside her but screaming at Lorraine wouldn't help the situation, and she really didn't want to fight with the older woman.

Fortunately, Lorraine only gave her a slight smile before retreating. Mikki called out a goodbye, closed the door, then leaned against it.

"Perry told his mother?"

How could he? He knew Lorraine worked for her. They saw each other nearly every day, if not at the store, then at one another's houses. The whole family frequently had dinner together.

What if she said something to the kids? What if Perry did?

Mikki groaned, then grabbed her bag and headed for the

garage. Twenty minutes later she parked in front of the equipment rental building and stalked into Perry's office. She found him on the phone.

He took one look at her, then told the person on the other end that he would call him back.

"Your mother came to see me," she said as soon as the receiver rested in the cradle. "Your *mother*. She thinks it's wonderful that you're still in love with me and made it clear she thinks we should absolutely get back together. It was peachy keen."

Perry winced. "I'm sorry."

"Sorry? You told your *mother*." She belatedly remembered she'd also told her own mother, but then reminded herself that was different. Rita wouldn't say anything to anyone and she certainly wasn't pushing for a reconciliation.

"I'll talk to her." Perry stood. "She won't discuss it again."

"Like I believe that. Who else have you told? Are you planning to spring your emotional revelation on our children so you can use them to manipulate me?"

"I wouldn't do that."

She glared at him.

"I won't do that," he amended. "I'm sorry about Mom. I needed someone to talk to and she was there."

"Call a friend. Go see a shrink. She's my mother-in-law. She works for me. Do you know how incredibly awkward this is?"

"She won't mention it again."

"She doesn't have to. I'll see it in her eyes. Why would you do that?"

"I wanted her thoughts on how to win you back."

"Not like this!"

"I'm sorry." He circled the desk. "Mikki, I really do apologize. You're right, I was wrong."

She stared at him, surprised at his sincerity. Perry had always been the kind of guy who muttered he was sorry and then expected her to never bring up his transgression again.

"I know I have a lot of work to do," he said. "You don't see me as a love interest anymore, but I'm hoping to change your mind." He gave her a smile. "You're kind of hard to get over."

"Perry," she began.

"I'll stop." He took her hand. "Did she know you were pissed?"

"She guessed. Now I feel bad for yelling at her."

"You didn't yell. You were never a screamer." His mouth turned up in a smile. "Except for that one time when—"

She snatched her hand back. "Don't you dare bring up sex."

"At least we got that part right, didn't we?"

Her anger dissipated. "Yes, but we got a lot wrong."

"The love didn't die, Mikki. It got ignored and went into hiding. We were both busy. We didn't take care of each other or prioritize our marriage, but we never killed the love."

"We didn't have to. It died on its own."

"Not for me. At least consider what I'm saying. Spend a little time thinking about the good times and how we could have them again. Twenty years, Mikki. Isn't that worth a second look?"

Which was what Ashley had said the other night, she thought with surprise.

Before she could figure out what to say, he leaned in and kissed her. The feel of his mouth was warm and familiar. She'd always liked kissing Perry and had felt that after they were married, they didn't do it enough.

This time, though, he lingered just long enough to confuse her. They stared at each other.

"I'll take care of my mother," he said. "And again, I apologize. I was wrong."

Her lips tingled, her emotions swirled and she didn't know what had just happened.

"Um, thank you."

She nodded once, then opened the door and stepped out into

the hallway. It was just a kiss, she told herself as she walked to the car. It didn't mean a thing.

Bree had long ago learned to live with her hair. The stubborn curls were resistant to chemicals, so straightening them took time and effort, with no sure result. She'd spent most of high school trying different processes to get long, sleek hair like most of her friends. The summer she'd turned seventeen, she'd spent a month's vacation with a girlfriend at her family's summer place in the Hamptons.

The house was a sprawling mansion on the beach. There were servants and parties every weekend. Guest lists included everyone from politicians to movie stars. The second day there, Bree's friend had reconnected with a guy she'd known forever. Their summer fling had left Bree on her own.

The father of her friend had been working some deal in Asia, spending most of his days, and nights, on the phone, leaving his relatively new second, or possibly third, wife by herself. She'd only been a few years older than Bree and despite being incredibly beautiful, she'd been friendly.

Bree and Chandra had met by the pool and quickly discovered they read the same books, didn't get everyone's obsession with lobster salad and liked to watch cartoon reruns. They also shared thick, unruly hair.

Chandra had taught Bree how to embrace her curls and had initiated her into the strange and wonderful world of hair products. Bree had learned how to keep the curls tight and uniform, or let them soften into almost ringlets. Chandra had also shown her how to apply makeup such that she could pass for twenty-four and had explained the importance of birth control and making a guy wear a condom.

In Chandra's world, sex was power. At first, Bree hadn't been sure she understood the lesson—her boarding school experiences hadn't included many guys. But at her new friend's urging, she'd put on a string bikini at the next pool party and had learned that yes indeed, men did pay attention to her body.

She took Chandra's lessons to heart and although the two women didn't stay in touch, Bree thought of that month fondly. She'd spent the next year experimenting with how to attract a guy who interested her. She'd been careful and selective, finally giving her virginity to a sweet young man from Australia who'd been so nervous, he'd come twice against her leg before finally holding it together long enough to penetrate her.

At college she'd sampled plenty, practicing on who she wanted and letting them practice on her. She was meticulous about condoms and birth control. She'd discovered she liked sex a whole lot more than relationships—at least until her idiotic heart had fallen for Lewis.

All of which left her comfortable with both her hair and her sexuality, but unwilling to risk her heart. Which meant dating Harding was going to be a problem. Not that they were involved in any way. She was only thinking about it. Sort of.

In the meantime, she had the OAR fundraiser to get ready for. She was oddly nervous about the whole thing—she was going with Harding on what could only be described as a date, and she didn't know what he expected of her. Was she there to be eye candy? Did he want her to speak to specific donors, and if so, what was she supposed to say? They hadn't talked about anything beyond his invitation and a text telling her what time he would pick her up.

Ashley had said cocktail attire, so Bree used three different products to keep her curls tightly controlled. By the time she'd gotten the shape and texture exactly how she wanted, her hair looked two inches shorter, but each curl had perfect shine and definition.

She slipped out of her robe and, wearing only a thong, stood in front of her closet. *Sexy but not too sexy*, she thought. Hint at cleavage without letting the girls fly free.

Her cocktail dress assortment was limited—her lifestyle was more casual—but she had a couple of classic LBDs and one or two that were more fun.

She pulled out a black beaded dress she'd bought on sale and had never worn. The tank top style was simple, the scoop in front not too low. The dress fell to midthigh. What made it special was the overlay of looped beading that started at her shoulders and fell to just below the hemline.

She put on a push-up bra, then stepped into the dress and pulled it into place. She checked herself from all angles, then slipped on the small diamond hoops Lewis had bought her when they'd first gotten together. She rarely wore them, but tonight they seemed appropriate.

Last, she stepped into classic black pumps with a four-inch heel. Her feet would be whimpering by midnight, but the shoes looked good on her and she had a feeling knowing that would help her get through the evening.

Five minutes before Harding was due to arrive, she slipped off the heels and walked downstairs barefoot. They'd gone back and forth about him picking her up. She'd said no and he'd insisted. Explaining she didn't let anyone come to her house hadn't impressed him. He'd promised not to cross the threshold, even if he had to use the bathroom.

His attempt at humor had made her even more uneasy about the evening, him, them and life in general, but somehow she'd agreed.

She paced nervously until his truck pulled into the driveway, then she put on her shoes, picked up her slim evening bag and stepped out onto the porch.

Harding got out of the truck, pressed a hand to his chest, then gave a slightly strangled laugh. "You look incredible. You're taking my breath away, which will make it hard to ask people for money."

"You look good yourself."

He did. The dark suit and tie contrasted with the white shirt. His eyes were greener than usual, his jaw freshly shaven.

Nerves settled in her stomach, but she ignored them. It was just a fundraiser, not anything romantic. She would be fine. She was good at being fine.

He escorted her to the truck, then held open the door.

"Can you make the step in that dress?" he asked, eyeing the distance. "I could lift you into place."

She smiled at him. "The skirt isn't that tight. I'll be fine."

She put her hand on his shoulder, then stepped up into the cab.

"Damn," he muttered. "I was hoping you'd flash me a little something."

"I'm wearing a thong. It would be more than a little something."

A muscle twitched in his jaw. "Did you have to tell me that? I'm supposed to have intelligent conversations with people over the next few hours and you tell me you're wearing a thong."

She smiled unrepentantly. "Fortunately, I'm wearing a bra, otherwise the visual would be worse. Of course it's a black push-up bra and it matches the thong so there's that."

He smiled. "You're not playing fair."

"No, I'm not."

"I like that." He leaned close and whispered, "I don't want to mess up your lipstick, so I'll do this instead," before pressing his mouth against the side of her neck.

The warm pressure sent shock waves through her body. Her insides clenched and her nipples tightened. Wanting slammed into her and now she was the one who couldn't breathe.

He kissed her neck, then nibbled his way down to her collarbone. At the same time he put his hand on her knee and slid it up her thigh. He moved purposefully until he reached the top, then lightly, so lightly, brushed his thumb against her mound.

Their gazes locked. His eyes burned with desire. Her throat

went dry as need grew desperate. He swallowed then carefully drew back his hand and straightened.

"Okay," he said, his voice tight. "That was supposed to be me playing with you, but the plan backfired. I need a minute."

She thought about making a joke about his erection, but somehow that didn't feel right. The moment wasn't funny...it was a connection.

"I used three different hair products tonight," she said quietly. "One of them contains a lot of alcohol, so let's keep me away from any open flames."

He managed a smile. "This is you helping by distracting me?"

"Yes."

"Thank you." He hung his head. "I can't remember the last time I nearly lost it in my pants."

"You were probably fifteen and touching a girl's breast."

"Something like that." He looked at her. "The things you do to me."

Only she hadn't done anything. Not really.

"Sometimes you scare me," she admitted.

He smiled. "Good, because you scare me, too. The difference is you're terrified I'll destroy you, while my nightmare is you'll run."

Because he knew her.

"Ready to go to a party?" he asked.

She nodded.

He closed the door and walked around to the driver's side of the truck.

Thirty minutes later he handed his keys to a valet. Bree waited until he opened her door, then again put her hand on his shoulder as she carefully stepped to the ground. The parking lot in front of the OAR building was filled with cars. Music flowed from the open doors, and volunteers in bright T-shirts stood ready to welcome them.

The night was a celebration of achievement. Students who'd

made it into college would be awarded scholarships, and a new program would be announced. Corporate sponsors had provided the food, a record label had provided entertainment and there would be a straight-out ask for money.

Bree had a check for five thousand dollars in her purse. She'd never been one to donate to a good cause, something hanging out with Harding had made her rethink. She'd made a list of charities she cared about—protecting the environment, a women's shelter, OAR and a cat rescue in Torrance. She was putting together a budget for giving on a quarterly basis. Tonight's gift was her first foray into thinking financially about someone else.

Inside the building the huge main space was filled with well-dressed guests laughing and talking. Servers circulated with appetizers while there were bars in each corner. Harding pulled several tickets from his pocket.

"I scored some drink coupons," he said with a grin. "I know a guy."

She'd just taken one when two women walked up to Harding. The younger woman smiled briefly at Bree before turning to him.

"There are several people who want to meet you. I've been keeping a list. The Martins represent a foundation looking to expand their mission, and they think OAR is a good match." She laughed. "Mrs. Martin has read both your books and is a huge fan, so she's the driver, just so you know."

As she spoke, the circle around them grew as guests realized Harding had arrived. The buzz of conversation increased in pitch.

Bree knew what it was like to be around the star of the show. She'd learned how to act about the time she'd learned to walk, attending events with her parents. She was expected to be pleasant, attractive, friendly and most of all, quiet. The evening wasn't about her.

Later, with Lewis, his celebrity had been more in his mind

than reality but the expectations were the same. He needed to be the center of attention. She'd made herself useful, circulating with drinks and food, careful to stay in the background and never offer an opinion.

The first couple of years of their marriage, she'd assumed he was right and she couldn't possibly have anything interesting to say. As time had passed she'd started to realize narcissists simply couldn't be bothered with anyone else. That revelation had occurred shortly before she'd discovered he'd already been diagnosed with cancer when he'd asked her to come back. If one blow hadn't been enough to kill her love, the second certainly had.

She pushed thoughts of him from her head and walked toward one of the bars. As she waited in line, she studied the champagne selection and knew Mikki would shudder at the inexpensive options. When it was her turn, she asked for a glass of white wine. Not her favorite, but something she could hold for several hours without refreshing.

As she scanned the room, looking for Ashley, she felt someone come up behind her. She turned to find a man, maybe forty and movie-star handsome, smiling at her.

"Hello. I'm Jefferson."

He was six three, with broad shoulders and an easy, practiced smile. She would guess the suit was custom and that somewhere out in the parking lot was a very expensive car. His nails were buffed, his shoes designer.

Movie mogul? Venture capitalist?

"No," she said quietly and turned away.

"I could make you happy."

She glanced back at him. "No, you couldn't."

She found Ashley and Seth talking to another couple. Seth had his hand on the small of Ashley's back and watched her with a combination of pride and love that even Bree recognized.

He was crazy about her, so what was the deal about marrying

her? Bree wondered if his reluctance was as clear-cut as he made it or if there was some hidden wound he didn't want to admit to.

Ashley, beautiful in a shimmering emerald dress that flattered her red hair and green eyes, saw her.

"You're here. Let's air kiss. I've only been air kissing with people I don't care about and I'd like that to change."

Bree obliged, then looked at Seth. "Did she get started on the cocktails early?"

"I'm not drunk," Ashley insisted. "Just a little wound up. How are you? You look amazing."

"So do you. Love the dress."

Ashley spun in a circle. "It's fancy, huh? I rented it for the event. I'd need a second job to afford pretty dresses for all my events this summer. Renting is so easy." She pressed a hand to her mouth. "I sound drunk. I swear I've only had one glass of wine."

"With no food," Seth said, putting his arm around her waist. "I should have asked if you'd eaten." He smiled at Bree. "Excuse us. I need to get some food into her. I don't want her blood sugar to crash."

"It's not that bad," Ashley protested, waving as Seth led her away.

"There you are." Harding appeared next to her, frowning slightly. "Why did you disappear?"

"I didn't. You're Harding Burton. Everyone's here to see you. I just got out of the way so you could have your moment in the sun."

"That's not how it works." He took her hand in his. "You're with me, Bree. I didn't ask you here so you could stand in the corner and wait for me to be done."

"I never thought you did. I really was just trying to give you room to do your hosting duties."

"I don't need room. I need you with me."

"Then I'll be with you."

NINETEEN

Bree and Harding circulated through the room, pausing for him to greet people he knew and introduce her. She had no trouble with him saying she was the owner of The Boardwalk Bookshop, but when he called her his girlfriend, she nearly spilled her drink.

"I'm not your girlfriend," she whispered when they were alone. "We're barely dating and we haven't had sex yet." Nor were they going to, but why get into that right now?

He took her drink, put it on a table, then took both her hands in his and stared into her eyes.

"We are dating," he told her. "And you *are* my girlfriend."

Panic fluttered in her chest. "I'm not good at that kind of thing."

"You mean relationships."

"Yes. Or making bread. I can't get the yeast to rise."

He continued to look at her. "Dating," he said firmly. "Girlfriend."

"Whatever."

"Bree, I'm serious."

Why was this so hard? Why was he doing this?

"Hey, you two." Dave rolled up, a striking blonde at his side. "This is Dionne. You know Harding, and this is Bree."

"Hi," Bree murmured. "Nice to meet you." She smiled at Dave. "You look good in a suit. It's a guy thing, isn't it?"

They chatted for a few minutes. Bree kept waiting for Harding to toss around the G word, but he didn't and eventually she relaxed.

"Time to find our seats," Dave said, then chuckled. "I already know where mine is."

They moved toward the tables across the room. She wasn't surprised to find their names at one of the VIP tables near the front. Dave and his date were at the table next to theirs, and Ashley and Seth were in the back.

As more guests joined them, Bree braced herself for the introductions. Everyone already knew Harding, so she became the center of attention.

"This is Bree Larton," he said.

"Oh, the girlfriend," an older woman said with a laugh. "We've heard all about you. The Boardwalk Bookshop is one of my favorite places by the beach. And that charming gift store."

"My friend Mikki runs that."

"My new go-to place for when I need a little something for a friend."

Another woman leaned across the table. "We're going to pepper you with questions, dear. Harding rarely brings a date to these things. There was one young woman a few years ago. Nowhere near as pretty as you." The woman paused. "Oh, dear. That sounds terribly old-fashioned. Should I compare your accomplishments instead?"

"Oh, Doris, don't ever change," her husband said affectionately.

Harding shook his head. "Obviously, I've known everyone here for years. They've supported OAR from the beginning. I apologize in advance for anything they might say."

Everyone laughed. Bree wasn't sure if she should join in or

bolt. She settled on smiling and hoping they would change the subject.

Fortunately, Harding took charge of the conversation and shifted to the scholarship students, and Bree was able to sit back and simply listen.

Dinner was served and the presentations began. During a lull, the woman next to her leaned close.

"He's happy with you. We can all see it. He's more relaxed than usual, but with an air of purpose. I don't know if I'm making sense, but I wanted you to know, it's nice to see him this way. You're very good for him."

Bree murmured a quick "Thank you," because she was unable to manage more than that. Probably smart, because what else was there to say? That she wasn't good for Harding? The truth, yes, but it would make for an awkward shift in the evening.

Her good mood vanished. What was she doing here? She wasn't Harding's girlfriend. She barely knew what the word meant and couldn't see herself ever being anything like that. She wasn't *good for him*, because she wasn't good for anyone. She was flawed, suspicious and defaulted to assuming the worst. When threatened by something—real or imagined—she retreated. She wouldn't fight for Harding, she wouldn't take care of him. When things got bad, she would run.

No, it was worse than that. She wouldn't let things get good enough to later get bad. A relationship required a level of faith she didn't have anymore.

By the time the evening ended, she'd worked herself up into a decent-size mad. She refused to hold his hand on the walk outside and barely thanked him as he held open the truck door.

Once they were out of the parking lot, Harding pulled to the side of the road and angled toward her.

"Too much?" he asked calmly. "Too many people asking too many questions? Or was it the assumptions about us?"

"I have no idea what you're talking about."

"You're pissed. At me or the world, I don't know."

"I'm not having sex with you tonight."

"I know."

"Or maybe ever."

He grimaced. "That's tough to accept. I can wait, but never is a really long time. A guy can only masturbate so many times before he starts feeling pathetic."

"No one would ever think of you as pathetic."

"You don't know how many times a week I jerk off."

She felt her lips twitch and forced them into a straight line. "I'm serious."

"Me, too. We've never discussed the number. Speaking of which, you're not getting any right now. So how often do you take care of business? And if you don't mind sharing, is it manually or is there equipment involved?"

He leaned back in the seat and closed his eyes. "I picture you in bed, on your back, legs spread. Trimmed bush. The whole nothing-down-there look isn't my thing. You start out slow, circling your clit, then going faster and faster."

He opened his eyes and glanced at her. "I want to say there's more to it than that, but by the time you're arching your head back, I'm pretty much coming, so that's where it ends."

He was fearless, she thought in terror, even as liquid desire filled her. People said she was brave, but she wasn't. Not like him. She took what she wanted and walked away when she said, but that wasn't brave. She didn't put anything on the line so she had nothing to lose. Walking away didn't mean anything when she left no part of herself behind. There were so many walls and barriers around her heart, she couldn't remember the last time she'd felt genuine affection for someone, let alone love. After what Lewis had done, she wasn't sure she was capable.

"This is going to end badly," she whispered. "You think there's something inside of me, waiting to get out. You think I'm holding back, that I'm capable of great love, so you're willing to wait, but what if you're wrong? This is all there is, Harding. It's all I have to give and I'm not interested in more."

He drew her hand to his mouth and kissed her knuckles. "My parents are in town next week. Join us for dinner. Ashley and Seth will be there, so just the six of us." He turned her hand and pressed a kiss to the palm.

"For the record, I heard what you just said," he continued. "I'm not sure how to respond, so I'm not going to. Unless you count my invitation to dinner."

"With your parents."

"Yes."

"I've never met anyone's parents before."

He stared at her. "That's not possible. Most people have parents. What about your friends from school? You said you traveled with their families. You met parents there."

She pulled her hand free. "You know what I mean."

He pretended puzzlement, then flashed her a grin. "Oh, you've never met the *boyfriend's* parents."

"Lewis's had died years before I knew him."

"It's no big deal. I'm sure you can read about it online. So that's a yes?"

Five minutes ago she'd been pissed and ready to end things. Four minutes ago she'd been desperate to have sex with him, and three minutes ago she'd been, yet again, ready to end things. She needed to pick an emotion and stay there for a full half hour or else get some professional help.

"I love you, Bree," he said into the silence. "I know I promised not to say that, but I lied. I really do love you. I know you don't find those words comforting, but I believe that you want to love me back. You just have to find your way." His smile returned. "I'm willing to bet my heart on that."

"And when your heart gets broken?"

"Then we'll be a matched set. So yes on the parents?"

She nodded slowly.

"Excellent." He started the engine. "Now I'm going to take you home and not have sex with you."

Which he did. He escorted her to her front door, kissed her on the cheek, then walked away without looking back. Bree went inside and slipped out of her shoes. In the bedroom she stripped out of her clothes, pulled on a nightgown and washed her face. Alone in bed, she stared at the ceiling.

Images from the night swirled in her brain, moving too fast for her to analyze, but after a few minutes she circled back to one conversation. Smiling, she picked up her phone.

No toys, just my fingers. As you said, on my back, legs spread.

She sent the text, then waited. Seconds later dots appeared.

Naked?

I just pulled up my nightie.

You're killing me.

Not the goal. Now what?

She could practically hear him chuckling.

I think you know what's next. Meet back in five?

She smiled.

Really? It's gonna take you five minutes?

No, but I was trying to impress you. Text when you're done.

She put down the phone and closed her eyes as she trailed her hand down her belly and settled it between her legs. She was already wet and swollen. Ready. She thought about Harding and what he was doing right this second.

Her orgasm took less than two minutes. She waited another two before texting.

Done?

Yes. For a while now.

She laughed out loud.

How was it?

Not as good as if you were here. Did you think of me?

I did.

Are you surprised at how big I am?

She laughed again.

I'm very impressed. Night, Harding.

Night, Bree. I'm not going to say it, but you know what I'm thinking.

She did. He was thinking that he loved her. Words that always made her uncomfortable to the point of wanting to run. Just not tonight.

Mikki debated showing up for her morning of trash pickup on the beach. She wasn't sure if she wanted to spend the time with Perry. But not showing up felt wrong, somehow, so she went.

There were about ten volunteers. After getting their equipment and assignment, they got in Perry's car and drove to their section of beach and started walking along the sand.

"I wasn't sure you'd be here," Perry said, scooping up a couple of empty beer cans.

"Why? We're friends. We pick up trash every other week. It's no big deal."

Brave words she hadn't been feeling forty-five minutes ago, she thought but didn't say.

"You're not still mad?"

"I was never mad." She paused. "Well, except about your mother."

"Are things better now?"

"She's not mentioning us getting back together, but it's still awkward. We'll get there."

She hoped. Lorraine was a great employee.

They walked in silence for a few minutes.

"It seemed like you were mad at me, too," he told her.

She used her grabbers to pick up some paper and put it in her trash bag.

"You changed the rules. We were living our lives and being friends and you announced, out of the blue, that you're still in love with me and want to get back together. Who does that? I had no warning, nothing. It's not fair. It's not where we are."

He stopped walking. "I want to change where we are."

"I don't." She faced him. "Perry, I'm seeing someone."

His face fell. "Still? I thought you'd stopped seeing him."

"I haven't. We're still dating and I don't have plans to stop. You and I aren't getting back together."

He looked past her. "I thought you'd at least give us a try."

"We tried already."

He returned his attention to her. "No, we didn't. We drifted apart. We got busy. But you and I never sat down, discussed what was wrong and then tried to fix it. We just let our marriage go. Don't you ever wonder what would have happened if we'd both made the effort?"

While she hadn't ever wondered, she knew he had a point

about the rest of it. They hadn't made any effort—not counseling or trying to work things out on their own. Maybe there was a message in that.

"I've changed," he added. "You should take a little time and explore the new me." He smiled. "I didn't mean that exactly how it came out."

She was both amused and exasperated. "Dammit, Perry. What's really going on here? You're making me crazy with all this. Are you sure you want me back and this isn't just because I'm finally seeing someone I like? I find your timing highly suspicious. You've had three years to figure this all out but you only come to this conclusion when you find out about Duane?"

"It's not like that. I've been working on this for a while. Learning about the other guy moved up my timing a little. Just on the telling-you part. I'd already bought the house. You have to admit, you like it."

"For you, yes. It's great."

"The addition was for us." He took a step toward her. "The kids will be around for a while, coming back for summers or holidays. But there's going to be a third bedroom."

He paused as if that bit of information was significant.

"For a guest room?" she asked, not sure who would come stay with them. All their family was nearby.

"No, for that baby you always wanted. We could do it, Mikki. Have a third child. I have real regrets about not agreeing when you asked before."

The grabber fell to the sand as she opened her mouth, then closed it. *No way*, she thought, feeling light-headed and horrified at the same time.

"What is wrong with you?" she asked, her voice uncomfortably loud. "A baby? I'm nearly forty. I don't want a baby now. Seriously, is that what you've been thinking? We'd have another kid?"

"You wanted one."

"Eight years ago. Not today. My children are nearly grown. I'm ready to move on. I want an adult-based life with travel and going out and doing all the things you can't do with a baby in the house."

She picked up her grabber and marched down the beach. "A baby! Talk about harebrained. No. Just no." She picked up a bottle and thrust it into the trash. "There is something seriously wrong with you, Perry Bartholomew. You should get some help."

"I swear this shopping mall gets bigger every time I visit," Joy Burton said with a laugh as she and Ashley carried their shopping bags out of the Nordstrom at Del Amo Fashion Center.

Other malls were closer to Ashley's apartment and her parents' hotel, but Del Amo was the one they always visited.

"Bigger is better when it comes to shopping," Ashley pointed out. She motioned toward the parking garage where they'd left Ashley's SUV. "Look at how great that sale was."

Her parents were in town for a quick visit. They flew in from Portland a few times a year or Ashley met them up there. The flight was easy—less than two hours.

"I'm very proud of my savings," her mother said. "I'm not sure your father will agree."

"Oh, Mom, you know he doesn't care."

"That's true but he does like to tease me."

They put their bags in the back of Ashley's SUV.

"The hotel?" Ashley asked.

"Yes, please. I'm ready to put my feet up. I'm sure your father will, as well, when he gets back."

While she and her mom had spent the day shopping, Harding had taken their father to Griffith Park Observatory.

Ashley headed for Pacific Coast Highway. This time of day the surface streets would be as fast as the freeway and the view was prettier. Her parents were staying in Santa Monica, at a beachfront hotel.

"You look good, darling," her mother said. "A little tired, but otherwise happy."

"I'm feeling fine," Ashley lied. "Busy with work and volunteering."

If her mother believed she was happy, then she was faking it better than she thought. Not that she was pleased to be lying to her parents, but there was no way to discuss the whole Seth situation without everyone overreacting. And she wasn't exactly unhappy. Just confused.

"Your brother's doing well," her mother continued. "He says he's making progress on his book."

"That's what he tells me, but I've yet to see actual pages," Ashley teased.

Her mother laughed. "Harding is nothing if not a hard worker. I'm not worried." She relaxed back against the seat. "He's come so far. If I hadn't lived through his accident, I'd have a hard time believing it ever happened." She looked at Ashley. "I still have nightmares."

"Me, too. I was so scared he would die."

Her mother squeezed her arm. "You were very brave."

"I stood on the sidelines and watched. He's the one who had to recover, then learn to walk again."

"You did more than you think. You were there for all of us. You took care of yourself so we could be with Harding. You never complained."

Ashley stopped at a light, then smiled at her mom. "Is my halo on straight? I can never tell."

Her mother laughed again. "I'm serious."

"I'm serious, too. Mom, I did okay, but I'm not the hero of the story. But I will admit that as awful as it was, going through Harding's accident made us all stronger emotionally. And more connected."

"We learned hard lessons. You thrived afterward. Look at you, owning a successful business before thirty. I'm so proud of you."

"Thanks. I'm happy with how Muffins to the Max is going."

"I'm proud of both my children," her mother said. "And a little bit smug about your father and I. Several nurses warned us they'd seen couples torn apart by the stress of an accident like that. Your father and I made a conscious decision to always be there for each other. Our marriage is stronger than ever."

Joy shook her head. "All right. Enough talk about that horrible time. Let's change the subject to something more cheerful. How's Seth?"

"He's good. Busy. He'll be working on the next Johnny Blaze movie."

"Oh, Johnny Blaze. He's so good-looking."

Ashley grinned. "Into younger men now, are we? You know he's happily married with a couple of kids."

"Why would that matter? I'm just saying he's good-looking."

They talked about celebrities and who was dating whom in that crazy world. Ashley managed to focus enough to follow the conversation, but after she dropped off her mother, she found herself wanting to pull over and have a good cry.

Ridiculous, she told herself. Nothing was wrong with her life. She was fine. Her business, as her mother had pointed out, was doing well. She had friends and a man who adored her. Which all sounded great but disguised the actual problem: she and Seth wanted different things. No, not things, plural. Just the one.

She drove home and went into the apartment. Seth wouldn't be home for another hour or two, which was plenty of time to feel sorry for herself before pulling it all together.

She curled up on the bed and gave in to the tears that had been threatening. They poured down her cheeks and soaked her pillow as she wondered why he had to be the way he was. Why couldn't he understand how important this was to her and how wrong he was not to want to marry her?

Her body shook and she went through nearly a box of tissues. Only the thought of how blotchy her skin would be and how swollen her eyes would look had her struggling for a whisper of control. She sat up and told herself to breathe, but sucking in air made her start crying again. She had to—

"Ashley?"

She swallowed her sob and frantically wiped her face. But before she could begin to brush away the tears, Seth walked into the bedroom and saw her.

"What's wrong?" he asked, racing to her side and pulling her close. "Are you sick? Did you get in a car accident? Ashley, what's going on?"

She wanted to sag against him and cry into his strong shoulder. Maybe then, for a second or two, she could pretend she was strong enough to do what he asked.

"I'm fine," she whispered. "Just sad."

"About what?" He drew back so he could look at her. "Baby, what's happening? How can I fix it?"

He looked worried and confused and completely in love with her. That was the hell of it—she honest to God believed he loved her.

"I'm trying," she told him, wiping her face. "I really am. I'm reading everything you suggested and I think a lot about our future. But things happen. My mom was talking about how awful it was when Harding was in the hospital but how she and my dad committed to making their marriage survive what they went through. They didn't want to lose each other."

"And they didn't." He touched her cheek. "I don't get it."

"I want that. I want us to grow stronger every year we're together. I want us to always be in love."

"Me, too. You know that."

"But it feels like I'm going to be auditioning all the time. You worry that I'll get complacent and I don't know what that means. What if I gain ten pounds or don't do the laundry the day you think I should? Will you leave? I don't want to spend my life waiting for you to decide I'm not trying hard enough."

He pulled her close. "Ashley, no. That's not what I mean. It's not an audition. It's forever. It's both of us committing to each other."

He shifted back. "I've been thinking, too, and I'm starting to understand why people have weddings."

She swallowed. "You do?"

"It's a representation of a couple's plan for the future. Their moment to tell the world they're starting this journey together. We're all witnesses to the moment."

Hope ignited, but she ignored the sensation. "I don't know what that has to do with us."

"We should do the same thing."

Was he saying what she thought he was saying? "Have a wedding?"

He brushed away that comment with a flick of his wrist. "Not that. A commitment ceremony. We'll pledge our love in front of everyone we know." He smiled. "No chair covers, though. I just can't get into them."

Her heart sank. She felt it collapse in her chest as that whisper of hope extinguished. She closed her eyes and thought about what that day would be like. Not them getting married, not her in a dress, no traditional words, no signing of the marriage certificate. Just the two of them in front of their friends and family saying they absolutely weren't getting married.

He leaned in and kissed her forehead. "Think about it, okay?"

She nodded slowly, knowing if she tried to speak, she would scream. She would say things that couldn't be unsaid and in the saying, she would destroy what they had.

"One hour before we have to leave," he added. "What can I do to help?"

"Nothing," she whispered, leaning into him again and feeling his arms hold her close. At least this time she wasn't lying, she thought grimly. Seth absolutely didn't understand her point of view. Worse, she had no idea how to change him, or herself. Which left them on the edge of a precipice, teetering toward disaster.

TWENTY

"This is such a bad idea," Bree said as she stepped outside and shut the door.

Harding smiled at her. "You're really not going to let me into your house, are you?"

"No."

Why was that an issue? There was no need to go inside—they were on their way to dinner. A dinner that she in no way wanted to attend.

"You're kind of repressed emotionally," he said before he kissed her.

"You're just now getting that? I have massive issues, which you are triggering, by the way. I'm barely willing to admit we're dating and you're taking me to meet your parents, which is a horrible idea. I don't do well with parents."

Especially not her own, but why go there?

She'd stressed all day about the dinner, not sure what to say or how to act. She hoped his parents were nice, but who knew? What if they grilled her about her past? What if they saw through her facade of normalcy and called her out on all her flaws in front of Harding and Ashley? What if—

"Hey," he said before lightly kissing her. "Get out of your head."

"You have no idea what I'm thinking. Maybe I'm considering getting a kitten."

Harding didn't look convinced. "They're going to adore you."

"You are such a damned Pollyanna. It's really annoying. Am I dressed okay? I had no idea what to wear."

She'd chosen one of her two "nice" summer dresses. A simple sleeveless fit-and-flare style in a lemony yellow. The color flattered her tan and brown eyes. She'd sprung for a fresh pedicure, so her toes would look good in her strappy sandals.

"You look great. I like the shoes. They're sexy."

"I bought them on sale."

He chuckled, then put his hand on the small of her back and guided her to his truck. Once she was in the passenger seat, he moved close and stared into her eyes.

"You're beautiful, funny, smart and caring, Bree. You're a hell of a catch and I don't know what you see in me but I'm glad you're willing to almost date me."

He sounded sincere and she knew enough about him to know he meant what he said. What she didn't understand was why he was so eager to overlook the truth about her. Hadn't he figured out the reason she didn't want to know he loved her was because she wasn't capable of love herself?

"I don't want to hurt you," she admitted. "I really don't."

His look of affection never wavered. "Then don't."

"It's not that simple."

"It could be." He kissed her again, then closed the door and walked around to his side of the truck.

They arrived at the Santa Monica restaurant long before she was ready. As she stepped down, she told herself to breathe and smile and not assume the worst until it happened.

Ashley and Seth were waiting in the entryway.

"We waited for you," Ashley said, "so we'd all walk in together. I figured meeting the parents wasn't your thing."

The unexpectedly sweet gesture left Bree both happy and

unsettled. She was about to thank her friend when she noticed something in Ashley's eyes.

"Are you okay?"

"Great. I spent the day with Mom, which was fun. Harding and Dad went to the Observatory. Did he tell you?"

Harding took Bree's hand and grinned. "No, I don't want her knowing about my geeky side just yet. Let's let her revel in my charm and good looks for a while first."

"He's charming?" Seth asked Ashley, pretending confusion. "Huh, I didn't know that. Is it new?"

The three of them laughed. Bree smiled, but kept her attention on Ashley. Was it her or had her friend deftly shifted attention away from herself? Bree briefly wished Mikki was with them. Mikki would absolutely know if Ashley was hiding something or if Bree was overreacting.

Before she could decide, Seth turned to her. "I've known Ashley's folks for a while now. They're good people. Try to relax."

"Great. So you can tell I'm nervous."

They walked into the restaurant. Ashley waved to a couple sitting at a table in the back. Bree instinctively tightened her grip on Harding's hand as they approached.

His parents were a nice-looking couple in their late fifties. Joy looked a lot like her daughter, with red hair and big blue eyes. Kevin Burton had Harding's build and easy smile. His hair was a little darker, with flecks of gray at the temples.

Joy and Kevin rose. They kissed Ashley's cheek, hugged Seth and Harding, then turned to her.

"Such a pleasure to meet you," Joy said, giving Bree a warm smile. "Ashley adores you and Harding is clearly smitten."

Smitten? What did that mean? She shot him a worried look, hoping he hadn't actually used the L word with his parents.

Harding leaned close. "She means I can't stop talking about you. I never mentioned that tattoo you have."

Joy glanced between them. "What's your tattoo? I have a little dove on my shoulder. I got it the day Harding left the hospital, my symbol of hope."

"That's lovely," Bree murmured. "Harding's being funny. I don't have a tattoo."

They took their seats. Bree found herself between Harding and Seth, across from Kevin.

"I've taken the liberty of ordering champagne," Harding's father said. "I hope that's all right."

Ashley looked at Bree and grinned. "I don't know, Dad. Mikki, our business partner, has kind of turned us into champagne snobs. We have expectations."

Her dad laughed. "Then you'll have to tell me if I meet them."

Joy leaned toward Seth. "Ashley said you're working on the new Johnny Blaze movie. I'm so excited that you get to meet him."

"Money managers rarely go to the set, Joy, so Johnny and I won't be hanging out."

"Oh, pretend you will be, then tell me all about it."

"Promise."

Conversation flowed easily. Bree relaxed as the five of them talked and joked with each other. Kevin and Joy were obviously comfortable with Seth and he with them. Bree watched how Seth kept looking at Ashley, his expression happy and full of love. From the outside the man was head over heels, so what was the deal on getting married?

Not that she would ask tonight. She was fairly sure Ashley hadn't discussed the issue with her parents.

The champagne arrived. Kevin asked Ashley and her for their opinions.

"I'm not getting in the middle," Bree said easily. "I appreciate the bubbles and am happy with whatever you choose."

"A diplomat," Joy said approvingly as Kevin filled their glasses.

Harding mentioned how the OAR fundraiser had exceeded their two-million-dollar goal.

"We want to expand our ability to get our kids into trade school," he explained. "College isn't for everyone, but somehow supporting that is more popular than helping a student learn to repair HVAC units or be electricians. We'd like to help with scholarships, plus housing and a stipend."

"That's ambitious," Joy said.

"We're trying. I've been approached by a company that recycles shipping containers into homes for nonprofits who combat the housing crisis. We're thinking we could create a little village for our kids. Transitional housing. We've been promised a couple of plots of land that could work. I don't know—like you said, it's ambitious, but Dave thinks we can pull it off."

Bree was surprised. Harding hadn't mentioned the land or the shipping-container homes to her.

"How much would each home cost?" Joy asked.

"It depends. We think we can get the containers donated, along with some of the materials. We're also thinking students could donate a certain number of hours of labor in exchange for free rent."

"You should come up with a shopping list for your donors," Bree added. "Price out windows or appliances so their donation buys something tangible. I think they'd find it satisfying to buy a thousand square yards of flooring, rather than writing a check for something nebulous."

Harding looked at her. "Great idea. The specificity of the donation would make the project more interesting and real."

Their server told them about the specials, then took their orders. Joy asked Ashley about her new muffin flavors. After that, conversation shifted to the weather differences between Los Angeles and Portland. Bree relaxed as she mostly listened. This reminded her of spending holidays with different friends from boarding school. Some families had been more formal, but many had been easygoing and open, like Harding's parents.

How would she have been different if her parents had actually wanted her around? What would it have been like to grow up nurtured? While it was difficult to miss something she'd never had, she would admit to a sense of regret for what could have been.

"How long have you and Harding been dating?" Joy asked.

Bree took a second to realize the question was directed at her.

"About two months," Harding said, putting his arm around her. "I did a signing at her store." He winked at her. "She thought I was charming."

Bree smiled. "Even if I hadn't, he wouldn't have noticed. Have you been to one of his signings? The women line up for hours. I sold a lot of books that day."

"I know. I'm both impressed and confused by the crowds," Joy admitted. "Some of the women are very intense."

Kevin looked at his son with pride. "Harding can handle himself in any situation. Something he learned while he was in the hospital and rehab. Every day there was something new to manage."

"I had my bad days," Harding said lightly.

"Not many."

Joy glanced at Bree. "I think I heard you'd been married before. Am I right?"

"Yes. I'm a widow."

"Oh, I'm sorry."

"Thank you. It's been a few years."

"You didn't have children." Joy's voice was friendly, but her expression turned speculative. "Because you didn't want any?"

A jog in subject Bree hadn't seen coming. She tensed, not sure what to say. She'd been ambivalent about children. Yes, if none of them would ever feel about her the way she felt about *her* mother. There were times when she'd told herself she was a different person than Naomi. That she might not know what to do but she sure as hell knew what not to do. But she'd quickly discovered that the bigger problem had been Lewis.

"My late husband wasn't a fan of the idea," she said.

"But you would have had one or two?"

"Mom, I think we've taken this subject about as far as we should," Harding said easily. "You've known Bree an hour. Let's give her a break."

Ashley shot her a sympathetic look. "Mom and I found some real bargains today," she said quickly.

Joy glanced at her daughter. "Shall we tell everyone about the shoes we bought?"

Harding reached under the table and took her hand in his. She saw him mouth the word "Sorry." She faked a smile, as if she was fine.

She hadn't thought about having children in years. Not since well before she and Lewis had separated. After he'd died, she'd been too determined to remove any trace of him from her life to have regrets about nonexistent children.

But if she'd found someone else, she thought briefly, and maybe if she had half of Mikki's parenting skills, she would trust herself enough to have kids.

She glanced at Harding as he laughed at something Ashley had said. He would want a family, she realized. He would want a wife and kids and pets. The trappings of normal. Big family dinners and summer vacations and annual traditions that marked the passage of time.

If he loved her, did he want that with her? The thought that he might terrified her. She wasn't an ordinary-life kind of person. She wouldn't even let the man in her house—how was she supposed to host Christmas? Or have a baby or be part of a family?

Yes, she'd wanted those things once, before Lewis had destroyed her trust and shredded her heart. Harding said he liked her broken parts—that they fit his. But he thought she'd healed, that she was stronger for the wounds. But she wasn't. She was like cracked glass. The tiniest pressure would shatter her into a thousand pieces and once that happened, she would never be

SUSAN MALLERY

able to put herself together. Worse, if she let herself care about Harding, she risked taking him down with her.

The salads arrived. As each of them accepted or declined the offer of cracked pepper and Kevin ordered a bottle of wine for the table, Bree allowed herself a second to pretend everything would work out. That she would grow and change enough to be able to handle what Harding wanted to give her. That hazel-eyed babies and a strong, loving man were a part of her future. Then, as she had learned as a child, she mentally turned her back on the image and reminded herself that wishing didn't change anything. Her course had been set and there was no changing it now.

"I understand the reasons, but I don't agree with them," Duane said, then smiled. "We probably shouldn't talk politics. What if we fight?"

"About Brexit?" Mikki laughed. "I view the decision from a great distance. You forget my sad, travelless life doesn't include quick trips all over the world to talk economics. I just make a list of what I want to see and hope I can understand the money."

She paused. "That really does sound unsophisticated, doesn't it? I have to get out more."

"I could show you the world," Duane told her, his fingers laced with hers. He paused. "Isn't that a line from a Disney song?"

"*Aladdin,*" they both said together, then laughed.

"The joys of children," Mikki teased. "The songs of their youth are stuck in our heads forever."

"I'm glad my kids were too old to want to see *Frozen* eighty-seven times. I actually like the song, 'Let it Go,' but that's because I've only heard it occasionally."

"I like 'Do You Want to Build a Snowman?'" She looked around at the gardens. "I had no idea there were so many types of palm trees in the world, let alone practically in my backyard."

Duane had brought her to the UCLA Mildred E. Mathias Botanical Garden.

"I like coming here," he told her. "If I have a couple of hours between classes, it's a great place to think."

She would guess what he mulled about in a day and what she did were totally different. She knew nothing about economics and had signed up for a beginning class online, starting in September. Not that she would mention that to him. While she'd hoped to get her AA way back when, she'd never seriously considered a four-year degree. She had no idea if she was smart enough to get through beginning economics, which, by the way, wasn't even called that. Instead, the book she'd both downloaded and bought in print was macroeconomics. If she completed the course and was still sane at the end, next up was microeconomics.

She was hoping those two classes would give her a basic understanding of what Duane actually taught and did in his nonprofit work. Money was complicated. She still remembered a couple of episodes of *The Crown* where the prime minister had talked about devaluing the pound and she'd had no idea what that meant.

"We need to go through the Habitat Garden," he said. "We'll see hummingbirds and butterflies."

"One of the few acceptable bugs," she said. "Along with ladybugs and bees."

"You like bees?"

"From a distance. My affection is more because of their important place in the ecosystem. The bee population is being threatened. Some cities in Europe are using every available bit of space to create native gardens meant to feed bees, roadsides and medians, on top of bus stops." She sighed. "I wish we'd do something like that here. We have plenty of unused corners of land to help bees."

Duane smiled at her.

She put her free hand on her hip. "You're about to say something mocking, aren't you? You think I'm silly about the bees."

"I think you're absolutely right about the bees and I would never mock you. I might tease, but not mock."

She studied him. There was something in his dark eyes. "What aren't you telling me?"

He surprised her by turning away. "I'm fine, Mikki. Let's go look at butterflies."

She pulled her hand free of his. "Wait. Something's wrong. I can feel it."

Did he think she was idiotic with her bee talk? Was he finding her boring? Fat? Should she research interesting things to talk about and maybe start exercising?

For a second he stood with his back to her, tension in his shoulders. Worry knotted in her stomach. She'd hoped she was wrong about some kind of problem, but she hadn't been. He was—

He turned toward her, his expression grim.

"I'm fine," he began.

"You don't look fine."

"I'm trying not to be a jerk." His mouth straightened. "I really enjoy spending time with you. It's fun and easy and I like being around you."

No! He was going to break up with her! She knew it. Why? How had she messed up? She thought she'd been doing all right. They laughed a lot. They texted daily and… Was that it? Did he think she was needy?

"I don't understand," she whispered. "I thought you liked what we had."

"What?" He frowned at her. "I just said I did."

"But you're breaking up with me." She blinked away instant tears. No! She wasn't going to cry. "I thought—" She cleared her throat. "I guess it doesn't matter what I thought." She faked a smile. "It's fine. Thank you for letting me know."

Duane made a strangled noise low in his throat. He crossed to her, hauled her against him then kissed her with an unmistakable passion. His mouth claimed hers, his tongue danced with hers. She couldn't help leaning into him and wrapping her arms around him. Their bodies pressed together, bringing his very large erection in contact with her belly.

Wait a second. She pulled back and stared at him. "I don't understand."

One corner of his mouth turned up. "I kind of figured that from what you said. Mikki, I don't want to end things. I want to keep seeing you. If you sense anything different, it's because I'm having a little trouble with how much I want you. Most of the time I can keep control, but every now and then, being with you, watching you move or seeing a curve or a flash of—" He waved toward her chest. "It hits me and when that happens I need a few minutes to remember to act civilized. You need time and I'm determined not to rush you."

Wait, what? "This is about sex?" Relief poured through her. He didn't want to end things, he wanted to do it with her.

He moved close again and put his hands on her waist. "Some sex, some making love, depending on whatever fantasy I'm having that day."

He assumed there was a difference. If she had to guess, she would say sex was fast and orgasm-driven while making love was about the experience.

"Why would you think you had to keep waiting?" she asked.

He moved a little closer, his smile sexy, and his hands shifted to her butt.

"You haven't dated much. I'm not sure there's been a guy between Perry and me." The smile widened. "Not counting Earl, of course."

She waved away talk of Earl. "There was one a few months after the divorce. It was pretty awful." And fast and ultimately depressing.

She closed the last inch between them, pressing her belly against his erection. He reacted by digging his fingers into her butt and squeezing. She liked that and put her hands on his chest.

"You're hard," she whispered, then felt herself blush.

"Nearly every second I'm with you."

"Really? I haven't noticed."

"I try to be discreet."

She glanced down at the impressive bulge. "I'm not sure there's a good way to hide that."

He laughed, then kissed her. "Okay, so we're clear. I don't want to break up with you and I'm hoping you feel the same about me."

"Absolutely."

He stepped back and took her hand. "Then it's probably best to go look at some natural habitats. We'll have to walk slowly, until things calm down."

He was an amazing man, she thought, slightly stunned by all he'd told her. Not pushing her into something when he thought she wasn't ready. Always kind and thoughtful.

"I think we should go back to your place," she told him.

"You mean get takeout?"

Now who was being obtuse? She told herself that he'd been willing to tell her what he wanted when it came to their relationship. She should be willing to be just as brave.

She glanced around to make sure no one was nearby, then brought both his hands up to her breasts.

"Not for takeout. At least not at first."

Understanding dawned in his eyes, with passion quickly following. His hands moved and his thumbs brushed against her suddenly tight nipples.

"You sure?" he asked.

Heat burned through her. In seconds she felt the telltale ache starting between her thighs.

"Very. But we'll have to stop and get condoms. I don't have any with me."

Duane put his arm around her and started walking toward the car. *Quickly* walking.

"I thought we had to go slow," she teased.

"I'm motivated. I can work through the discomfort. And I have condoms at home."

TWENTY-ONE

Close to midnight Mikki pulled into her garage. Duane had wanted her to spend the night, but she wasn't comfortable staying there until she could tell the kids where to find her. They were both with Perry this week, so they weren't waiting up, but every now and then one of them came home early, or needed her for something.

She opened her car door, then wondered if she had the strength to walk the few feet to the house. She'd heard the phrase "boneless" before but had never had occasion to apply it to herself. Not until tonight.

She forced herself to stand, then laughed as her legs wobbled. She staggered inside and up the stairs to her bedroom where she quickly stripped down to take a shower. As she waited for the water to heat up, she caught sight of her body in the full-length mirror on the wall. Normally, looking at her saggy boobs and poofy tummy with its stretch marks depressed her. But not tonight.

For reasons she couldn't understand but would not question, Duane loved every inch of her body. He loved her breasts and her butt and her jiggly thighs. He'd explored every inch of her, had nibbled, licked and caressed until she'd been forced to climax again and again.

She stepped into the shower. The hot water reminded her of

his tongue and how he'd used it between her legs. The first time, she'd been embarrassed to come in less than thirty seconds. He'd teased her about a do-over, which she hadn't thought possible, but apparently was. She'd come again, screaming out her pleasure, unable to keep from begging him not to stop.

She shampooed her hair, washed all over and quickly rinsed before stepping out of the shower.

He'd been more impressive naked than she'd imagined. Fit with a perfect dick that had slid inside in such a way as to make her wonder what she'd been thinking, depending on Earl all this time. Men, or maybe just Duane, were ten times better.

Mikki dried her hair, then pulled on her pajamas before falling into bed. She was still smiling when she fell asleep.

But her eyes popped open at five twenty-seven as second thoughts and guilt threw mental rocks at her. She shot up and looked around the room, tired, disoriented and emotionally confused about the night before.

She reached for her phone.

> I need someone to talk to. Can you come by this morning? Please? I'm up and I'm going to make coffee. And maybe cinnamon rolls.

She glanced at the clock, then added,

> Is it too early?

She waited anxiously until the three dots appeared on her screen. Bree's answer showed up seconds later.

> You okay?

> I'm not bleeding. I'm in shock. I need to talk.

> I got that. On my way. You better not be lying about the cinnamon rolls.

Mikki dressed then went down to the kitchen and started on the rolls. When they were in the oven, she measured out coffee and paced by the front door until she heard Bree's Mini pull into the driveway. She met her friend out front.

Bree eyed her suspiciously. "Should I be worried?"

"No. Everything's fine. It's great. I'm fine."

"If you were fine, you wouldn't be texting me at five thirty in the morning."

They walked inside.

"Did I wake you?" Mikki asked anxiously.

"No. I was up. I was thinking of taking a spin class or going for a run." She led the way into the kitchen and breathed in the scent of cinnamon and butter. "This is better."

Mikki motioned to the island. She poured them each a mug of coffee and put out milk. She'd already made the frosting so when the timer went off, they would only have to wait for the rolls to cool for a couple of minutes.

"Did you want eggs?" she asked. "Or fruit? I have—"

"Stop." Bree cradled her mug before taking a sip. "Don't feed me. Just tell me what happened. From the beginning."

Mikki took a seat and picked up her coffee. Then put it down. Fortunately, the timer went off and she was able to busy herself pulling the cinnamon rolls out of the oven. But while she waited for them to cool, she had nothing to do and Bree was watching her patiently.

She sucked in a breath and faced her friend. "I slept with Duane."

Bree's smile was immediate. "Good for you. How was it? Earl-worthy?"

"Amazing. He's beautiful and the things he does. I'd forgotten what it was like to have the whole skin-on-skin experience. I don't even know how many times we did it."

Bree's expression turned smug. "I doubt that."

Mikki held in a grin. "Okay, I do know."

She lifted the rolls from the pan, then slathered on icing. After pushing them close to Bree, she got out two plates and took her seat.

"He wore a condom every time," she admitted, feeling herself blush. "And he's very enthusiastic. I practically floated home. It was great."

"But you're feeling guilty."

Mikki's head snapped up. "How did you know?"

Bree reached for a cinnamon roll. "You haven't been dating since the divorce. Not really. I think you mentioned a couple of guys, but they weren't significant and even if you slept with them, it wasn't the same. You're not the type who enjoys a variety of men. You like Duane, he obviously likes you, so while it's great, it's also new and uncomfortable."

"Exactly that," Mikki told her. "I was so happy when I went to bed and I woke up feeling like I cheated. I hate that. I didn't. I don't owe Perry anything." She leaned toward Bree. "It's because Perry's been all about getting back together, isn't it? He's got me thinking, even if I'm not interested I can't help wondering about what he said. Plus, he's the father of my children and we're friends."

"I'm your friend and I don't make you feel guilty about sleeping with Duane. I totally support it. I think you should do it more."

"So what's wrong with me? Am I freaked so I'm trying to find a problem? And what's with Perry? Part of me wonders if he really does want to get back together. I can't help thinking that he simply doesn't want someone else to have me."

Bree finished her roll and licked her fingers. "Delicious. Worth every calorie. Why do you care what Perry thinks? This is your life, Mikki, and your decision. What do you want? More Duane?"

"Yes, please. I really like him. It's just with Perry—"

Bree shook her head. "Stop it. Like you said, you don't owe Perry anything. You two are finished. Whatever his reasons for trying again, it's not your rock. Put it down. You've told him no, so just get on with your life."

Sound advice, Mikki thought. Really smart stuff.

"He's talking about us having another baby."

Bree nearly choked on her coffee. "You and Perry?"

"Yeah. About eight years ago I wanted a third kid. Perry was totally against it, so I let the idea go. He brought it up the other day and I was shocked. I told him it's too late. My kids are nearly grown. I don't want to start over."

"Does Duane want a baby?"

"I don't think so. It's never come up. When we talk about the future, it's always places we'll travel. Experiences we want. I think he's done with kids."

"Are you?"

"I said I was."

Bree's gaze was steady. "Did you mean it?"

Mikki nibbled at her roll and she considered the question. "I don't want more children. I really am ready to do adult things. I'm happy with that part of my life."

"And Duane."

Mikki smiled. "Especially with Duane. Last night was amazing. Not just the sex but how he sees me and thinks about me."

"Uh-huh. Told you so. He thinks you're a walking invitation to fuck."

"He kind of does."

"So why does Perry wanting to get back together rattle you so?"

"I don't know," she admitted. "But it's the right question, isn't it? And finding out the answer is going to help me figure out what I want to do next."

"And with whom."

★ ★ ★

"I've never seen Bree nervous before," Mikki murmured. "It's making me uncomfortable."

Ashley nodded as she watched Bree pace the length of the bookstore. "Yes, like discovering that mountains really do move. I mean if you can't depend on a mountain, what else is there?"

Mikki eyed her. "That's a really strange analogy. You think of Bree as a mountain?"

"No, but something solid and strong. You can scream at a mountain all you want, but it's not going to back down."

"You're weird."

Ashley laughed. "Probably."

She glanced at her watch. The signing was due to start in a couple of hours. There were chairs in place, a podium with a microphone, and a table with a stack of Naomi Days's latest literary masterpiece. Ashley had read a couple of reviews along with a book club discussion transcript. Apparently, the book was about a perfectly ordinary woman who unexpectedly spirals into madness. At the end of the book she sets herself on fire and dies. Not exactly upbeat.

"When does she get here?" Ashley asked.

"The author?" Mikki wrinkled her nose. "I mean Bree's mom. No idea. I've been watching for her, but I haven't seen anyone who looks like her."

Bree glanced at them, then walked over. "Stop talking about me."

"How do you know we're talking about you?" Ashley asked.

"You're looking at me, pointing and talking. It's not a big leap."

"We're worried about you," Mikki said bluntly. "So we want you to know we've got your back."

Bree offered a tight smile. "I'm fine."

"You're not," Ashley told her. "But you will be. You're stronger than you think."

"I wish that were true." Bree's shoulders slumped forward. "Why did I agree to the signing? I don't want to see her. We have nothing to talk about. She's going to find some way to remind me how unimportant I am to her and then she'll leave."

"If she says something mean, I'll take her on." Ashley curled her hands into fists. "I know self-defense."

"You're going to hit a woman in her late fifties?" Mikki asked.

"Oh. Right. No, I guess not. But I'll do something."

Bree's worry faded a little. "You're very brave, little kitten, but no one is hitting anyone. It's no big deal. I've dealt with her all my life. I can get through one signing."

"We'll be right here," Ashley reminded her. "We're taking turns so it's not creepy, but you're not going to be alone with her."

Bree looked puzzled. "I don't understand."

Ashley glanced at Mikki, not sure what wasn't clear.

"One of us will be hovering at all times," Ashley said. "Mikki, me, Rita and Lorraine. We have a plan."

"I can take care of myself."

Mikki smiled. "Yes, but you don't have to. That's the point. You're stuck with us. Accept it."

"I don't even know what to do with that information," Bree muttered before returning to her pacing.

Ashley watched her walk away. "I'll take the first shift," she said. "I'm feeling fiercely protective."

"I got that, what with the threats of physical violence. So unlike you."

"I know, right? I can't tell you where that came from, but I meant it."

She would take care of her friend, no matter what. Because she cared about Bree. Not news, but still, the concept caused her to pause.

She was worried about her friend and would do everything she could to keep her safe. With no expectation of something in return. With no rules or requirements. She was acting out of a giving heart.

Is that what Seth meant when he talked about a relationship where both partners showed up because they wanted to and not because they had to? Was he trying to explain an attitude rather than an audition? She wasn't sure, but if she was right, then maybe they weren't as far apart as she thought. She could completely embrace the idea of giving and caring to show love for another. Committing out of love and treating every day as an opportunity to make the partnership stronger and safer.

Something for her to think about, she told herself. Later, when she wasn't worried about protecting her friend from her scary, coldhearted mother.

Bree quickly realized Ashley hadn't been kidding about her friends watching over her. Lorraine was hovering by the front door, Rita kept muttering about "some people don't know how to treat their only child" and Ashley and Mikki were sticking close.

She wanted to tell them all she was totally fine, but somehow she couldn't speak the words—probably because she *wasn't* fine. She was nervous and unsettled.

In her head she knew that the event was meaningless. Her mother didn't care about her or the store—she simply wanted to be able to tell her friends she'd been here. Bree was nothing more than a means to an end.

Her heart was in a different place. No matter how she tried to disconnect emotionally, deep inside she was still that twelve-year-old girl whose parents regretted having her.

At the door Lorraine started doing some kind of alert dance, her arms high above her head. They stilled and fell suddenly. The moment had arrived.

She braced herself and walked to the front of the store. Her mother breezed in, a younger woman at her side. No doubt Idalina, the publicist. Naomi didn't travel alone.

Bree watched her mother pause and glance around. She wondered if Naomi would appreciate the high ceilings, the carefully thought-out displays of gifts and books, the appealing scent of chocolate and orange from a fresh batch of cupcakes. Trying to see the store as a stranger would, Bree felt a flush of pride. She and her friends had done well here.

She turned her attention back to her mother. Naomi looked as she always did—well dressed in tailored pants and a silk blouse. Her hair, as curly as Bree's, had been straightened and trimmed into a tidy bob. Her jewelry was tasteful, her shoes expensive and timeless. Everything about her screamed an attention to detail, a concern about having things "just so."

Her mother continued to study the store, her mouth becoming more pinched by the second. She murmured something to Idalina before turning her head and spotting Bree.

"Oh, good. You're here." Naomi walked toward her. "Hello, Bree. This is my publicist, Idalina. You've spoken on the phone. Are we ready for the signing or do you need to prepare?"

Idalina glanced between them, her confusion obvious. Bree understood her point. Mother and daughter reunited after more than a year apart. Shouldn't there be more?

She waited to feel the slap of the snub, the regret at the coldness, but there was only a sense of familiarity at the lack of connection.

"Everything's ready to go," she said.

"I hope that's true."

Bree caught sight of Ashley only a couple of feet away and Lorraine closing in fast. But before either of them intervened, Harding appeared at her side. He winked, then flashed her mother a smile.

"Mrs. Days, nice to meet you," he said. "Harding Burton. I'm the boyfriend."

The boyfriend? Bree held in a groan. She didn't want to discuss her personal life with her mother.

"Naomi, please. This is Idalina, my publicist." Naomi frowned. "Why is your name familiar? Have we met?"

"I'm a writer," he said easily. "Not in your league, of course. My work is nonfiction."

Her mother brightened. "Of course. The memoir. I read it. A very compelling story. Well written. Your prose could be better. You might think about taking some poetry classes to help with imagery and word choice."

She turned her attention to Bree. "So you're dating."

"Apparently so."

"Interesting. Shall we go get set up?"

Bree led the way to the rows of chairs. Her mother inspected the podium and the table, then nodded.

"This is fine. I'll wait in your office."

"Let me show you the way."

Before she moved in that direction, Harding pulled her against him. "I'll be here if you need me."

Past him was Ashley, with Rita stacking and restacking the books. Bree felt herself relax.

"You'll have to get in line," she teased.

"We all care about you."

Something Bree hadn't been able to count on before. Backup. It felt good.

She walked her mother to the office. It was only after her mother had taken a seat by the desk that Bree realized Idalina hadn't come with them. Which meant conversation would be required.

"How was your flight?" Bree asked.

Her mother sighed. "Next you'll be asking about the weather. Did you expect us to have dinner afterward?"

She hadn't seen her mother since Lewis had died. They rarely spoke so it was reasonable to assume after all this time, there would be much to say. Only there wasn't. Naomi had no interest in her life and the opposite was also true. Excluding their biological connection, they were strangers forced together for a few hours.

She remembered when she was younger how she'd wanted to talk to her mother. She would come up with what she hoped were interesting topics they could discuss. Sometimes she did research or made notes, but while her mother would occasionally engage on the subject, her interest was fleeting. After a few minutes she would need to get back to work, and Bree would be alone again. Until boarding school, her world had been small and lonely.

But it wasn't anymore. She had friends. According to Harding, she even had a boyfriend. None of the games she and her mother played mattered anymore.

"Let's skip dinner and you can take an earlier flight back to New York."

Her mother gave her a genuine smile. "That would be better for me."

"Then you should ask Idalina to change your ticket. Excuse me. I want to check in the readers. I'll come back for you when it's time."

She stepped out of her office and closed the door behind herself. As she turned, she bumped into Harding.

"Were you listening?" she whispered.

He pulled her toward the store. "I was keeping track of things."

"That's so tacky." She leaned against him. "Thank you."

"How are you holding up?"

"Okay, considering the fact that she's my mother. I thought I'd be more hurt, but I kind of feel nothing. I think that's a good thing."

"I do, too." He stared into her eyes. "She's an emotionally

stunted person and you did a good job of raising yourself. You should be proud."

"You're biased."

"I'm a writer, which makes me a trained observer."

"You're not infallible."

"No, but I'm really good-looking."

That made her laugh. "Yes, you are. Now I have work to do."

Bree saw about thirty people waiting. Not a great turnout, but then she didn't really have a literary-leaning clientele. She put away a couple of rows of chairs so the area didn't look so sad and empty. Exactly at two, she tapped on the office door before opening it.

"We're ready."

Her mother followed her out and waited while Bree introduced her to the modest crowd.

Rather than give any kind of talk, Naomi read from her book, then took a few questions. Bree hadn't mentioned their relationship and her mother didn't address it, either. It wasn't until people lined up to get their books signed that the topic came up.

"You must be very proud of your daughter," Rita said, holding open her copy.

Naomi stared at her in surprise. "Why on earth would you say that?"

Ashley immediately took a step toward her. Harding grabbed her arm and held her back. Lorraine looked pained and Mikki groaned.

"Because she owns this store and she's very successful."

"But it's retail."

Rita snatched up the book and snapped it closed. "I've changed my mind. I don't want an autographed copy after all."

She walked away, head held high. Bree watched her go, feeling warm and loved. She looked back and saw all her friends watching her with concern.

"I'm fine," she told them, ushering the next customer to

the table. The most amazing part of that statement was that it was true.

An hour later the signing was over. Bree had her mother sign an extra ten books. Signed books always sold—people bought them as gifts.

Naomi collected her handbag from the office, then turned to Bree.

"Our flight leaves in two hours. We're going directly to the airport." She paused, as if considering her words. "Thank you for hosting the signing. I know my type of book isn't your thing."

"I'm sure my customers enjoyed the change." Bree walked her through the store to the front. "Safe flight."

"Yes, and I'll tell your father that you're doing well."

They faced each other. Bree wondered if her mother felt the sadness of the moment or if she was incapable of any emotion that didn't include her husband or a character. Would Naomi ever understand what had been lost?

Unlikely, Bree thought, as Idalina pulled up in a rental car.

"Goodbye, Mother," she said.

"Bree."

Her mother walked to the waiting vehicle. She got in, shut the door and they drove away.

Harding came up and put his arm around her waist.

"You okay?"

"Mostly. I'm not upset like usual. At first, I didn't feel anything, but now I'm sad. We should've been a family."

"Do you want that?"

"There's no reaching her or my father. I spent the first twelve years of my life thinking of ways to make them care about me. They aren't interested and I'm done trying. I wish them the best, but I don't need anything from them. Not anymore."

She looked back at the store. Rita was helping a customer. Mikki was chatting with Lorraine while Ashley rang up a purchase.

Her friends had been there for her, protecting her, ready to do battle if necessary. As had Harding.

"Are you going to take a poetry class?" she asked.

He grinned. "You know, I just might. Then I can write a sonnet about you."

"Not a dirty limerick?"

He chuckled. "Those I can do already. Shall I show you?"

"Rain check. I need to get back to work." She put her hand on his chest. "Thanks for coming today."

His hazel gaze locked with hers. "Always, Bree. Always."

TWENTY-TWO

Mikki sat crossed-legged on Duane's bed. His bedroom was big, with a large deck with a peekaboo view of the Pacific Ocean. The en-suite bath had a shower big enough for two, along with double vanities and a tub. She wasn't a condo kind of person, but she had to admit, his was nice. And given that he was a single guy who traveled a fair amount, it made sense.

She watched him put socks and underwear into the carry-on suitcase he was packing.

"I couldn't do it," she admitted. "You're gone for four days. How can you take so little? I'm not sure all my cosmetics would fit in that tiny thing."

He chuckled. "You know you're too beautiful to need makeup, right?"

"I wish. So how does it work? You take a couple of shirts, assume your jeans are going to stay clean and that's it?"

"Yup. If I need new ones, I'll buy them there, but it's just a four-day conference." He held up a pair of dark pants. "For dinners out."

"Fancy."

Duane was heading to Madrid for an economics meeting. He'd mentioned her coming along, but when he'd shown her the schedule, they'd both realized he would be working eight to ten hours a day, leaving her on her own. She'd already been to one foreign city by herself and she hadn't enjoyed the experience.

"I appreciate that you thought about bringing me," she said.

He looked puzzled. "What else would I do? I'll miss you. I have a trip to Japan in October. I'm trying to get the schedule ahead of time so we can figure out if it makes sense for you to come with me. I'm hoping there's more free time."

Japan? As in Japan? "That's a long flight."

"We're on the west coast of the US. Everything's a long flight. Have you finished your merchandise orders for Christmas?"

"There's a change in subject."

"My classes start in less than a month. That made me think of fall and the holidays. I know you have to get your orders in early to meet demand."

She laughed. "Yes, Duane. I've placed my orders. Want to see my confirmations?"

His brows rose, as his mouth curved in a smile. "I'll look at anything you want to show me."

A tempting invitation, but they were on a time crunch. She pointed at the suitcase. "Keep packing, mister."

She watched him check his shaving kit. He worked efficiently—no doubt because of lots of practice. He paid attention to the little things.

"Were you a good husband?" she asked.

He glanced at her. "I tried to be." His expression turned rueful. "I got better with practice. Unfortunately, she became less interested in me with time. I think I was a good dad. I liked it a lot and sometimes I wish they still needed me as much as they used to."

"I worry about that next stage," she admitted. "Sydney's already in college. I only have another year with Will. It's going to be hard to see them go."

She glanced down at the comforter, then back at him. "Did you ever think about having more children?"

His wide-eyed shock was answer enough, she thought, even as he said, "No. I miss them but I'm not looking to repeat the process. Do you want more children?"

"No, I was just asking." Because the idea had been on her mind. Not having kids so much as Perry being ridiculous about it.

He dropped the shaving kit into the suitcase, then sat next to her. "Mikki, I had a vasectomy years ago."

"You did? But you use a condom."

He touched her face. "Not for birth control, but to keep you safe. I'm hoping we're in a place where we can each get tested and then stop using condoms." He paused. "Well, I guess only I have to get tested. I don't think Earl is much of a risk."

Tested for STDs. Because that was what people did these days. So not part of her regular life.

"It would mean we're committing to a monogamous relationship," he added. "Are you ready for that?"

Holy crap! "I realize this is a very sweet moment and I'm having all the feels, but I can't get past the fact that you think I'm capable of sleeping with two men at once. I'd never do that. Not just because I would think it was wrong, but because it would totally freak me out. Seriously. I couldn't do it."

He laughed. "Point taken. I've never been the cheating type, either. So I get tested and we're taking this to the next level?"

She wasn't totally sure what all that meant, but she was excited to find out. Dating Duane was so much more than she'd ever hoped a real grown-up relationship could be.

"I'm in," she told him. "And thank you for using a condom."

"I want to take care of you."

"I want to take care of you, too." She stared into his eyes. "I know it's only four days, but I'm going to miss you."

"I feel the same." He kissed her. "So it's forty-five minutes until I leave for the airport. Want to show me how much you'll miss me?"

She pulled off her T-shirt and unfastened her bra. "I thought you'd never ask."

Bree watched as Harding paddled to shore. He'd managed to get up on his board twice and even ridden in a wave. But from her place on the sand, she could see he was cold and tired.

Worry gripped her, making her want to wade out and drag him in. He pushed himself too far and always ended up shaking from exhaustion. He wasn't a morning person. Most nights he went to bed well after one or two, so why would he get up for a predawn surfing class week after week?

By the time he staggered out of the water, she'd worked herself into a pretty decent mad. She stalked toward him and dropped to her knees so she could unfasten his board, then she snatched it away and glared at him.

"What is wrong with you?" she demanded. "Why do you do this to yourself? This isn't your sport. You're practically blue. You're trembling and pale. Go back to cycling. You don't have to do this to impress me. We're already almost dating. Call it a win and quit scaring me every damn week."

He managed a faint smile. "I don't come here because of you. I like surfing."

"That's so much bullshit and you know it."

"Then sleep with me and I'll give up surfing."

She nearly smacked him with the board. "You're kidding, right? That's your offer? I have sex with you and you'll stop acting like a fool?"

"Oh, I'll still act like a fool, but just in a different way."

Men were idiots, she thought, more worried about him than offended by what he'd said. She unzipped his wet suit and dragged it down his torso while he pulled his arms free, then she reached for a large towel and began rubbing him dry.

Sometimes he protested, saying he wasn't a child, but this morning he let her have her way with him. She moved against the thick muscles in his arms and back. He balanced himself against his truck as he pulled off the rest of the wet suit. His teeth were chattering and his lips were blue.

"You're a mess," she told him.

"That's hot, right? Because perfect guys are so boring."

She looked at him, the way his wet hair fell across his forehead and how, despite how crappy he must feel, he was smiling at her. Harding showed up. She would give him credit for that. He was patient and sexy and funny and for reasons not clear to her at all, he thought he was in love with her.

"Can you drive?" she asked.

"Since I was sixteen. There was that year I was in the hospital and stuff, but otherwise, I've been driving for a while now."

"Very funny. Are you capable of driving or are you shaking too much?"

"I can drive." Some of the humor faded from his eyes. "You heading home?"

"Yes." She paused. "With you."

She watched as he processed the statement. Confusion morphed into surprise. His brows rose.

"To do what?" he asked.

She shoved his board into the back of his truck and started toward the Mini.

"I'm going to need a shower first. Get rid of the salt water. Make sure the water's hot when I get there."

He took off a little bit above the speed limit. She followed more slowly, figuring there was no need for both of them to get a ticket.

She parked behind his truck in the driveway, then went inside. After locking the front door, she toed off her sandals and carried her tote bag upstairs.

While she hadn't exactly planned the morning, she'd considered the possibility. She had clean panties and a bra, along with jeans and a T-shirt with her. Oh, and a box of condoms because sometimes guys forgot the basics.

As she moved into the bedroom, she heard the sound of running water coming from the bathroom. She got her shampoo out of her tote, slipped off her sundress and stepped out of her tank swimsuit. She hung it over the back of the desk chair, then walked naked into the bathroom.

Harding stood by the steaming shower, still in his trunks. His erection strained against the fabric. He was shaking but looked less cold.

She knew making love with him was crossing a line. That she would find herself smack in the middle of whatever she'd been trying to avoid. Harding was dangerous to her in ways no man had ever been—not since Lewis. Her late husband had destroyed her ability to believe in a man ever again. Or so she'd thought. Here she was—practically believing in Harding.

A slick road to hell, she told herself, even as she walked over to him and put her hands on his chest.

"I have to wash my hair," she told him. "Not especially sexy, but it's a thing. Once I'm finished I'm available for whatever you can think of that you want to do with me." She raised herself up and kissed his mouth. "Then we'll do what I like. If you're still alive after that, I'll make you brunch."

He had to clear his throat before he could speak. "You cook?"

She laughed. "Under the right circumstances."

She started for the shower, pausing to glance back at him as she opened the door. "You're welcome to come in and watch. Just let me finish with my hair before touching."

He had his trunks off in an eighth of a second. The shower was plenty big, with good water pressure. She stood with her back to the spray and saturated her hair, then used her ridiculously expensive shampoo to wash out the coconut oil she'd sprayed on before going into the ocean.

As she worked she was aware of Harding watching her. His gaze drifted over her body, pausing where she would expect. She did a little looking of her own, taking in the broad shoulders, flat belly and large erection. Being this close to him, both of them naked, with the promise of sex only minutes away, aroused her. Her breasts ached and her clit swelled.

She had a feeling they were going to be good together. He would make sure she was satisfied and she would be his willing partner in any sexual game he liked.

She tilted her head to rinse the shampoo out of her hair. She'd just finished when she felt his hands on her thighs. She glanced down and saw him kneeling on the tile. Seconds later his tongue stroked against her clit. Just one little flick that made her gasp and part her legs.

Hunger burned. She hadn't been with a man in months and unlike Mikki, she didn't enjoy her own Earl at home. When she needed to get laid, she wanted the real thing. But since meeting Harding, she hadn't bothered with her usual practice of finding a man for a night or two. She was aroused, she was horny and she was more than ready.

"Don't play," she told him. "Just eat me like you mean it."

He immediately parted his lips to suck on her, pulling hard enough to make her gasp with pleasure. At the same time he shoved two fingers deep inside before withdrawing them again. The combination of actions had her bracing her hands against the wall to keep herself upright. Her legs started to tremble.

He loved her with his tongue, pressing hard, then sucking again. He curled the fingers inside her and found her G-spot. He rubbed the swollen flesh, matching the speed and intensity of his tongue and lips, until she found herself screaming out an unexpected climax that nearly sent her to her knees.

Shudders rippled through her, leaving her helpless to do anything but beg him not to stop. Her orgasm went on and on, her muscles convulsing around his fingers, her clit taking more and more until at last, the glory of it all began to fade and she could once again think rationally.

Harding stood and faced her, a faintly satisfied smile tugging at his mouth.

"I like it when you wash your hair."

She didn't know what to say. Part of the deal of sex with someone was both partners getting off. She enjoyed an orgasm as much as the next person. They just weren't usually so...explosive. Nor did they leave her desperate for more.

She turned him so he was under the spray. For a second she considered returning the favor by going down on him, but she was too selfish. She wanted to feel him inside her. The blow job could wait for another time.

While the water rinsed him, she pressed her body against his and drew his hands to her breasts. As they kissed and their tongues mingled, she felt his fingers on her nipples. He pressed and teased and squeezed exactly how she liked it. Hard enough to get her panting but not so hard that it hurt.

His erection pressed against her belly, big with all kinds of promise. She broke free and tugged him toward her.

"I need you," she said.

His gaze locked with hers. She saw his hunger and it fueled her own. She turned off the water and stepped out of the shower. He followed. She grabbed two towels and headed for the bedroom. She wrapped one around her hair and put the other on the comforter, then lay on her back.

Harding paused to open a nightstand and pull out several condoms. He slid one onto his dick before kneeling between her thighs. She reached up to wrap her arms around his neck and kiss him. Just before her mouth settled on his, she whispered, "Do me."

He plunged inside her, his stroke deep and true. She gasped as he filled her completely, then withdrew. He pushed in again, the delicious friction making her moan. She wrapped both her legs around his hips, pulling him in deeper. He braced himself on his arms and stared into her eyes.

"Come for me," he told her. "I want to watch."

Even as his movements pushed her closer and closer to release, Bree wasn't sure about his request. She knew what he wanted—letting him see her climax was a kind of intimacy. In that moment of pure pleasure there was nowhere to hide. It wasn't something she normally agreed to, but somehow with Harding, saying no wasn't possible.

He moved faster, pushing her closer. The feel of him, the thickness, the pressure, all conspired to bring her to her release. She dug her nails into his back as she half rose off the bed, getting right on the edge of falling.

"Open your eyes."

The gentle request could not be denied. She gave herself over to the orgasm and called out his name as she opened her eyes and stared into his. Pleasure claimed her and her breath, leaving her gasping. Not two seconds later he shoved in one last time and came inside her. His hazel eyes darkened as she watched him surrender to her body.

When the aftershocks had faded, Harding disposed of the condom, then rolled onto his back and started laughing.

"I don't think I can walk," he admitted. "My legs are still shaking from this morning and possibly what we just did."

She got up and pulled the comforter over him. "Go to sleep. I'll wake you in an hour."

He grabbed her hand. "You're not leaving, are you?"

"No." She smiled. "I promised you brunch."

"I just don't want you to go."

"I'll be here."

Bree collected her clothes and went downstairs. She dressed and then made coffee. After filling a mug, she sat out on the patio and breathed in the warm morning air.

She was fine. Having sex with Harding had been inevitable

from the start, but it wasn't a big deal. If anything, she should think of herself as growing and changing in a positive way. She'd slept with someone she cared about. They were dating and sex was the next logical step in their relationship. She was totally okay with that. Really.

Only she didn't feel fine. Yes, her body hummed with all the feel-good hormones coursing through her, but there was also an underlying sense of unease. It was like knowing there was a storm coming—sure, the skies were blue now, but for how long? And when the storm did hit, how bad would it be?

She sipped her coffee and tried to relax, but tension built inside her until she wanted to run. She had her car, she could write a note and be gone. What was the big deal? Except where, exactly, was she supposed to go? And what would happen when she got there?

She returned to the kitchen. Manuscript pages were stacked by chapters on the breakfast bar. Handwritten notes covered many of them. She picked a random chapter and started to read.

After thirty-two years of marriage, Maggie Truxillo lost her husband. For the first time in her adult life, she was alone and struggling to find out where she fit in what she'd come to think of as "the hell of new normal."

Maggie explains: "Hopelessness is harder to live with than sadness. I was sad for the first year, but then that turned into hopelessness. Without hope, what's the point? There's nothing to live for. I know this sounds crazy but I crawled out of that big, dark pit because my neighbor asked me to look after her kitten.

He was about four months old—a scrawny, feisty thing who didn't like me at all. He would hiss when I tried to feed him and forget about playing with him. He clawed my hand so bad. My neighbor was on vacation for two weeks, so I was stuck. So I went online and read how to make friends with kittens. I realized he was scared, not mean. I went slower with him, letting him come to me.

The first time I petted him and he purred, I started to cry. Ri-

diculous, but that rumbly sound really got to me. Then he crawled into my lap to sleep and I sat there crying for everything I'd lost. Not just because Rob died, but for the months when I hadn't been there for my kids or grandkids because I was too sad. They were suffering, too, and I just couldn't deal with them.

Grief is natural, but when left alone it grows into something bigger. Something that steals hope. You shut down and no one gets in. The walls get bigger. I see that in my grief group. Some of them are healing but others may be lost in their pain forever."

Bree put down the pages, willing to admit his work was interesting, but it had nothing to do with her.

"Hey."

Harding walked into the kitchen. He'd pulled on jeans, and his hair was mussed. He looked sleepy and sexy and she wanted to rush into his arms. Instead, she tapped the manuscript.

"I'm not stuck in grief."

He poured himself a mug of coffee. "Okay."

"I mean it. I'm not. I don't feel any grief in my life, so we're not going to talk about it."

Harding faced her and leaned against the counter. "You're right. We're not. I never should have asked you before. I apologize."

"Good. Because I don't feel grief. Not even a little."

"Everybody grieves, Bree. Big things, small things. It happens."

"Not to me. You think I was sad when Lewis died?" She glared at him from across the breakfast bar. "I wasn't. I hated him. Loathed him. He played me and I hated him for that."

"Because he knew about the cancer before he asked you back," Harding said quietly, his gaze locked on her face.

"Yes. He showed up out of the blue, saying he'd made a horrible mistake. That he loved me and wanted me back." She thought about how she'd felt when she'd heard the words. "I was so grateful. What an idiot. I believed him. For the first time in months, I was happy. Until the diagnosis."

"Of course."

"It felt so unfair—that we'd finally found our way back to being in love and then his diagnosis. I was there for every treatment, every consultation. I cooked the foods he could tolerate, I cleaned up his puke. I loved him."

She had. With every fiber of her being. Heart and soul, all in. Until she'd started to realize he was simply going through the motions. That whatever love he'd felt before was gone.

She'd told herself she was wrong, that she was looking for trouble. But the feeling never went away, and a few months later she discovered he'd known about the cancer before he'd asked her to come back.

"He didn't want to die alone," she said aloud. "That's why he'd come back to get me. He knew I still loved him and would be grateful for a second chance. He knew I wouldn't leave him, even when I found out the truth. And I didn't. I was there to the end, hating him and watching him die, but unable to walk away and leave him like the bastard he was."

She looked at Harding. "I didn't grieve and I don't. I vowed then and there I would never love anyone again. I would never care enough to be hurt. You can't touch me because no one touches me. If you want to fuck, let's do that, but if you're looking for more, I don't have it in me."

Harding looked more sad than surprised. She waited for him to yell at her, to accuse her of leading him on, of being flawed and unlovable, not at all who he thought she was. She braced herself for the impact and told herself she would be fine regardless.

He put down his coffee. "I've always been impressed by your strength. There's been so much pain in your life, so much betrayal. Yet, look at you, standing there. Tough. Vibrant. Alive. When I was hit by that car, I had a long road to recovery. It was hard, but I was never alone. My family was with me. The doctors and nurses were there. Strangers prayed for me. Kids at schools halfway across the country sent handmade cards. If I got tired or wanted to give up, there was always someone there, cheering me on. I didn't do anything alone."

He looked at her. "It wasn't like that for you. There weren't any fans, no loving family. But you got through it. You figured out boarding school would be better for you and you made it happen. You kept moving forward. You're resilient and you're brave and I'm grateful to have you in my life."

"Don't be grateful," she snapped. "What a stupid thing to say. I'm not someone you admire. This is it, Harding. I can't do better. You want a regular life where we fall in love and get married and have kids. You want me to love you and have Christmas with your family."

"You want that, too."

"Yes, but I can't do it. I can't trust you and I sure as hell can't trust myself. I'll never give my heart again. Never. I'm done. I've tried. Loving Lewis and having him do what he did nearly killed me. I can't be hurt like that one more time."

"I wouldn't do that."

"Now," she said sharply. "You say it now, but you're asking me to trust you in the future. You're asking me to risk my heart on you and I won't. I don't have another break in me. I know that and I've learned to protect myself. Here's the thing. When we're done, I won't grieve you. I'll walk away and never think I made a mistake. You can't be important to me because I won't let you. You don't matter to me. You never will."

Raw pain swept across his face. His muscles contracted as if she'd slapped him. The starkness of his reaction, the realization of what she'd said, had her clutching her midsection, as if to hold the sides of a wound together.

"I knew you were scared," he said quietly. "I could deal with that. I'll admit it never occurred to me you just plain weren't interested." He glanced down, then back at her. "You're not in love with me."

"No."

"And you don't care if I love you."

"Hearing you say it makes me uncomfortable."

"And what we just did. That was sex."

"Good sex," she said. "But it didn't mean anything."

Lies, all lies, she thought. But telling them made her feel safe. Not admitting her feelings, not risking herself, was the best course. If she was vulnerable, he would hurt her. If she didn't take care of herself, no one else would do it.

"I told you," she whispered. "I warned you from the beginning that I would hurt you." *I knew I wasn't worth it.*

He shocked her by circling the breakfast bar and wrapping his arms around her. For a second she allowed herself to hang on because holding him always felt right.

"You're going to run now," he whispered into her hair. "Probably for the best because I'm about five seconds from crying and it's not a good look for me. I think you're lying about most of this, but I can't figure out if that's true, or wishful thinking. Or maybe you're lying to yourself. I don't know. I'm just a guy who loves you with his whole heart. I mean that, Bree. You're right when you say I want it all. To marry you, have babies and holidays with my family. And a dog. I'd really like a dog."

He drew back enough to kiss her.

"Go get your shit together, then come back to me. Because letting me go is a really stupid idea. Guys like me don't come along very often—not because I'm so great, but because we're great together. I love you. I'm committed to you and I will lay down my life for you, so if you lose out on me, you're going to regret it for a long time." He jerked his head toward the ceiling. "And what happened up there wasn't just sex. We didn't fuck. We made love. Both of us. And it mattered."

Tears burned in her eyes. She turned away before he could see them. She raced out of the kitchen and went upstairs where she grabbed her bag. He wasn't waiting for her when she got back downstairs. She ran to her car and drove away, telling herself this was a lucky escape and not the last desperate act of someone without the courage to embrace the best thing that had ever happened to her.

TWENTY-THREE

"But that doesn't make any sense," Ashley said, trying to take in what her brother had told her. "You two belong together. How could she walk away?"

"She's scared and she's reacting." Harding picked up his beer. "At least, that's what I tell myself. I hope I'm right—otherwise, it's going to be a long, cold, lonely winter."

Ashley had impulsively stopped by with sandwiches from the deli he liked, only to find him exhausted and defeated. His shoulders were slumped, his eyes filled with pain.

He'd told her about Bree ending things, which Ashley hadn't seen coming.

"She's been home sick for the past couple of days," she said slowly. "A stomach bug."

"Yeah, it's not that."

She just couldn't believe what had happened. "But she cares about you. I know she does. And you love her."

They were on his back patio, the untouched sandwiches on the table between them.

"You have to fight for her," Ashley said, then winced. "That sounds really dumb. Sorry. I just don't know what to say. I'm in shock."

"Me, too, although I should have known better. With her past and her trust issues, it was always going to be a crapshoot."

She reached across the table and squeezed his hand. "I'm here for you. Tell me what to do and I will. I can hate her if you want."

Harding swallowed hard. "Don't do that. She's going to need her friends around her. You have to be there for her."

Ashley snatched back her hand and glared at him. "I'm not choosing that bitch over my brother. She hurt you, which, by the way, I warned you would happen."

His gaze met hers. "Don't call her names. This isn't her fault."

"That's crap. Of course it is."

"She warned me dozens of times that she wasn't into relationships or looking for love. I'm the one who didn't listen. This is on me."

"You can't possibly be that rational at this moment. You're a mess. You're hurting."

He shrugged. "Price of doing business." He set down his beer. "I miss her with every breath. I've been in love before, but not like this. I was starting to think there was something wrong with me. Why couldn't I find a woman I wanted to settle down with? Was it the fame? Had the accident messed me up emotionally?"

"There's nothing wrong with you, Harding. You just hadn't met the right person."

He stared at the table. "I have now. She's incredible and I love her. I want to marry her and spend the rest of my life being the luckiest guy on the planet. But that's not going to happen—not unless she's willing to take a chance on me. I can't force that and the risk is I could lose her forever." He picked up his beer. "A hell of a thing."

I want to marry her and spend the rest of my life being the luckiest guy on the planet.

The words echoed in Ashley's head, cutting her with their simplicity and earnestness. Harding loved Bree and wanted to marry her. Because that was what people did.

She forced her attention back on her brother. "What can I do to help?"

"You brought me a sandwich. That's enough."

"Are you going to eat it?"

"Maybe later."

She put the food in the refrigerator and got out fresh fruit and milk. She found protein powder in the pantry and made him a berry chocolate protein drink, then glared at him until he finished it. They sat together another hour until he tossed her out.

"You have a life," he said, walking her to the door and hugging her. "I'll be fine."

"You look like crap."

He managed a weak chuckle. "Thanks. It's what I was going for."

She studied him, wishing she could make him feel better. "I won't tell the folks. Maybe things will work out."

"Maybe." He didn't sound very hopeful. "Don't blame Bree. This isn't on her. It just is."

"I won't yell at her, but I'm going to be a little less friendly. That's the best I can do."

She drove back to the store, her heart heavy with concern and worry. She'd wanted to be wrong about Bree, had wanted things to work out. But her friend was unable to change, despite being loved by a great man.

Because love didn't transform a person into someone else, she thought as she parked in her spot. Love wasn't a cure or a solution. Love might make a person want to be their best self but it didn't fundamentally alter beliefs. Ashley was pretty sure Bree was in love with her brother but that love wasn't enough to keep Bree from reacting from fear. And no matter how much Seth loved her or how many articles, books or bride magazines he read, or how much they talked, he was never going to want to marry her.

That realization followed her all afternoon. She set out muffins and cupcakes, rang up purchases and texted with Oscar about blueberries. It combined with the sadness she felt about Harding and left a knot in her stomach.

A little after six she drove to OAR where she was holding a workshop on figuring out a career path. She'd given the talk before and was grateful to already have the notes she needed.

About a dozen teens showed up. She talked about the differences between college and trade school and explained about financial resources. She told them that what they wanted now could change and to be open to the possibility.

"Did you always want to be a baker?" Tyra asked.

Ashley cringed. "No. I totally messed up my career path. I went to college to be a physical therapist because of Harding's accident and rehabilitation. I got my bachelor's degree, but I realized I didn't want to get my doctor of physical therapy. So I worked in a lab, which I hated. So there I was—twenty-three with a bachelors and a job that depressed me."

"Were you scared?" Tyra asked.

"A little," Ashley admitted. "I was also discouraged and embarrassed. I'd put so much time and effort into my degree, only to discover that I didn't want to use it. I'd always loved baking and decided to go to culinary school. I saved for a year, took in a roommate to share expenses and got a loan to help pay for it. By the time I graduated, I was selling muffins and cupcakes in a co-op by the Santa Monica pier. Now I have a shared store by the beach."

Several of the teens glanced at the tray of cupcakes she'd brought in with her.

"Yes," she said with a laugh. "Please, help yourself. If you have any other questions, let me know."

She stayed with the teens another half hour, mostly reminding them about the resources that were available through OAR. Just before eight the workshop wrapped up. Ashley picked up stray trash and started to leave. On her way out she swung by

Dave's office. Despite the late hour he was behind his desk, typing away on his computer.

"Still putting in fourteen-hour days?" she asked as she walked in.

He looked up and smiled at her. "I was just finishing up with a few emails. How was the workshop?"

"Good. I'm trying to get everyone to use the resource center."

"That's why it's there." He waved her into a seat. "You're a great volunteer, Ashley. We all appreciate your time and effort."

"I like helping out."

She thought about what Harding was going through but didn't know if he'd shared the news with his friend. As she wasn't sure, she decided not to mention it.

But thinking about Bree and her brother brought her back to the topic she'd been wrestling with for hours. Seth and how he felt about marriage.

"Do you want to get married?" she asked abruptly.

"Sudden," Dave said calmly, looking at her. "Unexpected, but sure. We can get married. Oh, and in case you were wondering, the equipment works."

Despite her swirling emotions, she laughed. "I can't believe you said that."

"Are you talking about my acceptance of your proposal or the line about the equipment?"

"You know I didn't propose. Do you want to get married someday?"

"No comment on the other thing?"

"I already knew. One of your ex-girlfriends was very explicit about that."

"Was she complimentary?"

"Dave! I'm serious."

"So am I." He chuckled. "Okay, I'll play along. Why would you ask that? Sure, I want to get married. I want to fall in love, have a wedding, have a family." He paused. "Wait. This isn't about me, is it? What's going on?"

"Nothing. Okay, not nothing, but it's no big deal."

She was surprised to feel her eyes burning.

"Seth doesn't believe in marriage." She held up her hand to stop him from speaking. "He loves me and wants to commit to forever. A house, kids, the whole thing. Just not marriage."

Dave watched her without speaking.

"We're trying to work it out," she continued. "See things from each other's point of view. It's not like I've been planning my wedding since I was six. But I always saw myself getting married."

She shook her head. "Why does even saying that make me feel weak and needy? I'm not. I just, I don't know. I think the relationship is stronger with marriage. But maybe I'm putting too much emphasis on the institution. I've been trying to let go of the idea of being a wife. But every time I almost get there, I can't take that final step. I can't convince myself it would be okay not to be married. I don't know why that's so hard for me."

"Want to know what I think?"

"Very much." She trusted Dave to be honest and she cared what he had to say.

"It's bullshit. I don't know what Seth's problem is but he's feeding you a line. Seth claims to love you and wants to spend his life with you, but he's not willing to do the one thing that makes your life together possible. You want to get married. That's where you are. He either gets with the program or he's a dick."

He leaned toward her. "The reason you can't get there is it doesn't feel right to you. You're not comfortable trusting your future and your kids' future to fate. You want certainty."

"Marriage isn't certain. We could get a divorce."

"Yeah, but you probably won't. Besides, it's what you want, Ashley. You deserve that."

What he said felt right, she thought grimly. And if he was right, then she and Seth were in trouble.

"I could change."

"Why should you have to? You're not asking for anything unreasonable. In fact, he's the unreasonable one. I hope he appreciates how much you love him, because he's sure not acting like it."

"I'm trying to be patient and wise."

"You're giving him too much slack."

"You have very strong opinions."

He grinned. "You knew that when you asked me what I thought."

"Yes, I did."

His humor faded. "Don't settle. Stand up for yourself and insist he listen to you."

"Be strong," she said. "I'm not always good at that."

"Then this is a great time to get in a little practice."

"Don't you dare quote OAR philosophy to me."

He chuckled. "I wouldn't."

She rose. "Thanks for listening. I feel better and worse, if that makes sense."

"Happy to offer my opinion any time you want. You know where to find me. Oh, and just so we're clear—I want a church wedding. I don't care where the reception is, but I want to be married before God."

"Traditional," she said. "I wouldn't have guessed."

"I don't want any surprises later."

She laughed. "I'll keep that in mind."

Mikki was feeling torn in two directions. Okay, three. On the one hand, she was worried about Bree and what was happening with Harding. Technically, nothing had been discussed—at least not among Bree and Ashley and Mikki. But Harding had told Ashley, who'd told Mikki. After two days of claiming to be sick, Bree had returned to the store, pale, thin and tired. Under any other circumstances, Mikki would have totally believed the stomach flu excuse.

While she and Ashley had agreed not to discuss the "Harding thing" until Bree brought it up, Mikki was questioning their decision. Bree obviously needed her friends right now, and waiting for her to cough up the truth was hard on all of them. On the other hand, Bree wasn't someone who shared things easily. Pushing her might cause her to retreat even more. It was a conundrum.

At the other end of her life spectrum, Duane was still gone. The British Prime Minister had asked him to stop by after Madrid, so sometime today Duane would fly to London for a little chitchat with whomever ran the money side of Britain. He'd been very apologetic late last night, which had been early morning for him. He'd also sent her beautiful roses and had been texting with the regularity of a teenager. It was lovely and had her smiling, but to be honest, she would rather have the man instead of the texts and the flowers.

She missed him. It wasn't as if they spent every second together, but knowing he was so far away and staying longer than he'd planned, made her sad. She'd been looking forward to their reunion, to hearing about the conference, to spending another night in his bed.

But that would have to wait. At least the flight from London would be direct—albeit nine hours.

She sniffed her flowers. They sat on the counter, by the main cash register. She'd debated keeping them in her office, where they were less conspicuous, but had decided she wasn't going to hide the fact that she was dating Duane. Lorraine wanted her to get back together with Perry, but Mikki had other plans. Better to be honest about it.

The UPS guy walked into the store, pulling an overflowing trolley. She, Ashley and Bree kept the guy busy delivering boxes.

"Tell me you brought parchment paper, Grant," Ashley said, walking to meet the man.

"Hey, what's in the boxes is up to you. My job is to get them here in one piece."

Ashley studied the boxes. "Books, books, mugs, frames, books. Ooh, my flavored sugars. I'm excited."

Mikki was about to tease her friend for her unnatural interest in all the packages when she heard a sharp cry from the back of the store. She turned in time to see Lorraine go completely white and stumble—her phone held to her ear.

"No! When? Where are you taking him?" Tears spilled down her cheeks. "I'll be there. Tell him I'll be there."

Mikki ran to her mother-in-law. "What happened?"

Lorraine's lips trembled. "Chet collapsed. The medics think he had a heart attack. They're taking him to the hospital." She grabbed Mikki's arm. "He can't die. He can't."

Mikki ignored the cold wash of panic that swept through her. She would freak out later—right now Lorraine needed her.

"Which hospital?"

"City General."

One of the best, Mikki thought, and part of the UCLA Medical Center.

"They'll take care of him there. Come on, I'll drive."

Lorraine looked at her in confusion. "I don't understand. He was fine this morning. I made him an omelet."

She put her arm around her mother-in-law. "Let's go find out what's happening. Maybe it's something else." *Something less scary than a heart attack*, she thought desperately.

Ashley hovered. "How can I help?"

Mikki realized she and Lorraine were the only ones working her store that morning. "Call in a couple of the part-time people to take over. I don't know how long I'll be gone."

Bree and Rita walked over.

"What happened?" Rita asked, rushing to her friend.

"It's Chet," Lorraine said, collapsing in Rita's arms. "They think it's a heart attack."

Mikki silently willed her mother not to say anything awful. "He's going to die for sure" was very much Rita's style. But her mom only murmured, "It's going to be all right, Lorraine. You'll see."

"We're going to the hospital," Mikki told her.

"I'll take care of the store until you can get other people in to help," her mom said, surprising her. "I remember how it all works."

"Thanks."

Bree, looking wan and sad, moved closer. "What can I do?"

"I think we're good for now. I'll call as soon as we know something."

She and her mother-in-law collected their handbags, then hurried to Mikki's car. She drove to the massive hospital and parked by the emergency room. Between the parking lot and the entrance, Lorraine started crying. Mikki pulled her close and kept them moving.

Inside, she looked around for a reception desk or a—

She spotted Perry talking to a nurse. Relief swept through her.

"Perry's here," she said.

They raced over to him. He nodded at the nurse and pulled them both close. Mikki leaned against him, knowing he would be strong through whatever they were dealing with. When there was a crisis, Perry was a rock.

"He's stable," he said. "Not in a lot of pain. They're going to run tests to determine if it was a heart attack. We'll be able to see him shortly."

Lorraine began to sob. Mikki moved back so Perry could hold his mother. Her ex-husband looked as worried as she felt.

"I want to wait to tell the kids," she said. "Let's find out what happened before we scare them."

He nodded.

"How are things at work?" she asked. "Do I need to go by and do anything?"

"They're handling things. I'll update them later."

"I'll call," she told him. "You take care of your mom." She pointed to several empty chairs in a corner. "Let's go sit."

Once Perry and Lorraine were seated, Mikki got everyone coffee from the kiosk down the hall. As she waited her turn, she texted her mother to let her know what was happening.

We're all praying, her mother texted back.

That was all they could do, Mikki thought. Pray and wait.

Four hours later Mikki watched in surprise as her mother, followed by a very tough-looking man with a shaved head and plenty of tattoos, walked into the waiting room. Rita spotted her and headed in her direction. Her companion followed closely, nodding as she spoke.

"Mom, you made it."

Mikki rose and hugged her mother, then turned to the man. "Hi."

"I brought sandwiches," he said, setting a large box on the nearest table. "Drinks. Cupcakes. Ashley sent me."

"This is Oscar," Rita said. "My daughter, Mikki. Oscar was in prison but he's fine now."

Mikki tried not to wince at the blunt statement. "Nice to meet you. I hope my mother wasn't too much for you to handle."

Oscar surprised her with a smile. "She's got attitude, but I respect that. Sorry about your father-in-law. I hope he's going to be all right."

"We think he will be. They're just finishing up surgery to put in a stent." One of the nurses had come by to say everything was going well and the doctor would be out shortly.

Rita studied her. "Are you just saying that to be polite?"

"It's what they said. With a few lifestyle changes, Chet should make a full recovery."

"I'll head back to the store," Oscar said.

"Ashley called in volunteers from OAR," Rita said, "to handle things. Bree's taken charge, putting everyone to work. How's Lorraine?"

Mikki motioned to the corner of the waiting room where Sydney and Will sat with their grandmother and Perry.

"Shaken. We all are."

Rita looked at Oscar. "I'm going to stay here. Mikki or one of my grandkids can give me a ride back to the store. Thank you for your help."

"Anytime." Oscar nodded and left.

Mikki hugged her mom. "Thanks for bringing food. I'm sure everyone is hungry." Not that she could imagine eating, but the kids would want food and maybe Perry.

"I just hope Chet doesn't die."

"They said he'd be fine."

"What else are they going to say? That he's hanging on by a thread? Hearts are tricky things." She sniffed and wiped her eyes. "Plus, Lorraine still loves him. It would hit her so hard." She cleared her throat. "Don't worry. I'll be strong and I won't say anything about his imminent death."

With that, she squared her shoulders and walked over to greet Lorraine. The two longtime friends embraced. Sydney made room for her maternal grandmother on the sofa, while Perry walked over to Mikki.

"There's food," she said as he approached. "Ashley sent it."

Instead of answering, he held open his arms. She stepped into his familiar embrace and hung on.

"I can't believe it," he told her, his body pressed against hers. "Dad's so damned strong all the time. He's a healthy guy. How could this happen?"

"Chet never liked to go to the doctor. You know your mom's been bugging him about his blood pressure for years. He wouldn't do anything about it."

She stepped back and stared into Perry's sad eyes. "You heard the nurse. He's going to be fine. This is a good lesson for him. Now he'll start to do all the things he should. You'll see. This time next year, your dad will be running marathons."

Perry started to laugh, then collapsed onto a nearby sofa and covered his face with his hands.

"We could have lost him," he said, his voice thick with tears.

She sat next to him and put her arm around him. "But we didn't. He's going to get through this. We all are."

He wiped his face. "You're always the strong one. When something bad happens, you're a rock."

He took her hand. "I love you, Mikki. I don't mean that any way other than I love you and I'm grateful you're here. I know it's because of my dad, but I like us being a family again."

Before she could answer, Sydney walked over and sat next to Mikki. She snuggled close to her mom.

"I hate the waiting," she admitted. "The worrying. I love you guys. Never get sick, okay?"

Mikki pulled her close. "We'll do our best."

Will joined them. He sat on the coffee table in front of the sofa. "Grandma Lorraine's a mess. I'm glad Granny Rita is here to take care of her. I didn't know what to say."

"There are sandwiches," Mikki said, pointing to the table in the corner. "From Ashley and Bree. Probably sodas and cup-cakes."

"I'm not hungry." Sydney rubbed her belly. "My stomach's too upset from worrying."

"I'm starved," Will admitted, getting to his feet and ambling over to the spread.

Sydney stretched out her hand toward her father. "I need you to start exercising, Dad. And eat more broccoli. And salad in general."

"Now you sound like your mother," he said, winking at Mikki.

"I never nagged you to take care of yourself," she protested. "I was more subtle than that."

"Meatless Mondays," Sydney and Perry said together.

"Remember those bean tacos that gave us all gas?" Perry asked.

"Or the zucchini fritters that tasted like green dirt?"

"Hey, some of my meatless meals were a success."

"I did like the Portabella burgers," Perry admitted. "All they needed was a little hamburger and they would have been perfect."

They were still laughing when the surgeon walked into the waiting area. Instantly, the room went silent as everyone came to their feet.

"He's fine," she said easily. "Resting comfortably." Her gaze found Lorraine, who was clinging to Rita. "You'll be able to see him shortly. We'll keep him in the hospital a couple of days, just to monitor him, then he can go home. If all goes well, he'll be back to regular activities in ten days or so."

Perry asked a few questions, then the doctor left. The grandkids hugged their grandmothers while Perry hung on to Mikki.

"We're not going to lose him," he said, sounding shocked.

"Not for a long time."

The kids joined them, hugging and jumping in place. The connection, the sense of belonging, was familiar. As if after a long time gone, she'd finally found her way home.

Only she and Perry weren't a couple anymore. They would always be family, but as former spouses and friends. Not husband and wife. She looked into the face of the man she'd loved most of her adult life and wondered if moving on really was what she wanted or if, as Perry suggested, they had given up too soon.

TWENTY-FOUR

Bree would never admit it to Mikki, but she was actually grateful for Chet's heart attack. Filling in for her friend, coordinating the volunteers who covered shifts at the bookstore and gift shop, kept her busy. It was easier to get through the day when there wasn't time to think.

With Oscar's help, she and Ashley had shifted the cash registers closer together. It was easier to keep track of things when they weren't constantly running from one end of the store to the other. With Mikki, Rita and Lorraine all gone, there was more work than hours. Bree took care of inventory, stocking shelves, logging in deliveries and placing orders where she could, while Ashley managed the customer flow.

They worked well together, never mentioning what had happened. Whatever thoughts Ashley had about how Bree had treated her brother, she kept them to herself. A fact for which Bree was grateful.

When she was by herself—in the storeroom, loading shelves before the store opened—she was willing to admit she missed Harding desperately. His absence was a tangible ache every second she was awake. Worse, he haunted her in her sleep, filling her dreams with his laughter, his touch, his smile. She wanted to tell him she'd changed her mind, that of course she could be all he wanted and they would be fine.

But she knew herself—knew she was incapable of the very thing he needed from her. Trust. Not in him but in herself. She couldn't believe that she was strong enough to survive whatever happened between them. Better to not take the chance. Better to lose all of it.

But knowing she'd done the right thing and living through it were not the same. She was exhausted, not eating, barely able to function, but she drove herself forward, clear on the fact that her friend needed her. Or more honestly, grateful that the crisis gave her a place to hide.

She rolled a cart of books out into the store and started shelving them. She'd just finished with the cozy mysteries when she heard someone behind her.

"Hello, Bree."

She turned and her heart sank. Sad Guy stood there, his hair mussed, the print of his Hawaiian shirt as loud as ever. Mingling with the wish that he would go away was a bit of embarrassment about what had happened the last time she'd seen him. Given how she'd offered sex then had thrown up, she probably owed him an apology. Fortunately, he spoke before she could figure out how to phrase one.

"I wanted to let you know I've sold my surf shop," he said, his gaze unreadable. "I'm moving to Maui. I have some friends who own a place and I'll go in with them."

"Congratulations."

He ignored that. "I can't stay here and see you every day when I know the truth." He shook his head. "I used to think you were some amazing woman—elusive and beautiful. That if I could just figure you out, I could make you fall in love with me. But after what happened that night, I've realized you're an empty shell pretending to be a person. I can't believe how much time I wasted wanting something that turned out to be nothing."

He left then, just walked out of the store without looking back. Bree stared after him, her skin cold and clammy, her heart pounding. For a second she thought she was going to throw up the way she had that last night at his place, but after a few deep breaths her stomach calmed down.

Ashley raced over, her expression outraged.

"What was that? I only heard part of what he said, but what the hell? Asshole. He's such a jerk. Are you okay? I wish I'd hit him. I should call Oscar. He's always offering to take care of any guy who bugs me. I'll have him take care of Sad Guy."

"I don't feel anything," Bree told her. "I'm fine."

"How can you say that?"

Because it was the truth. Because he was one of the few people who had actually seen her for who she was. Sure, there was surprise and a little embarrassment, but none of it was news.

"I'm okay," she repeated. "He's moving to Maui. I hope he'll be happy."

Ashley grabbed her upper arms. "Why are you so calm? He was awful. He hurt you."

"He didn't. He can't. I don't feel anything. I don't get hurt or sad or upset. None of this touches me."

She thought Ashley might recoil or even slap her, but instead she surprised Bree by smiling.

"You are so full of shit. Seriously? You don't feel anything? You miss my brother so much, you're wasting away in front of my eyes. You're texting Mikki every fifteen minutes to see if she needs something. You ask about Seth, take care of both stores, you have a very twisted relationship with your mother. None of that is an example of not feeling. If anything, you feel everything and you don't know how to handle it."

Ashley hugged her. "Oh, Bree, I worry about you. How can you not see yourself the way we see you? We're a family now. That's going to be awkward with Harding, I know, and at some point we have to talk about how stupid you are, but we'll get through it."

Bree pulled back. "We're not family. How can you say that?

We're work associates, nothing more. Don't make it something it isn't. You're being ridiculous."

"So are you. You think you're so tough, but you're not the only one. I'm tough, too."

"So tough you can't tell your boyfriend to either suck it up and propose or you're done?"

Bree immediately wanted to call back the words. She saw the flash of pain in Ashley's eyes and instinctively moved toward her, only to stop herself. She had a point to prove and that mattered more than how the other woman felt.

"You're right," Ashley said, surprising her. "You're absolutely right. I've tried and I've tried but I don't want to do it anymore. I don't want to pretend it's okay when it isn't."

Bree's icy heart melted and she grabbed Ashley. "I'm such a bitch. I'm sorry. I shouldn't have said that. I felt cornered, so I reacted. Don't be mad and I'm sorry I hurt you. I just don't know what to do with all my feelings. Everything's wrong."

Ashley stared into her eyes. "No, only one thing's wrong. You're in love with Harding and you're either too stupid or too scared to admit it." One corner of her mouth turned up. "And I've never thought you were stupid."

"You're talking really tough today."

"I learned from an expert."

Bree stepped back and closed her eyes. "I can't do it. I can't be with him. You were right to tell him to avoid me. I can only go so far and then I get scared and I run. That's why I keep things casual. It's easier."

"But you love him."

She opened her eyes. "I don't want to and thinking I might terrifies me. Don't romanticize this, Ashley. Don't think I'm going to figure it out. I'm not. I'm going to destroy what Harding and I have because I understand the pain. I trust the pain. It's the being happy I don't believe in."

No, she corrected silently. Not the happy—it was what came

later. It was letting her guard down for a second, and then having him obliterate her. The way her parents had over and over again, and then Lewis. She'd only ever loved and cared for him and he'd used her in the worst way possible. He'd allowed her to believe they could have their love back, when he'd been playing her the whole time.

"You're so messed up," Ashley told her. "You're going to lose him, you know. One day he's going to heal and move on."

"That's what I'm hoping for. He deserves better than this."

Ashley groaned. "I want to shake you. What about what you deserve? Don't you get to have a great life with a wonderful man who adores you?"

Bree shook her head. "Not this life. Maybe I'll do better next time."

"That's a defeatist attitude."

"It's realistic. I know what I'm capable of and what I'm not. I know Harding is hurting now, but in the long run, he'll be grateful I let him go."

"That's just an excuse."

"Maybe, but it's also the truth."

Ashley watched the clock, waiting for Seth to get home from work. Her discussion with Bree had provided the final piece she'd needed to understand what she wanted and what compromises she was willing to make.

She loved being with Seth. They liked the same things, shared a set of values, laughed at the same jokes. They loved Thai food, were wary of small monkeys, preferred dogs to cats, books to e-readers, were close to their families. Their house-hunting adventures had shown them that they disagreed on wall color but both wanted big, open kitchens and a killer master bath. They'd settled on two kids, unless she was up for more—a decision to be made later.

He'd researched what it would take to franchise Muffins to

the Max and already had an idea about an investor. He talked about building an empire together. They shared a vision of the future and the possibilities.

But he was still opposed to marriage. He loved her, wanted to be with her forever, would commit to her in every way possible. Except for one.

The front door opened and he walked into the apartment.

"Hey," he said with a smile. "When did you get home?" His smile faded. "Something's happened. Is Chet all right?"

"He's fine. Back home and being fussed over."

Seth crossed to the sofa and sat angled toward her. "Did you have it out with Bree? I know you're upset about what she did."

He thought this was about Bree?

"I'm fine with her," she said, wondering how he could get it so wrong. "I know she's hurting and confused, but she didn't end things to be mean. She can't handle the emotions. She doesn't have the skills or trust herself enough. Harding's been trying to explain it to me for a while now, but I finally got it today with Sad Guy."

"Then what's wrong?"

She hesitated, not sure how to say what she was thinking, only to realize the truth was always the best answer.

"I haven't changed my mind about wanting to get married," she told him.

He sagged against the back of the sofa. "Ashley," he began.

She held up her hand to stop him. "Let me finish. I love you and I believe you love me. I understand your reluctance and I know you have your reasons, but this isn't about you. It's about me. I want a commitment that makes me feel safe. Telling me you love me and will always be there for me isn't enough. I need the ceremony—you and me standing in front of our friends and family, telling the world we'll always love each other. I don't need a fancy wedding, but I need something tangible. A marriage certificate, a ring, a couple of pictures. I want to know that we are legally bound together."

"And if I don't want that? Is this an ultimatum?"

She felt herself flinch at the question, instantly feeling defensive. What was it about certain words? What was it about her?

"I don't have all the answers," she admitted. "I'm just letting you know that your way isn't going to work for me."

"And if I say the same?"

Her stomach twisted as her chest tightened. What would happen then? If neither of them was willing to bend, was their relationship over?

Tears filled her eyes. "I don't want to think about that."

He pulled her close and held her tight. "Me, either. We have to figure this out, Ashley."

Then damn well marry me. But she didn't say the words aloud. Because forcing him wasn't a solution. She couldn't make him want to do something. But she also couldn't be happy with his view of their future.

"I love you," he whispered, then kissed her. "Please know that."

"I do." She faked a smile. "I love you, too."

"There's a solution. We'll find it. I know we will."

He spoke with conviction, which should have reassured her, but didn't. And even as she leaned her head against him and told herself they would get through this, the thick tendrils of doubt began to wrap themselves around her heart.

"How does this work?" Mikki asked, wondering if she sounded as doubtful as she felt.

Bree pulled her T-shirt over her head, revealing a body-fitting workout tank over a sports bra. "It's spin class. You ride a bike. This is a short one—only thirty minutes. I didn't think you'd want to go longer."

"I get that, but are there any things I should know like how I keep up and am I expected to shout or something?"

"You know these are stationary bikes, right? They don't move, so you don't have to worry about keeping up."

"You know what I mean."

Bree, still pale and thin, with dark circles under her eyes, smiled. "We'll get bikes in the back. Just follow along and you'll be fine."

Mikki was already regretting her impulsive text to Bree, asking to join her next spin class. But she'd spent the past few days unable to focus and she wasn't sleeping well. Everyone always said intense exercise cleared the mind, so here she was, ready to try something new.

Okay—maybe *ready* was a little strong, but she'd shown up, so yay her.

She followed Bree into the main exercise room, or whatever it was called. As promised, they chose bikes in the back. Bree adjusted the incredibly small and hard seat.

"I'm supposed to sit on this for half an hour?" Mikki asked as she shifted in a futile attempt to get comfortable.

"You won't be sitting very much."

"It's a bike. What else would I do?"

Bree's smile turned genuine. "Stand. It's the only way to get up the hills."

Thirty-five minutes later Mikki managed to almost step, almost fall off her bike. She was dripping sweat, her thighs were shaking and she wasn't sure her heart rate would ever return to normal.

"You did great," Bree said, not bothering to hide her amusement.

"I'll hate you forever," Mikki muttered, holding on to the bike until she was sure she could stand on her own. "I can't believe you do this on purpose."

"It's fun."

"It's torture. I'm sweating. I don't sweat. It's why I do Pilates. Everything is slow. Difficult, but there's no sweating."

"Sweat is good for you."

Mikki's legs steadied enough for her to hobble toward the locker room. "Did I mention the hate? I'm not kidding."

"Come on. I'll buy you a milkshake."

Mikki eyed her suspiciously. "You're messing with me. It's not really going to be a milkshake, is it? You're taking me to some vegan place where a coconut drink is supposed to fool me."

Bree laughed. "I promise actual cream, sugar and chocolate."

True to her word, Bree drove to In-N-Out Burger. They each got a milkshake and split an order of fries, then took their food to an outdoor table in the shade. Mikki sat down, trying not to wince from the pain in her thighs. If she hurt this much now, how bad would it be later?

"So," Bree said, unwrapping her straw. "What's going on?"

Mikki could pretend not to know what her friend was asking, but that would only be stalling.

"I'm confused," she admitted. "Chet's heart attack threw me."

"You said he's going to be fine."

"He is. It's not him, exactly. It's more how it was. Perry and me and the kids. Like we were before. He was a rock to everyone else, but he needed me to help him be strong. We were a team."

Bree looked at her. "You're having second thoughts about him wanting the two of you to get back together."

"Not exactly." She picked up a fry. "I'm just, I don't know, questioning myself."

"And that's different from second thoughts how?"

Mikki ignored that. "I like Duane a lot. I like being with him. The sex is amazing. He's a great guy. I could see myself really falling for him."

"Why is that a problem? Were you thinking about being with Perry before he mentioned it?"

"No. I like where we are. But now that he's talked about it, I can't seem to let it go. And being with him and the kids in the hospital kind of shifted things. It's like I can see how it would be. He's different now. More mature. More interested in making things work. If he'd been like that three years ago, I don't think we would have divorced. Although I'd checked out, too, so maybe."

Bree watched her without speaking.

"It feels like if I walk away from Perry, we'll be breaking up all over again."

"Are you still in love with him?"

"I don't know," she admitted, not sure what she felt. "I like him. I like where we are. I don't want to go back."

"But?"

"What if it's not going back? What if it's going forward? I loved him for twenty years. Is that really done? And why did I wait three years to finally start dating? Was I getting over my marriage? Was I hiding or was I secretly hoping Perry and I would get back together?"

"I don't know."

"Someone has to."

Bree sipped her milkshake. "Yeah, and that someone would be you."

"I need you to tell me what to do."

"You really don't, but I'll play along for now. What if you hadn't met Duane? Would you want to get back together with Perry?"

An interesting question, Mikki thought. Would she? "I don't know. I think I might have been more willing to consider it."

"Because you were lonely and he was better than living like your mom?"

"Yikes, don't say that. It makes me sound terrible."

"I'm just asking the obvious question."

"Would I settle for Perry rather than be alone?"

Bree shrugged. "Only you can answer that."

"I'm not that shallow," Mikki said, hoping it was true. "I went looking for Duane. Not him exactly, but a man. Perry came looking for me."

"Does that matter?"

"I don't know. Does it?" Mikki ate more fries. "Okay, what about this. Would I have given Perry another thought if he hadn't brought up reconciling? If he was with someone else, would I care?" She considered her own questions. "I felt weird when Perry dated someone. Left out and discarded, but not shattered."

"What if Perry hadn't changed the rules? Would you be falling in love with Duane?"

"Yes."

"Are you still?"

Mikki groaned. "Possibly. He's so great."

"The obvious solution is to keep them both."

Despite her mixed emotions, Mikki laughed. "I can't do that. I'm not like you."

"I've never been into two guys at the same time."

"How about just the one?"

"You're going to distract me by mentioning Harding?"

Mikki leaned toward her friend. "You miss him."

"It's over. How I feel is something I deal with."

"You love him."

Bree's dark gaze sharpened. "No, I don't."

"We can all see it. You two are so good together."

"Back to Perry and Duane."

Mikki sighed. "Fine. Back to Perry and Duane."

"Is it possible you've been in love with Perry this whole time but didn't want to admit it?"

"I want to say no, but I'm not sure."

If she had been in love with Perry, it would explain why she'd been unable to brush off his attempts to get them back together.

If she'd been in love with him, she would know why she couldn't stop thinking about them having another baby together.

"I need to figure this out," Mikki said, picking up her milkshake.

"Not today. Or even tomorrow, but at some point, yes."

"Sure you won't tell me what to do?"

Bree laughed. "I want to, but I won't."

"You're a good friend. Annoying, but good."

TWENTY-FIVE

Ashley tried to act as if nothing was wrong, and Seth did the same. They cooked together, talked at dinner, went hiking on Saturday morning and to a few open houses on Sunday. To any observer, they were exactly where they'd always been—happy and in love. Only they weren't.

She had no idea what he was thinking or feeling, but she spent her days feeling like she had really bad PMS every day. She was moody, sad and mentally bracing herself for disaster. It wasn't an easy way to live.

Over the next few days, she volunteered extra shifts at OAR, worked on a few new muffin recipes and faked cheerful as much as possible. She took Harding to lunch where his pain distracted her from her own—at least in the moment. But eventually, she returned to the apartment she shared with Seth and had to face the reality of their impasse.

On Wednesday he texted her to say he was bringing home dinner. He walked in, right on time, carrying takeout from their favorite Thai place, a dozen red roses and a small blue bag with Tiffany written on the side.

"I can't live like this anymore," he said, after he'd put everything on the kitchen table. "I don't think you can, either."

She told herself to stop staring at the small bag and focus on what he was saying. But it was hard to look away and deep inside she felt a happy, fluttering sensation. It wasn't her birthday or Valentine's Day. Seth had no reason to visit Tiffany's. As far as she knew, he'd never been inside the store before.

Relief joined the happy. Finally, she thought, fighting the need to throw herself at him. He'd realized what she needed and was taking the next step.

"It's been tough," she admitted. "But you're important to me."

"And you're important to me, too. I love you, Ashley. You're the one I want to spend the rest of my life with."

He reached for the bag and drew out a small box. When he opened it, she saw a beautiful diamond wedding band.

"You changed your mind," she blurted. "You want to get married."

He frowned. "No. It's just last week you talked about the ceremony and the ring and I thought maybe if I gave you this, it would be enough."

It took her a full three seconds to understand what he'd said. Realization came like a slap. Hope died. Anger flared, disguising the underlying pain, but for right now she would take it.

"You think this is about a ring?" she asked in disbelief. "You think some piece of jewelry solves the problem?"

She told herself Seth wasn't a cruel man. He hadn't done this to hurt her or dismiss her feelings or make her feel unheard and insignificant. He'd been looking for a compromise, at least as he saw it.

"You're upset."

"Of course I'm upset. Did you think I'd be grateful you bought me a wedding ring when you have no intention of marrying me?"

As quickly as her temper had come to life, it died, leaving her with the emptiness of truth. It had been there the whole time and she'd refused to see it.

Seth would never marry her. He'd said he wouldn't and he'd meant it.

She knew all the arguments. Did she really want to get married more than she wanted to be with the man? What if he was the one and she never fell in love again? Blah, blah, blah.

"I've handled this badly," he said, looking and sounding miserable. "I'm sorry. Ashley, please, help me get this right."

"You didn't do anything wrong," she said, her tone soft. "You believe what you believe and I believe what I believe. Neither of us is ever going to change."

She looked at his familiar face, at the mouth she loved to kiss and the eyes that usually shone with love and affection. He was a good man and she would miss him desperately. But staying wasn't an option.

"I'll go," she said quietly. "You keep the apartment."

"What?" He paled. "No! Don't leave. Ashley, we love each other. What we have is incredible. You can't walk away from that."

Tears filled his eyes. He dropped the ring box to the floor and reached for her. She leaned in, feeling the warmth of his body. His arms held her tight as he stroked her hair.

"Don't go. I love you."

"I love you, too. But it's not enough. I'm sorry." She pulled back, surprised by how calm she felt. Later the pain would hit her, but right now she was ready to do what needed to be done.

"I'll take a few things tonight and come back when you're at work. It'll take me a few days to figure out what I'm going to do."

He wiped away tears. "Don't go."

"I'm sorry."

He collapsed on the sofa, hands over his face. His shoulders shook. She started toward him, then stopped herself. Better for her to leave.

She quickly filled a suitcase with cosmetics and clothes, then left the apartment without speaking again. Once in her car, she closed her eyes and told herself she would be fine. Only she knew she wouldn't.

The sobs came out of nowhere, shocking her with their intensity. They shook her body and made it impossible for her to catch her breath. She loved Seth with her entire being and she'd just left him. What the hell?

She started to get out of the car, then fell back into her seat. Tears poured down her cheeks. Her heart ached, her throat burned. Even as she struggled to breathe, she reached for her phone, intending to call her brother. But instead, she found herself pushing the button for another number.

"Hi," Bree said, picking up immediately.

Ashley was crying too hard to speak.

"Ashley? What's wrong? Are you okay?"

"No. It's Seth."

"Was he in an accident? Tell me what's happening."

"I left him."

She thought about mentioning the ring, but that seemed like too much to explain. She wiped her face and repeated, "I left him."

"Where are you?"

"In the parking lot at the apartment. I'm going to stay with my brother." Ashley swallowed. "Can I come there instead?"

A ridiculous ask. Mikki and Ashley had talked several times about Bree's odd need for privacy. Neither had been to her house.

"Of course," Bree said without hesitation. "I'll make up the spare room right now. Can you drive? Do you need me to come get you?"

"I can make it. I just need the address. Are you sure? I know you're not always a people person."

"I'm going to make an exception for you."

"Thanks." Ashley wiped away more tears. "I hurt so much."

"It's going to get worse before it gets better."

"That's cheerful."

"It's also the truth."

"I know. I'll see you soon."

Ashley hung up, then started her car. Seconds later her phone lit up with the text of an address. She pulled out of the parking lot. Whether she'd done the right thing or not, there was no going back. Not anymore.

"Then the goats started kind of shoving," Will said, grinning broadly. "The kids—"

"Human kids," Sydney added.

He looked at his sister and chuckled. "Right. The human kids totally freaked, screaming and running everywhere, which only made the goats more excited. They started jumping around and bumping into the students. The teacher was screaming."

Mikki laughed at the memory. "Why are we telling this story? It doesn't make me look good."

Will shook his head. "Mom, you saved us." He looked at Duane. "So she rips off her sweatshirt."

"I had a T-shirt underneath," Mikki added quickly.

"She runs to the goats, waving the shirt like she's a matador, yelling, 'Come get me! Come get me!'"

Duane chuckled. "Did they?"

"Yup. They chased her to the far end of the pen. The teacher got the rest of us out, and one of the workers at the petting zoo came in with corn or something so Mom could escape."

Mikki drew in a breath and picked up her glass of wine. "It was harrowing. I haven't liked petting zoos since."

Duane smiled at her. "You were brave, sacrificing yourself for the children."

"I didn't know what else to do. That teacher was useless, flapping her arms and screaming. They shouldn't take little kids to petting zoos. Not on school outings. Stick to museums where nothing is alive."

"At least not during the day," Sydney joked, referencing *Night at the Museum*, a family favorite.

Duane grinned. "I have an image in my head I'll carry with me forever."

"Don't say that," Mikki told him. "That's not how I want to be remembered."

"Too late. Besides, you look very empowered."

Their eyes met. Mikki felt heat in her belly—not that anything would be happening with her kids around. Which was fine. Duane had gotten home two days ago and they'd had a very long and glorious night in his bed. Remembering that would help her control herself for the next couple of hours.

"So dessert," she said, coming to her feet. "I have ice cream and brownies. There are some cookies in the freezer, if you can wait the twenty minutes it will take them to defrost."

"We're going to Grandma's house to hang," Sydney said, grabbing the salad bowl. "Grandpa wants Will to play some video game with him, and Grandma and I are going to watch *The Great British Baking Show*. We'll be back by ten."

"They go to bed early," Will added with a smirk.

"Old people," Duane teased. "What are you going to do."

"Yeah," Will agreed. "But we love them."

With everyone helping, they cleared the table and tidied the kitchen quickly, then the kids piled into Will's car and drove away. Mikki and Duane walked into the family room where he pulled her close and kissed her.

"I've missed you," he murmured against her mouth.

"You saw me last night."

He grinned. "While I want to see you in that very way tonight, I get that it's not going to happen, what with your children running in and out."

Mikki wanted to say that they would be at their grandparents' house for a couple of hours, but she didn't. Not when they could pop in at any second.

"You're very understanding," she told him. "And I missed you, too. I'm glad you're back."

They sat on the sofa. Duane put his arm around her and took her hand in his.

"You had a lot going on while I was in Europe," he said. "I'm glad Chet's better."

"He's doing great. The doctor says he can go back to work. He's starting his heart-healthy lifestyle classes next week. Lorraine's going with him, so they'll both have the information."

She leaned against him. "It really was tough, having him in the hospital like that. I know the kids were scared. When we lost my dad, it was sad, but different for them. After the divorce, he went off and lived his own life, doing all the things he couldn't with my mom. So we only saw him every few weeks, then briefly. Sydney and Will hang out with Chet and Lorraine all the time."

"That's nice. My kids were close to their grandparents as well. I've always been happy about that. And speaking of my kids, I have them for Thanksgiving this year."

She shifted so she could see his face. "But they're over eighteen. Are you still following your parenting plan?"

He smiled. "They are. They're free to do what they want, so every year they decide where they're spending the holidays. This year I get Thanksgiving and their mom gets Christmas. So I was thinking it would be nice if you could meet them."

"I'd like that," she said, immediately fighting nerves. What would they think of her? What would she think of them? Ack!

"And," he added, staring into her eyes. "Maybe you and I could talk about going to Paris for Christmas. I know it will be cold, but the city is beautiful in the winter and there's so much to see."

"Paris for Christmas? I can't. I mean it sounds lovely, but Christmas is a family time. We have traditions and everyone has a stocking and we have turkey on Christmas Eve, then go to church. I make a prime rib on Christmas Day. Will's going to be graduating from high school and then what? I don't know how often they'll come home."

She couldn't seem to stop talking. Worse, she felt her eyes burning. As if she was going to cry, which was ridiculous. A hunky guy wanting to take her to Paris was hardly tear-worthy, but here she was, sniffing and snuffling like an idiot.

"I'm just not sophisticated enough to have Christmas in Paris. I'm sorry, but it's the truth. I want my ornaments and making cookies and my ugly Christmas sweater collection and complaining that it's eighty degrees, only I don't really mind because that's how it's supposed to be here."

"Hey, it's okay." Duane touched her under her chin, forcing her to look into his kind eyes. "I get it. Christmas is a big deal. I should have thought of that before I said something. You're a great mom and you take care of everyone you know. It was the wrong question. I take it back."

She brushed away tears. "You do? Because you don't want to go to Paris with me?"

He laughed and pulled her against him. "Mikki, you're amazing. I don't know how to resist you. Of course I want to go to Paris with you. Is New Year's an option?"

New Year's in Paris? She drew back and smiled at him. "It is. Totally. I'd love that."

"Great. We'll spend Christmas with your family, then fly out on the twenty-seventh. I know exactly where I want us to stay. There's this great hotel with big suites that have fireplaces in the bedrooms."

He was saying all the right things, but all she could hear was, "We'll spend Christmas with your family." A logical assumption, considering the conversation they were having. To be honest, she'd already sort of agreed to have Thanksgiving with his kids, so this was just more of the same. Only when she had a second to think about it, she wasn't sure how it was going to work.

Would everyone come to her house? In the past she and Perry had alternated hosting, but Duane going to Perry's bungalow would be weird. And how would Lorraine and Chet feel about the whole thing? While Lorraine had been good about not mentioning the reconciliation again, Mikki knew it was on her mind. And since the heart attack—

"I've lost you," Duane told her. "What happened?"

"Sorry. I'm trying to work out logistics. In the past Perry and I have alternated where we held the holidays. But he's moved out of his parents' house and into his own place, so I'm not sure about bringing you there. I mean, it would be weird, right? So I guess I can have everything here."

"Why am I a problem? Perry's brought girlfriends to holidays, hasn't he?"

"Not really. I mean we met a few of the women he dated early on, but no one came to anything big like a birthday or Thanksgiving."

Duane shifted back a little. "Are you saying you'd rather I wasn't there, either?"

"No," she said a little too heartily. "That's silly. We're dating. They all know that. Lorraine's seen you at the store. I've told Perry a bunch of times. It's just since the heart attack things have been..." Wait, that wasn't right. "Sometimes Lorraine thinks that we should be just family and..."

She paused, not sure what to say. However she tried to explain the situation, it sounded really bad—as if she'd been involved with Perry while dating Duane, which wasn't true at all.

"Mikki, what's going on? You're not making any sense."

Dread swept through her as she hesitated, thinking there was really no good way to tell him and maybe she should just blurt it out and hope he would understand.

"Perry thinks he and I should get back together. That we gave up on our marriage too quickly. His mother knows, so that's been awkward and then his dad had a heart attack, so it's just been really complicated."

Duane slid back even farther and stared at her. She couldn't tell if he was mad or hurt or both, but he sure wasn't happy.

"You've been seeing Perry?"

"Like dating? No. Never. I see him when I usually see him. The stuff you know about. Picking up trash on the beach, hanging out with the kids. Okay, I've been helping him with the house a little but it's not…"

She pressed her lips together, aware she wasn't helping her situation.

"He wants to get back together with you?" he asked with a slight edge in his voice.

"He thinks he's still in love with me. He's not," she added hastily. "I'm a convenient excuse to avoid moving on."

"You never thought to mention that to me? Did it occur to you I might want to know your ex wants to get back together with you?"

"I didn't think it mattered."

He stood and glared at her. "You would be wrong about that."

She scrambled to her feet. "Duane, I'm sorry. I'm handling this badly. It's not anything."

"It sounds like something to me. When did this sudden interest happen? After we started going out? Am I a way to make Perry jealous?"

"What?" Her voice came out as a shriek. She consciously lowered the pitch and volume. "No! How can you think that? You know I wasn't dating before I met you. I hadn't been dating anyone for years. Then I found you and it's been great. I should have said something about Perry. I see that now. It's just at first it wasn't anything, but then he started talking about being in love with me and having another baby and—"

Mikki slapped her hand over her mouth, desperate to claw back the words, but it was too late. Duane's eyes narrowed.

"He wants more children. That's why we talked about it a few weeks ago. So what's the deal? You're taking each of us for a test drive and figuring out who you want to be with?"

"It's not like that, Duane. I wasn't doing that."

"Explain to me how it's different." Sadness filled his eyes. "I believed you, Mikki. I trusted you. Not two weeks ago we agreed we were in a committed monogamous relationship. Now I find out you've been seeing Perry the whole time. I knew from the start a lot of things could go wrong, but I'll admit I never thought you'd cheat on me. I was a fool."

He started for the door. Mikki raced after him. "No. Duane, please, listen to me. It wasn't like that. I'm not dating Perry."

He stopped and looked at her. "Since he told you he's still in love with you and wants to get back together, have you ever once considered reconciling?"

She opened her mouth and closed it. "*Considered* is really strong," she whispered.

He turned away. She grabbed his arm.

"Wait. It was a lot to take in. Then Chet had his heart attack and we were a family again and I didn't know how to deal with that."

"Are you sleeping with him?"

"No! I wouldn't do that."

"I don't know why not. You're doing everything else."

The tears returned, but this time they had nothing to do with Christmas.

"Duane, please. Let me explain."

"I think we can both agree you've said enough. I thought we had something special and were moving toward a future together." His mouth twisted. "I was going to tell you my blood tests came back all clear. I thought we'd celebrate."

Her tears fell faster and harder, making it hard to see him. "Duane, I'm so sorry. I've screwed this up. I'm not dating Perry."

"I think that you are, whether you want to admit it or not.

I think you're still in love with him and you needed to date someone else to figure it out. I don't think you set out to play me, but now that it's happened, I'm not sure motivation counts for very much. Goodbye, Mikki."

He walked out and closed the door behind him. Seconds later she heard him drive away.

Mikki sank to the floor and pulled her knees to her chest. If she made herself small enough, maybe she could disappear and none of this would have happened. Only physics didn't work that way, so she was stuck, alone, sobbing her heart out, just having lost a great man for no reason other than she was an idiot. Which eventually she would deal with. It was losing Duane that was going to haunt her for the next forty-plus years.

TWENTY-SIX

Bree stepped out of the shower and dried off. Her morning surfing hadn't gone well. Unable to focus, she'd fallen off her board more than she'd stayed on. She'd avoided class for a couple weeks until Dalton texted her that Harding had canceled his surf lessons. When she'd shown up that morning, Dalton had asked if she'd wanted to talk about anything. She'd told him no, and that had been that. Except for her inability to stay on her board.

Now she dressed and dried her hair before going downstairs. She was surprised to see Ashley sitting at the kitchen table. Her new roommate was generally up early and out before Bree stirred. In fact, since moving in a few days before, Ashley had mostly made herself scarce.

That first night Ashley had huddled on the sofa, sobbing but not saying much. Bree knew that something had happened to cause Ashley to leave Seth, but she was short on particulars. At work Ashley did her job and mostly kept to herself. Bree wanted to talk to Mikki about the situation but Mikki had been keeping herself busy with an unscheduled inventory and then had taken a couple of days off. She also hadn't answered any of Bree's texts.

"Hey," Bree said, putting a pod in the Nespresso machine. "How are you feeling?"

"Sick, tired."

Ashley was pale, with dark circles under her eyes. Her gorgeous red hair was dull and there was a downward bend to her mouth.

"Are you drinking enough water? Are you eating?"

Her lips briefly curved up. "You sound like my mom."

"You've talked to her?" That was good news, Bree thought. Ashley needed to be talking to someone.

"No, but that's what she would say if she knew."

"When was the last time you ate?"

Ashley waved vaguely. "I don't know. A few days ago. I'm not hungry."

"Coffee will chew up your stomach."

Bree walked to the refrigerator and pulled out eggs, grated cheddar and all the veggies she could find. She had bagels in the freezer and a couple of bananas.

She set the bagels out on the counter to start defrosting, then started chopping vegetables.

Without looking at Ashley she said, "Tell me what happened."

Ashley stared out the window. "Nothing. Everything." Her mouth twisted. "It was so romantic. Seth came home with take-out, roses and a wedding ring from Tiffany. He had the little blue bag and everything."

Bree nearly dropped her knife. "He proposed?"

"What? Seth violate his sense of self? How could you even ask? Of course he didn't propose. Marriage is just an excuse for people to stop trying. Life should be a constant audition. Are you doing good enough for him to stick around? What about those ten extra pounds from that third baby you popped out? That's on you, not on him. Sorry, gotta go. And here's the thing. What if we'd had kids and one of them had a heart defect or something? Would he have stuck around? Wouldn't that break the whole 'you're not trying hard enough' rule because if I'd tried harder, the baby would have been perfect."

"You're angry."

"I don't think the word *angry* comes close to defining how I feel. I'm furious. I'm enraged. He brought a Tiffany bag into our home, pulled out the box and showed me the most perfect, most exquisite, ring I have ever seen. Like a fool, like a ridiculous, wannabe princess, I believed that he'd changed his mind. But alas, no. He was simply trying to give me something I wanted. Not marriage. God forbid he move on his principles. So not marriage, but a ring. He was giving me a ring."

Bree began sauteing mushrooms. "Like you were supposed to wear the ring without being married."

"I guess. I don't know what he was thinking. But as I stared at him and the ring and felt my hopes shatter, I knew it was never going to happen. I'm in love with a man who simply isn't willing to marry me. He never will be. He was never going to change his mind and I can't change mine so fuck him and the horse he rode in on."

"I've never heard you use the F word before."

"I know. That's your thing. Sorry to steal the glory but I am so pissed. At him, at myself. At the world. I feel used and ridiculous and weak and stupid. I tried. I really tried to understand his point of view. I read those articles and books. I tried to figure out how to do what he wanted. Well, you know what? He should have been getting down on his knees and begging me to marry him because I'm the best thing to ever happen to him."

Bree continued to fix breakfast, knowing at some point Ashley's anger was going to fade and all she would be left with was her broken heart. Because no matter how much she was pissed now, the truth was she loved Seth and getting over him would not be easy. Bree had a little experience in that department herself.

She'd known ending things with Harding would be difficult, but she hadn't expected it to be crushing. She missed him with every breath. The ache inside had only grown. She was so desperate, she'd considered trying to fake normal so they could be together for a little while longer—at least until he figured out how broken she was and walked away.

But she couldn't pretend to be someone else and she sure wasn't willing to risk her heart for real, which left her back where she'd started. Hurting them both so he would be able to heal and go have a good life somewhere else.

She whipped the eggs in a bowl and put the bagels into the toaster.

"For what it's worth, you did the right thing," she said. "It was never going to work with Seth."

"What?" Ashley shrieked. "You're the one who told me to see things from his side. You're the one who said I should consider the possibility of not getting married."

"I did. What if you'd realized you were fine with it? That would have changed everything. But you weren't and if he's not going to change, then the breakup was inevitable."

Ashley stretched her arms out on the table and dropped her head onto them. "I hate my life."

"No, you hate being in pain. Anger is easy. It gives you energy but underneath, there's just a world of hurt."

She cut the omelet in half and slid it onto a plate, along with a bagel and the banana.

"Eat," she said, pushing the food toward her friend. She took the other half for herself and sat at the table.

Ashley poked at the omelet, then took a bite. She chewed reluctantly, but then perked up. "This is really good. I am hungry. I didn't know."

Bree started on her own breakfast. "Can you take off this morning?"

"Sure. Why?"

"We're going to do a paintball course in the Valley."

"What are you talking about? Paintball? No."

"Yes. It's a great way to process anger. You get to shoot things.

I can ask the guy to change all the targets into human silhouettes. You can pretend they're Seth."

"So this is therapy." For the first time since showing up three days ago, Ashley smiled. "I'm in."

Mikki pulled two bottles of Larmandier-Bernier Latitude Extra Brut from the refrigerator in the break room. She tucked them in the tote she carried, hesitated, then added a third bottle. It had just been that kind of week with a great suckatude of emotions. Sadness, depression, self-flagellation for how incredibly stupid and thoughtless she'd been. And the week ahead showed no signs of getting better.

After collecting glasses and her blanket, she walked to the front of the store where Bree and Ashley were waiting. They each held a big bag from a restaurant she hadn't heard of.

"Food," Ashley said, raising her bag. "We decided we needed it after this week."

Mikki patted her tote. "I have three bottles of champagne, so we're on the same page."

Together they trooped out to the sand and found a relatively quiet spot. The day had started out overcast, so the temperatures were only in the low eighties—perfect for a comfortable sunset. Now the sky was a rainbow of colors, with the lingering clouds bathed in red and yellow. Once they were settled in their places, Mikki went to work on the first bottle while Bree and Ashley set out the food.

"Fried chicken bites with three different dipping sauces," Bree said. "Pancetta, pear and pecan puffs, fruit and cheese kabobs, and cut up raw veggies with dill dip because, you know, vegetables."

Mikki's stomach growled.

Ashley pointed to her display. "Cheesecake-filled strawberries, mini apricot-and-lemon meringue pies."

"I'm suddenly starving," Mikki admitted.

Bree looked at her. "Good, because you haven't been eating."

"How would you know that?"

"You look wan."

"But not skinny? I want to look skinny."

"Sorry. You have too many curves for that. We've talked about this. You need to embrace them."

"I'd rather have Duane do that."

The words came out before Mikki could stop them. Worse, she unexpectedly started crying.

"I'm such an idiot," she said, wiping her face with a napkin. "The dumbest of the dumb."

She felt more than saw Bree and Ashley exchange a look.

"We knew something happened," Ashley said quietly. "But we didn't know what. Are you ready to talk about it?"

"I don't care if you are or not." Bree's tone was harsh, her words blunt. "You've been holding whatever it is inside too long. You're festering."

Mikki sniffed. "I thought I was wan." She sighed, knowing her friend was right. She hadn't told anyone what happened because it was just too awful, but at some point she had to get the words out there.

"I screwed up with Duane," she began, then quickly filled them in on the disaster that was their last evening together.

"He was so hurt," she said when she'd finished. "So disappointed. The look in his eyes—it was awful. I never meant anything bad to happen. I wasn't dating Perry at the same time."

"Oh, please," Ashley snapped. "Of course you were. You've been using your relationship with him to keep from moving on. Don't pretend you weren't. Holidays together? Picking up trash on the beach? Cozy dinners at his new place discussing wallpaper? What else would you call it?"

The attack, possibly justified, was nonetheless unexpected. "We never talked about wallpaper," Mikki murmured. "I'm not a fan."

Ashley surprised her by laughing. "Okay, then tile. But you get my point. Come on—you've been totally using him for everything but sex. Frankly, your relationship with Earl is way more healthy than the one you have with Perry."

"But we did it for the kids."

Bree sipped her champagne. "If that were true, you wouldn't be fighting with Duane."

"We're not fighting," Mikki said flatly. "He broke up with me."

Both women stared at her. "I thought he was only mad," Ashley said.

"It's more than that." Mikki shifted on the blanket. "We'd just talked about having an exclusive relationship that was getting serious." She didn't mention the blood test. "I think I'm falling in love with him. Then I blew the whole thing because of Perry."

"Because you don't know how you feel about him," Bree pointed out.

"I'm so bad at this," Mikki admitted. "Dating and men in general. I don't know what's going on with Perry. I can't stop thinking about what he said about getting back together and I don't know what that means."

"Oh, boo-hoo." Ashley waved her glass. "Poor you, with two amazing men who desperately want to be with you. How awful. How do you stand it? Just admit that you love the attention and that's why you won't decide. It's way more fun to have them both."

The accusation stung. Mikki felt herself flush as she stared at Ashley. "It's not like that. I'm not that person."

Bree picked up one of the food containers. "Pear puff?"

Mikki ignored her. "Ashley, is that what you really think?"

"Yes, because that's what it is. I'm not saying I would act any differently. It's nice to be popular. Just don't pretend you don't see what's really happening."

The harsh words were unsettling and painful to hear, Mikki

thought. She wanted to keep protesting, or maybe stalk away. Instead, she forced herself to sit there and admit the possibility that she was in this predicament because she'd been self-centered. Not exactly behavior to make herself proud.

"I don't know what to say," she whispered. "I'm a terrible person."

"You're not," Bree told her. "You had a bad moment. Move on."

Ashley filled their glasses. "You're probably not the one to be telling anyone to move on, girlfriend."

Bree looked unfazed by the advice. "Those who can, do. Those who can't, tell other people what to do."

Mikki was still caught up in Ashley's uncomfortable truth. Had she really been pretending to be unsure because she liked the attention? Was she that shallow?

While she didn't want to admit the possibility, she couldn't escape a little voice inside whispering it was probably true. And if she accepted that, then she'd screwed up more than one life because she'd been flattered and a little smug.

"I hate myself," she muttered.

"Don't say that," Ashley said. "You're lovely. Annoying, but we love you anyway. So what's the verdict?"

"I'm not in love with Perry." Mikki spoke without planning her words and was more than a little surprised by them. "I don't love Perry," she repeated, more certain this time. "He's a good man and we have great kids, but it's done. It's been done. I don't want to go backward."

Bree held out her glass. "Congratulations. You have clarity."

"I could have used it two months ago. Before I screwed up with Duane."

"There is that," Bree admitted. "You should talk to him."

"I need to talk to Perry first." And she would. She would get her thoughts together, then go explain how they needed to move on. It was the only way to be happy.

"Okay, one down, two to go," she said. "Who wants to be healed next?"

"I'd love to be healed." Ashley nibbled on a fried chicken bit. "I miss Seth. I want us to be together. I want him to walk up to me and propose so we can live happily ever after."

"Have you heard from him at all?"

Ashley shook her head. "Not really. I texted him when I'd be coming by with Harding to get the rest of my stuff. He said that was fine and that was it." She paused. "I don't regret what I did. I know I'm right. I just wish it didn't hurt so much."

Mikki wished she had great advice, but she couldn't think of any. In her opinion, Seth was wrong not to give in on getting married. She was equally sure his friends were telling him to stand strong. It was an impossible situation.

"I'm sorry," she said.

"Thanks. I appreciate that. And the champagne." She turned to Bree. "You've been amazing. I don't like to say that too much because it freaks you out, but you have been."

Bree looked uncomfortable and ready to run. Instead, she grabbed a fruit kabob and sighed. "I have a nurturing side. I try to hide it, but it comes out every now and then."

"Remnants of your time with Lewis?" Mikki asked.

"No. Ashley is a much better person. I like being there for her. Lewis was a toad." Bree turned to Ashley. "I'm sorry about Harding. You said I would hurt him and I did."

"You're the scorpion," Ashley told her. "From the scorpion and the frog."

Bree grimaced. "Not very flattering."

"No one wants to be the scorpion." Mikki thought about the old fable. "Or the frog. He ends up dead. Maybe we should avoid amphibian and insect references."

"I don't think scorpions are insects," Bree murmured.

"My point is," Ashley continued, rolling her eyes. "You did what you said you would. You're clear about who you are." She bumped Bree's arm. "I was mad at you, but not anymore. You're hurting as much as he is. I know you love him and I also know you can never admit that. In fact, in about three seconds, you're going to forcefully say you don't love him."

Bree pressed her lips together, then blurted. "I don't love him."

"You should have bet on that," Mikki told Ashley.

"I didn't think of it in time."

"I don't love him," Bree repeated. "I don't love anyone."

"All evidence to the contrary," Mikki said, holding her glass out to Ashley. They toasted each other, then Mikki put her arm around Bree. "We love you, too. Even if you are a sad little husk of a human being."

"Shut up."

Mikki laughed. "You sound so tough, but we're not buying it. Now let's eat."

Ashley went through the motions of her life. Sometimes she thought maybe she was starting the healing process, but other times she was convinced she would never escape the sadness that had invaded down to her bones.

With her brother's help, she moved her things out of the apartment. She told her parents what had happened, which had been followed by her mother flying down for three days of commiseration, fancy dinners and lots of hugs and shopping. She sold her muffins and cupcakes, volunteered at OAR and had started surfing with Bree on Thursdays.

She supposed the biggest surprise of the past few weeks had been her relationship with Bree. A week after she'd moved in, Bree had shocked her by replacing the old futon she'd been sleeping on with an actual bed. A few days later Bree had gruffly told her she was welcome to stay as long as she liked. They'd agreed that Ashley would commit to being a roommate for three months, then they'd reassess. Ashley had insisted on paying rent, but Bree had refused any security deposit.

"What the fuck do you think you're going to do that requires a security deposit? Start making meth in the living room?"

That visual had caused them both to laugh, then they inexplicably dissolved into tears as they realized how screwed up their personal lives were.

Ashley forced her attention back to work. She'd brought in batches of almond cupcakes with salted caramel frosting and carrot cake cupcakes with white chocolate cream cheese frosting, part of her transition to fall. Labor Day was next Monday. A couple of weeks later she would go full in with pumpkin muffins and a great candy corn cupcake.

"Those look good."

She smiled when she saw Dave on the other side of the display case. "Hi, what are you doing here?"

He shrugged. "I was in the neighborhood and thought I'd stop by. Do you have time for a walk?"

She eyed him suspiciously. "You want to give me a talking-to, don't you? I'm not a project." Nor had she told him what had happened with Seth. No doubt her brother had shared the news.

"No, you're a friend and I thought you might like to have a friendly shoulder for a bit."

"No lecture?"

He smiled. "Would I do that?"

"In a hot minute, but I'll go on a walk with you anyway."

She put a couple of cupcakes in a small to-go box, then told her cashier she'd be back in an hour. She and Dave went along the boardwalk until they found an empty bench in the shade. She sat on the end and he pulled up next to her.

She offered him an almond cupcake. "The salted caramel frosting is addictive."

"I consider myself warned. How are you?"

"Sad. Resigned. I know I made the right decision but I can't shake the feeling that I was the girl who needed to get married. Just saying that makes me feel uncomfortable. Am I pathetic?"

Dave ate a cupcake in three bites. "That's really good. And no, you're not pathetic. You know what I think?"

She sighed. "That Seth is making a big mistake and that he should compromise. What about me? I'm being just as stubborn."

"Is it being stubborn or is it something more?"

Ugh. The question she didn't want to answer. "I can't plan a future with Seth if we're not married."

She had more she wanted to say, but suddenly, she was crying. "Why doesn't he want to marry me? What's wrong with me?"

Dave drew her close. She leaned into him, burying her head in his strong shoulder.

"Nothing. Seth's an asshole and for the rest of his life, he'll regret letting you go."

"I wish that was more comforting," she whispered. "I miss him, which makes me a fool. It's just I really loved him."

"I know, Ashley. You gave him everything you had. This isn't on you."

Maybe not, but knowing that didn't make the pain go away, nor stop her from questioning herself.

"I thought he'd come after me," she admitted. "I wasn't testing, so much as I thought once I was gone, he'd change his mind. Dumb, huh?"

"Only on his part."

"I wish I was stronger," she told him. "I wish I could move on and not miss him."

"You're doing great. Don't be so hard on yourself."

She sniffed, then raised her head and stared into his eyes. "Maybe this would be a good time to give me some solid OAR advice. Something about getting back on the horse."

"I never got the whole horse thing. How about if I offer to give you a ride back to work?"

She managed a shaky smile as she straightened. "I'll walk. I wouldn't want your latest girlfriend thinking I was hitting on you."

"I'm between women right now."

"I didn't know. Want me to introduce you to some of my single friends?"

He shook his head. "I can get my own girl."

The tears returned. "I know. And then you'll marry her in a church wedding. But Seth is never going to marry me."

Dave swore softly. Before she knew what was happening, he'd lifted her onto his lap and wrapped his arms around her. She'd thought she might feel awkward, but she didn't. She felt safe and comforted.

Warmed by his presence, she gave in to the tears. So much for Seth's promise to love her forever. He'd just let her go. An act that made her wonder how much he'd cared in the first place. Eventually, she would get over him but right now she let herself get lost in the sadness and pain.

TWENTY-SEVEN

Mikki waited several days before texting Perry and asking to see him. She'd wanted to be sure about her feelings and how she would handle things in the future. Then she had to figure out the right location for their conversation. Her place, his place or somewhere neutral? As long as they weren't going to be interrupted, she didn't much mind the where, although in the end, she asked him over to her house because it made the most sense.

Right on time, Perry knocked. Mikki wiped her suddenly sweaty hands on her capris, then opened the front door and let him in.

He smiled as he walked into the living room. Everything about him was familiar—his eyes, his body, the way he walked. Once he'd been her world. They'd made kids together.

She motioned for him to take a seat, then took the chair across from his.

"We have to talk," she began.

His smile never faded. "I figured that from your text. What's up?"

She drew in a breath and reminded herself it was past time for this conversation.

"Perry, we're divorced and there's a good reason for that. We tried to make our marriage work and it didn't. We both have responsibility in that. I think we did a good job when we split up. We kept the kids safe and emotionally secure, we stayed friends with our in-laws. All that is good."

His smile slowly faded.

"We need to move on," she continued. "I've been proud of the fact that you and I are friends, but now I think we've been using each other to stay stuck. We get just enough emotional engagement that we don't really need anyone else. I want that to change."

"You don't want to be friends with me?" He sounded hurt.

"It's not about being friends," she said, trying not to be distracted. "It's about everything else. We're not getting back together. It was never going to happen and I'm sorry you started down that path. We're not in love, Perry. We're convenient. Trying to take us back to what we were isn't good for either of us."

"No. You don't mean that. Mikki, we can make it. I know we can."

"We can't. I don't want to go back. I'm sorry to be blunt, but I'm not in love with you. I haven't been for a while. I also don't think you're in love with me. Planning a future with me is easier than getting out there. Believe me, I know how scary that is. But there's nothing to go back to. We weren't wrong to get a divorce."

He sagged back in the chair, his expression shocked and sad. "I love you."

She did her best to ignore the guilt. "I'm sorry if that's true. I don't love you anymore. Not romantically. You're a good man and the father of my children. I'll always be grateful for both. But there's nothing else between us. Thinking there is isn't healthy."

She forced herself to keep going. "I think it would be best if we saw less of each other. No more lunches or having me over to the house or picking up trash on the beach. Not until we've both moved on."

"You won't even see me?"

"We need a clean break. With the kids, we'll always have

communication, but we need to take some time away from each other."

She consciously gentled her voice. "Perry, think about putting yourself out there. You're a catch. I mean that. You need to start dating."

He stood and glared at her. "I'm in love with you. Don't tell me to date someone else. I don't want anyone else. I want you. I want us back together."

She rose. "There is no us. Not anymore."

He looked away. "I guess that says it all, doesn't it? You've made your position clear. I won't bother you again."

She recognized the stiff pride in his posture and the pain in his eyes. She knew she'd hurt him, had hurt them. She knew he would move to anger and refuse to communicate with her for a couple of weeks, then, hopefully, he would start to see she was right. Or at least be less upset with her.

He walked past her without saying anything and she let him go. When the door slammed behind him, she sank back onto the chair and told herself to keep breathing. If she was right, then he would quickly realize living without her wasn't as difficult as he'd expected. With a little luck he would start dating again and they could return to friendship.

If she was wrong…well, she didn't want to think about that. She might not be in love with Perry, but she didn't want to break his heart. But right or wrong, she knew there was simply no going back to what they'd had. As for moving forward—she still hadn't figured out what that meant. But having resolved things with Perry she could now focus her attention on the man she had fallen for. If only she hadn't screwed up so much that he was unwilling to give her a second chance.

Bree paddled out on the ocean. The morning was warm, promising a hot day, even at the beach. Overhead, the sky was that perfect California blue, and seagulls circled lazily as if they, too, were enjoying the last days of summer.

Beside her Ashley paddled earnestly, her expression tight with concentration. She'd only been coming to class for a few weeks, but she'd gotten up her first try and continued to make improvement. Bree couldn't tell if she actually liked surfing, but she was ready at five thirty every Thursday morning, her board leaning up against the front door of Bree's house.

Having a roommate was unexpectedly nice, Bree thought. Comforting, in a way. They didn't hang out together every second, but knowing there was another heartbeat in the house was often enough to get her through the bad moments. They'd agreed to never discuss Harding and so far were holding to that promise. Every now and then Bree saw traces of him in Ashley. Her smile, a gesture, a word choice. The recognition was immediately followed by the sharp pain of realization that whatever she and Harding could have had would never be.

Sometimes she told herself to grow a pair and risk it all. Was she really such a coward that she couldn't take a chance on him? But even thinking about the possibility of trusting someone again made her instantly retreat. She couldn't do it. Being with Harding was risking emotional death. Self-preservation won every time.

She turned and waited for the swells to become a wave she would ride in, judging the movement by the feel of her board on the water. A few seconds later she began paddling to shore, then moved smoothly into a crouched position before standing. She instinctively shifted to keep her balance as her board settled on the crest of the wave. Exhilaration filled her, clearing her mind.

She stayed upright until the last possible second, before dropping back onto her board. She paddled closer to the beach. When the water was shallow enough, she slipped off and carried her board the rest of the way.

Dalton stood by her towel. "Great ride."

"The waves are perfect today."

His gaze flicked to the left. "I don't know what happened with you and Harding, but I wanted to give you a heads-up. He's here. Waiting by your car."

A thousand emotions jolted through her. Before she could stop herself, she turned and saw a familiar silhouette next to her Mini. She was too far away to see his expression, but just knowing he was there made her both want to race toward him and run in the opposite direction.

Did she want to see him? Talk to him? Touch him? Her heart offered a very loud *yes*, but her gut and her brain were more wary. Fear battled with anticipation.

"You got this?" Dalton asked.

She reached for her towel. "I'm good."

"I'm here if you need me."

"Thanks."

She started toward her car. Harding stayed where he was, his gaze locked on her. As she got closer she found herself walking faster and consciously slowed down. Her chest was tight, her breathing rapid.

He looked good. Thinner, maybe, but still strong and tanned. As she approached, she tried to read him, but he was keeping it all inside. Only his faint smile told her he was happy to see her.

"You look good out there," he said, taking her board.

"The waves are just right."

While she peeled off her wet suit and toweled off, he secured her board to the Mini's roof. She slipped her sundress over her suit and brushed a few strands of hair off her face.

"Ashley surfs with me now. Did you two plan this?"

Harding faced her. "No. Until about ten seconds ago, she had no idea I'd be here."

Six months ago Bree would have assumed he was lying. She would never have trusted anyone not to set her up. Now she found herself accepting his words—Harding had never lied to her, and Ashley frequently had her back.

They looked at each other. Every cell in her body told her to take those few steps forward, to close the distance between them. To surrender to the inevitable and let this man love her. Yes, in the end, that love would destroy her, but what a great way to go.

Only the fear was still there, too. Just as strong, keeping her in place. The instinct to survive was locked in her DNA, strengthened by everything Lewis had put her through. Yes, she wanted Harding, but there was no way in hell she would ever trust him with her heart.

"I've missed you," he said.

"I've missed you, too."

"Yeah?"

The flash of hope in his hazel eyes hit her like a semi, but before she could tell him hope was for suckers, he went on.

"I've been giving you time," he told her. "I know this is hard for you. I still love you, Bree. I still think you're the one. I'm going to wait for as long as it takes you to figure it out. I just need to know you believe we could have a future together."

Was that all? Couldn't he ask for something simple like one of her lungs?

"Don't do this," she said, turning away. "Harding, don't. I can't be what you want. No, I won't be. I'm not taking the chance. I wish you could understand that."

He shifted so he was facing her again. "I won't hurt you. I'll always be there for you. I'm a good guy—you know that. Can't you believe in me even a little?"

She raised her gaze to his and flinched at the pain she saw. "No. I'm sorry. I don't want to hurt you. I…" She swallowed against the tightness in her throat. "You've gotten close. I'll give you that. Closer than anyone. If I thought it was possible, that I could trust you, I would want to. But that's never going to happen. I won't take the chance."

She felt as if she was ripping out her own heart, but she knew she had to do it and make him see there was nothing between them. There never had been.

"You're wasting your time on me," she said flatly. "I'm not worth it." She thought of what Sad Guy had said. "I'm an empty shell, not a real person. Go find someone else to love—someone who can love you back."

"I don't want anyone else, Bree. I want you. I love you."

His words were physical blows. She felt her knees start to buckle and had to grab on to the car to keep from falling.

"Just go," she whispered, turning away again.

There was no answer, no anything. After a few seconds she turned around and he was gone. Just like she'd asked.

She released her hold on the car and sank into a crouch. Her sobs came in bursts, almost guttural, as she fought against the sense of drowning in pain. The broken pieces of her psyche rubbed against each other, creating an agony she'd never experienced before. She wasn't going to survive this, she thought desperately. No way one person could get through this much and still function.

"Oh, Bree."

The soft voice warned her of Ashley's presence. Her friend pulled her to her feet and hugged her tight.

"How badly did you just screw that up?"

Bree managed to suck in enough air to speak. "You know me. It was bad."

"I should hate you, but you're just too pitiful."

Bree hung on tight. "You *should* hate me. I hate myself. I just can't do what he wants. I can't risk it. I'm sorry I hurt him. I really am."

"I know. You're also a fool to let him go, but hey, you know that." Ashley shifted so she was next to Bree. "Come on. Let's go home. I'll drive. You need a shower and some food."

"I can't eat. I'll throw up."

"I'll make you a smoothie. You'll be able to keep that down."

Bree didn't want to let go, but she forced herself to stand on her own. "Why are you being nice to me?"

"You're my friend. I love you. I'm not going to leave you alone to deal with this. Harding has a lot of places to go for support. Who else do you have but me and Mikki?"

"No one," Bree whispered, knowing it was true. "Absolutely no one."

"You broke Lorraine's heart."

Mikki pressed her lips together in an attempt to keep from snapping at her mother.

"She's devastated," Rita added. "She can barely get out of bed."

"Stop," Mikki told her. "You're not helping. Besides, you told me not to reconcile with Perry. I thought you'd be happy."

"You hurt Lorraine."

"How could I tell Perry no without doing that?"

Her mother sniffed. "No idea. I'm just telling you where things are. How you fix them is up to you."

"Okay. I appreciate the update."

With that, Mikki left the storage area and walked back into her gift shop. She hated the sense of impending doom that followed her. She'd known her mother-in-law wasn't happy, but maybe there was more going on than just disappointment.

"Next time no family members working in the business," she muttered to herself. "Strangers only. Preferably people I don't like."

She busied herself helping customers. A mother-daughter duo bought eight tote bags with matching flip-flops for the bridesmaids in the daughter's wedding. An older woman fussed over teapots for an hour and left without buying anything. A little before one Lorraine walked into the store. Mikki met her by the break room.

"Hi," Mikki said cheerfully. "Do you have a minute?"

Lorraine nodded and led the way inside. After storing her handbag in her locker, she faced Mikki, careful not to meet her eyes.

Mikki held in a groan. Maybe her mother was right. Maybe things were worse than she thought.

"You're upset," Mikki said, trying to keep any hint of accusation out of her voice. "Can we talk about that?"

"I'm fine."

"You're not. You've called in sick twice this week, you're barely speaking to me and you won't even look at me." Mikki paused. There were a thousand things she could say in her own defense, but none of them would be helpful right now.

"I'm sorry things didn't work out between Perry and me. We were over three years ago. I wish we could have both remembered that from the beginning."

Her mother-in-law glanced at her, tears in her eyes. "I thought you were getting back together. He's still so in love with you. It's like we're going through the divorce all over again."

"I didn't want that to happen. I should have been clearer with Perry the first time he mentioned reconciliation." She gentled her tone. "It was never going to work. We've moved on. We're different people now."

"But he loves you."

Mikki was less sure about that. "I suspect he'll recover quicker than you think. It would help if you'd encourage him to start putting himself out there."

"He doesn't want to date anyone else."

Her stubbornness was starting to be annoying. "Lorraine, we need to figure this out if we're going to keep working together." An awful thought occurred to her. "Do you want to quit?"

"What? No, of course not. I love my job. I just thought you were going to work it out."

"We're not. You have to accept that." Mikki figured if she

was going to be honest, she might as well go all the way. "You know I was seeing someone?"

Lorraine nodded, looking even more miserable. "Yes, that Duane man. You're still seeing him?"

A complicated question. Mikki went for the easy lie. "Yes, and if things work out the way I'm hoping, I'll continue to see him. So it's not just about work. It's about our lives. He'll be hanging out with the kids, spending holidays with us. Which means dinner with all of us."

Lorraine pressed a trembling hand to her mouth. "At Christmas?"

"Yes. Birthdays, picnics, whatever."

A single tear slipped down her cheek. "I just wanted my family back."

"No one went anywhere. You still have your family. You'll always have me around, just not as Perry's wife."

Lorraine's head lowered. "You're not going to change your mind?"

"No. I love you and respect you, but I won't pretend just to make things easier for you. It's not good for me and it sure isn't good for Perry."

Lorraine nodded slowly. "All right. I understand. I won't mention it again. I just wish…" She sniffed, then straightened her shoulders. "What I wish doesn't matter." She reached in her locker for her work apron. "Did those crystal clocks come in?"

Mikki hesitated. "Are we okay?"

Lorraine patted her arm. "Yes. It's going to take me a bit to get over all this, but I'll figure it out. And I'll talk to Perry about trying to meet someone. He's been focused on you for so long, he's let everything else go. Now, tell me about the clocks."

Not exactly words designed to make Mikki feel like anything but slime. Still, she didn't complain—Lorraine was due her time to grieve.

"The clocks are a bit of a disappointment. They look a little tackier than I was hoping."

"Oh, dear. Let me see them. Maybe in the right display, they'll show better."

"If anyone can fix it, you can."

"You're rushing things," Oscar said, staring at the bags of candy corns. "It's too soon to start baking fall cupcakes and muffins."

Ashley ignored unexpected irritation. "We always start this week in September."

"No, we start in two weeks. You want time to go faster because of Seth, but life doesn't work that way. You need to work the steps, and in your situation that means feeling the pain, processing it and healing. If you don't do the work, you'll stay stuck where you are forever."

It was barely 6 a.m. Ashley had come in to do inventory and pick up cupcakes and muffins. She was cranky, hungry and she'd forgotten her coffee at home.

"Me bringing in candy corns has nothing to do with Seth and me breaking up."

"You're wrong."

They were practically toe to toe, glaring at each other. Ashley ignored the fact that Oscar was half a foot taller, about seventy pounds of muscle heavier and a man who had, in fact, already committed murder. For real.

"You're really pissing me off," she yelled into his face.

"Yeah, you're no picnic these days. Work the steps, Ashley."

She blinked first, stepping back. "Whatever." But her lips were twitching as she spoke.

"Drama queen."

"Felon."

Oscar chuckled. "Good. You're feeling better."

"A little." She glanced at the bags of candy corn and sighed.

"You're right. It's too early. I'll put them in the pantry until we're ready."

"Put them in the lunchroom. We'll need new ones in two weeks. We're not using old candy corns."

She was about to call him out on his ridiculous standards when she heard a familiar voice speak her name. Even as her heart stopped in her chest, Seth walked into the kitchen.

He looked awful. He was pale, with dark circles under his eyes. His clothes were wrinkled and hung on him as if they'd been made for someone else. Shock at seeing him followed that thought, along with a jolt of pain, but mostly she couldn't get past how bad he looked. As if he were—

"Are you sick?" she asked, hearing the panic in her voice. She remembered Bree talking about how Lewis had been diagnosed with lung cancer, even though he'd never smoked. Did Seth have something like that, or maybe leukemia? She didn't want him to die.

"Can we talk?"

Oscar stepped between them. He didn't say anything, but he was a menacing presence. Ashley shook her head at him, then pulled Seth by the arm into the hallway. As the kitchen door closed behind them, she turned to him.

"What's going on?"

He touched her arm. "God, it's good to see you. You look great. I've missed you so much."

"Seth, talk to me. Are you sick?"

"No. Not the way you mean." His mouth trembled. "I can't do it. I've tried and tried, but I can't get over you. I love you, Ashley, heart and soul. I've waited for you my whole life. I thought I'd be fine, but I'm not. I need you and I love you."

Which was all really nice to hear, but she had no idea what he was talking about.

"Do you want to sit down?" she asked.

"No. I want to ask you to marry me."

The statement came out of nowhere. At first, she didn't think she'd heard him correctly, but then he pulled a diamond solitaire out of his shirt pocket and handed it to her.

"I want you to be happy," he told her, staring into her eyes. "I want us to be together, like we talked about. With kids and a house and a dog. I love you, Ashley, and if getting married is what it takes to keep you with me always, then I'll marry you."

What? She closed her fingers around the ring, feeling the smooth edges and the shape of it. Her skin went cold, then hot, her breathing hitched in her chest.

"You're proposing?"

"Yes. Marry me, please. Say we can be together. I want this. I want us."

She heard the sincerity in his words, felt it in the way he watched her. He'd changed his mind—he was willing to get married.

She waited for the relief, the rightness of the moment. She waited for happiness and all the emotions that would propel her into his arms so they could start their lives together. She waited for the certainty, the joy, the...

"I can't," she whispered. "I can't marry you."

Seth looked stricken. "How can you say that? I'm proposing. You said you wanted to get married. Let's do it. We can elope right now. This is what you wanted."

It was. It was the dream.

"It *is* what I want," she told him. "But I can't. I'm sorry, but somehow it went wrong between us. We had our time, all those weeks ago. We were in that place where it should have happened, but didn't and now it's gone."

"You're punishing me for waiting?" he asked in disbelief.

"No. It's not that. Please don't think it is." She struggled to explain. "I'll always be the one who wanted to get married and you'll always be the guy who was forced into it. That will never work. I'll feel guilty and you'll get resentful. Eventually, that would rip us apart."

She looked into his eyes. "You still don't want to get married. You're only doing this for me."

"Why does that matter? I'm giving you what you want!"

"I'm sorry."

"Sorry isn't good enough. Don't I matter at all?"

"You do." She looked at the ring she held, wishing things could have been different, then she held it out to him. "It's not going to work. Not anymore."

She waited for the accusations, the angry words, but Seth simply snatched back the ring, spun on his heel and walked away. Ashley stayed where she was, watching him go. The shock of the moment disguised the pain to come, but she knew it was just a matter of time until this all hit her.

"You weren't wrong."

She turned and saw Oscar in the doorway of the kitchen.

"You were listening?"

"Sure. Wouldn't you?"

"Probably."

He shrugged. "You weren't wrong. He came back because he's looking for an easy fix to how he feels. But in time he would resent you, just like you said. You were doomed."

"That's cheerful."

"Maybe not, but it's the truth." He waved her into the kitchen. "Come on, boss. I'll make you a cup of coffee."

"I'd rather you went out with Carrie. You'd make such a cute couple."

"Shut up."

"You know you would."

He grumbled something she couldn't hear, then walked to the coffeemaker. But when he handed her the full mug, he put his hand on her shoulder and squeezed gently.

"You done good. It's gonna hurt like a son of a bitch for a while, but you'll be stronger for doing the right thing."

She clutched her coffee. "Work the steps, right?"

"Every single one of them."

TWENTY-EIGHT

"Tell him you had a head injury and it's not your fault," Bree offered helpfully.

"That's insane." Ashley stretched out on the chaise. "Just be honest. You didn't mean to mess up—you were caught up in a situation you didn't recognize. The truth is better."

"I'd go with the head injury."

Mikki sat in a comfortable deck chair on Bree's back porch, listening to her friends' advice on how to approach Duane. She'd debated several options—writing him a long letter, going by his place. But the most fair and nonweird course of action was probably to call the man.

"I'm not faking a head injury," Mikki told them.

"I could shave part of your head," Bree offered with a grin. "For authenticity."

"Ignore her," Ashley said, sipping her iced tea.

The Sunday afternoon was warm and beautiful as only mid-September could be. Mikki had a ton of things she could be doing at home, but hanging out here was way more fun. Sharing their pain seemed to help.

"I'm calling," Mikki said, standing and waving her phone. "I doubt he'll pick up but if he does, I'll ask if we can talk in person. Otherwise, I'll leave a message."

"You have a plan." Bree smiled at her. "Good for you. Remember, you only screwed up because you're a really bad dater."

"Ignorance as my defense?"

"Something like that."

Mikki walked into the house and scrolled through her contacts. She sucked in a breath, then pushed the button. Seconds later the phone rang five times, then went to voice mail.

"You've reached Duane. Leave a message."

Just the sound of his voice made her all fluttery inside. How could she have been so dumb as to risk—

Beep.

"Um, hi. It's Mikki. I was hoping we could talk for a few minutes. In person, if that's all right. I'd like to see you and, well, I just…" Ack! Why hadn't she planned what she was going to say? "I'd appreciate it if you'd give me a chance to tell you a few things. I hope I hear from you."

She ended the call and returned to the patio. Both Bree and Ashley watched her expectantly.

"I didn't get him," she said. "But I do feel nauseous."

"Ashley's pregnant," Bree said cheerfully.

"I'm not!" Ashley's voice was a yelp. "Why would you say that?"

Mikki stared at both of them. "What's going on?"

Bree looked smug. "Just distracting you."

Ashley pressed a hand to her stomach. "Don't even joke about that. I got my period last week. I'm not pregnant. There's something really wrong with you, Bree."

Bree's grin was unrepentant. "I think we can all agree on that."

Mikki's phone buzzed. The three of them went still as Mikki glanced at the screen.

I'll be home at four, if you want to come by.

The churning sensation in her stomach returned, but this time it had a slightly more hopeful quality.

"He says I can come by this afternoon." She clutched the phone to her chest. "I don't know what to say."

Bree swung around so her feet were on the patio pavers. "Be honest. Tell him you screwed up and that you'd like a second chance. If you're feeling especially brave, tell him you're falling in love with him."

"Don't mention love," Ashley corrected. "He might feel like that's a trap. Just apologize and explain, then wait. Let him talk. You'll want to babble and then he won't feel heard."

They both looked at her. She shrugged. "I've been reading some self-help books and talking to one of the therapists at OAR. Just, you know, casually."

"I probably need therapy," Bree muttered.

"It wouldn't hurt," Mikki told her. "But we'll deal with that later." She glanced at her watch. "It's only eleven. How am I supposed to get through the next five hours?"

Bree gave an evil laugh. "Funny you should ask. I happen to know a spin class starting in an hour. Let's all go."

Mikki sweated her guts out, then joined her friends for a post-workout meal at a local taco truck. She ran a few errands on her way home, arriving at her place a little before three. By then the tacos had settled but the second thoughts and worry were grinding away, creating disastrous scenarios in her head, each worse than the one before.

She showered, blew out her hair, then debated what to wear and how much makeup to apply. She wanted to look nice, but not as if she was trying too hard. So nothing sexy and nothing too sophisticated. She settled on light wash jeans and a simple pink T-shirt, along with flats. She applied waterproof mascara and lip gloss, and at three thirty, got in her SUV to make the drive to Duane's place.

She could feel her heart pounding in her chest, and every few minutes she wondered if she was about to have her very first panic attack. To distract herself, she found an oldies station on the radio and cranked up the volume to join in with the Beach Boys as they sang "Barbara Ann."

She arrived early and sat in her car, hyperventilating, until exactly four. During the short walk to his condo's front door, she reminded herself that the act of apology was the most important. Everything else was gravy. Hopefully, he would want to talk after she'd groveled. She'd made a few notes, which she'd gone over that afternoon, although she wasn't sure preparation helped much with matters of the heart.

She knocked once and waited. Seconds later he opened the door. They stared at each other.

He looked good, she thought, trying to ignore her shaking legs. Tall and gorgeous, with broad shoulders. He wore a short-sleeved shirt over jeans. His mouth was a firm straight line and his dark gaze unreadable.

He stepped back to let her in without saying anything. The lack of warmth, the determined set of his spine, had her hopes withering. He was obviously willing to hear her out but he didn't seem the least bit happy to see her.

Closure, she told herself. She was here to do the right thing and ask for what she wanted. He didn't owe her anything. She would be mature and calm and honest. If she accomplished that, she would be proud of herself.

In the living room he pointed to a club chair. He took a seat on the sofa.

At least he wasn't expecting her to talk while standing, she thought, trying to slow her breathing. That was good. Maybe.

"I'm sorry," she began. "I'm sorry for not telling you what was happening with Perry. I was totally and completely wrong to keep that from you. I hope you believe me when I tell you I wasn't hiding anything. It honestly didn't occur to me there was anything to share. He and I weren't dating. I was seeing him the same way I always had, so that wasn't different for me. When he talked about getting back together, I was more pissed than intrigued."

She twisted her hands together and forced herself to meet his gaze. "I don't date. You know that. Not since I was a teenager. I forgot that when you're with someone you like, you treat them honestly and with respect. I should have told you the second Perry brought up reconciling. I shouldn't have continued helping with his new house or the beach walks. I'm not saying being with you means Perry and I can't be friends. Of course we can, but looking at the situation objectively, I see now how he and I were in a strange middle ground. Divorced, but still involved emotionally. I didn't get that before. Now I do."

She paused, hoping he would say something, but he only continued to watch her.

"I've figured out that I was using that not-involved, not-not-involved middle ground to keep myself from having to get out there and find a great guy. But I didn't know that when I met you, so it was easy to get pulled back in with Perry." She leaned toward him. "I swear I never thought I was cheating or being disrespectful. I was so unaware and dumb about the whole thing."

"The man asked you to have his baby."

She pressed her lips together. "Yes, he did. And I knew that was a big deal and it was confusing and it should have been a wake-up call." She ducked her head. "I think maybe after twenty years of being just a mom and a wife and not very special, a part of me liked getting attention from both of you. It was a fun problem to have, although not my most mature hour."

She looked at him. "I was shallow and thoughtless, which is really hard to say because I've never thought of myself as a bad person, but maybe I am in ways I didn't realize."

She paused again, but he remained silent.

"I wanted to apologize. Also, I want you to know that Perry and I are no longer enmeshed in each other's lives. We're not doing anything together, or having lunch or hanging out. We talk about the kids and we'll see each other at family events and that's all. What we were doing wasn't good for either of us. When the kids were younger, we needed to be a team, but then it turned into something unhealthy and I swear, I just didn't realize it. You opened my eyes. I'm sorry you had to get caught up in my co-dependency."

She cleared her throat. "I really like you, Duane. I've enjoyed getting to know you. I like how we laugh together and the things we talk about. You're an amazing man and I am so grateful for what we had. I want all the things we talked about before. I want to keep seeing you. Only you. Exclusively."

He stiffened. The action was subtle, but she caught it and knew there wasn't going to be a second chance. It took all her courage and strength to stay in the chair and finish what she had to say rather than just run, but she'd promised herself to do the right thing, no matter what it cost.

"I'd like the chance to earn back your trust. I think what we had was special and rare. I'm sorry I messed up so badly and I'm hoping you'll give us another try."

She wanted to mention how she'd talked to Lorraine about his coming over for Christmas, but that felt too random, so she stopped talking.

He looked at her, then away. "You hurt me."

She nodded, telling herself she wasn't going to cry. She didn't want Duane to think she was manipulating him with tears.

"I trusted you, Mikki. I believed in us. I was falling in love with you."

Now it was her turn to flinch. He'd loved her? Duane had loved her and she'd blown it? Pain squeezed her from every direction and against her will, tears fell. She brushed them away angrily and held in the need to explain again, to plead again.

She couldn't convince him with a volume of words, nor was it right to badger him.

"I need to think about what you said," he told her.

The tears stopped as quickly as they'd started. She stared at him.

"You're not going to toss me into the street?"

"I couldn't. My condo faces the other way."

Was that humor? Was he being funny? And if he was, could she hope that was a good sign?

He stood and loomed over her. "Dammit, Mikki, your ex-husband? Who does that? Did you sleep with him?"

"No. I haven't slept with anyone since the divorce except for that one awful experience and Earl. It's just me and Earl."

He stalked to the far end of the room, then turned to glare at her. "Did you kiss him?"

"Once." She paused to check her math. "Yes, once." She hesitated, then risked adding, "Earl and I don't kiss."

"I would imagine you don't talk much, either." He rubbed the back of his neck. "You're trouble, Mikki Bartholomew. I always knew you would be. It's the how of it that's thrown me."

"I didn't mean to be slutty. I had no idea what I was doing. I accept I am totally in the wrong, but I genuinely wasn't doing any of it on purpose." She decided to press her point. "I talked to Lorraine about you. I told her that you were a part of my life and that you'd be joining us for all the holidays. I mean, if you still wanted to."

"That can't have been an easy conversation."

"She's a strong woman. She'll adjust. My kids already like you and I'm excited to meet your kids."

She wanted to go to him and hold him, but she knew he hadn't completely made his decision. Given the circumstances, he had to be the one to come to her.

His mouth flattened into a line. "I've missed you. I nearly called you a dozen times. I drove by your house twice. I almost stopped and knocked on the door, but I knew I wasn't ready and I had no idea where you were. For all I knew, you'd eloped with Perry."

"That was never an option. I'm glad you waited. I had to figure a lot of things out. Not how I feel about you. That was never in doubt. But how I let things get so out of control. I needed to spend some time looking at myself and the poor choices I'd made. I hurt a lot of people because I was thoughtless. I'm not proud of that."

One corner of his mouth turned up. "You do give a great apology." He took a step toward her. "You *are* going to have to earn back my trust."

Her body froze. Did that mean he was offering her another chance?

"I want to do that," she said softly. "But I have no idea how, so maybe you can help me figure it out?" She paused. "You know, it would probably be good for you to meet Perry. I'm not saying be friends or anything, but once you see each other, we'll have a shared frame of reference. The kids can be there. And maybe Bree and Ashley. So it's a crowd, not a thing."

"I don't want to meet your ex, but your point's a good one. Only let's get on a little firmer ground first, all right? I want to know you and I are back where we were."

She pressed her hands together. "Are you giving me another chance?"

His beautiful, wonderful smile returned. "I am. With ground rules."

"Absolutely. Starting with exclusive. Totally and completely exclusive. Just us. No one else. Ever."

"Agreed." He paused. "I missed you."

Before she could reply, he pulled her close and held her so tight she could barely breathe, but she found it didn't really matter. She hung on, inhaling the scent of him, feeling the steady beat of his heart.

After a few minutes he cupped her face and kissed her.

"I missed you," he repeated, staring into her eyes. "You got into my life and my head and I was lost without you."

"I missed you, too. So much. I'm sorry for what I did. Really sorry."

"I know. Stop apologizing. I want to move forward, not look back. Starting right this second."

"Me, too. So Thanksgiving with your kids and Christmas with my former in-laws?"

"Yes," he whispered. "And Paris at New Year's."

She looked at him. "I love you, Duane. I want you to know that you have my heart. I love you."

She hadn't planned on saying the words, nor did she know what his reaction would be. As she watched, wonder and joy filled his eyes.

"I love you, too," he whispered. "More than you know."

She was so happy, she thought maybe she could float. Although on a practical note, she had some other things in mind.

"While we're confessing things, I wanted to let you know that Earl and I are no longer a thing. Not since you and I first made love."

His eyebrows rose. "But it's been nearly a month since we were together."

"I know, but it didn't seem right to, um, use him."

"Interesting. Because from what I've read, a woman your age is in her sexual prime."

"I've heard that, too."

"We wouldn't want that to go to waste."

"That would be sad."

He put his arm around her and led her toward the bedroom. "I have a brand-new blood test that might interest you."

Wanting spiraled out from her belly. "So no more condoms? We should check that out."

"I agree."

★ ★ ★

Bree followed Ashley and Mikki into the OAR building. They'd talked her into volunteering on a project involving literacy, which under any other circumstances, she would have been on board with. It was just the whole Harding-OAR connection that had her worried.

She wanted to ask, yet again, if they were sure he wasn't around. But they'd already promised he wasn't and she really did trust her friends.

"What ages are the children?" Bree asked, catching up with her friends. "You didn't say."

Ashley and Mikki exchanged a look.

"First through third grade."

"Preteens."

They spoke at the same time. Mikki rolled her eyes. "It's a mixed group."

"That doesn't make any sense," Bree said, following them upstairs. "You can't mix age groups like that. The older kids will intimidate the younger ones and—"

They stopped outside a door. Bree stared at the sign and knew immediately that she'd been played. Anger joined hurt.

"Counseling?" she said, taking a step back. "There isn't a literacy project, is there?"

Mikki inched between her and the exit. "No. We lied to get you here."

"It's an intervention," Ashley added.

"No way."

Bree turned to leave, but Ashley grabbed her arm and half pushed, half shoved her toward the door. Mikki opened it, stepped in after them, then leaned against it as if she would physically prevent Bree from escaping.

"We're asking for thirty minutes," Ashley said quickly. "Just half an hour. That's all." Her tone softened. "We love you and we want you to be happy."

Bree couldn't shake the sense of betrayal. "You tricked me." She couldn't believe it. "I trusted you."

"We know there's a risk," Ashley admitted, grabbing Bree's hand. "We've sweated over this. But you're in pain all the time and we don't know how to help."

"I don't need your kind of help." Bree pulled her hand free. "I'm leaving."

"Wait!" Mikki waved for Ashley to join her at the door. "Just listen to what she has to say. It's an hour out of your life. Then you can walk away."

"I thought it was thirty minutes."

She was about to physically force her friends away from the door when a woman walked into the waiting area. She was in her midfifties, with curly gray hair and a kind face.

"Ashley, are you blocking the door so Bree can't leave?"

"Maybe."

"Do you think that's wise? We talked about this when you came to me last week. I don't see patients against their will." The woman turned to Bree and held out her hand. "Hello. I'm Kimberley."

The moment felt surreal—her friends kidnapping her, the therapist, all of it.

"Nice to meet you," Kimberley added, then raised her eyebrows. "Ashley, step away from the door."

She and Mikki both moved. Mikki introduced herself. They all stood looking at each other.

Kimberley smiled at Bree. "I take it you don't want to be here."

"No. I thought I was volunteering."

Kimberley made a tsking sound. "For what it's worth, your friends acted with the best of intentions. Although, if it were me, I'd feel both loved and insulted."

"And betrayed," Bree muttered.

Ashley winced. Mikki dropped her head.

Kimberley motioned to her office. "I have a free hour. Why don't we talk for a bit? After all, you're here, so why not? If you don't want to stay, you're welcome to leave at any time."

Leaving made the most sense. Bree knew she was a flawed person and she was fine with that. Okay, not fine, but she'd learned to live with the reality. Yes, sometimes it was hard, like when she'd had to walk away from Harding, but that was a small price to pay to protect herself.

"I can't be fixed," she said flatly.

Kimberley surprised her by smiling. "I know. You're not a cabinet with a loose door. People don't get fixed. But I'm guessing you do see there's a problem."

Bree nodded. "I don't feel things other people feel. I don't let anyone in."

"Of course," Kimberley said kindly. "That's very typical for abuse victims. Trust requires opening ourselves and isn't that the most difficult thing of all?"

Bree stared at her. "I wasn't abused. Is that what they told you? My parents never hit me and or sexually assaulted me."

She looked around and realized that Ashley and Mikki had left. She wasn't sure when they'd crept away, but as she was alone with Kimberley, it made sense to follow her into her small office.

"I wasn't abused," Bree repeated forcefully as she sat in one of the comfortable leather chairs.

"Abuse comes in many forms," Kimberley told her. "Emotional abuse is just as damaging as physical or sexual, but maybe you'd be more comfortable with the word *neglect*."

"Yes, that makes sense to me."

"We can get used to nearly anything. The younger we are, the easier it is to set the pattern. Eventually, the pain becomes something we not only accept but understand and, oftentimes, look for. It's why the children of alcoholics frequently marry alcoholics. They don't have that illness themselves, but they understand it and know the rules. It's when they start getting involved with nonalcoholics that there can be trouble. Suddenly, the rules don't make sense and they don't know how to act or what's expected."

Kimberley smiled. "I'm generalizing but you get my point."

Bree blinked several times. "You're saying I look for patterns in relationships, so I'm comfortable, but when I step out of those patterns, it's harder for me."

The concept made sense, even if she'd never articulated it before. "Lewis was like my parents. I fell in love with him and kept thinking how great it was going to be because he cared about me in ways they never did. Only it wasn't real."

She paused. "Those guys I slept with—I keep them at a distance. I do to them what my parents did to me. I'm the one who decides."

As for the rest of it, was Kimberley right? Did the pain come from trying to break the patterns? "It was hard to like Ashley and Mikki. To trust them." Her mouth twisted. "And look what they did to me."

"I don't think Ashley and Mikki are quite as guilty as some other people in your life, but the rest of it sounds right. You've been thinking about this, haven't you?"

"Some." Bree turned away. "Ashley's reading all these self-help books. She leaves them lying around the house. Sometimes I pick them up. Just, you know, out of curiosity."

And because every now and then she wondered what it would be like to be the same as everyone else. Part of her longed for the freedom of being normal, but she wasn't sure of the price she would pay.

"I can't risk it," she said aloud. "I don't have one more break in me."

Kimberley nodded. "Makes sense. You've been through so much already. Just one quick question before you go. What if you didn't have to break?"

Bree froze in her chair. "What does that mean?"

The gentle smile returned. "Crap happens all the time. You can't avoid it, but you can develop skills to deal with it. Bad things are in your future, Bree. I can't tell you what or when, but they're going to happen. The secret isn't to avoid them. The secret is to be strong enough to survive them. Right now you think you're incapable of getting through emotional pain. That your heart is so mangled and brittle, it will shatter into a thousand pieces. No one lives through that. I'm suggesting there are ways to strengthen your sense of self and to add to your emotional tool kit, if you will, so that when the bad stuff happens, you can cope. If your heart doesn't shatter, then why not take a chance on the relationships that could bring you joy and happiness?"

No way Bree was buying into that. "It's not that easy."

"You're right. It's not easy. The work is hard, but it's very doable. Part of it would be learning skills you were never taught as a child. Part of it is breaking unhealthy patterns. What we would do together is slow and tedious and frustrating."

Bree stared at the therapist, desperate to believe something better was possible, but unwilling to be played. "How do you know I can change?"

"You're strong, you're motivated, you have an emotional support system. That's more than a lot of people have, so while I won't guarantee anything, I have a good feeling about what we could accomplish together." Kimberley met her gaze. "Let's meet weekly for a month, then assess. If it's not going well, you can fire my ass and walk away."

Bree looked around at the small space, with the flower prints on the wall and the desk in the corner. "I don't want to run into Harding."

"I have an office a few miles from here. We could meet there."

"You really think you can fix me?"

"I'm sure I can't fix you, but I know you could heal yourself and let go of the fear that's holding you back. Want to try?"

Bree sensed the importance of the moment. She was being given a chance and she could either take it or she could continue to live her small, frightened life. From the outside it looked as if she had it all, but she knew the truth. She knew she was exactly what Sad Guy had claimed.

"I want to be stronger."

"Then let's make that our first goal. How does next Tuesday evening work for you?"

TWENTY-NINE

"Have you decided?" Ashley asked her brother.

Harding considered the cookies. "One chocolate chip and two peanut butter."

She glared at him across the table. "You know what I mean."

"Hey, why don't you care what cookies I want?" Dave asked.

The three of them were having lunch at OAR to catch up. Ashley was pleased that Harding looked better than he had. He'd obviously been eating and sleeping. He looked sad but healthy.

She knew the same could be said about herself. Day by day she was healing. She'd started a yoga class that left her feeling like the least flexible person on the planet, but she knew the movement was good for her. She was surfing and working hard on her business.

She passed homemade cookies to the guys. "There are oatmeal raisin, too," she said.

Dave shuddered. "Raisins are gross."

"But you like grapes and wine."

"Really?" he asked, his dark eyes bright with humor. "Logic?"

She laughed before turning her attention back to Harding. "Well?"

"I've renewed the lease on my house," he said. "I want to stay in LA."

"I'm happy and concerned equally," she admitted. After what

had happened with Bree, she'd half expected Harding to take off. But he hadn't.

"My decision has nothing to do with Bree," he told her. "LA has always been my home." He grinned. "Besides, there's a good airport down the road."

"You're going to start traveling again?"

That was good news. Harding had been a little too solitary lately.

He nodded. "My publicist is sending me on tour. I'm going to combine that with research on the grief book. I have some people to interview. I'll be gone a couple weeks at a time."

She studied him. "You okay?"

"I'm getting better. I still miss her, but I can't force her to love me." He glanced at the table, then back at her. "I want to ask how she is."

"We agreed not to talk about that."

"I know, but she's okay, right?"

Ashley thought about how Bree was doing in her life. She worked long hours, surfed every Thursday, lost herself in spin class twice a week and, most surprising of all, continued to see Kimberley faithfully.

"Harding, don't put me in the middle."

Her brother gave her a sad smile. "Sorry." He grabbed a couple of cookies. "I'm going to head out. See you two soon."

He circled the table and kissed the top of her head, then nodded at Dave before leaving. Ashley watched him go.

"He's still in pain," she murmured.

"He gave his heart. It's going to take a long time to get over that. And speaking of recovery, how are you doing?"

"Better," she told him. "I don't get angry anymore and I've stopped crying over the breakup. There are things I miss and things I don't. I think what gets me through is I wasn't wrong to ask for what I wanted. It took me a long time to see that, but I made the right decision and I was strong. I'll probably never know what Seth's issue was, but that's okay. I need to take care of myself and toward the end of our relationship, I wasn't."

She reached for a cookie. "It's a process."

"You're impressive," he said. "You're being proactive in your healing."

"Is this where you start in on the OAR platitudes?"

He drew back in pretended insult. "Platitudes? These are life's pearls of wisdom."

"Uh-huh. Sell it somewhere else."

"Fair enough. So the Saturday after Thanksgiving? Do you have any plans?"

She looked at him. "The Saturday after Thanksgiving? That's in like two months. Why would I have plans?"

"It's a holiday weekend. You could be traveling or going to a concert."

Was it just her, or was he being weird? "Harding and I are flying up to have Thanksgiving with Mom and Dad. He's staying the weekend, but I'll be back Friday morning because of work. It's Black Friday, followed by Small Business Saturday."

"Want to have dinner that night?"

"Is there an OAR event? If it's not too early, I could go. Bree, Mikki and I have agreed we're keeping to regular business hours that weekend, so we're closing at five on Saturday. We have shorter hours in the winter because it gets dark earlier."

"It's not an OAR event."

There was something in his tone that she didn't understand and he was watching her with an expression she couldn't read.

"I'm confused. You're asking me to dinner the Saturday after Thanksgiving but it's not an OAR event."

"Yes."

"Then what is it?"

"A date."

She put down the cookie she'd been holding and carefully

wiped her fingers on a napkin. A thousand thoughts took flight in her head and she couldn't seem to capture even a single one.

"A date," she repeated slowly, wondering if there was a definition to the word that she couldn't remember.

"As you pointed out earlier, it's two months away," he said, his tone casual, but his gaze oddly intense. "I'm not saying you'll be completely over Seth by then, but you'll be on your way. I'll admit it's a timing problem. Obviously, I want you well on the road to recovery, but I don't want to wait so long that you get involved with someone else."

Okay, she was going to start at the beginning and walk through this slowly. Dave had asked her to dinner. In two months. On a date.

"You're asking me out," she confirmed.

"Yes."

"Like a boy-girl thing."

"I prefer man-woman, but yes."

"On a date."

He chuckled. "I remember you being brighter than this."

"Don't you get all with the attitude. Years ago I had a mad crush on you. I told you and you practically patted me on the head like a puppy. You said I was Harding's little sister and you'd never see me any other way. You broke my heart."

His humor faded. "I squashed your ego a little, but nothing was broken. You were a kid, Ashley."

"Seventeen."

"A kid," he repeated. "You had your whole life ahead of you. I was still learning how to be in this chair and I didn't want you to be collateral damage." He glanced away, then back at her. "I didn't want you to feel obligated."

She would deal with her reaction to that revelation later. "Why now?"

"We've had timing issues. Five or six years ago I figured I was ready to pursue you, but you were involved, then I was involved.

Then Seth came along. That was a nightmare. But you're done and while I don't think you're ready to start dating right now, I'm not willing to risk you falling for another guy between now and November." He flashed her a smile. "Let's face it—emotionally you're kind of flighty."

She didn't know if she should throw something at him or plop herself on his lap and kiss him. Both possibilities had merit.

"I don't know what to say," she admitted, trying to process everything he'd told her.

"*Yes* would be my first choice."

She looked at him. "Yes, Dave. I would very much like to have dinner with you the Saturday after Thanksgiving."

"Then it's a date."

"It is."

"If you want to go out with other guys between now and then, I'll understand. Just don't fall in love with one of them."

"I promise."

She looked at him, feeling happy and giddy and a little shy. He surprised her by wheeling close.

"Okay, so let's get this part over with. I'm not presuming anything, but just in case things go well, you're going to have questions about how it all works. I have full control over my bathroom functions. Believe me, that's a big deal. The equipment is fine." He flashed her a grin. "As we've discussed."

She swallowed. "Yes, we have. You were very impressed with yourself."

"You will be, too." The smile faded. "There are things I can do and things I can't. It's a lot about leverage and strength and control. I'm never going to walk again, Ashley. There's no miracle waiting for me. But I'm more than capable of being everything you need."

He touched her face. "I'll email you a list of books to read. They'll answer a lot of your questions. Anything else you want to know, ask me directly. If, after you've read them, you decide this isn't for you, I'll understand. No hard feelings."

The raw honesty of the moment touched her more than anything had maybe ever. He was laying himself bare, telling her how it would be. She wasn't sure how she was supposed to resist that. Or him.

"I'll read every word," she promised. "And come to you with questions."

"I'll be here."

She knew that was true. No matter what, Dave would be there for her. He was smart, determined, loyal, kind and strong. And he wanted a big church wedding.

"I should get back to work," she murmured, wanting nothing more than to kiss him. Only she knew he was right about her needing time.

"Me, too."

She stood and walked to the door, then turned back. "You should call me tonight. Just to talk."

"Nine work for you?"

"Nine works just fine."

Bree struggled to type fast enough to keep up with her thoughts. She used a computer for work and shopping, but writing was new to her. Kimberley had suggested keeping a journal, which Bree had resisted for at least three weeks before giving in. She spent twenty minutes every morning writing down what she was feeling.

It was a pain in her ass and she hated it, but after a solid week of putting in the time, she'd found herself looking forward to the morning mental cleanse. That had grown into her taking a half hour or so in the evening to write about other things. Her parents, Lewis and after another week, Harding.

She still missed him, but the pain was familiar now. Like breathing. She was desperate to ask Ashley about him, although she didn't. She liked her roommate and didn't want to mess up what they had. They'd both agreed to never mention him. Ashley saw her brother away from the house. He never came to the store. And if Bree sometimes drove to the corner of his street where she could almost see his place from the safety of her car, well, she never told anyone about that. But she wrote about it.

Most days she deleted what she'd written—she wasn't looking to write a novel, God forbid, or anything anyone else would read. Her gut told her the process was what would help her, not the final output. But every now and then, she saved part of her work into a file and in late October, she had five pages on the subject of grief.

She reread the file.

Discovering opens wounds decades after the fact doesn't make them any less inclined to fester. They have to be treated and fussed over. They have to be given attention, or they won't heal. The pain is constant but sometimes knowing why I hurt, why I act the way I do, is its own reward.

For me, grief is alive. She's a cold, unforgiving bitch who lurks in the shadows. When I'm tired or stressed, she's always ready to pounce, to make me feel weak and incapable. Sometimes she frightens me with how big she is, but with help, I'm learning to beat her back, and now when she attacks, she's a little smaller than the last time.

Healing is a choice. I made the decision to heal. It wasn't easy or pleasant or anything I wanted to do but the alternative was to continue to live in pain and I just couldn't do that anymore. The pain sucks me dry and I was at risk of shriveling up and blowing away.

So every morning I decide to be a little bit better. Sure, there are days I screw up completely, but then I start again. I initiated a hug with a friend. No big deal for most people, but for me it was an act of courage. Tiny steps add up. At least that's the plan.

You have to decide to acknowledge the grief and heal anyway. Heal despite. And one day, when you're not paying attention, you have a moment of being happy. Just one moment. The grief returns, she makes you pay for that happiness, but then there's another moment and another. And one day you realize the grief isn't so big and bad anymore and sometimes you can even feel sorry for her.

Bree saved the file, then hit the print button. When the pages had printed, she put them in an envelope and went downstairs.

It was late, just after midnight. She grabbed her bag, then went out to the car.

The sky was clear. No stars, of course—this was Los Angeles and the lights of the city were too bright—but she could see airplanes on approach and they glittered nearly as bright.

The drive to Harding's house didn't take long. As she expected, lights shone from several windows. The man was such a night owl. She parked a few houses away and turned off her car, then walked quietly to his front porch.

She desperately wanted to see him, just for a few seconds. She wanted to look into his eyes and see him smile. She wanted to feel his arms around her as he pulled her close and held on like he would never let go. She wanted him to take her to his bed and do all the delicious things he'd done to her, with her, before.

She closed the distance to the door and put her hand flat on the hard surface. But she didn't knock or press the bell. She couldn't. She wasn't ready, and reaching out to him would only cause him pain. She needed to get stronger.

So despite the need and the hunger and the pain—although the pain was a reminder of what mattered—she dropped her arm to her side, then placed the envelope on the mat and quietly walked away.

"Bring a jacket," Mikki said in her "I'm the mother" tone.

Ashley resisted the urge to roll her eyes. "It's not that cold."

"It's in the sixties. You need a jacket or a hoodie."

September had rolled into October. The days were noticeably shorter and the beach was less crowded during the week. Happily, the store stayed busy.

They'd rented out the extra space at the OAR building. Ashley and Mikki coordinated much of the work there so Bree didn't have to go often. When she did, Ashley made sure Harding wouldn't be there. These days that was less difficult—he was on the road more than half the time.

Ashley gave in to the inevitable and grabbed a sweatshirt. She pulled it over her head, then reached for the bottle of Piper-Heidsieck Brut she'd chosen for tonight. They'd agreed to go back to a single bottle of champagne every Friday and had let go of the snacks. Life was returning to normal.

She met her friends at the front of the store. Mikki, happy in her relationship with Duane, practically glowed. Her hair had a healthy shine and was longer now, her eyes were bright, her smile constant. She studied the bottle's label.

"We're going to love this," she announced. "Shall we?"

Ashley fell into step with Bree. "Is it just me or is she even more cheerful than usual?"

"She is," Bree agreed. "I'm trying not to take it personally."

"Young love. It sucks when it's not us."

"You have young love waiting in the wings so you don't get to complain."

Ashley smiled. "It's not a sure thing."

Bree groaned. "Really? The man is here practically every day. You hang out all the time, but maintain some weird pretense that you're not dating."

"We're not. We're getting to know each other as friends. We haven't even kissed."

Mikki put her arm around Ashley. "You should definitely be kissing. It's the best."

"We're waiting. Dave wants me to be totally over Seth."

"Are you?" Bree asked.

Some of Ashley's good mood faded. "Mostly. I don't miss him anymore, but I still struggle with regret. Who did what wrong when. It's a process."

"He did everything wrong," Mikki told her. "Hang on to that."

"You're both to blame," Bree added. "Relationships are rarely one-sided. You have fault."

"You're right and yet I find you annoying."

Bree only laughed.

They settled in their usual spot. There weren't many people out this time of year and the surf seemed louder. Ashley expertly opened the bottle, as Mikki had taught them, then poured them each a glass of the bubbly liquid. They took turns discussing the hint of ginger and smooth finish.

"Ladies Know Wine says this is a great date night champagne," Mikki said.

"Well, then, it must be so," Bree teased.

"Are you mocking my favorite wine blog?"

Bree hugged her. "I wouldn't do that."

They talked about the week's business and had a brief argument about how many Christmas trees to put in the store.

"Customers still need to be able to walk around," Ashley pointed out.

"But it's Christmas trees," Mikki said. "More is better."

Ashley shook her head. "You're annoying when you're happy."

"She's right about that," Bree said before sipping on her champagne. "Five trees. No more."

"I agree," Ashley said.

"Fine. Scrooges." Mikki glanced at Ashley. "You're really not sleeping with Dave?"

"No. We're exploring friendship until the Saturday after Thanksgiving."

"Okay, then." Mikki reached into her jacket pocket and pulled out a rectangular box about eight inches long. "For you. From both of us."

Ashley glanced between them. "You bought me a present? Why?"

Bree and Mikki exchanged a smile.

"Open it," Mikki said.

Ashley ripped open the pretty floral paper only to stare in disbelief at the picture on the box. There was a small pink plastic rabbit attached to what looked like a tree, and fancy script promising her "endless delight and pleasure."

"Holy shit, you bought me a vibrator."

Mikki and Bree burst into laughter.

"It's not a vibrator. It's your very own Earl. The website said this model is very popular with the younger crowd."

Bree grinned. "It's just to tide you over until things get hot with Dave."

Ashley felt her cheeks burn. "You bought me a vibrator. What were you thinking?"

"That a girl has needs. Earl got me through some tough times."

Mikki and Bree held up their glasses. Ashley put down Earl and touched her glass to theirs.

"Thank you," she said. "I think."

"Oh, you'll thank us later," Mikki teased.

Bree shook her head. "I just hope Ashley isn't a screamer. That could make my life very uncomfortable."

THIRTY

"Is it just me, or is there more wrapping paper now than this morning?" Mikki asked with a laugh.

Bree held up the trash bag overflowing with holiday paper. "Where does it come from? I've already been through the family room twice."

"It reproduces when we're not looking. Hey, stop cleaning. It's Christmas."

"I like bringing order to chaos," Bree said. "I'll do one more pass and then I'll be done. I swear."

Mikki pressed her lips together, as if trying not to protest. Bree knew her friend understood today had been a test for her. Hanging out with over a dozen loud, friendly people who were filled with the spirit of the day. She'd wanted to stay home by herself, but she knew this was better. Healthier. And to be honest, a little nicer than solitude.

In the lull between unwrapping presents and dinner, most of the group was outside. Lorraine and Rita were overseeing a volleyball game, Chet acting as referee. Perry played on the same side as his new girlfriend, a pretty blonde about twelve years younger. Bree wondered if she was the only one who noticed the woman's resemblance to Mikki. But she kept her mouth shut. Perry's new girlfriend was very sweet and her two young girls were adorable.

Sydney and Will played on opposite sides. They'd both wanted Duane on their side, but he'd gone with Sydney, leaving Will to grumble. Duane had brightened the teen's spirits by offering to let him drive his car after dinner.

After putting the trash bag in the can, Bree washed her hands, then helped Mikki set the table. Knowing her friend as she did, Bree wasn't surprised by the holiday dishes, the Santa and Mrs. Claus salt-and-pepper shakers or the holly-embroidered linen napkins.

Last night had been a traditional turkey dinner. Today there was prime rib, Yorkshire pudding, which Bree had never made, vegetables and every pie imaginable. Bree had brought a fruit tart with a made-from-scratch crust. Her baking lessons with Oscar were paying off.

"You doing all right?" Mikki asked casually, setting out the flatware.

"Yes. This has been fun. Thanks for having me."

Mikki put down a gravy boat and moved in front of Bree. "You're ready. Call him."

There was no need to ask who "he" was. "It's been four months. He's moved on."

"Why do you say that? You haven't. You're just as wild about him as you were the day you tossed his yummy ass to the curb."

Bree managed a smile. "That's a very strange visual."

"I stand by it. Come on, it's Christmas. Give yourself a little something fun."

"He's seeing someone else."

Mikki's mouth dropped open. "What?" she asked, her voice a shriek. "Since when? Ashley never said a word. She's always telling me he's busy with work and travel and there's no one. How can you know there's someone else? That bastard!"

"Women throw themselves at him. Trust me, there's a woman."

"Oh, I get it. You're *speculating*. And if you tell yourself he's got a girlfriend, you get to be all self-righteous and not take a chance on telling him you're still in love with him. Is that deflection or just plain candy-assed cowardice?"

"Stop saying ass, please. I'm the one who swears in this relationship."

"I notice you didn't deny being in love with him."

Bree sighed. "No."

Kimberley had helped her see the truth, or maybe just admit it. She had been in love with Harding. That was why she'd acted so badly—she'd been terrified of what he could do to her.

"But you're not going to call him?"

"What am I supposed to say?" Bree asked. "Hey, it's me. I'm slightly less damaged than I used to be. Want to hang out or go to the movies?"

"That's a start."

"He's not interested."

"You don't know that. He could still care about you or he could be sleeping with every flight attendant from here to Miami. We should ask Ashley." Mikki started to look around for her phone.

"No," Bree said firmly. "We're not bothering Ashley on Christmas."

She and her parents, along with Dave and Harding and possibly some woman Harding was seeing, were having dinner at Dave's house. He was cooking and everything. Humorously, Ashley and Dave had spent so much time "just being friends" that their first date had turned into an all-weekend sleepover. Ashley had barely made it into work on Monday. They'd been together ever since.

Which was nice, Bree thought wistfully. Falling in love and letting yourself be loved in return.

"I'll finish setting the table," Bree said. "You need to check on your prime rib. It seemed a little too brown around the edges last time I looked."

Mikki shrieked and raced to the kitchen. Bree felt momentarily guilty for the lie, but she didn't want to talk about Harding anymore. Knowing what she'd lost made her sad. Having the skills to deal with the pain didn't make the pain any less sucky.

Fortunately, Mikki got distracted by the roast and a few minutes later the volleyball game ended. Everyone moved back into the house, which meant there was too much conversation and activity for introspection.

Mikki put Bree in charge of the Yorkshire pudding. Thirty minutes and several gray hairs later Bree proudly dropped the light and fluffy muffins into a napkin-lined basket. Mikki, Bree and Lorraine carried the food to the table. Once seated, they joined hands and Chet said grace.

This, she thought an hour later, as Duane joked with Perry and the girls, and Rita laughed with Lorraine. This was what she wanted for herself. Family, friends, happiness.

A house, kids, a dog. And you. I love you.

Harding's words echoed inside her head. He'd told her he loved her. He'd said he wanted forever and while she believed him, she'd been unable to trust him enough to try.

No, she reminded herself. None of this was on him—she was the one who hadn't been brave enough, strong enough, to believe she could make it through whatever happened. She was the one who had decided it was better to be safe and small, not happy, but never risking her heart. Never having more.

She'd come a long way, she told herself. She'd learned a lot, was in a much better place. But was it enough? And even if it was, had Harding waited?

After the pies had been eaten and everyone had gone into the family room to watch *It's a Wonderful Life*, Bree pulled Mikki out of the room and hugged her.

"Thank you for the best Christmas ever," she said.

Mikki held her tight. "I'm so glad you came." She stepped back. "Call him. There isn't anyone else. I asked. *Call* him."

The words immobilized Bree. For a second she couldn't breathe or move or think. "You talked to Ashley?"

"Yes, and she had what she described as a very not-subtle conversation with her brother." Mikki held up a hand. "She didn't mention you at all. She badgered him about not moving on and at least finding someone to have sex with. He said he wasn't ready, he was still in love with you."

Tears prickled in Bree's eyes, but she blinked them back.

"I'm scared."

"Of course you are. Love is always scary, but it's worth the risk. You already know that. Trust yourself. Trust Harding. And if he turns out to be a jerk, we'll have Oscar beat the crap out of him."

"I don't know."

Mikki touched her shoulder. "Yes, you do."

Bree hugged her again, then left. She drove home, then paced the length of her living room, phone in hand.

Mikki's words gave her hope, but the fear was still so big.

She thought about loving Lewis, how he'd used her and broken her. She thought about her parents, especially her mother, and knew those wounds might never heal. Then she thought about how there were no guarantees, no promises, just this moment and what she did with it.

> **I wondered if maybe we could talk later—when you're done with your family.**

She sent the text, then stared at her phone, willing an answer to appear. When it didn't, she grabbed a jacket and went outside.

Christmas lights twinkled from every house. She could see lit trees and new bikes on porches. In the distance there was laughter and a dog barking. A mother called her children into the house for cake. Overhead airplanes headed for the airport, their lights bright against the inky sky. Her phone buzzed.

I'll be there in thirty minutes.

Bree kept walking. She circled the block until it was nearly time, then waited on her front steps, watching for a familiar truck to drive down the street. After what felt like three eternities, Harding pulled into her driveway and turned off the engine. He got out and walked toward her.

Her first thought was that he looked good. Her second was that he'd already proven himself to be the kind of man who didn't give up. No matter what life handed them, he would be there, at her side. He wouldn't get scared or betray her or use her. He was, in fact, the best man she'd ever known.

She stood as he approached. "I have trust issues. I never learned how to be in a family and when I get scared, I run. I'm learning to stay put, to deal with it all, but there's a better than even chance I'll never be like everyone else." She wrinkled her nose. "I want to say *normal*, but Kimberley says my definition of normal is totally blown out of proportion. That I assume no one else has problems or fails or whatever."

She shoved her hands in her back pockets. "I'm not like you. I'm not brave. I'm trying but it's hard and sometimes I just want to say fuck it and walk away. Which is totally the wrong thing to do, so I'm trying to stare down the fear. Having said that, I'm never going to have a relationship with my parents, so you'd need to just let that go. Not everything broken can be made whole again."

He watched her with an intensity that should have scared her but instead made her feel warm and safe and happy.

"I never wanted to love you," she whispered. "But I do. Very much. And I thought you should know."

He reached for her at the exact second she threw herself at him. He pulled her hard against him, pressing his mouth to hers. She wrapped her arms around his neck then gave herself over to all he was willing to give. His mouth was warm and familiar and she knew, she *knew* this was what she'd been looking for, even when she'd decided to run.

"Took you long enough," he said with a shaky laugh as he pulled away and stared into her eyes.

"I'm a slow learner. I've been in remedial love classes."

"How have they been going?"

"I guess you'll be the one to decide." She touched his face. "I'm sorry for what I put you through. It wasn't on purpose."

"I know. You needed time."

"What I need is you."

"Yeah." He leaned his forehead against hers. "You have me, Bree. Heart and soul." He chuckled. "So that's why Ashley was grilling me on my sex life."

"She wanted to know if you were cheating on me."

"Hey, we weren't together."

She stared into his eyes. "We weren't. Whatever happened is totally fine. I don't even want to know."

"Nothing happened. Without you, there wasn't a point."

"I didn't sleep with anyone, either," she said quickly. "I was too busy having my emotional guts ripped out by my therapist. Plus, you know. The in-love thing."

She led the way inside and closed the door behind him. When they were in the living room, she faced him.

"I don't know how to do this," she admitted. "A real relationship. Ashley's pretty much living with Dave, so if you want to move in here, that would be good. Or is it too soon to say that? Should we date first? You know, it would help if you told me the rules."

He kissed her again. "Love me, Bree. That's the only rule."

"That one I've got."

"Then you and I are going to be just fine."

★ ★ ★ ★ ★

THE
BOARDWALK
BOOKSHOP

SUSAN MALLERY

BOOK CLUB DISCUSSION GUIDE

Red, White and Blueberry Muffins

2 cups all-purpose flour
2 tsp baking powder
8 tbsp butter, softened
1 cup sugar
2 eggs
½ cup sour cream
1 tsp vanilla
2/3 cup each fresh blueberries, raspberries*
and white chocolate chips

Preheat oven to 375°F. Line 18 standard-sized muffin cups with paper cups.

Sift together flour and baking powder. Set aside. With a mixer, cream together butter and sugar on medium speed until butter is a very pale yellow. Add eggs, one at a time, mixing well after each addition. Mix in sour cream and vanilla. Dump flour mixture into the wet ingredients and mix on low speed just until combined. Fold in the berries and chips.

Fill each paper muffin cup about 2/3 full. Bake until golden brown and a toothpick inserted into the center of a muffin comes out clean, 18–25 minutes.

*You can use frozen blueberries and raspberries. Thaw them under running water, then dry on paper towels before adding to the dough.

A note from Susan Mallery on champagne...

You might have been inspired by the story to serve champagne at your book club meeting. I encourage it! In fact, if you do and your group isn't camera shy, please post a picture on Facebook or Instagram and tag @susanmallery.

True champagne is only from France and comes from the Champagne region. Everything else is sparkling wine. A brut champagne is more dry and less sweet. It will also pair very well with food. Sweeter champagnes tend to work well for toasts and for stand-alone drinking.

If you're on a budget, try prosecco. It's from Italy, and there are dozens of modestly priced options. One of my favorite cocktails for special occasions is a French 75. It's gin, lemon juice, simple syrup and a champagne float. Fancy, right? When I make them at home, I use prosecco rather than cracking open a bottle of champagne and only using a few tablespoons. Of course, you could save the champagne and have mimosas for brunch the next day!

Susan recommends...

Domaine Ste. Michelle. A shout-out to a local Washington winery and their sparkling wine. They have a brut and a rosé. Both are lovely.

Schramsberg sparkling wines come in a variety of price points, from about twenty dollars to well over sixty. They're a fave for me. If you're celebrating and have a little extra cash, their Blanc de Blancs is lovely and should be around forty to fifty dollars.

If you're going to blow the budget, then you can't go wrong with any of the champagnes I mention in the book. They are all fabulous. See them below.

Perrier-Jouët Blason Rosé
Veuve Clicquot
Taittinger Brut La Francaise
Larmandier-Bernier Latitude Extra Brut
Piper-Heidsieck Brut

These questions contain major spoilers about the book. We recommend that you wait until after you've finished the book to read the questions.

1. What did you think of the way *The Boardwalk Bookshop* came into being, with three business owners agreeing to lease space together? Which of the three businesses would you like to own, and why?

2. In the beginning of the book, Bree, Mikki and Ashley were really just starting to become friends, having met only six months prior. How did their friendship grow and develop through the book? What brought them closer together? By the end, how did you feel about their friendship?

3. Which of the three women grew and changed the most and in what ways? Which of the characters is most like you? How so?

4. Bree was a wounded soul. Discuss the things that happened in her life to inflict those emotional wounds. Did your opinion about Bree change as the story progressed and you learned more of her backstory? If so, how so? What made Harding fall in love with Bree?

5. In the beginning, Ashley was worried that Bree would break Harding's heart. That's exactly what happened, and yet instead of being angry with Bree, Ashley pitied her, and their friendship deepened because of it. Why do you think Ashley was so quick to forgive Bree for hurting her brother?

6. For many readers, Susan Mallery is an autobuy, while others probably read the back cover before picking up *The Boardwalk*

Bookshop. How about you? For those of you who didn't read the back cover first, were you surprised when Ashley realized that Seth didn't ever want to get married, or did you have a feeling that was coming? Would you have broken up with the perfect partner if they didn't want to get married, or could you be happy without saying "I do"? Was Seth wrong not to propose? Why or why not? When he finally did propose, were you surprised by Ashley's reaction?

7. Before the book started, Mikki took a solo trip to London and discovered that she didn't like traveling alone. Have you ever taken a trip by yourself, and if so, did you enjoy it? Are you comfortable eating in a restaurant alone? For those of you who have tried online dating, how did it go? Did you think that Mikki was going to end up with her ex-husband? Why or why not? Would you have given Perry a second chance? Why or why not?

8. Which of the men in the story did you like best, and why? (We're guessing that no one will choose Sad Guy.)

9. What surprised you while reading?

10. How did you feel about the way each story line concluded?

#1 *New York Times* bestselling author
Susan Mallery delivers a warm and witty new novel
about two friends and the one Christmas that
wil change their lives forever.

Enjoy this preview of
Home Sweet Christmas.

ONE

"Your teeth are lovely, Camryn. Did you wear braces as a child?"

Camryn Neff reminded herself not only that the woman sitting across from her was a very wealthy potential client, but also that her own mother had raised her to be polite to her elders. Still, it took serious effort to keep from falling out of her chair at the weirdness of the question.

"No. This is how they grew."

Hmm, that didn't sound right, although to be honest, she didn't have a lot of experience when a conversation turned dental.

She refocused her mind to the meeting at hand. Not that she knew for sure why Helen Crane, leader of Wishing Tree society (such as it was) and sole owner of the very impressive Crane hotel empire, wanted to meet with her. The summons had come in the form of a handwritten note, inviting her to the large sprawling estate on Grey Wolf Lake. Today, at two.

So here Camryn was, wearing a business suit that had been hanging in her closet for over a year. The dress code for retail in Wishing Tree and the dress code for the job in finance she'd left back in Chicago were very different. While it had been fun to dust off her gorgeous boots and a silk blouse and discover her skirts still fit, she was ready to get to the point of the invitation.

"How can I help you, Mrs. Crane?" she asked.

"Helen, please."

Camryn smiled. "Helen. I'm happy to host a wrapping party, either here or at the store. Or if you'd prefer, I can simply collect all your holiday gifts and wrap them for you."

She casually glanced around at the high ceilings of the sitting room. There was a massive fireplace, intricate molding and a view of the lake that, even with two feet of snow on the ground, was spectacular. And while there were lovely fall floral displays on several surfaces, there wasn't a hint of Christmas to be found. Not in Wishing Tree, eight days before Thanksgiving. Those decorations didn't appear until the Friday after.

"I have some samples for custom wrapping paper," she said, pulling out several sheets of paper from her leather briefcase. "The designs can be adjusted and the colors coordinated with what you have planned for this holiday season. Wrapped presents under a tree are such an elegant touch."

"You're very thorough," Helen murmured. "Impressive." She made a note on a pad. "Are you married, dear?"

"What?" Camryn clutched the wrapping paper samples. "No."

Helen nodded. "Your mother passed away last year, didn't she?"

A fist wrapped around Camryn's heart. "Yes. In late October."

"I remember her. She was a lovely woman. You and your sisters must have been devastated."

That was one word for it, Camryn thought grimly, remembering how her life had been shattered by the loss. In the space of a few weeks, she'd gone from being a relatively carefree, engaged, happy junior executive in Chicago to the sole guardian of her twin sisters, all the while trying to keep Wrap Around the Clock, the family business, afloat. The first few months after her mother's death were still a blur. She barely remembered anything about the holidays last year, save an unrelenting sadness.

"This year the season will be so much happier," Helen said firmly. "Victoria and Lily are thriving at school. Of course they still miss their mother, but they're happy, healthy young adults." The older woman smiled. "I know the teen years can be trying, but I confess I quite enjoyed them with Jake."

Camryn frowned slightly. "How do you know about the twins?" she asked.

Helen's smile never faded. "It's Wishing Tree, my dear. Everyone knows more than everyone else thinks. Now, you're probably wondering why I invited you over today."

"To discuss wrapping paper?" Although even as Camryn voiced the question, she knew instinctively that was not the real reason.

Helen Crane was close to sixty, with perfect posture and short dark hair. Her gaze was direct, her clothes stylish. She looked as if she'd never wanted for anything and was very used to getting her way.

"Of course, you'll take care of all my wrapping needs," Helen said easily. "And I do like your idea of custom paper for faux presents under the tree. I'll have my holiday decorator get in touch with you so you two can coordinate the design. But the real reason I asked you here is to talk about Jake."

Camryn was having a little trouble keeping up. The order for wrapping and the custom paper was great news, but why would Helen want to discuss her son?

She knew who Jake was—everyone in town did. He was the handsome, successful heir to the Crane hotel fortune. He'd been the football captain in high school, had gone to Stanford. After learning the hotel business at the smaller Crane hotels, he was back in Wishing Tree, promoted to general manager of the largest, most luxurious of the properties.

They'd never run in the same circles back when they'd been kids, in part because she was a few years younger. She'd been a lowly freshman while he'd been a popular senior. Her only real connection with Jake was the fact that he'd once been engaged to her friend Reggie.

Helen sighed. "I've come to the conclusion that left to his own devices, Jake is never going to give me grandchildren. I lost my husband eighteen months ago, which has been very hard for me. It's time for my son to get on with finding someone, getting married and having the grandchildren I deserve."

Well that put the whole "did you wear braces" conversational gambit in perspective, Camryn thought, not sure if she should laugh or just plain feel sorry for Jake. His mother was a powerful woman. Camryn sure wouldn't want to cross her.

"I'm not sure what that has to do with me," she admitted.

Helen tapped her pad of paper. "I've come up with a plan. I'm calling it Project: Jake's Bride. I'm going to find my son a wife, and you're a potential candidate."

Camryn heard all the words. Taken individually, she knew what Helen was saying. But when put together, in that exact way, the meaning completely escaped her.

"I'm sorry, what?"

"You're pretty, you're smart. You've done well at Wrap Around the Clock. You're nurturing—look how you've cared for your baby sisters." Helen smiled again. "I confess, I do like the idea of instant grandchildren, so that's a plus for you. There are other candidates, of course, but you're definitely near the top of the list. All I need is confirmation from your gynecologist that you're likely to be fertile and then we can get on with the business of you and Jake falling in love."

"You want to know if I'm fertile?"

Camryn shoved the samples back in her briefcase and stood. "Mrs. Crane, I don't know what century you think we're living in, but this isn't a conversation I'm going to have with you. My fertility is none of your business. Nor is my love life. If your plan is genuine, you need to rethink it. And while you're doing that, you might want to make an appointment with your own doctor, because there's absolutely something wrong with you."

Helen looked surprisingly unconcerned. "You're right, Camryn. I apologize. Mentioning fertility was going a bit too far. You're the first candidate I've spoken to, so I'm still finding my way through all this." She wrote on her pad. "I won't bring that up again. But as to the rest of it, seriously, what are your thoughts?"

Camryn sank back on her chair. "Don't do it. Meddling is one thing, but you're talking about an actual campaign to find your son a bride. No. Just no. It's likely to annoy him, and any woman who would participate in something like this isn't anyone you want in your family."

Helen nodded slowly. "An interesting point. It's just they make it look so easy on those reality shows."

"Nothing is real on those shows. The relationships don't last. Jake's going to find someone. Give him time."

"I've given him two years. I'm not getting younger, you know." Her expression turned wistful. "And I do want grandchildren."

"Ask me on the right day and you can have the twins."

Helen laughed. "I wish that were true." Her humor faded. "Do you know my son?"

"Not really."

"We could start with a coffee date."

Camryn sighed. "Helen, seriously. This isn't going to work. Let him get his own girl."

"He's not. That's the problem. All right, I can see I'm not going to convince you to be a willing participant. I appreciate your time." She rose. "I meant what I said about the wrapping. I'll arrange to have all my gifts taken to your store. And my holiday decorator will be in touch about the custom paper."

"Is the holiday decorator different from the regular decorator?" Camryn asked before she could stop herself.

Helen chuckled. "Yes, she is. My regular decorator is temperamental and shudders at the thought of all that cheer and tradition. He came over close to Christmas a few years ago and nearly fainted when he saw the tree in the family room."

She leaned close and her voice dropped to a conspiratorial whisper. "It's devoted to all the ornaments Jake made for me when he was little. There are plaster handprints and little stars made out of popsicle sticks. My favorite is a tuna can with a tiny baby Jesus in the manger tucked inside. There's bits of straw and a star." She pressed both hands to her heart. "I tear up thinking about it."

Baby Jesus in a tuna can? Helen was one strange woman.

Camryn collected her briefcase and followed Helen to the front door. Helen opened it, then looked at her.

"You're sure about not being a part of Project: Jake's Bride?"

"Yes. Very." Camryn kept her tone firm, so there would be no misunderstanding.

"A pity, but I respect your honesty."

Camryn walked to her SUV and put her briefcase in the back seat. Once she was behind the wheel, she glanced at the three-story house rising tall and proud against the snow and gray sky.

The rich really were different, she told herself as she circled the driveway and headed for the main road. Different in a cray-cray kind of way.

She turned left on North Ribbon Road. When she reached Cypress Highway, she started to turn right—the shortest way back to town. At the last minute, she went straight. Even as she drove north, she told herself it wasn't her business. Maybe Jake knew about his mother's plans. Maybe he supported them.

Okay, not that, she thought, passing the outlet mall, then turning on Red Cedar Highway and heading up the mountain. She might not know Jake very well, but Reggie had dated him for months. Reggie was a sweetie who would never go out with a jerk. So Jake had to be a regular kind of guy, and regular guys didn't approve of their mothers finding them wives.

Besides, she doubted Jake needed any help in that department.

He was tall, good-looking and really fit. She'd caught sight of him jogging past her store more than once and was willing to admit she'd stopped what she was doing to admire the view. He was also wealthy. Men like that didn't need help getting dates.

The sign for the resort came into view. She slowed for a second, then groaned as she drove up to the valet. Maybe she was making a mistake, but there was no way she couldn't tell Jake what had just happened. It felt too much like not mentioning toilet paper stuck to someone's shoe.

If he already knew, then it would be a short conversation. If he didn't care, then she would quietly think less of him and leave. If he was as horrified as she thought he might be, then she'd done her good deed for the week and yay her. Whatever the outcome, she would have done the right thing, which meant she would be able to sleep that night. Some days, that was as good as it was going to get.

Jake Crane stood at his office window, gazing out at the mountain. The air was still, the sky gray. About six inches of fresh powder had fallen overnight. His two o'clock meeting had been moved to next week, and sunset wasn't for two and a half hours. There was no reason he couldn't grab his gear and get in an hour or so of snowboarding, then return to work later and finish up. One of the advantages of his position was the ability to adjust his hours if he wanted. Except he didn't want to go snowboarding.

Oh, he loved the sport, the rush of speed, the trick of staying balanced, testing himself on the mountain. He enjoyed the cold, the sounds, the sense of achievement as he mastered a difficult run. He was a typical guy who enjoyed being outdoors. Just not by himself.

He had friends he could call. Dylan had the kind of job where he could take off and make up the time later, and Dylan was always up for snowboarding. Only that wasn't the sort of company Jake was looking for. He missed having a woman in his life.

He'd been avoiding that truth for a while now. Given his incredibly disastrous track record, he'd sworn off getting involved. As he saw it, the only way to keep from screwing up in the romance department was to not get romantically entangled. An easy, sensible solution. What he hadn't counted on was being... lonely.

Sex was easy. He could head to Seattle or Portland, meet someone, have a great few days, then head home. No commitment, no risks of breaking her heart, no getting it wrong. Except he'd discovered he didn't enjoy those kinds of relationships. He wanted more. He wanted to get to know someone and have her get to know him. He wanted shared experiences, laughter and, worst of all, commitment. He wanted what other people made look easy.

But if he got involved, he would completely mess up. Or he could turn into his father, and he refused to do that. So he did nothing. A solution that was no longer working for him, which left him where he'd started. Staring at the mountain with no idea what to do with his personal life.

The phone on his desk buzzed.

"Jake, there's a Camryn Neff here to see you. She doesn't have an appointment, but says it's about something personal."

Camryn Neff? The business community in Wishing Tree was small enough that he knew who she was. She owned Wrap Around the Clock—a store that sold wrapping paper and wrapped and shipped gifts for people. The hotel referred guests to her when they wanted items they'd bought sent to friends and family or simply shipped home.

He knew her well enough to say hello at a business council meeting, but little else. He thought she might have younger sisters.

He pushed a button on his phone. "I'll be right there."

He crossed the length of his large office and stepped out into the foyer of the executive offices. Camryn, an attractive redhead with a cloud of curls and big brown eyes, stood by Margie's desk.

Wishing Tree was a casual kind of place, so he was surprised to see her wearing an expensive-looking suit and leather boots with three-inch heels. Her posture was stiff, her expression bordering on defensive. Camryn hadn't stopped by to sell him wrapping paper, he thought, wondering what was wrong and how he'd gotten involved.

"Hello, Camryn," he said easily.

"Jake." She seemed to force herself to smile. "Thanks for seeing me on such short notice. I wasn't sure I should come, but then I couldn't not talk to you and..." She pressed her lips together. "Can we go into your office?"

"Of course." He motioned to show her the way, then followed her inside. He pointed to the corner seating area, where the couch and chairs offered a more informal setting.

"Can I get you something to drink?" he asked. "Coffee? Water? Bourbon?"

At the latter, she managed a sincere smile. "I wish, but it's a little early in the day for me. Plus, I'm not a bourbon kind of woman. Brown liquor isn't my thing."

"We have a nice selection of vodkas in the main bar."

Camryn chuckled and relaxed a little in her chair. "Tempting, but no."

Jake had taken a seat on the sofa. He leaned toward her and asked, "How can I help you today?"

Her body instantly tensed and the smile faded. She crossed and uncrossed her legs. "Yes, well, I wanted to tell you something. It's not my business, really." She paused and met his gaze. "It would have been if I'd said yes, but I didn't. I want to be clear about that."

"Please don't take this the wrong way, but so far you haven't been clear about anything." He smiled. "Except not liking brown liquor."

"I know. I'm sorry. I'm trying to find the words. I should just say it. Blurt it out."

He considered himself a relatively easygoing guy who could handle any crisis, but she was starting to make him uncomfortable. What could she possibly want to tell him? Not that she was pregnant—they'd never been on a date, let alone slept together. He doubted she needed money. The store was successful, and if she did need a loan, why would she come to him? While they knew a lot of the same people, they didn't hang out together, so an issue with a mutual friend seemed unlikely.

"I saw your mother today."

Jake held in a groan. Those five words always meant trouble and mostly for him.

Camryn met his gaze, her brown eyes filled with sympathy and concern. "She invited me to the house. I didn't know why but hoped it was to buy custom wrapping paper. We can design nearly anything and have it printed. In fact, I have some ideas for custom paper for the resort. I've been playing with the logo and there are—"

"Camryn?"

She blinked. "Yes?"

"My mother."

"Oh, right. That." She swallowed and looked at him. "She wants to find you a wife. She had a plan. It's called Project: Jake's Bride. She's interviewing women as potential candidates. Apparently she's done waiting for you to find someone on your own."

He stood, then wasn't sure what to do. Pace? Run? Shout? His mother had always been a meddler, but this was bad, even for her. Project: Jake's Bride? Seriously? *Seriously?*

"She wants grandchildren," Camryn added helpfully.

He sank back on the sofa and resisted the urge to rest his head in his hands. "She's losing her mind."

"I don't think so. She's very lucid and completely in control. I wasn't sure if you knew."

He stared at her. "I didn't know."

"Yeah, I can tell by the look on your face."

"Horror and murderous rage?"

She smiled. "You're not mad. Resigned, maybe. You love your mom, so you can't hate her. But I get this isn't ideal."

Jake collapsed back against the sofa. "The woman is trying to find me a wife, Camryn. I think 'not ideal' undersells the moment."

He swore silently as he realized he had no idea what he was going to do about the problem. Telling his mother to back off was the equivalent of looking at the sky and discussing the weather. The exchange was frequently unsatisfying and ultimately futile.

"I'm shipping her off to Bali. She enjoys tropical weather. I'll buy her a nice condo, supply a staff. She can take up painting. Like that painter." He paused. "What's his name? Oh, Paul Gauguin. But that was Tahiti, not Bali. Which is fine. They're both beautiful this time of year."

"What makes you think she'd agree to go?" Camryn asked. "Your mother seems highly invested in your personal life."

"I'll trick her. I could do that." He would tell her he was eloping and wanted her there for the wedding. Then he would lock her in the newly bought condo and—

He looked at Camryn. "Why did she tell you all this?"

She ducked her head, but not before he saw color flare on her cheeks. "She, ah, thought I would be a good candidate."

Jake hadn't realized the situation could get worse, which he should have. When it came to Helen Crane, that was always a possibility.

"My mother invited you to her house to discuss the possibility of us marrying?"

Camryn nodded slowly. "Although she did say she thought we should start dating first. Get to know each other."

"You're defending her?"

"No, it's just she was impressive and talking about it like this makes her sound…"

"Outrageous? Impossible?"

"A little. I understand why you're upset. She actually wanted me to provide proof of fertility, which is what set me off."

Proof of— He stood again, only to realize there still wasn't anywhere to go.

"I'm sorry about all of this," he said stiffly. "That she butted into your life and dragged you into one of her crazy schemes. I'll make this go away."

Somehow. There had to be a way to get her to stop what she was doing.

Camryn rose. "There are other candidates. I don't know who they are, but she mentioned them. Some might have kids. She said my younger sisters were a plus. She called them *instant grandchildren.*"

He held in a groan. Other candidates? Unsuspecting women who were going to be approached by his mother?

She looked at him. "She's lonely, Jake. She lost her husband less than two years ago and she's by herself in that huge house. I know she has friends and a life, but it's not like having a husband around. Wanting grandchildren is pretty common at her stage of life." She held up a hand. "Still not defending her. It's just—I get what she's doing and when you think about it, she's really very sweet."

"Then we'll let her find you a husband. See how sweet she seems then."

Camryn laughed. "Point taken. Anyway, I wanted you to know."

"I appreciate you coming here and warning me. I owe you."

Her eyes brightened. "Really? Because I could bring some

custom wrapping paper samples by for you. They'd look lovely under the dozens of trees I know you'll be putting up. Your mother is ordering them for the house."

"Sure. Make an appointment with Margie and bring them by. We support local whenever we can."

"Then I'll see you again soon. Samples in hand."

"I look forward to it."

He escorted her out of his office. Once she'd left, he turned off his computer, grabbed his coat and then headed for the door. He paused by his assistant's desk.

"I'm going to be gone a couple of hours. Text me if there's an emergency. Otherwise, I'll be back around four."

Margie, a fortysomething brunette with three teenaged sons and a husband who adored her, frowned. "You okay, boss? You look, I don't know, stressed maybe."

"I'm fine," he lied. "I'm going to stop by and see my mother, then I'll be back."

Margie sighed. "I hope when my boys are grown, they're as good to me as you are to her."

Jake only nodded, because he couldn't say what he was thinking. That the whole Bali/Tahiti plan made the most sense, but if she wouldn't agree, he was going to hire some kind of keeper. And take all her electronics away. And possibly her car. He understood she was missing his father and he wanted to be there for her, but there was no way in hell he was letting her move forward with Project: Jake's Bride. Not now. Not ever. No. Just no.

Need to know what happens next?
Preorder your copy of Home Sweet Christmas *today!*